THE
TIN SOLDIER

TEMPLE BAILEY

1ˢᵗ WORLD
LIBRARY
Literary Society

The Tin Soldier

Temple Bailey

© 1st World Library, 2006
PO Box 2211
Fairfield, IA 52556
www.1stworldlibrary.com
First Edition

LCCN: 2006938115

Softcover ISBN: 978-1-4218-3413-9
Hardcover ISBN: 978-1-4218-3313-2
eBook ISBN: 978-1-4218-3513-6

Purchase *"The Tin Soldier"*
as a traditional bound book at:
www.1stWorldLibrary.com/purchase.asp?ISBN=978-1-4218-3413-9

1st World Library is a literary, educational organization
dedicated to:

- Creating a free internet library of downloadable ebooks

- Hosting writing competitions and offering book
publishing scholarships.

Interested in more 1st World Library books?
contact: literacy@1stworldlibrary.com
Check us out at: www.1stworldlibrary.com

1st World Library Literary Society

Giving Back to the World

"If you want to work on the core problem, it's early school literacy."

- James Barksdale, former CEO of Netscape

"No skill is more crucial to the future of a child, or to a democratic and prosperous society, than literacy."

- Los Angeles Times

Literacy... means far more than learning how to read and write... The aim is to transmit... knowledge and promote social participation."

- UNESCO

"Literacy is not a luxury, it is a right and a responsibility. If our world is to meet the challenges of the twenty-first century we must harness the energy and creativity of all our citizens."

- President Bill Clinton

"Parents should be encouraged to read to their children, and teachers should be equipped with all available techniques for teaching literacy, so the varying needs and capacities of individual kids can be taken into account."

- Hugh Mackay

CONTENTS

BOOK THREE - THE BUGLE CALLS

BOOK ONE

ON THE SHELF

"I cannot bear it," the Tin Soldier said, standing on the shelf, "I cannot bear it. It is so melancholy here. Let me rather go to the wars and lose my arms and legs."

HANS ANDERSEN: The Old House.

CHAPTER I

THE TOY SHOP

The lights shining through the rain on the smooth street made of it a golden river.

The shabby old gentleman navigated unsteadily until he came to a corner. A lamp-post offered safe harbor. He steered for it and took his bearings. On each side of the glimmering stream loomed dark houses. A shadowy blot on the triangle he knew to be a church. Beyond the church was the intersecting avenue. Down the avenue were the small exclusive shops which were gradually encroaching on the residence section.

The shabby old gentleman took out his watch. It was a fine old watch, not at all in accord with the rest of him. It was almost six. The darkness of the November afternoon had come at five. The shabby old gentleman swung away from the lamppost and around the corner, then bolted triumphantly into the Toy Shop.

"Here I am," he said, with an attempt at buoyancy, and sat down.

"Oh," said the girl behind the counter, "you are wet."

"Well, I said I'd come, didn't I? Rain or shine? In five minutes I should have been too late—shop closed—" He lurched a little towards her.

She backed away from him. "You—you are—wet—won't you take cold—?"

"Never take cold—glad to get here—" He smiled and shut his eyes, opened them and smiled again, nodded and recovered, nodded and came to rest with his head on the counter.

The girl made a sudden rush for the rear door of the shop. "Look here, Emily. Poor old duck!"

Emily, standing in the doorway, surveyed the sleeping derelict scornfully. "You'd better put him out. It is six o'clock, Jean—"

"He was here yesterday—and he was furious because I wouldn't sell him any soldiers. He said he wanted to make a bonfire of the Prussian ones—and to buy the French and English ones for his son," she laughed.

"Of course you told him they were not for sale."

"Yes. But he insisted. And when he went away he told me he'd come again and bring a lot of money—"

The shabby old gentleman, rousing at the psychological moment, threw on the counter a roll of bills and murmured brokenly:

"Ten little soldiers fighting on the line, One was blown to glory, and, then there were nine—!"

His head fell forward and again he slept.

"Disgusting," said Emily Bridges; "of course we've got to get him out."

Getting him out, however, offered difficulties. He was a very big old gentleman, and they were little women.

"We might call the police—"

"Oh, Emily—"

"Well, if you can suggest anything better. We must close the shop."

"We might put him in a taxi—and send him home."

"He probably hasn't any home."

"Don't be so pessimistic—he certainly has money."

"You don't know where he got it. You can't be too careful, Jean—"

The girl, touching the old man's shoulder, asked, "Where do you live?"

He murmured indistinctly.

"Where?" she bent her ear down to him.

Waking, he sang:

> "Two little soldiers, blowing up a Hun—
> The darned thing—exploded—
> And then there was—One—"

"Oh, Emily, did you ever hear anything so funny?"

Emily couldn't see the funny side of it. It was tragic and it was disconcerting. "I don't know what to do. Perhaps you'd better call a taxi."

"He's shivering, Emily. I believe I'll make him a cup of chocolate."

"Dear child, it will be a lot of trouble—"

"I'd like to do it—really."

"Very well." Emily was not unsympathetic, but she had had a rather wearing life. Her love of toys and of little children had kept her human, otherwise she had a feeling that she might have hardened into chill spinsterhood.

As Jean disappeared through the door, the elder woman moved about the shop, setting it in order for the night. It was a labor of love to put the dolls to bed, to lock the glass doors safely on the puffy rabbits and woolly dogs and round-eyed cats, to close the drawers on the tea-sets and Lilliputian kitchens, to shut into boxes the tin soldiers that their queer old customer had craved.

For more than a decade Emily Bridges had kept the shop. Originally it had been a Thread and Needle Shop, supplying people who did not care to go downtown for such wares.

Then one Christmas she had put in a few things to attract the children. The children had come, and gradually there had been more toys—until at last she had found herself the owner of a Toy Shop, with the thread and needle and other staid articles stuck negligently in the background.

Yet in the last three years it had been hard to keep up the standard which she had set for herself. Toys were made in Germany, and the men who had made them were in the trenches, the women who had helped were in the fields—the days when the bisque babies had smiled on happy working-households were over. There was death and darkness where once the rollicking clowns and dancing dolls had been set to mechanical music.

Jean, coming back with the chocolate, found Emily with a great white plush elephant in her arms. His trappings were of red velvet and there was much gold; he was the last of a line of assorted sizes.

There had always been a white elephant in Miss Emily's window. Painfully she had seen her supply dwindle. For this last of the herd, she had a feeling far in excess of his value, such as a collector might have for a rare coin of a certain minting, or a bit of pottery of a pre-historic period.

She had not had the heart to sell him. "I may never get another. And there are none made like him in America."

"After the war—" Jean had hinted.

Miss Emily had flared, "Do you think I shall buy toys of Germany after this war?"

"Good for you, Emily. I was afraid you might."

But tonight a little pensively Miss Emily wrapped the old mastodon up in a white cloth. "I believe I'll take him home with me. People are always asking to buy him, and it's hard to explain."

"I should say it is. I had an awful time with him," she indicated the old gentleman, "yesterday.'

She set the tray down on the counter. There was a slim silver pot on it, and a thin green cup. She poked the sleeping man with a tentative finger. "Won't you please wake up and have some chocolate."

Rousing, he came slowly to the fact of her hospitality. "My dear young lady," he said, with a trace of courtliness, "you shouldn't have troubled—" and reached out a trembling hand for the cup. There was a ring on the hand, a seal ring with a coat of arms. As he drank the chocolate eagerly, he spilled some of it on his shabby old coat.

He was facing the door. Suddenly it opened, and his cup fell with a crash.

A young man came in. He too, was shabby, but not as shabby as the old gentleman. He had on a dilapidated rain-coat, and a soft hat. He took off his hat, showing hair that was of an almost silvery fairness. His eyebrows made a dark pencilled line—his eyes were gray. It was a striking face, given a slightly foreign air by a small mustache.

He walked straight up to the old man, laid his hand on his shoulder, "Hello, Dad." Then, anxiously, to the two women, "I hope he hasn't troubled you. He isn't quite—himself."

Jean nodded. "I am so glad you came. We didn't know what to do."

"I've been looking for him—" He bent to pick up the broken cup. "I'm dreadfully sorry. You must let me pay for it."

"Oh, no."

"Please." He was looking at it. "It was valuable?"

"Yes," Jean admitted, "it was one of Emily's precious pets."

"Please don't think any more about it," Emily begged. "You had better get your father home at once, and put him to bed with a hot water bottle."

Now that the shabby youth was looking at her with troubled eyes, Emily found herself softening towards the old gentleman. Simply as a derelict she had not cared what became of him. But as the father of this son, she cared.

"Thank you, I will. We must be going, Dad."

The old gentleman stood up. "Wait a minute—I came for tin soldiers—Derry—"

"They are not for sale," Miss Emily stated. "They are made in Germany. I can't get any more. I have withdrawn everything of the kind from my selling stock."

The shabby old gentleman murmured, disconsolately.

"Oh, Emily," said the girl behind the counter, "don't you think we might—?"

Derry Drake glanced at her with sudden interest. She had an unusual voice, quick and thrilling. It matched her beauty, which was of a rare quality—white skin, blue eyes, crinkled hair like beaten copper.

"I don't see," he said, smiling for the first time, "what Dad wants of tin soldiers."

"To make 'em fight," said the shabby old man, "we've got to have some fighting blood in the family."

The smile was struck from the young man's face. Out of a dead silence, he said at last, "You were very good to look after him. Come, Dad." His voice was steady, but the flush that had flamed in his cheeks was still there, as he put his arm about the shaky old man and led him to the door.

"Thank you both again," he said from the threshold. Then, with his head high, he steered his unsteady parent out into the rain.

It was late when the two women left the shop. Miss Emily, struggling down the block with her white elephant, found, in a few minutes, harbor in her boarding house. But Jean lived in the more fashionable section beyond Dupont Circle. Her father was a doctor with a practice among the older district people, who, in spite of changing administrations and fluctuating populations, had managed, to preserve their family traditions and social identity.

Dr. McKenzie did not always dine at home. But tonight when Jean came down he was at the head of the table. He was a big, handsome man with crinkled hair like his daughter's, copper-colored and cut close to his rather classic head.

Hilda Merritt was also at the table. She was a trained nurse, who, having begun life as the Doctor's office-girl, had, gradually, after his wife's death, assumed the management of his household. Jean was not fond of her. She had repeatedly begged that her dear Emily might take Miss Merritt's place.

"But Hilda is much younger," her father had contended, "and much more of a companion for you."

"She isn't a companion at all, Daddy. We haven't the same thoughts."

But Hilda had stayed on, and Jean had sought her dear Emily's company in the little shop. Sometimes she waited on customers. Sometimes she worked in the rear room. It was always a great joke to feel that she was really helping. In all her life her father had never let her do a useful thing.

The table was lighted with candles, and there was a silver dish of fruit in the center. The dinner was well-served by a trim maid.

Jean ate very little. Her father noticed her lack of appetite, "Why don't you eat your dinner, dear?"

"I had chocolate at Emily's."

"I don't think she ought to go there so often," Miss Merritt complained.

"Why not?" Jean's voice was like the crack of a whip.

"It is so late when you get home. It isn't safe."

"I can always send the car for you, Jean," her father said. "I don't care to have you out alone."

"Having the car isn't like walking. You know it isn't, Daddy, with the rain against your cheeks and the wind—"

Dr. McKenzie's quick imagination was fired. His eyes were like Jean's, lighted from within.

"I suppose it is all right if she comes straight up Connecticut Avenue, Hilda?"

Miss Merritt had long white hands which lay rather limply on the table. Her arms were bare. She was handsome in a red-cheeked, blond fashion.

"Of course if you think it is all right, Doctor—"

"It is up to Jean. If she isn't afraid, we needn't worry."

"I'm not afraid of anything."

He smiled at her. She was so pretty and slim and feminine in her white gown, with a string of pearls on her white neck. He liked pretty things and he liked her fearlessness. He had never been afraid. It pleased him that his daughter should share his courage.

"Perhaps, if I am not too busy, I will come for you the next time you go to the shop. Would walking with me break the spell of the wind and wet?"

"You know it wouldn't. It would be quite—heavenly—Daddy."

After dinner, Doctor McKenzie read the evening paper. Jean sat on the rug in front of the fire and knitted for the soldiers. She had made sweaters until it seemed sometimes as if she saw life through a haze of olive-drab.

"I am going to knit socks next," she told her father.

He looked up from his paper. "Did you ever stop to think what it means to a man over there when a woman says 'I'm going to knit socks'?"

Jean nodded. That was one of the charms which her father had for her. He saw things. It was tired soldiers at this moment, marching in the cold and needing—socks.

Hilda, having no vision, remarked from the corner where she sat with her book, "There's no sense in all this killing—I wish we'd kept out of it."

"Wasn't there any sense," said little Jean from the hearth rug, "in Bunker Hill and Valley Forge?"

Hilda evaded that. "Anyhow, I'm glad they've stopped playing the 'Star-Spangled Banner' at the movies. I'm tired of standing up."

Jean voiced her scorn. "I'd stand until I dropped, rather than miss a note of it."

Doctor McKenzie interposed:

"'The time has come,' the Walrus said,
'To talk of many things,
Of shoes—and ships—and sealing wax—
Of cabbages—and kings—'"

"Oh, Daddy," Jean reproached him, "I should think you might be serious."

"I am not just twenty—and I have learned to bank my fires. And you mustn't take Hilda too literally. She doesn't mean all that she says, do you, Hilda?"

He patted Miss Merritt on the shoulder as he went out. Jean hated that. And Hilda's blush.

With the Doctor gone, Hilda shut herself up in the office to balance her books.

Jean went on with her knitting, Hilda did not knit. When she was not helping in the office or in the house, her hands lay idle in her lap.

Jean's mind, as she worked, was on those long white hands of Hilda's. Her own hands had short fingers like her father's. Her mother's hands had been slender and transparent. Hilda's hands were not slender, they had breadth as well as length, and the skin was thick. Even the whiteness was like the flesh of a fish, pale and flabby. No, there was no beauty at all in Hilda's hands.

Once Jean had criticised them to her father. "I think they are ugly."

"They are useful hands, and they have often helped me."

"I like Emily's hands much better."

"Oh, you and your Emily," he had teased.

Yet Jean's words came back to the Doctor the next night, as he sat in the Toy Shop waiting to escort his daughter home.

Miss Emily was serving a customer, a small boy in a red coat and baggy trousers. A nurse stood behind the small boy, and played, as it were, Chorus. She wore a blue cape and a long blue bow on the back of her hat.

The small boy was having the mechanical toys wound up for him. He expressed a preference for the clowns, but didn't like the colors.

"I want him boo'," he informed Miss Emily, "he's for a girl, and she yikes boo'."

"Blue," said the nurse austerely, "you know your mother doesn't like baby talk, Teddy."

"Ble-yew—" said the small boy, carefully.

"Blue clowns," Miss Emily stated, sympathetically, "are hard to get. Most of them are red. I have the nicest thing that I haven't shown you. But it costs a lot—"

"It's a birfday present," said the small boy.

"Birthday," from the Chorus.

"Be-yirthday," was the amended version, "and I want it nice."

Miss Emily brought forth from behind the glass doors of a case a small green silk head of lettuce. She set it on the counter, and her fingers found the key, then clickety-click, clickety-click, she wound it up. It played a faint tune, the leaves opened—a rabbit with a wide-frilled collar rose in the center. He turned from side to side, he waggled his ears, and nodded his head, he winked an eye; then he disappeared, the leaves closed, the music stopped.

The small boy was entranced. "It's boo-ful—"

"Beautiful—" from the background.

"Be-yewtiful—. I'll take it, please."

It was while Miss Emily was winding the toy that Dr. McKenzie noticed her bands. They were young hands, quick and delightful hands. They hovered over the toy, caressingly, beat time to the music, rested for a moment on the shoulders of the little boy as he stood finally with upturned face and tied-up parcel.

"I'm coming adain," he told her.

"Again—."

"Ag-yain—," patiently.

"I hope you will." Miss Emily held out her hand. She did not kiss him. He was a boy, and she knew better.

When he had gone, importantly, Emily saw the Doctor's eyes upon her. "I hated to sell it," she said, with a sigh; "goodness knows when I shall get another. But I can't resist the children—"

He laughed. "You are a miser, Emily."

He had known her for many years. She was his wife's distant cousin, and had been her dearest friend. She had taught in a private school before she opened her shop, and Jean had been one of her pupils. Since Mrs. McKenzie's death it had been Emily who had mothered Jean.

The Doctor had always liked her, but without enthusiasm. His admiration of women depended largely on their looks. His wife had meant more to him than that, but it had been her beauty which had first held him.

Emily Bridges had been a slender and diffident girl. She had kept her slenderness, but she had lost her diffidence, and she had gained an air of distinction. She dressed well, her really pretty feet were always carefully shod and her hair carefully waved. Yet she was one of the women who occupy the background rather than the foreground of men's lives—the kind of woman for whom a man must be a Columbus, discovering new worlds for himself.

"Yon are a miser," the Doctor repeated.

"Wouldn't you be, under the same circumstances? If it were, for example, surgical instruments—anaesthetics—? And you knew that when they were gone you wouldn't get any more?"

He did not like logic in a woman. He wanted to laugh and tease. "Jean told me about the white elephant."

"Well, what of it? I have him at home—safe. In a big box—with moth-balls—" Her lips twitched. "Oh, it must seem funny to anyone who doesn't feel as I do."

The door of the rear room opened, and Jean came in, carrying in her arms an assortment of strange creatures which she set in a row on the floor in front of her father.

"There?" she asked, "what do you think of them?"

They were silhouettes of birds and beasts, made of wood, painted and varnished. But such ducks had never quacked, such geese had never waddled, such dogs had never barked—fantastic as a nightmare—too long—too broad—exaggerated out of all reality, they might have marched with Alice from Wonderland or from behind the Looking Glass.

"I made them, Daddy."

"You—."

"Yes, do you like them?"

"Aren't they a bit—uncanny?"

"We've sold dozens; the children adore them."

"And you haven't told me you were doing it. Why?"

"I wanted you to see them first—a surprise. We call them the Lovely Dreams, and we made the ducks green and the pussy cats pink because that's the way the children see them in their own little minds—"

She was radiant. "And I am making money, Daddy. Emily had such a hard time getting toys after the war began, so we thought we'd try. And we worked out these. I get a percentage on all sales."

He frowned. "I am not sure that I like that."

"Why not?"

"Don't I give you money enough?"

"Of course. But this is different."

"How different?"

"It is my own. Don't you see?"

Being a man he did not see, but Miss Emily did. "Any work that is worth doing at all is worth being paid for. You know that, Doctor."

He did know it, but he didn't like to have a woman tell him. "She doesn't need the money."

"I do. I am giving it to the Red Cross. Please don't be stuffy about it, Daddy."

"Am I stuffy?"

"Yes."

He tried to redeem himself by a rather tardy enthusiasm and succeeded. Jean brought out more Lovely Dreams, until a grotesque procession stretched across the room.

"Tomorrow," she announced, triumphantly, "we'll put them in the window, and you'll see the children coming."

As she carried them away, Doctor McKenzie said to Emily, "It seems strange that she should want to do it."

"Not at all. She needs an outlet for her energies."

"Oh, does she?"

"If she weren't your daughter, you'd know it."

On the way home he said, "I am very proud of you, my dear."

Jean had tucked her arm through his. It was not raining, but the sky was full of ragged clouds, and the wind blew strongly. They felt the push of it as they walked against it.

"Oh," she said, with her cheek against his rough coat, "are you proud of me because of my green ducks and my pink pussy cats?"

But she knew it was more than that, although he laughed, and she laughed with him, as if his pride in her was a thing which they took lightly. But they both walked a little faster to keep pace with their quickened blood.

Thus their walk became a sort of triumphant progress. They passed the British Embassy with the Lion and the Unicorn watching over it in the night; they rounded the Circle and came suddenly upon a line of motor cars.

"The Secretary is dining a rather important commission," the Doctor said; "it was in the paper. They are to have a war feast—three courses, no wine, and limited meats and sweets."

They stopped for a moment as the guests descended from their cars and swept across the sidewalk. The lantern which swung low from the arched entrance showed a spot of rosy color—the velvet wrap of a girl whose knot of dark curls shone above the ermine collar. A Spanish comb, encrusted with diamonds, was stuck at right angles to the knot.

Beside the young woman in the rosy wrap walked a young man in a fur coat who topped her by a head. He had gray eyes and a small upturned mustache—Jean uttered an exclamation.

"What's the matter?" her father asked.

"Oh, nothing—" she watched the two ascend the stairs. "I thought for a moment that I knew him."

The great door opened and closed, the rosy wrap and the fur coat were swallowed up.

"Of course it couldn't be," Jean decided as she and her father continued on their wonderful way.

"Couldn't be what, my dear?"

"The same man, Daddy," Jean said, and changed the subject.

CHAPTER II

CINDERELLA

The next time that Jean saw Him was at the theater. She and her father went to worship at the shrine of Maude Adams, and He was there.

It was Jean's yearly treat. There were, of course, other plays. But since her very-small-girlhood, there had been always that red-letter night when "The Little Minister" or "Hop-o'-my-Thumb" or "Peter Pan" had transported her straight from the real world to that whimsical, tender, delightful realm where Barrie reigns.

Peter Pan had been the climax!

Do you believe in fairies?

Of course she did. And so did Miss Emily. And so did her father, except in certain backsliding moments. But Hilda didn't.

Tonight it was "A Kiss for Cinderella"—! The very name had been enough to set Jean's cheeks burning and her eyes shining.

"Do you remember, Daddy, that I was six when I first saw her, and she's as young as ever?"

"Younger." It was at such moments that the Doctor was at his best. The youth in him matched the youth in his daughter. They were boy and girl together.

And now the girl on the stage, whose undying youth made her the interpreter of dreams for those who would never grow up, wove her magic spells of tears and laughter.

It was not until the first satisfying act was over that Jean drew a long breath and looked about her.

The house was packed. The old theater with its painted curtain had nothing modern to recommend it. But to Jean's mind it could not have been improved. She wanted not one thing changed. For years and years she had sat in her favorite seat in the seventh row of the parquet and had loved the golden proscenium arch, the painted goddesses, the red velvet hangings—she had thrilled to the voice and gesture of the artists who had played to please her. There had been "Wang" and "The Wizard of Oz"; "Robin Hood"; the tall comedian of "Casey at the Bat"; the short comedian who had danced to fame on his crooked legs; Mrs. Fiske, most incomparable Becky; Mansfield, Sothern—some of them, alas, already gods of yesterday!

At first there had been matinees with her mother—"The Little Princess," over whose sorrows she had wept in the harrowing first act, having to be consoled with chocolates and the promise of brighter things as the play progressed.

Now and then she had come with Hilda. But never when she could help it. "I'd rather stay at home," she had told her father.

"But—why—?"

"Because she laughs in the wrong places.'

Her father never laughed in the wrong places, and he squeezed her hand in those breathless moments where words would have been desecration, and wiped his eyes frankly when his feelings were stirred.

"There is no one like you, Daddy," she had told him, "to enjoy things." And so it had come about that he had pushed away his work on certain nights and, sitting beside her, had forgotten the sordid and suffering world which he knew so well, and which she knew not at all.

As her eyes swept the house, they rested at last with a rather puzzled look on a stout old gentleman with a wide shirt-front, who sat in the right-hand box. He had white hair and a red face.

Where had she seen him?

There were women in the box, a sparkling company in white and silver, and black and diamonds, and green and gold. There was a big bald-headed man, and quite in the shadow back of them all, a slender youth.

It was when the slender youth leaned forward to speak to the vision in white and silver that Jean stared and stared again.

She knew now where she had seen the old gentleman with the wide shirt front. He was the shabby old gentleman of the Toy Shop! And the youth was the shabby son!

Yet here they were in state and elegance! As if a fairy godmother had waved a wand—!

The curtain went up on a feverish little slavey with her mind set on going to the ball, on Our Policeman wanting a shave, on the orphans in boxes, on baked potato offered as hospitality by a half-starved hostess, on a waiting Cinderella asleep on a frozen doorstep.

And then the ball—and Mona Lisa, and the Duchess of Devonshire, and The Girl with the Pitcher and the Girl with the Muff—and Cinderella in azure tulle and cloth-of-gold, dancing with the Prince at the end like mad—.

Then the bell boomed—the lights went out—and after a little
moment, one saw Cinderella, stripped of her finery, staggering
up the stairs.

Jean cried and laughed, and cried again. Yet even in the midst
of her emotion, she found her eyes pulled away from that
appealing figure on the stage to those faintly illumined figures
in the box.

When the curtain went down, her father, most surprisingly,
bowed to the old gentleman and received in return a genial
nod.

"Oh, do you know him?" she demanded.

"Yes. It is General Drake."

"Who are the others?"

"I am not sure about the women. The boy in the back of the
box is his son, DeRhymer Drake."

Derry!

"Oh,"—she had a feeling that she was not being quite candid
with her father—"he's rather swank, isn't he, Daddy?"

"Heavens, what slang! I don't see where you get it. He is rich,
if that's what you mean, and it's a wonder he isn't spoiled to
death. His mother is dead, and the General is his own worst
enemy; eats and drinks too much, and thinks he can get away
with it."

"Are they very rich—?"

"Millions, with only Derry to leave it to. He's the child of a
second wife."

Oh, lovely, lovely, lovely Cinderella, could your godmother do more than this? To endow two rained-on and shabby gentlemen with pomp and circumstance!

Jean tucked her hand into her father's, as if to anchor herself against this amazing tide of revelation. Then, as the auditorium darkened, and the curtain went up, she was swept along on a wave of emotions in which the play world and the real world were inextricably mixed.

And now Our Policeman discovers that he is "romantical." Cinderella finds her Prince, who isn't in the least the Prince of the fairy tale, but much nicer under the circumstance—and the curtain goes down on a glass slipper stuck on the toes of two tiny feet and a cockney Cinderella, quite content.

"Well," Jean drew a long breath. "It was the loveliest ever, Daddy," she said, as he helped her with her cloak.

And it was while she stood there in that cloak of heavenly blue that the young man in the box looked down and saw her.

He batted his eyes.

Of course she wasn't real.

But when he opened them, there she was, smiling up into the face of the man who had helped her into that heavenly garment.

It came to him, quite suddenly, that his father had bowed to the man—the big man with the classic head and the air of being at ease with himself and the world.

He did things to the velvet and ermine wrap that he was holding, which seemed to satisfy its owner, then he gripped his father's arm. "Dad, who is that big man down there—with the red head—the one who bowed to you?"

"Dr. McKenzie, Bruce McKenzie, the nerve specialist—"

Of course it was something to know that, but one didn't get very far.

"Let's go somewhere and eat," said the General, and that was the end of it. Out of the tail of his eye, Derry Drake saw the two figures with the copper-colored heads move down the aisle, to be finally merged into the indistinguishable stream of humanity which surged towards the door.

Jean and her father did not go to supper at the big hotel around the corner as was their custom.

"I've got to get to the hospital before twelve," the Doctor said. "I am sorry, dear—"

"It doesn't make a bit of difference. I don't want to eat," she settled herself comfortably beside him in the car. "Oh, it is snowing, Daddy, how splendid—"

He laughed. "You little bundle of—ecstasy—what am I going to do with you?"

"Love me. And isn't the snow—wonderful?"

"Yes. But everybody doesn't see it that way."

"I am glad that I do. I should hate to see nothing in all this miracle, but—slush tomorrow—"

"Yet a lot of life is just—slush tomorrow—. I wish you need never find that out—."

When Jean went into the house, and her father drove on, she found Hilda waiting up for her.

"Father had to go to the hospital."

"Did you have anything to eat?"

"No."

"I thought I might cook some oysters."

"I am really not hungry." Then feeling that her tone was ungracious, she tried to make amends. "It was nice of you to think of it—"

"Your father may like them. I'll have them hot for him."

Jean lingered uncertainly. She didn't want the food, but she hated to leave the field to Hilda. She unfastened her cloak, and sat down. "How are you going to cook them?"

"Panned—with celery."

"It sounds good—I think I'll stay down, Hilda."

"As you wish."

The Doctor, coming in with his coat powdered with snow, found his daughter in a big chair in front of the library fire.

"I thought you'd be in bed."

"Hilda has some oysters for us."

"Fine—I'm starved."

She looked at him, meditatively, "I don't see how you can be."

"Why not?"

"Oh, on such a night as this, Daddy? Food seems superfluous."

He sat down, smiling. "Don't ever expect to feed any man over forty on star-dust. Hilda knows better, don't you, Hilda?"

Hilda was bringing in the tray. There was a copper chafing-dish and a percolator. She wore her nurse's outfit of white linen. She looked well in it, and she was apt to put it on after dinner, when she was in charge of the office.

"You know better than to feed a man on stardust, don't you?" the Doctor persisted.

Hilda lifted the cover of the chafing-dish and stirred the contents. "Well, yes," she smiled at him, "you see, I have lived longer than Jean. She'll learn."

"I don't want to learn," Jean told her hotly. "I want to believe that—that—" Words failed her.

"That men can live on star-dust?" her father asked gently. "Well, so be it. We won't quarrel with her, will we, Hilda?"

The oysters were very good. Jean ate several with healthy appetite. Her father, twinkling, teased her, "You see—?"

She shrugged, "All the same, I didn't need them."

Hilda, putting things back on the tray, remarked: "There was a message from Mrs. Witherspoon. Her son is on leave for the week end. She wants you for dinner on Saturday night—both of you."

Doctor McKenzie tapped a finger on the table thoughtfully, "Oh, does she? Do you want to go, Jeanie?"

"Yes. Don't you?"

"I am not sure. I should like to build a fence about you, my dear, and never let a man look over. Ralph Witherspoon wants to marry her, Hilda, what do you think of that?"

"Well, why not?" Hilda laid her long hands flat on the table, leaning on them.

Jean felt little prickles of irritability. "Because I don't want to get married, Hilda."

Hilda gave her a sidelong glance, "Of course you do. But you don't know it."

She went out with her tray. Jean turned, white-faced, to her father, "I wish she wouldn't say such things—"

"My dear, I am afraid you don't quite do her justice."

"Oh, well, we won't talk about her. I've got to go to bed, Daddy."

She kissed him wistfully. "Sometimes I think there are two of you, the one that likes me, and the one that likes Hilda."

With his hands on her shoulders, he gave an easy laugh. "Who knows? But you mustn't have it on your mind. It isn't good for you."

"I shall always have you on my mind—."

"But not to worry about, baby. I'm not worth it—."

Hilda came in with the evening paper. "Have you read it, Doctor?"

"No." He glanced at the headlines and his face grew hard. "More frightfulness," he said, stormily. "If I had my way, it should be an eye for an eye, a tooth for a tooth. For every man they have tortured, there should be one of their men— tortured. For every child mutilated, one of theirs—mutilated. For every woman—."

He stopped. Jean had caught hold of his arm. "Don't, Daddy," she said thickly, "it makes me afraid of you." She covered her face with her hands.

He drew her to him and smoothed her hair in silence. Over her head he glanced at Hilda. She was smiling inscrutably into the fire.

CHAPTER III

DRUSILLA

The thing that Derry Drake had on his mind the next morning was a tea-cup. There were other things on his mind—things so heavy that he turned with relief to the contemplation of cups.

Stuck all over the great house were cabinets of china—his father had collected and his mother had prized. Derry, himself, had not cared for any of it until this morning, but when Bronson, the old man who served him and had served his father for years, came in with his breakfast, Derry showed him a broken bit which he had brought home with him two nights before. "Have we a cup like this anywhere in the house, Bronson?"

"There's a lot of them, sir, in the blue room, in the wall cupboard."

"I thought so, let me have one of them. If Dad ever asks for it, send him to me. He broke the other, so it's a fair exchange."

He had it carefully wrapped and carried it downtown with him. The morning was clear, and the sun sparkled on the snow. As he passed through Dupont Circle he found that a few children and their nurses had braved the cold. One small boy in a red coat ran to Derry.

Temple Bailey

"Where are you going, Cousin Derry?"

"Down town."

"To-day is Margaret-Mary's birf-day. I am going to give her a wabbit—."

"Rabbit, Buster. You'd better say it quick. Nurse is on the way."

"Rab-yit. What are you going to give her?"

"Oh, must I give her something?"

"Of course. Mother said you'd forget it. I wanted to telephone, and she wouldn't let me."

"Would a doll do?"

"I shouldn't like a doll. But she is littler. And you mustn't spend much money. Mother said I spent too much for my rab-yit. That I ought to save it for Our Men. And you mustn't eat what you yike—we've got a card in the window, and there wasn't any bacon for bref-fus."

"Breakfast."

"Yes. An' we had puffed rice and prunes—"

Nurse, coming up, was immediately on the job. "You are getting mud on Mr. Derry's spats, Teddy. Stand up like a little gentleman."

"He is always that, Nurse, isn't he? And I should not have on spats at this hour in the morning."

Derry smiled to himself as he left them. He knew that Nurse did not approve of him. He had a way as it were of aiding and abetting Teddy.

But as he went on the smile faded. There were many soldiers on the street, many uniforms, flags of many nations draping doorways where were housed the men from across the sea who were working shoulder to shoulder with America for the winning of the war—. Washington had taken on a new aspect. It had a waked-up look, as if its lazy days were over, and there were real things to do.

The big church at the triangle showed a Red Cross banner. Within women were making bandages, knitting sweaters and socks, sewing up the long seams of shirts and pajamas. A few years ago they had worshipped a Christ among the lilies. They saw him now on the battlefield, crucified again in the cause of humanity.

It seemed to Derry that even the civilians walked with something of a martial stride. Men, who for years had felt their strength sapped by the monotony of Government service, were revived by the winds of patriotism which swept from the four corners of the earth. Women who had lost youth and looks in the treadmill of Departmental life held up their heads as if their eyes beheld a new vision.

Street cars were crowded, things were at sixes and sevens; red tape was loose where it should have been tight and tight where it should have been loose. Little men with the rank of officer sat in swivel chairs and tried to direct big things; big men, without rank, were tied to the trivial. Many, many things were wrong, and many, many things were right, as it is always when war comes upon a people unprepared.

And in the midst of all this clash and crash and movement and achievement, Derry was walking to a toy shop to carry a tea-cup!

He found Miss Emily alone in the big front room.

She did not at once recognize him.

"You remember I was in here the other night—and you wouldn't sell—tin soldiers—."

She flushed a little. "Oh, with your father?"

"Yes. He's a dear old chap—."

It was the best apology he could make, and she loved him for it.

He brought out the cup and set it on the counter. "It is like yours?"

"Yes." But she did not want to take it.

"Please. I brought it on purpose. We have a dozen."

"Of these?"

"Yes."

"But it will break your set."

"We have oodles of sets. Dad collects—you know— There are dishes enough in the house to start a crockery shop."

She glanced at him curiously. It was hard to reconcile this slim young man of fashion with the shabby boy of the other night. But there were the lad's eyes, smiling into hers!

"I should like, too, if you don't mind, to find a toy for a very little girl. It is her birthday, and I had forgotten."

"It is dreadful to forget," Miss Emily told him, "children care so much."

"I have never forgotten before, but I had so much on my mind."

She brought forth the Lovely Dreams—"They have been a great success."

He chose at once a rose-colored cat and a yellow owl. The cat was carved impressionistically in a series of circles. She was altogether celestial and comfortable. The owl might have been lighted by the moon.

"But why?" Derry asked, "a rose-colored cat?"

"Isn't a white cat pink and puffy in the firelight? And a child sees her pink and puffy. If we don't it is because we are blind."

"But why the green ducks and the amethyst cows?"

"The cows are coming tinkling home in the twilight—the green ducks swim under the willows. And they are longer and broader because of the lights and shadows. That's the way you saw them when you were six."

"By Jove," he said, staring, "I believe I did."

"So there's nothing queer about them to the children—you ought to see them listen when Jean tells them."

Jean—!

"She—she tells the children?"

"Yes. Charming stories. I am having them put in a little pamphlet to go with the toys."

"She's Dr. McKenzie's daughter, isn't she? I saw her last night at the play."

"Yes. Such a dear child. She is usually here in the afternoon."

He had hoped until then that Jean might be hidden in that rear room, locked up with the dolls in a drawer, tucked away in a box—he had a blank feeling of the futility of his tea-cup—

Then, suddenly, the gods being in a gay mood, Jean arrived!

At once his errand justified itself. She wore a gray squirrel jacket and a hat to match—and her crinkled copper-colored hair came out from under the hat and over her ears. She carried a little muff. Her eyes—the color of her cheeks! A man might walk to the world's end for less than this—!

He was buying, he told her, pink pussy cats and yellow owls. Had she liked the play last night? He was glad that she adored Maude Adams. He adored—Maude Adams. Did she remember "Peter Pan"? Yes, he had gone to everything— glorified matinees—glorified everything! Wasn't it remarkable that his father knew her father? And she was Jean McKenzie, and he was Derry Drake!

At last there was no excuse for him to linger. "I shall come back for more—Lovely Dreams," he told Miss Emily, and got away.

Alone in the shop the two women looked at each other. Then Emily said, "Jean, darling, how dreadful it must be for him."

"Dreadful—."

"With such a father—."

"Oh, you mean—the other night."

"Yes. He isn't happy, Jean."

"How do you know?"

"He has lonesome eyes."

"Oh, Emily."

"Well, he has, and it must be dreadful."

How dreadful it was neither of them could really know. Derry, having lunched with a rather important committee, went to Drusilla Gray's in the afternoon for a cup of tea. He was called almost at once to the telephone. Bronson was at the other end. "I am sorry, Mr. Derry, but I thought you ought to know—"

Derry, with the sick feeling which always came over him with the knowledge of what was ahead, said steadily, "That's all right, Bronson—which way did he go?"

"He took the Cabin John car, sir. I tried to get on, but he saw me, and sent me back, and I didn't like to make a scene. Shall I follow in a taxi?"

"Yes; I'll get away as soon as I can and call you up out there."

He went back to Drusilla. "Sing for me," he said. Drusilla Gray lived with her Aunt Marion in an apartment winch overlooked Rock Creek. Marion Gray occupied herself with the writing of books. Drusilla had varying occupations. Just now she was interested in interior decoration and in the war.

She was also interested in trying to flirt with Derry Drake. "He won't play the game," she told her aunt, "and that's why I like it—the game, I mean."

"You like him because he hasn't surrendered."

"No. He is a rather perfect thing of his kind, like a bit of jewelled Sevres or *Sang de boeuf.* And he doesn't know it. And that's another thing in his favor—his modesty. He makes me think of a little Austrian prince I once met at Palm Beach; who wore a white satin shirt with a high collar of gold embroidery, and white kid boots, and wonderful rings—and his nails long like a Chinaman's. At first we laughed at him—called him effeminate—. But after we knew him we didn't laugh. There was the blood in him of kings and rulers—and presently he

Temple Bailey

had us on our knees. And Derry's like that. When you first meet him you look over his head; then you find yourself looking up—"

Marion smiled. "You've got it bad, Drusilla."

"If you think I am in love with him, I'm not. I'd like to be, but it wouldn't be of any use. He's a Galahad—a pocket-edition Galahad. If he ever falls in love, there'll be more of romance in it than I can give him."

It was to this Drusilla that Derry had come. He liked her immensely. And they had in common a great love of music.

She had tea for him, and some rather strange little spiced cakes on a red lacquer tray. There was much dark blue and vivid red in the room, with white woodwork. Drusilla herself was in unrelieved red. The effect was startling but stimulating.

"I am not sure that I like it," she said, "the red and white and blue, but I wanted to see whether I could do it. And Aunt Marion doesn't care. The red things can all be taken out, and the rest toned down. But I have a feeling that a man couldn't sit in this room and be a slacker."

"No, he couldn't," Derry agreed. "You'd better hang out a recruiting sign, Drusilla."

"I should if they would let me. The best I can do is ask them to tea and sing for them."

It was right here that Bronson's message had broken in, and Derry, coming back from the telephone, had said, "Sing for me."

Drusilla lighted two red candles on the piano in the alcove. She began with a medley of patriotic songs. With her voice never soaring above a repressed note, she managed to give the effect of culminating emotion, so that when she reached a climax in the Marseillaise, Derry rose, thrilled, to his feet.

She whirled around and faced him. "They all do that," she said, with a glowing air Of triumph. "It's when I get them."

"Why did you give the Marseillaise last?"

"It has the tramp in it of marching men—I love it."

"But why not the 'Star Spangled Banner'?"

"That's for sacred moments. I hate to make it common—but I'll sing it—now—"

Still standing, he listened. Drusilla held her voice to that low note, but there was the crash of battle in the music that she made, the hush of dawn, the cry of victory—

"Dear girl, you are a genius."

"No, I am not. But I can feel things—and I can make others feel—"

She rose and went to the window. "There's a new moon," she said, "come and see—"

The curtains were not drawn, and the apartment was high up, so that they looked out beyond the hills to a sky in which the daylight blue had faded to a faint green, and saw the little moon and one star.

"Derry," Drusilla said, softly. "Derry, why aren't you fighting?"

It was the question he had dreaded. He had seen it often in her eyes, but never before had she voiced it.

"I can't tell you, Drusilla, but there's a reason—a good one. God knows I would go if I could."

The passion in his voice convinced her.

"Don't you know I'd be in it if I had my way. But I've got to stay on the shelf like the tin soldier in the fairy tale. Do you remember, Drusilla? And people keep asking me—why?"

"I shouldn't have asked it, Derry?"

"You couldn't know. And you had a right to ask—everybody has a right—and I can't answer."

She laid her hand on his shoulder. "When I was a little girl," she said, softly, "I used to cry—because I was so sorry for the—tin soldier—"

"Are you sorry for me, Drusilla?"

"Dreffly sorry."

They stood in silence among the shadows, with only the red candles burning. Then Derry said, heartily, "You are the best friend that a fellow ever had, Drusilla."

And that was as far as he would play the game!

CHAPTER IV

THE QUESTION

Whatever else might be said of General Drake, his Bacchanalian adventures were those of a gentleman. Not for him were the sinister streets and the sordid taverns of the town. When his wild moods came upon him, he struck out straight for open country. Up hill and down dale he trudged, a knight of the road, finding shelter and refreshment at wayside inns, or perchance at some friendly farm.

The danger lay in the lawless folk whom he might meet on the way. Unshaven and unshorn he met them, travelling endlessly along the railroad tracks, by highways, through woodland paths. They slept by day and journeyed by night. By reversing this program, the General as a rule avoided them. But not always, and when the little lad Derry had followed his strange quests, he had come now and then upon his father, telling stories to an unsavory circle, lord for the moment of them all.

"Come, Dad," Derry would say, and when the men had growled a threat, he had flung defiance at them. "My mother's motor is up the road with two men in it. If I don't get back in five minutes they will follow me."

The General had always been tractable in the hands of his son. He adored him. It was only of late that he had found anything to criticise.

Derry, driving along the old Conduit road in the crisp darkness, wondered how long that restless spirit would endure in that ageing body. He shuddered as he thought of the two men who were his father—one a polished gentleman ruling his world, by the power of his keen mind and of his money, the other a self-made vagabond—pursuing an aimless course.

The stars were sharp in a sable sky, the river was a thin line of silver, the bills were blotted out.

Bronson was waiting by the big bridge. "He is singing down there," he said, "on the bank. Can you hear him?"

Leaning over the parapet, Derry listened. The quavering voice came up to him.

> "*He has sounded forth the—trumpet—that shall never call— retreat—He is sifting out the—hearts of men—before his judgment—Oh, be swift, my soul, to answer him! Be jubilant, my feet—*"

Poor old soldier, beating time to the triumphant tune, stumbling over the words—held pathetically to the memory of those days when he had marched in the glory of his youth, strength and spirit given to a mighty cause!

The pity of it wrung Derry's heart. "Couldn't you do anything with him, Bronson?"

"No, sir, I tried, but he sent me home. Told me I was discharged."

They might have laughed over that, but it was not the moment for laughter. In the last twenty years, the General had discharged Bronson more than once, always without the least idea of being taken at his word. To have lost this faithful servant would have broken his heart.

"I see. It won't do for you to show yourself just now. You'd better go home, and have his hot bath ready."

"Are you sure you can bring him, Mr. Derry?"

"Sure, Bronson, thank you."

Bronson walked a few steps and came back. "It is freezing cold, sir, you'd better take the rug from the car."

Laden thus, Derry made his way down. His flashlight revealed the General, a humped-up figure on the bank of a little frozen stream.

"Go home, Derry," he said, as he recognized his son. "I want to sit by myself."

His tone was truculent.

Derry attempted lightness. "You'll be a lump of ice in the morning, Dad. We'd have to chip you off in chunks."

"You go home with Bronson, son, He is up there. Go home—"

He had once commanded a brigade. There were moments when he was hard pushed that he remembered it.

"Go home, Derry."

"Not till you come with me."

"I'm not coming."

Derry spread his rug on the icy ground. "Sit on this and wrap up your legs—you'll freeze out here."

His father did not move. "I am puf-feckly comfa'ble."

The General rarely got his syllables tangled. Things at times happened to his legs, but he usually controlled his tongue.

"I am puf-feckly comfa'ble—go home, Derry."

"I can't leave you, Dad."

"I want to be left."

He had never been quite like this. There had been moods of rebellion, but usually he had yielded himself to his son's guidance.

"Dad, be reasonable."

"I'd rather sit here and freeze—than go home with a—coward."

It was out at last. It struck Derry like a whiplash. He sprang to his feet. "You don't mean that, Dad. You can't mean it."

"I do mean it."

"I am not a coward, and you know it."

"Then why don't you go and fight?"

Silence! The only sound the chuckle of living waters beneath the ice of the little stream.

"Why don't you go and fight like other men?"

The emphasis was insulting. Derry had only one idea—to escape from that taunting voice. "You'll be sorry for this, Dad," he flung out at white heat, and scrambled up the bank.

When he reached the bridge, he paused. He couldn't leave that old man down there to die of the cold—the wind was rising and rattled in the bare trees.

But Derry's blood was boiling. He sat down on the parapet, thick blackness all about him. Whatever had been his father's shortcomings, they had always clung together—and now they were separated by words which had cut like a knife. It was useless to tell himself that his father was not responsible. Out of the heart the mouth had spoken.

And there were other people who felt as his father did—there had been Drusilla's questions, the questions of others—there had been, too, averted faces. He saw the little figure in the cloak of heavenly blue as she had been the other night,—in her gray furs as she had been this morning—; would her face, too, be turned from him?

Words formed themselves in his mind. He yearned to toss back at his father the taunt that was on his lips. To fling it over the parapet, to shout it to the world—!

He had never before felt the care of his father a sacrifice. There had been humiliating moments, hard moments, but always he had been sustained by a sense of the rightness of the thing that he was doing and of its necessity.

Then, out of the darkness, came a shivering old voice, "Derry, are you there?"

"Yes, Dad."

"Come down—and help me—"

The General, alone in the darkness, had suffered a reaction. He felt chilled and depressed. He wanted warmth and light.

Mounting steadily with his son's arm to sustain him, he argued garrulously for a sojourn at the nearest hostelry, or for a stop at Chevy Chase. He would, he promised, go to bed at the Club, and thus be rid of Bronson. Bronson didn't know his place, he would have to be taught—

Arriving at the top, he was led to Derry's car. He insisted on an understanding. If he got in, they were to stop at the Club.

"No," Derry said, "we won't stop. We are going home."

Derry had never commanded a brigade. But he had in him the blood of one who had. He possessed also strength and determination backed at the moment by righteous indignation. He lifted his father bodily, put him in the car, took his seat beside him, shut the door, and drove off. He felt remarkably cheered as they whirled along at top speed.

The General, yielding gracefully to the inevitable, rolled himself up in the rugs, dropped his head against the padded cushions and, soothed by the warmth, fell asleep.

He waked to find himself being guided up his own stairway by Bronson and the butler.

"Put him into a hot bath, Bronson," Derry directed from the threshold of his father's room, and the General, quite surprisingly, made no protest. He had his bath, hot drinks to follow, and hot water bags in his bed. When he drifted off finally, into uneasy dreams, he was watched over by Bronson as if he had been a baby.

Derry, looking at his watch, was amazed to find that the evening was yet early. He had lived emotionally through a much longer period than that marked by the clocks.

He had no engagements. He had found himself of late shrinking a little from his kind. The clubs and the hotels were crowded with officers. Private houses, hung with service flags, paid homage to men in uniform. He was aware that he was, perhaps, unduly sensitive, but it was not pleasant to meet the inquiring glance, the guarded question. He was welcomed outwardly as of old. But, then, he had a great deal of money. People did not like to offend his father's son. But if he had not been his father's son? What then?

He dined alone and in state in the great dining room. The portraits of his ancestors looked down on him. There was his mother's grandfather, who had the same fair hair and strongly marked brows. He had been an officer in the English army, and wore the picturesque uniform of the period. There were other men in uniform—ancestors—.

But of what earthly use was an ancestor in uniform to the present situation? It would have been better to have inherited Quaker blood. Derry smiled whimsically as he thought how different he might have felt if there had been benignant men in gray with broad-brimmed hats, staring down.

But to grant a man an inheritance of fighting blood, and then deny him the opportunity to exercise his birthright, was a sort of grim joke which he could not appreciate.

For dessert a great dish of fruit was set before him. He chose a peach!

Peaches in November! The men in the trenches had no peaches, no squabs, no mushrooms, no avacados—for them bully beef and soup cubes, a handful of dates, or by good luck a bit of chocolate.

He left the peach untasted—he had a feeling that he might thus, vicariously, atone for the hardships of those others who fought.

After dinner he walked downtown. Passing Dr. McKenzie's house he was constrained to loiter. There were lights upstairs and down. Was Jean McKenzie's room behind the two golden windows above the balcony? Was she there, or in the room below, where shaded lamps shone softly among the shadows?

He yearned to go in—to speak with her—to learn her thoughts—to read her heart and mind. As yet he knew only the message of her beauty. He fancied her as having exquisite sensibility, sweetness, gentleness, perceptions as vivid as her youth and bloom.

The front door opened, and Jean and her father came out. Derry's heart leaped as he heard her laugh. Then her clear voice, "Isn't it a wonderful night to walk, Daddy?" and her father's response, "Oh, you with your ecstasies!"

They went briskly down the other side of the street. Derry found himself following, found himself straining his ear for that light laugh, found himself wishing that it were he who walked beside her, that her hand was tucked into his arm as it was tucked into her father's.

Their destination was a brilliantly illumined palace on F Street, once a choice little playhouse, now given over to screen productions. The house was packed, and Jean and her father, following the flashlight of the usher, found harbor finally in a box to the left of the stage. Derry settled himself behind them. He was an eavesdropper and he knew it, but he was loath to get out of the range of that lovely laughter.

Yet observing the closeness of their companionship he felt himself lonely—they seemed so satisfied to be together—so sufficient without any other. Once Dr. McKenzie got up and went out. When he came back he brought a box of candy. Derry heard Jean's "Oh, you darling—" and thrilled with a touch of jealousy.

He wondered a little that he should care—his experiences with women had heretofore formed gay incidents in his life rather than serious epochs. He had carried in his heart a vision, and the girl in the Toy Shop had seemed to make that vision suddenly real.

The play which was thrown on the screen had to do with France; with Joan of Arc and the lover who failed her, with the reincarnation of the lover and his opportunity, after long years, to redeem himself from the blot of cowardice.

In the stillness, Derry heard the quick-drawn breath of the girl in front of him. "Daddy, I should hate a man like that."

"But, my dear—"

"I should hate him, Daddy."

The play was over.

The lights went up, and Jean stood revealed. She was pinning on her hat. She saw Derry and smiled at him. "Daddy," she said, "it is Mr. Drake—you know him."

Dr. McKenzie held out his hand. "How do you do? So you young people have met, eh?"

"In Emily's shop, Daddy. He—he came to buy my Lovely Dreams."

The two men laughed. "As if any man could buy your dreams, Jeanie," her father said, "it would take the wealth of the world."

"Or no wealth at all," said Derry quickly.

They walked out together. As they passed the portal of the gilded door, Derry felt that the moment of parting had come.

"Oh, look here, Doctor," he said, desperately, "won't you and your daughter take pity on me—and join me at supper? There's dancing at the Willard and all that—Miss McKenzie might enjoy it, and it would be a life-saver for me."

Light leaped into Jean's eyes. "Oh, Daddy—"

"Would you like it, dear?"

"You know I should. So would you. And you haven't any stupid patients, have you?"

"My patients are always stupid, Drake, when they take me away from her. Otherwise she is sorry for them." He looked at his watch. "When I get to the hotel I'll telephone to Hilda, and she'll know where to find us."

It was the Doctor who talked as they went along—the two young people were quite ecstatically silent. Jean was between her father and Derry. As he kept step with her, it seemed to him that no woman had ever walked so lightly; she laughed a little now and then. There was no need for words.

While her father telephoned, they sat together for a moment in the corridor. She unfastened her coat, and he saw her white dress and pearls. "Am I fine enough for an evening like this?" she asked him; "you see it is just the dress I wear at home."

"It seems to me quite a superlative frock—and I am glad that your hat is lined with blue."

"Why?"

"Your cloak last night was heavenly, and now this—it matches your eyes—"

"Oh." She sat very still.

"Shouldn't I have said that? I didn't think—"

"I am glad you didn't think—"

"Oh, are you?"

"Yes. I hate people who weigh their words—" The color came up finely into her cheeks.

When Dr. McKenzie returned, Derry found a table, and gave his order.

Jean refused to consider anything but an ice. "She doesn't eat at such moments," Doctor McKenzie told his young host. "She lives on star-dust, and she wants me to live on star-dust. It is our only quarrel. She'll think me sordid because I am going to have broiled lobster."

Derry laughed, yet felt that it was after all a serious matter. His appetite, too, was gone. He too wanted only an ice! The Doctor's order was, however, sufficiently substantial to establish a balance.

"May I dance with her?" Derry asked, as the music brought the couples to their feet.

"I don't usually let her. Not in a place like this. But her eyes are begging—and I spoil her, Drake."

Curious glances followed the progress of the young millionaire and his pretty partner. But Derry saw nothing but Jean. She was like thistledown in his arms, she was saying tremendously interesting things to him, in her lovely voice.

"I cried all through the scene where Cinderella sits on the door-step. Yet it really wasn't so very sad—was it?"

"I think it was sad. She was such a little starved thing—starved for love."

"Yes. It must be dreadful to be starved for love."

He glanced down at her. "You have never felt it?"

"No, except after my mother died—I wanted her—"

"My mother is dead, too."

The Doctor sat alone at the head of the table and ate his lobster; he ate war bread and a green salad, and drank a pot of black coffee, and was at peace with the world. Star-dust was all very well for those young things out there. He laughed as they came back to him. "Each to his own joys—the lobster was very good, Drake."

They hardly heard him. Jean had a rosy parfait with a strawberry on top. Derry had another.

They talked of the screen play, and the man who had failed. If he had really loved her he would not have failed, Jean said.

"I think he loved her," was Derry's opinion; "the spirit was willing, but the flesh was weak."

Jean shrugged. "Well, Fate was kind to him—to give him another chance. Oh, Daddy, tell him the story the little French woman told at the meeting of the Medical Association."

"You should have heard her tell it—but I'll do my best. Her eloquence brought us to our feet. It was when she was in Paris—just after the American forces arrived. She stopped at the curb one morning to buy violets of an ancient dame. She found the old flower vendor inattentive and, looking for the cause, she saw across the street a young American trooper loitering at a corner. Suddenly the old woman snatched up a bunch of lilies, ran across the street, thrust them into the hands of the astonished soldier. 'Take them, American,' she said. 'Take the lilies of France and plant them in Berlin.'"

"Isn't that wonderful?" Jean breathed.

"Everything is wonderful to her," the Doctor told Derry, "she lives on the heights."

"But the lilies of France, Daddy—! Can't you see our men and the lilies of France?"

Derry saw them, indeed,—a glorious company—!

"Oh, if I were a man," Jean said, and stopped. She stole a timid glance at him. The question that he had dreaded was in her eyes.

They fell into silence. Jean finished her parfait. Derry's was untouched.

Then the music brought them again to their feet, and they danced. The Doctor smoked alone. Back of him somebody murmured, "It is Derry Drake."

"Confounded slacker," said a masculine voice. Then came a warning "Hush," as Derry and Jean returned.

"It is snowing," Derry told the Doctor. "I have ordered my car."

Late that night when the Doctor rode forth again alone in his own car on an errand of mercy, he thought of the thing which he had heard. Then came the inevitable question: why wasn't Derry Drake fighting?

CHAPTER V

THE SLACKER

It was at the Witherspoon dinner that Jean McKenzie first heard the things that were being said about Derry.

"I can't understand," someone had remarked, "why Derry Drake is staying out of it."

"I fancy he'll be getting in," Ralph Witherspoon had said. "Derry's no slacker."

Ralph could afford to be generous. He was in the Naval Flying Corps. He looked extremely well in his Ensign's uniform, and he knew it; he was hoping, in the spring, for active service on the other side.

"I don't see why Derry should fight. I don't see why any man should. I never did believe in getting into other people's fusses."

It was Alma Drew who said that. Nobody took Alma very seriously. She was too pretty with her shining hair and her sea-green eyes, and her way of claiming admiration.

Jean had recognised her when she first came in as the girl she had seen descending from her motor car with Derry Drake on the night of the Secretary's dinner. Alma again wore the diamond-encrusted comb. She was in sea-green, which matched her eyes.

"If I were a man," Alma pursued, "I should run away."

There was a rustle of uneasiness about the table. In the morning papers had been news of Italy—disturbing news; news from Russia—Kerensky had fled to Moscow—there had been pictures of our men in gas masks! It wasn't a thing to joke about. Even Alma might go too far.

Ralph relieved the situation. "Oh, no, you wouldn't run away," he said; "you don't do yourself justice, Alma. Before you know it you will be driving a car over there, and picking me up when I fall from the skies."

"Well, that would be—compensation—." Alma's lashes flashed up and fluttered down.

But she turned her batteries on Ralph in vain. Jean McKenzie was on the other side of him. It would never be quite clear to him why he loved Jean. She was neither very beautiful nor very brilliant. But there was a dearness about her. He hardly dared think of it. It had gone very deep with him.

He turned to her. Her eyes were blazing. "Oh," she said, under her breath, "how can she say things like that? If I knew a man who would run away, I'd never speak to him."

"Of course. That's why I fell in love with you—because you had red blood in your veins."

It was the literal truth. The first time that Ralph had seen Jean McKenzie, he had been riding in Rock Creek Park. She, too, was on horseback. It was in April. War had just been declared, and there was great excitement. Jean, taking the bridle path over the hills, had come upon a band of workers. A long-haired and seditious orator was talking to them. Jean had stopped her horse to listen, and before she knew it she was answering the arguments of the speaker. Rising a little in her stirrups, her riding-crop uplifted to emphasize her burning words, her cheeks on fire, her eyes shining, her hair blowing under her three-cornered hat, she had clearly and crisply challenged the patriotism of the speaker, and she had presented to Ralph's appreciative eyes a picture which he was never to forget.

She had not been in the least embarrassed by his arrival, and his uniform had made him seem at once her ally. "I am sure this gentleman will be glad to talk to you," she had said to her little audience. "I'll leave the field to him," and with a nod and a smile she had ridden off, the applause of the men following her.

Ralph, having put the long-haired one to rout, had asked the men if they knew the young lady who had talked to them. They had, it seemed, seen her riding with Dr. McKenzie. They thought she was his daughter. It had been easy enough after that to find Jean on his mother's visiting list. Mrs. Witherspoon and Mrs. McKenzie had exchanged calls during the life-time of the latter, but they had lived in different circles. Mrs. Witherspoon had aspired to smartness and to the friendship of the new people who brought an air of sophistication to the staid and sedate old capital. Mrs. McKenzie had held to old associations and to old ideals.

Mrs. Witherspoon was a widow and charming. Dr. McKenzie was a widower and an addition to any dinner table. In a few weeks the old acquaintance had been renewed. Ralph had wooed Jean ardently during the short furloughs which had been granted him, and from long distance had written a bit cocksurely. He had sent flowers, candy, books and then, quite daringly; a silver trench ring.

Jean had sent the ring back. "It was dear of you to give it to me, but I can't keep it."

"Why not?" he had asked when he next saw her.

"Because—"

"Because is no reason."

She had blushed, but stood firm. She was very shy—totally unawakened—a little dreaming girl—with all of real life ahead of her—with her innocence a white flower, her patriotism a red one. If only he might wear that white and red above his heart.

As a matter of fact, Jean resented, sub-consciously, his air of possession, the certainty with which he seemed to see the end of his wooing.

"You can't escape me," he had told her.

"As if I were a rabbit," she had complained afterwards to her father. "When I marry a man I don't want to be caught—I want to run to him, with my arms wide open."

"Don't," her father advised; "not many men would be able to stand it. Let them worship you, Jeanie, don't worship."

Jean stuck her nose in the air. "Falling in love doesn't come the way you want it. You have to take it as the good Lord sends it."

"Who told you that?"

"Emily—"

"What does Emily know of love?"

He had laughed and patted her hand. He was cynical generally about romance. He felt that his own perfect love affair with his wife had been the exception. He looked upon Emily as a sentimental spinster who knew practically nothing of men and women.

He did not realize that Emily knew a great deal about dolls that laughed and cried when you pulled a string. And that the world in Emily's Toy Shop was not so very different from his own.

Alma, having turned a cold shoulder to Ralph, was still proclaiming her opinion of Derry Drake to the rest of the table. "He is rich and young and he doesn't want to die—"

"There are plenty of rich young men dying, Alma," said Mrs. Witherspoon, "and it is probably as easy for them as for the poor ones—"

"The poor ones won't mind being muddy and dirty in the trenches," said Alma, "but I can't fancy Derry Drake without two baths a day—"

"I can't quite fancy him a slacker." There was a hint of satisfaction in Mrs. Witherspoon's voice. Her son and Derry Drake had gone to school together and to college. Derry had outdistanced Ralph in every way; but now it was Ralph who was leaving Derry far behind.

Jean wished that they would stop talking. She felt as she might had she seen a soldier stripped of sword and stripes and shamed in the eyes of his fellows.

"Wasn't he in the draft?" she asked Ralph.

"Too old. He doesn't look it, does he? It's a bit hard for the rest of us fellows to understand why he keeps out—"

"Doesn't he ever try to—explain?"

Ralph shook his head. "Not a word. And he's beginning to stay away from things. You see, he knows that people are asking questions, and you hear what they are calling him?"

"Yes," said Jean, "a coward."

"Well, not exactly that—"

"There isn't much difference, is there?"

And now Alma's cool voice summed up the situation. "A man with as much money as that doesn't have to be brave. What does he care about public opinion? After the war everybody will forgive and forget."

Coolly she challenged them to contradict her. "You all know it. How many of you would dare cut the fellow who will inherit his father's millions?"

Mrs. Witherspoon tried to laugh it off; but it was true, and Alma was right. They might talk about Derry Drake behind his back, but they'd never omit sending a card to him.

Jean ate her duckling in flaming silence, ate her salad, ate her ice, drank her coffee, and was glad when the meal ended.

The war from the beginning had been for her a sacred cause. She had yearned to be a man that she might stand in the forefront of battle. She had envied the women of Russia who had formed a Battalion of Death. Her father had laughed at her. "You'd be like a white kitten in a dog fight."

It seemed intolerable that tongues should be busy with this talk of young Drake's cowardice. He had seemed something so much more than that. And he was a man—with a man's right to leadership. What was the matter with him?

The night before she had slept little—Derry's voice—Derry's eyes! She had gone over every word that he had said. She had risen early in the morning to write in her memory book, and she had drawn a most entrancing border about the page, with melting strawberry ice, lilies of France, Cinderella slippers, and red-ink lobsters, rather nightmarishly intermingled!

He had seemed so fine—so—she fell back on her much

overworked word *wonderful*—her heart had run to meet him, and now—it would have to run back again. How silly she had been not to see.

After dinner they danced in the Long Room, which was rather famous from a decorative point of view. It was medieval in effect, with a balcony and tapestries, and some precious bits of armor. There was a lion-skin flung over the great chair where Mrs. Witherspoon was enthroned.

Between dances, Jean and Ralph sat on the balcony steps, and talked of many things which brought the red to Jean's cheeks, and a troubled light into her eyes.

And it was from the balcony-steps that, as the evening waned, she saw Derry Drake standing in the great arched doorway.

There was a black velvet curtain behind him which accentuated his fairness. He did not look nineteen. Jean had a fleeting vision of a certain steel engraving of the "Princes in the Tower" which had hung in her grandmother's house. Derry was not in the least like those lovely imprisoned boys, yet she had an overwhelming sense of his kinship to them.

As young Drake's eyes swept the room, he was aware of Jean on the balcony steps. She was in white and silver, with a touch of that heavenly blue which seemed to belong to her. Her crinkled hair was combed quaintly over her ears and back from her forehead. He smiled at her, but she apparently did not see him.

He made his way to Mrs. Witherspoon. "I was so sorry to get here late. But my other engagements kept me. If I could have dined at two places, you should have had at least a half of me."

"We wanted the whole. You know Dr. McKenzie, Derry?"

The two men shook hands. "May I dance with your daughter?" Derry said, smiling.

"Of course. She is up there on the stairs."

Jean saw him coming. Ever since Derry had stood in the door she had been trying to make up her mind how she would treat him when he came. Somebody ought to show him that his millions didn't count. She hadn't thought of his millions last night. If he had been just the shabby boy of the Toy Shop, she would have liked his eyes just as much, and his voice!

But a slacker was a slacker! A coward was a coward! All the money in the world couldn't take away the stain. A man who wouldn't fight at this moment for the freedom of the world was a renegade! She would have none of him.

He came on smiling. "Hello, Ralph. Miss McKenzie, your father says you may dance with me—I hope you have something left?"

The blood sang in her ears, her cheeks burned.

"I haven't anything left—for you—" The emphasis was unmistakable.

Even then he did not grasp what had happened to him. "Ralph will let me have one of his—be a good sport, Ralph."

"Well, I like that," Ralph began. Then Jean's crisp voice stopped him. "I am not going to dance any more—my head aches. I—I shall ask Daddy to take me—home—"

It was all very young and obvious. Derry gave her a puzzled stare. Ralph protested. "Oh, look here, Jean. If you think you aren't going to dance any more with me."

"Well, I'm not. I am going home. Please take me down to Daddy."

It seemed a long time before the blurred good-byes were said, and Jean was alone with her father in the cozy comfort of the closed car.

"Do you love me, Daddy?"

"My darling, yes."

"May I live with you always—to the end of my days?"

He chuckled. "So that was it? Poor Ralph!"

"You know you are not sorry for him, Daddy. Don't be a hypocrite."

He drew her close to him. "I should be sorry for myself if he took you from me."

She clung to him. "He is not going to take me away."

"Was that what you were telling him on the balcony stairs?"

"Yes. And he said I was too young to know my own mind. That I was a sleeping Princess—and some day he would wake me—up—"

"Oh."

"And he is not the Prince, Daddy. There isn't any Prince."

She had shut resolutely away from her the vision of Derry Drake as she had seen him on the night of Cinderella. She would have no white-feathered knight! Princes were brave and rode to battle!

CHAPTER VI

THE PROMISE

It was Alma who gave Derry Drake the key to Jean's conduct.

"Did your ears burn?" she asked, as they danced together after Jean and her father had gone.

"When?"

"We were talking about you at dinner."

"I hope you said nice things."

"I did, of course." Her lashes flashed up and fluttered down as they had flashed and fluttered for Ralph. Every man was for Alma a possible conquest. Derry was big game, and as yet her little darts had not pierced him. She still hoped, however. "I did, but the rest didn't."

He shrank from the things which she might tell him. "What did they say?" His voice caught.

"I shan't tell you. But it was about the war, and your not fighting. As if it made any difference. You are as brave as any of them."

He glanced down at her with somber eyes. Quite unreasonably he hated her for her defense of him. If all women defended

Temple Bailey

men who wouldn't fight, what kind of a world would it be? Women who were worth anything girded their men for battle.

He knew now the reason for Jean's high head and burning cheeks, and in spite of his sense of agonizing humiliation, he was glad to think of that high-held head.

For such women, for such women men died!

But not for women like Alma Drew!

He got away from her as soon as possible. He got away from them all. He had a morbid sense of whispering voices and of averted glances. He fancied that Mrs. Witherspoon touched his hand coldly as he bade her "good-night."

Well, he would not come again until he could meet their eyes.

It was a perfectly clear night, and he walked home. With his face turned up to the stars, he told himself that the situation was intolerable—tomorrow morning, he would go to his father.

When he reached home, his father was asleep. Derry looked in on him and found Bronson sitting erect and wide-eyed beside a night lamp which threw the rest of the room into a sort of golden darkness. The General was in a great lacquered bed which he had brought with him years ago from China. Gilded dragons guarded it and princes had slept in it. Heavy breathing came from the bed.

"I think he has caught cold, sir," Bronson whispered. "I'm a bit afraid of bronchitis."

Derry's voice lacked sympathy. "I shouldn't worry, Bronson. He usually comes around all right."

"Yes, sir. I hope so, sir," and Bronson's spare figure rose to a portentous shadow, as he preceded Derry to the door.

On the threshold he said, "Dr. Richards has gone to the front. Shall I call Dr. McKenzie if we need someone—?"

"Has he been left in charge?"

"Yes, sir."

Derry stood for a moment undecided. "I suppose there's no reason why you shouldn't call McKenzie. Do as you think best, Bronson."

On his way to his own room, Derry paused for a moment at the head of the great stairway. His mother's picture hung on the landing. The dress in which she was painted had been worn to a dinner at the White House during the first Cleveland Administration. It was of white brocade, with its ostrich feather trimming making it a rather regal robe. It had tight sleeves, and the neck was square. Around her throat was a wide collar of pearls with diamond slides. Her fair hair was combed back in the low pompadour of the period, and there were round flat curls on her temples. The picture was old-fashioned, but the painted woman was exquisite, as she had always been, as she would always be in Derry's dreams.

The great house had given to the General's wife her proper setting. She had trailed her satins and silks up and down the marble stairway. Her slender hands, heavy with their rings, had rested on its balustrade, its mirrors had reflected the diamond tiara with which the General had crowned her. In the vast drawing room, the gold and jade and ivory treasures in the cabinets had seemed none too fine for this greatest treasure of them all. In the dining room the priceless porcelains had been cheapened by her greater worth. The General had travelled far and wide, and he had brought the wealth of the world to lay at the feet of his young wife. He adored her and he adored her son.

"It is just you and me, Derry," the old man had said in the first moment of bereavement; "we've got to stick it out together—"

And they had stuck it out until the war had come, and patriotism had flared, and the staunch old soldier had spurned this—changeling.

It seemed to Derry that if his mother could only step down from the picture she might make things right for him. But she would not step down. She would go on smiling her gentle painted smile as if nothing really mattered in the whole wide world.

Thus, with his father asleep in the lacquered bed, and his mother smiling in her gilded frame, the son stood alone in the great shell of a house which had in it no beating heart, no throbbing soul to answer his need.

Derry's rooms were furnished in a lower key than those in which his father's taste had been followed. There were gray rugs and gray walls, some old mahogany, the snuff-box picture of Napoleon over his desk, a dog-basket of brown wicker in a corner.

Muffin, Derry's Airedale, stood at attention as his master came in. He knew that the length of his sojourn depended on his manners.

A bright fire was burning, a long chair slanted across the hearthrug. Derry got into a gray dressing gown and threw himself into the chair. Muffin, with a solicitous sigh, sat tentatively on his haunches. His master had had no word for him. Things were very bad indeed, when Derry had no word for his dog.

At last it came. "Muffin—it's a rotten old world."

Muffin's tail beat the rug. His eager eyes asked for more.

It came—"Rotten."

Derry made room among the pillows, and Muffin curled up

beside him in rapturous silence. The fire snapped and flared, flickered and died. Bronson tiptoed in to ask if Derry wanted him. Young Martin, who valeted Derry when Bronson would let him, followed with more proffers of assistance.

Derry sent them both away. "I am going to bed."

But he did not go to bed. He read a letter which his mother had written before she died. He had never broken the seal until now. For on the outside of the envelope were these words in fine feminine script: "Not to be opened until the time comes when my boy Derry is tempted to break his promise."

It began, "Boy dear—"

"I wonder if I shall make you understand what it is so necessary that you should understand?" It has been so hard all of these years when your clear little lad's eyes have looked into mine to feel that some day you might blame—me. Youth is so uncompromising, Derry, dear—and so logical—so demanding of—justice. And life isn't logical—or just—not with the sharp-edged justice which gives cakes to the good little boys and switches to the bad ones. And you have always insisted on the cakes and switches, Derry, and that's why I am afraid of you.

"Even when you were only ten and I hugged you close in the night—those nights when we were alone, Derry, and your father was out on some wild road under the moonlight, or perhaps with the snow shutting out the moon, you used to whisper, 'But he oughtn't to do it, Mother—' And I knew that he ought not, but, oh, Derry, I loved him, and do you remember, I used to say, 'But he's so good to us, Laddie,—and perhaps we can love him enough to make him stop.'"

"But you are a man now, Derry. I am sure you will be a man before you read this, for my little boy will obey me until he comes to man's estate, and then he may say 'She was only a foolish loving woman, and why should I be bound?'"

"I know when that moment comes that all your father's money will not hold you." You will not sell your soul's honor for your inheritance. Haven't I known it all along? Haven't I seen you a little shining knight ready to do battle for your ideals? And haven't I seen the clash of those ideals with the reality of your father's fault?

Well, there's this to think of now, Derry, now that you are a man—that life isn't white and black, it isn't sheep and goats— it isn't just good people and bad people with a great wall between. Life is gray and amethyst, it is a touch of dinginess on the fleece of the whole flock, and the men and women whom you meet will be those whose great faults are balanced by great virtues and whose little meannesses are contradicted by unexpected generosities.

I am putting it this way because I want you to realize that except for the one fault which has shadowed your father's life, there is no flaw in him. Other men have gone through the world apparently untouched by any temptation, but their families could tell you the story of a thousand tyrannies, their clerks could tell you of selfishness and hardness, their churches and benevolent societies could tell you of their lack of charity. Oh, there are plenty of good men in the world, Derry, strong and fine and big, I want you to believe that always, but I want you to believe, too, that there are men who struggle continually with temptation and seem to fail, but they fight with an enemy so formidable that I, who have seen the struggle, have shut my eyes—afraid to look—.

"And now I shall go back to the very beginning," and tell you how it all happened. Your father was only a boy when the Civil War broke out. He came down from Massachusetts with a regiment which had in it the blood of the farmers who fired the shot heard round the world—. He felt that he was fighting for Freedom—he had all of your ideals, Derry; plus, perhaps, a few of his own.

"You know how the war dragged," four years of it—and much

of the time that Massachusetts regiment was in swamp and field, on the edge of fever-breeding streams, never very well fed, cold in winter, hot in summer.

"They were given for medicine quinine and—whiskey." It kept them alive. Sometimes it kept them warm, sometimes it lifted them above reality and granted them a moment's reckless happiness.

"It was all wrong, of course." I am making no plea for its rightness; and it unchained wild beasts in some of the men. Your father for many years kept his chained, but the beasts were there.

"He was almost fifty when I married him," and he was not a General. That title was given to him during the Spanish War. I was twenty when I came here a bride. There was no deception on your father's part. He told me of the dragon he fought—he told me that he hoped with God's help and mine to conquer. And I hoped, too, Derry. I did more than that. I was so sure of him—my King could do no wrong.

But the day came when he went on one of those desolate pilgrimages where you and I so often followed in later years. I am not going to try to tell you how we fought together, Derry; how I learned with such agony of soul that a man's will is like wax in the fire of temptation—oh, Derry, Derry—.

"I am telling you this for more reasons than one." What your father has been you might be. With all your ideals there may be in you some heritage of weakness, of appetite. Wild beasts can conquer you, too, if you let them in. And that's why I have preached and prayed. That's why I've kept you from that which overcame your father. You are no better, no stronger, than he was in the glory of his youth. But I have barred the doors against the flaming dragon.

I have no words eloquent enough to tell you of his care of me, his consideration, his devotion. Yet nothing of all this helped in those strange moods that came upon him. Then you were forgotten, I was forgotten, the world was forgotten, and he let everything go—.

"I have kept what I have suffered to some extent from the world." If people have pitied they have had the grace at least not to let me see. The tragedy has been that you should have been sacrificed to it, your youth shadowed. But what could I do? I felt that you must know, must see, and I felt, too, that the salvation of the father might be accomplished through the son.

"And so I let you go out into the night after him, I let you know that which should, perhaps, have been hidden from you. But I loved him, Derry—I loved you—I did the best I could for both of you."

"And now because of the past, I plead for the future. I want you to stay with him, Derry. No matter what happens I beg that you will stay—for the sake of the boy who was once like you, for the sake of the man who held your mother always close to his heart, for the sake of the mother who in Heaven holds you to your promise."

The great old house was very still. Somewhere in a shadowed room an old man slept heavily with his servant sitting stiff and straight beside him, at the head of the stairway a painted bride smiled in the darkness, the dog Muffin stirred and whined.

Derry's head was buried deep in the cushion. His hands clutched the letter which had cut the knot of his desperate decision.

No—one could not break a promise to a mother in Heaven. . .

He waked heavily in the morning. Bronson was beside his bed. "I am sorry to disturb you, sir, but Dr. McKenzie would like to speak to you."

"McKenzie?"

"Yes, sir. I had to call him last night. Your father was worse."

"Bring him right in here, Bronson, and have some coffee for us."

When Dr. McKenzie was ushered into Derry's sitting room, he found a rather pale and languid young man in the long chair.

"I hated to wake you, Drake. But it was rather necessary that I should talk your father's case over with you."

"Is he very ill?"

"It isn't that—there are complications that I don't care to discuss with servants."

"You mean he has been drinking?"

"Yes. Heavily. You realize that's a rather serious thing for a man of his age."

"I know it. But there's nothing to be done."

"What makes you say that?"

"We've tried specialists—cures. I've been half around the world with him."

The Doctor nodded. "It's hard to pull up at that age."

"My mother's life was spent in trying to help him. He's a dear old chap, really."

"There is, of course, the possibility that he may get a grip on himself."

Derry's languor left him. "Do you think there's the least hope of it? Frankly? No platitudes?"

"We are making some rather interesting experiments—psycho-analysis—things like that—"

He stood up. He was big and breezy. "What's the matter with you this morning? You ought to be up and out."

Derry flushed. "Nothing—much."

The Doctor sat down again. "I'd tell most men to take a cold shower and a two hours' tramp, but it's more than that with you—."

"It's a ease of suspended activity. I want to get into the war—"

"Why don't you?"

"I can't leave Dad. Surely you can see that."

"I don't see it. He must reap, every man must."

"But there's more than that. My mother tied me by a promise. And people are calling me a coward—even Dad thinks I am a slacker, and I can't say to him, 'If you were more than the half of a man I might be a whole one.'"

"Your mother couldn't have foreseen this war."

"It would have made no difference. Her world was centered in him. You know, of course, Doctor, that I wouldn't have spoken of this to anyone else—"

"My dear fellow, I am father confessor to half of my patients." The Doctor's eyes were kind. "My lips will be sealed. But if you want my advice I should throw the old man overboard. Let him sink or swim. Your life is your own."

"It has never been my own." He went to a desk and took out an envelope. "It's a rather sacred letter, but I want you to read it—I read it for the first time last night."

When at last the Doctor laid the letter down, Derry said very low, "Do you blame me?"

"My dear fellow; she had no right to ask it."

"But having asked—?"

"It is a moving letter, and you loved her—but I still contend she had no right to ask."

"I gave my sacred word."

"I question whether any promise should stand between a man and his country's need of him."

They faced each other. "I wonder—" Derry said, "I—I must think it over, Doctor."

"Give yourself a chance if you do. We can go too far in our sacrifice for others—." He resumed his brisk professional manner. "In the meantime you've a rather sick old gentleman on your hands. You'd better get a nurse."

CHAPTER VII

HILDA

The argument came up at breakfast two days before Thanksgiving. It was a hot argument. Jean beat her little hands upon the table. Hilda's hands were still, but it was an irritating stillness.

"What do you think, Daddy?"

"Hilda is right. There is no reason why we should go to extremes."

"But a turkey—."

"Nobody has said that we shouldn't have a turkey on Thanksgiving—not even Hoover." Hilda's voice was as irritating as her hands.

"Well, we have consciences, Hilda. And a turkey would choke me."

"You make so much of little things."

"Is it a little thing to sacrifice our appetites?"

"I don't think it is a very big thing." The office bell rang, and Hilda rose. "If I felt as you do I should sacrifice something more than things to eat. I'd go over there and nurse the wounded. I could be of real service. But you couldn't. With all your big ideas of patriotism you couldn't do one single practical thing."

It was true, and Jean knew that it was true, but she fired one more shot. "Then why don't you go?" she demanded fiercely.

"I may," Hilda said slowly. "I have been thinking about it. I haven't made up my mind."

Dr. McKenzie glanced at her in surprise. "I didn't dream you felt that way."

"I don't think I do mean it in the way you mean. I should go because there was something worth doing—not as a grandstand play."

She went out of the room. Jean stared after her.

The Doctor laughed. "She got you there, girlie."

"Yes, she did. Do you really think she intends to go, Daddy?"

"It is news to me."

"Good news?"

He shook his head. "She is a very valuable nurse. I should hate to lose her." He sat for a moment in silence, then stood up. "I shouldn't hold out for a turkeyless Thanksgiving if I were you. It isn't necessary."

"Are you taking Hilda's part, Daddy?"

"No, my dear, of course not." He came over and kissed her. "Will you ride with me this morning?"

"Oh, yes—how soon?"

"In ten minutes. After I see this patient."

In less time than that she was ready and waiting for him in her squirrel coat and hat and her little muff.

Her father surveyed her. "Such a lovely lady."

"Do you like me, Daddy?"

"What a question—I love you."

Safe in the car, with the glass screen shutting away the chauffeur, Jean returned to the point of attack.

"Hilda makes me furious, Daddy. I came to talk about her."

"I thought you came because you wanted to ride with me."

"Well, I did. But for this, too."

Over her muff, her stormy eyes surveyed him. "You think I am unreasonable about meatless and wheatless days. But you don't know. Hilda ignores them, Daddy—you should see the breadbox. And the other day she ordered a steak for dinner, one of those big thick ones—and it was Tuesday, and I happened to go down to the kitchen and saw it—and I told the cook that we wouldn't have it, and when I came up I told Hilda, and she laughed and said that I was silly.

"And I said that if she had that steak cooked I would not eat it, and I should ask you not to eat it, and she just stood with her hands flat on your desk, you know the way she does—I hate her hands—and she said that of course if I was going to make a fuss about it she wouldn't have the steak, but that it was simply a thing she couldn't understand The steak was there, why not eat it? And I said it was because of the psychological effect on other people. And she said we were having too much psychology and not enough common sense in this war!

"Well, after that, I went to my Red Cross meeting at the church. I expected to have lunch there, but I changed my mind and came home. Hilda was at the table alone, and, Daddy, she was eating the steak, the whole of it—." She paused to note the effect of her revelation.

"Well?"

"She was eating it when all the world needs food! She made me think of those dreadful creatures in the fairy books. She's— she's a ghoul—"

"My dear."

"A ghoul. You should have seen her, with great chunks of bread and butter."

"Hilda has a healthy appetite."

"Of course you defend her."

"My dear child—"

"Oh you do, Daddy, always, against me—and I'm your daughter—"

She wept a tear or two into her muff, then raised her eyes to find him regarding her quizzically. "Are you going to spoil my ride?"

"You are spoiling mine."

"We won't quarrel about it. And we'll stop at Small's. Shall it be roses or violets, to-day, my dear?"

She chose violets, as more in accord with her pensive mood, lighting the bunch, however, with one red rose. The question of Hilda was not settled, but she yielded as many an older woman has yielded—to the sweetness of tribute—to man's impulse to make things right not by justice but by the bestowal of his bounty.

From the florist's, they went to Huyler's old shop on F Street, where the same girl had served Jean with ice-cream sodas and hot chocolate for fifteen years. Administrations might come and administrations go, but these pleasant clerks had been cup-bearers to them all—Presidents' daughters and diplomats' sons—the sturdy children of plain Congressmen, the scions of noble families across the seas.

It was while Jean sat on a high stool beside her father, the sunshine shining on her through the wide window, that Derry Drake, coming down Twelfth, saw her!

Well, he wanted a lemonade. And the fact that she was there in a gray squirrel coat and bunch of violets with her copper-colored hair shining over her ears wasn't going to leave him thirsty!

He went in. He bowed to the Doctor and received a smile in return. Jean's eyes were cold above her chocolate. Derry bought his check, went to a little table on the raised platform at the back of the room, drank his lemonade and hurried out.

"A nice fellow," said the Doctor, watching him through the window. "I wonder why he didn't stop and speak to us?"

"I'm glad he didn't."

"My dear, why?"

"I've found out things—"

"What things?"

"That he's a—coward," with tense earnestness. "He won't fight."

"Who told you that?"

"Everybody's saying it."

"Everybody is dead wrong."

"What do you mean, Daddy?"

"What I have just said. Everybody is dead wrong."

"How do you know?"

"A doctor knows a great many things which he is not permitted to tell. I am rather bound not to tell in this case."

"Oh, but you could tell me."

"Hardly—it was given in confidence."

"Did he? Oh, Daddy, did he tell you?"

"Yes."

"And he isn't a slacker?"

"No."

"I knew it—."

"You didn't. You thought he was a coward."

"Well, I ought to have known better. He looks brave, doesn't he?"

"I shouldn't call him exactly a heroic figure."

"Shouldn't you?"

She finished her chocolate in silence, and followed him in

silence to his car. They sped up F Street, gay with its morning crowd.

Then at last it came. "Isn't it a wonderful day, Daddy?"

He smiled down at her. "There you go."

"Well, it is wonderful." She fell again into silence, then again bestowed upon him her raptures. "Wouldn't it be dreadful if we had loveless days, Daddy, as well as meatless ones and wheatless?"

That night, after Jean had gone to bed, the Doctor, having dismissed his last patient, came out of his inner office. Hilda, in her white nurse's costume, was busy with the books. He stood beside her desk. His eyes were dancing. "Jean told me about the steak."

"I knew she would—I suppose it was an awful thing to do. But I was hungry, and I hate fish—" She smiled at him lazily, then laughed.

He laughed back. He felt that it would be unbearable for Hilda to go hungry, to spoil her red and white with abstinence.

"My dear girl," he said, "what did you mean when you spoke of going away?"

"Haven't you been thinking of going?"

The color came up in his cheeks. "Yes, but how did you know it?"

"Well, a woman knows. Why don't you make up your mind?"

"There's Jean to think of."

"Emily Bridges could take care of her. And you ought to go. Men are seeing things over there that they'll never see again.

And women are."

"If my country needs me—"

Hilda was cold. "I shouldn't go for that. As I told Jean, I am not making any grand stand plays. I should go for all that I get out of it, the experience, the adventure—."

He looked at her with some curiosity. Jean's words of the afternoon recurred to him. "She's a ghoul—"

Yet there was something almost fascinating in her frankness. She tore aside ruthlessly the curtain of self-deception, revealing her motives, as if she challenged him to call them less worthy than his own.

"If I go, it will be because I want to become a better nurse. I like it here, but your practice is necessarily limited. I should get a wider view of things. So would you. There would be new worlds of disease, men in all conditions of nervous shock."

"I know. But I'd hate to think I was going merely for selfish ends."

She shrugged. "Why not that as well as any other?"

He had a smouldering sense of irritation.

"When I am with Jean she makes me feel rather big and fine; when I am with you—" He paused.

"I make you see yourself as you are, a man. She thinks you are more than that."

All his laughter left ham. "It is something to be a hero to one's daughter. Perhaps some day I shall be a little better for her thinking so."

She saw that she had gone too far. "You mustn't take the

things I say too seriously."

The bell of the telephone at her elbow whirred. She put the receiver to her ear. "It is General Drake's man; he thinks you'd better come over before you go to bed."

"I was afraid I might have to go. He is in rather bad shape, Hilda."

She packed his bag for him competently, and telephoned for his car. "I'll have a cup of coffee ready for you when you get back," she said, as she stood in the door. "It is going to be a dreadful night."

The streets were icy and the sleet falling. "You'd better have your overshoes," Hilda decided, and went for them.

As he put them on, she stood under the hall light, smiling. "Have you forgiven me?" she asked as he straightened up.

"For telling me the truth? Of course. You take such good care of me, Hilda."

Upstairs in her own room Jean was writing a letter. It was a very pretty room, very fresh and frilly with white dimity and with much pink and pale lavender. The night-light which shone through the rose taffeta petticoats of a porcelain lady was supplemented at the moment by a bed-side lamp which flung a ring of gold beyond Jean's blotter to the edge of the lace spread. For Jean was writing in bed. All day her mind had been revolving around this letter, but she had had no time to write. She had spent the afternoon in the Toy Shop with Emily, and in the evening there had been a Red Cross sale. She had gone to the sale with Ralph Witherspoon and his mother. She had not been able to get out of going. All the time she had talked to Ralph she had thought of Derry. She had rather hoped that he might be there, but he wasn't.

The letter required much thought. She tore up, extravagantly, several sheets of note-paper with tiny embossed thistles at the top. Doctor McKenzie was intensely Scotch, and he was entitled to a crest, but he was also intensely American, and would have none of it. He had designed Jean's note-paper, and it was lovely. But it was also expensive, and it was a shame to waste so much of it on Derry Drake.

The note when it was finished seemed very simple. Just one page in Jean's firm, clear script:

"Dear Mr. Drake:—

"Could you spare me one little minute tomorrow? I shall be at home at four. It is very important—to me at least. Perhaps when you hear what I have to say, it will seem important to you. I hope it may.

"Very sincerely yours,

"JEAN MCKENZIE."

She read it over several times. It seemed very stiff and inadequate. She sealed it and stamped it, then in a panic tore it open for a re-reading. She was oppressed by doubts. Did nice girls ask men to come and see them? Didn't they wait and weary [Transcriber's note: worry?] like Mariana of the Moated Grange—? "He cometh not, she said?"

New times! New manners! She had branded a man as a coward. She had condemned him unheard. She had slighted him, she had listened while others slandered—why should she care what other women had done? Would do? Her way was clear. She owed an apology to Derry Drake, and she would make it.

So with a new envelope, a new stamp, the note was again sealed.

It had to be posted that night. She felt that under no

circumstance could she stand the suspense of another day.

She had heard her father go out. Hilda was coming up, the maids were asleep. She waited until Hilda's door was shut, then she slipped out of bed, tucked her toes into a pair of sandals, threw a furry motor coat around her, and sped silently down the stairs. She shrank back as she opened the front door. The sleet rattled on the steps, the pavements were covered with white.

The mail-box was in front of the house. She made a rush for it, dropped in the precious letter, and gained once more the haven of the warm hall.

She was glad to get back to her room. As she settled down among her pillows, she had a great sense of adventure, as if she had travelled far in a few moments.

As a matter of fact, she had made her first real excursion into the land of romance. She found her thoughts galloping.

At the foot of the bed her silver Persian, Polly Ann, lay curled on her own gray blanket.

"Polly Ann," Jean said, "if he doesn't come, I shall hate myself for writing that note."

Polly Ann surveyed her sleepily.

"But it would serve me right if he didn't, Polly Ann."

She turned off the light and tried to sleep. Downstairs the telephone rang. It rang, too, in Hilda's room. Hilda's door opened and shut. She came across the hall and tapped on Jean's door. "May I come in?"

"Yes."

"Your father has just telephoned," Hilda said from the

threshold, "that General Drake's nurse is not well, and will have to be taken off the case. I shall have to go in her place. There is a great shortage at the hospital. Will you be afraid to stay alone, or shall I wake up Ellen and have her sleep on the couch in your dressing room?"

"Of course I am not afraid, Hilda. Nothing can happen until father comes back."

As Hilda went away, Jean had a delicious feeling of detachment. She would be alone in the house with her thoughts of Derry.

She got out of bed to say her prayers. With something of a thrill she prayed for Derry's father. She was not conscious as she made her petitions of any ulterior motive. Yet a placated Providence would, she felt sure, see that the General's sickness should not frustrate the plans which she had quite daringly made for his son.

CHAPTER VIII

THE SHADOWED ROOM

Derry had dined that night with his cousin, Margaret Morgan. Margaret's husband was somewhere in France with Pershing's divisions. Margaret was to have news of him this evening, brought by a young English officer, Dawson Hewes, who had been wounded at Ypres, and who had come on a recruiting mission, among his countrymen in America.

The only other guest was to be Drusilla Gray.

Derry had gone over early to have the twilight hour with Margaret's children. There was Theodore, the boy, and Margaret-Mary, on the edge of three. They had their supper at five in the nursery, and after that there was always the story hour, with nurse safely downstairs for her dinner, their mother, lovely in a low-necked gown, and father coming in at the end. For several months their father had not come, and the best they could do was to kiss his picture in the frame with the eagle on it, to put flowers in front of it, and to say their little prayers for the safety of men in battle.

It was Cousin Derry who dropped in now at the evening hour. He was a famous story-teller, and they always welcomed him uproariously.

Margaret Morgan, perhaps better than any other, knew in those days what was in Derry's heart. She knew the things against which he had struggled, and she had rebelled hotly, "Why should he be sacrificed?" she had asked her husband more than once during the three years which had preceded America's entrance into the war. "He wants to be over there driving an ambulance—doing his bit. Aunt Edith always idealized the General, and Derry is paying the price."

"Most women idealize the men they love, honey-girl." Winston Morgan was from the South, and he drew upon its store of picturesque endearments to express his joy and pride in his own Peggy. "And if they didn't where should we be?"

She had leaned her head against him. "I don't need to idealize you," she had said, comfortably, "but the General is different. Aunt Edith made Derry live his father's life, not his own, and it has moulded him into something less than he might have been if he had been allowed more initiative."

Winston had shaken his head. "Discipline is a mighty good thing in the Army, Peggy, and it's a mighty good thing in life. Derry Drake is as hard as steel, and as finely tempered. If he ever does break loose, he'll be all the more dynamic for having held himself back."

Margaret, conceding all that, was yet constrained to pour out upon Derry the wealth of her womanly sympathy. It was perhaps the knowledge of this as well as his devotion to her children which brought him often to her door.

Tonight she was sitting on a low-backed seat in front of the fire with a child on each side of her. She was in white, her dark hair in a simple shining knot, a little pearl heart which had been Captain Morgan's parting gift, her only ornament.

"Go on with your story," he said, as he came in. "I just want to listen and do nothing."

She glanced up at him. He looked tired, unlike himself, depressed.

"Anything the matter?"

"Father isn't well. Dr. McKenzie has taken the case. Richards has gone to the front. Bronson will call me if there are any unfavorable developments."

Margaret-Mary, curled up like a kitten in the curve of Cousin Derry's arm, was exploring his vest pocket. She found two very small squares of Washington taffy wrapped in wax paper, one for herself and one for Teddy. It was Derry's war-time offering. No other candies were permitted by Margaret's patriotism. Her children ate molasses on their bread, maple sugar on their cereal. Her soldier was in France, and there were other soldiers, not one of whom should suffer because of the wanton waste of food by the people who stayed softly at home.

"You tell us a story, Uncle Derry," Teddy pleaded as he ate his taffy.

"I'd rather listen to your mother."

"They are tired of me," Margaret told him.

"We are not ti-yard," her small son enunciated carefully, "but you said you had to fix the f'owers."

"Well, I have. May I turn them over to you, Derry?"

"For a minute. But you must come back."

She came back presently, to find the lights out and only the glow of the fire to illumine faintly the three figures on the sofa. She stood unseen in the door and listened.

"And so the Tin Soldier stood on the shelf where the little boy had put him, and nothing happened in the old, old house. There was just an old, old man, and walls covered with old, old portraits, and knights in armor, and wooden trumpeters carved on the door who blew with all their might,

"'Trutter-a-trutt, Trutter-a-trutt'—. But the old man and the portraits and the wooden trumpeters had no thought for the Tin Soldier who stood there on the shelf, alone and longing to go to the war. And at last the Tin Soldier cried out, 'I can't stand it. I want to go to the wars—I want to go to the wars!' But nobody listened or cared."

"Poor 'itte sing," Margaret-Mary crooned.

"If I had been there," Teddy proclaimed, "I'd have put him on the floor and told him to run and run and run!"

"But there was nobody to put him on the floor," said Derry, "so at last the Tin Soldier could stand it no longer. 'I will go to the wars, I will go to the wars,' he cried, and he threw himself down from the shelf."

The story stopped suddenly. "Go on, go on," urged the little voices in the dark.

"Perhaps you think that was the end of it, and that the Tin Soldier ran away to the wars, to help his country and save the world from ruin. But Fate wasn't as kind to him as that. For when the little boy came again to the old house, he looked for the Tin Soldier. But he wasn't on the shelf. And he looked and looked and, the old man looked, and the wooden trumpeters blew out their cheeks, 'Trutter-a-trutt, trutter-a-trutt—where is the Tin Soldier?—trutter-a-trutt—.'

"But they did not find him, for the Tin Soldier had fallen through a crack in the floor, and there he lay as in an open grave."

Drusilla's voice was heard in the lower hall, and the deeper voice of Captain Hewes. Margaret sped down to meet them, leaving the story, reluctantly, in that moment of heart-breaking climax.

When later Derry followed her, she had a chance to say, "I

hope you gave it a happy ending."

"Oh, did you hear? Yes. They found him in time to send him away to war. But Hans Andersen didn't end it that way. He knew life."

She stared at him in amazement. Was this the Derry whose supply of cheerfulness had seemed inexhaustible? Whose persistent optimism had been at times exasperating to his friends?

Throughout the evening she was aware of his depression. She was aware, too, of the mistake which she had made in bringing Derry and Captain Hewes together.

The Captain had red hair and a big nose. But he was a gentleman in the fine old English sense; he was a soldier with but one idea, that every physically able man should fight. Every sentence that he spoke was charged with this belief, and every sentence carried a sting for Derry.

More than once Peggy found it necessary to change the subject frantically. Drusilla supplemented her efforts.

But gradually the Captain's manner froze. With a sort of military sixth sense, he felt that he had been asked to break bread and eat salt with a slacker, and he resented it.

After dinner Drusilla sang for them. Sensitive always to atmosphere, she soothed the Captain with old and familiar songs, "Flow gently, sweet Afton," and "Believe me if all those endearing young charms."

Then straight from these to "I'm going to marry 'Arry on the Fifth of January."

"Oh, I say—Harry Lauder," was Captain Hewes' eager comment. "I heard him singing to the chaps in the trenches just before I sailed—a little stocky man in a red kilt. He'd laugh, and you'd want to cry."

Drusilla gave them "Wee Hoose among the Heather," with the touch of pathos which the little man in the red kilt had imparted to it as he had sung it in October in New York before an audience which had wept as it had welcomed him.

"Queer thing," Captain Hewes mused, "what the war has done to him, set him preaching and all that."

"Oh, it isn't queer," Margaret was eager. "That is one of the things the war is doing, bringing men back to—God—" A sob caught in her throat.

Drusilla's hands strayed upon the keys, and into the Battle Hymn of the Republic.

> "I have seen Him in the watch fires of a hundred circling camps, They have builded Him an altar in the evening dews and damps, I can read His righteous sentence by the dim and flaring lamps, His day is marching on—"

It was an old tune, but the words were new to Captain Hewes—as the girl chanted them, in that repressed voice that yet tore the heart out of him.

> "He has sounded forth the trumpet that shall never call retreat, He is sifting out the hearts of men before His judgment seat, Oh, be swift, my soul, to answer Him, be jubilant my feet, Our God is marching on—"

The Captain sat on the edge of his chair. His face was illumined.

"By Jove," he ejaculated, "that's topping!"

Drusilla stood up with her back to the piano, and sang without music.

"In the beauty of the lilies, Christ was born across the sea—
With the glory in His bosom that transfigures you and me,
As He died to make men holy, let us die to make men free,
While God is marching on—"

She wore a gown of sheer dull blue, there was a red rose in her
hair—her white arms, her white neck, the blue and red, youth
and fire, strength and purity.

When she finished the room was very still. The big
Englishman had no words for such a moment. The music had
swept him up to unexpected heights of emotion. While
Drusilla sang he had glimpsed for the first time the meaning of
democracy, he had seen, indeed, in a great and lofty sense, for
the first time—America.

Among the shadows a young man shrank in his seat. His vision
was not of Democracy, but of a freezing night—of a ragged
old voice rising from the blackness of a steep ravine—

"Oh, be swift, my soul—to answer—Him— Be jubilant
my feet—"

Why had Drusilla chosen that of all songs? Oh, why had she
sung at all?

A maid came in to say that Mr. Drake was wanted at the
telephone. The message was from Dr. McKenzie. The General
was much worse. It might be well for Derry to come home.

So Derry, with a great sense of relief, got away from the frigid
Captain, and from the flaming Drusilla, and from Peggy with
her flushed air of apology, and went out into the stormy night.
He had preferred to walk, although his shoes were thin. "It
isn't far," he had said when Margaret expostulated, "and I'll
send my car for Drusilla and Captain Hewes."

The sleet drove against his face. His feet were wet before he
reached the first corner, the wind buffeted him. But he felt

none of it. He was conscious only of his depression and of his great dread of again entering the big house where a sick man lay in a lacquered bed and where a painted lady smiled on the stairs. Where there was nothing alive, nothing young, nothing with lips to welcome him, or with hands to hold out to him.

He found when at last he arrived that the Doctor had sent for Hilda Merritt.

She came presently, in her long blue cloak and small blue bonnet. Hilda made no mistakes in the matter of clothes. She realized the glamour which her nurse's uniform cast over her. In evening dress she was slightly commonplace. In ordinary street garb not an eye would have been turned upon her, but the nun's blue and white of her uniform added the required spiritual effect to her rather full-blown beauty.

As she passed the painted lady at the head of the stairway she gave her a slight glance. Then on and up she went to her appointed task.

"It is pneumonia," Dr. McKenzie told Derry; "that's why I wanted Miss Merritt. She is very experienced, and in these days of war it is hard to get good nurses."

Derry found his voice shaking. "Is there any danger?"

"Naturally, at his age. But I think we are going to pull him through."

Derry went into the shadowed room. His father was breathing heavily. Something clutched at the boy's heart—the fear of the Thing which lurked in the darkness—a chill and sinister figure with a skeleton hand.

He could not have his father die. He would feel as if his thoughts had killed him—a murderer in intention if not in deed. Not thus must the Obstacle be removed. He raised haggard eyes to the Doctor's face. "You—you mustn't think that I store things up against him. He's all I have."

The Doctor's keen glance appraised him. "Don't get morbid over it; he has everything in his favor—and Miss Merritt is famous in such cases."

Hilda took his praise with downcast eyes Her manner with the Doctor when others were present was professionally deferential. It was only when they were alone that the nurse was submerged in the woman.

With her bonnet off and a white cap in its place, she moved about the room. "I shall be very comfortable," she said, when Derry inquired if anything could be done for her.

"We haven't any women about the place but Cook," he explained. "She has been in our family forever—"

"I'll put a day nurse on tomorrow," the Doctor said, "but I want Hilda with him at night; she can call me up if there's any change, and I'll come right over."

When the Doctor had gone, Derry, seeking his room, found Muffin waiting. Bronson bustled in to see that his young master got out of his wet clothes and into a hot bath. "All the time the Doctor was talking to you, I was worrying about your shoes. Your feet are soaked, sir. Whatever made you walk in the rain?"

"I couldn't ride—I couldn't."

The old man on his knees removing the wet shoes looked up. "Restless, sir?"

"Yes. There are times, Bronson, when I want my mother."

He could say it in this room to Bronson and Muffin—to the gray old dog and the gray old man who adored him.

Bronson put him to bed, settled Muffin among his blankets in a basket by the hot water pipes, opened the windows wide, said "God bless you," and went away.

"Sweet dreams, Muffin," said Derry from the big bed.

The old dog whuffed discreetly.

It was their nightly ceremony.

The sleet came down in golden streaks against the glow of the street lights. Derry lay watching it, and it was a long time before he slept. Not since his mother's death had he been so weighed down with heaviness.

He kept seeing Jean with her head up, declining to dance with him; on the high stool at the confectioner's, her eyes cold above her chocolate; the English Captain and his contemptuous stare; Alma, basely excusing him; Drusilla, in her red and blue and white—singing—!

He waked in the morning with a sore throat. Young Martin came in to light the fire and draw the water for his bath. Later Bronson brought his breakfast and the mail.

"You'd better stay in bed, Mr. Derry."

"I think I shall. How is Dad?"

"The nurse says he is holding his own."

"I am glad of that."

Bronson, feeding warm milk and toast to Muffin, ventured an opinion, "I am not sure that I like the nurse, sir."

"Why not?"

"She's not exactly a lady, and she's not exactly a nurse."

"I see." Derry, having glanced over a letter or two, had picked up an envelope with embossed thistles on the flap. "But she is rather pretty, Bronson."

"Pretty is as pretty does," sententiously.

Silence. Bronson looked across at the young man propped up among the pillows. He was rereading the letter with the thistles on the flap. The strained look had gone out of his eyes, and his lips were smiling.

"I think I'll get up."

"Changed your mind, sir?"

"Yes." He threw back the covers. "I've a thousand things to do."

But there was just one thing which he was going to do which stood out beyond all others. Neither life nor death nor flood nor fire should keep him from presenting himself at four o'clock at Jean McKenzie's door, in response to the precious note which in a moment had changed the world for him.

CHAPTER IX

ROSE-COLOR!

Jean found the day stretching out ahead of her in a series of exciting events. At the breakfast table her father told her that Hilda would stay on General Drake's case, and that she had better have Emily Bridges up for a visit.

"I don't like to have you alone at night, if I am called away."

"It will be heavenly, Daddy, to have Emily—"

And how was he to know that there were other heavenly things to happen? She had resolved that if Derry came, she would tell her father afterwards. But he might not come, so what was the use of being premature?

She sallied down to the Toy Shop in high feather. "You are to stay with us, Emily."

"Oh, am I? How do you know that I can make it convenient?"

"But you will, darling."

Jean's state of mind was beatific. She painted Lovely Dreams with a touch of inspiration which resulted in a row of purple camels: "Midnight on the Desert," Jean called them.

"Oh, Emily," she said, "we must have them in the window on

Christmas morning, with the Wise Men and the Star—"

Emily, glancing at the face above the blue apron, was struck by the radiance of it.

"Is it because Hilda is away?" she asked.

"Is what—?"

"Your—rapture."

Jean laughed. "It is because Hilda is away, and other things. But I can't tell you now."

Then for fear Emily might be hurt by her secrecy, she flew to kiss her and again call her "Darling."

At noon she put on her hat and ran home, or at least her heart ran, and when she reached the house she sought the kitchen.

"I am having company for tea, Ellen—at four. And I want Lady-bread-and-butter, and oh, Ellen, will you have time for little pound cakes?"

She knew of course that pound cakes were—*verboten*. She felt, however, that even Mr. Hoover might sanction a fatted calf in the face of this supreme event.

She planned that she would receive Derry in the small drawing room. It was an informal room which had been kept by her mother for intimate friends. There was a wide window which faced west, a davenport in deep rose velvet, some chairs to match, and there were always roses in an old blue bowl.

Jean knew the dress she was going to wear in this room—of blue to match the bowl, with silver lace, and a girdle of pink brocade.

Alone in her room with Polly-Ann to watch proceedings, she

got out the lovely gown.

"Oh, I do want to be pretty, Polly-Ann," she said with much wistfulness.

Yet when she was all hooked and snapped into it, she surveyed herself with some dissatisfaction in the mirror.

"Why not?" she asked the mirror. "Why shouldn't I wear it?"

The mirror gave back a vision of beauty—but behind that vision in the depths of limitless space Jean's eyes discerned something which made her change her gown. Quite soberly she got herself into a little nun's frock of gray with collars and cuffs of transparent white, and above it all was the glory of her crinkled hair.

Neither then nor afterwards could she analyze her reasons for the change. Perhaps sub-consciously she was perceiving that this meeting with Derry Drake was to be a serious and stupendous occasion. Throughout the world the emotions of men and women were being quickened to a pace set by a mighty conflict. Never again would Jean McKenzie laugh or cry over little things. She would laugh and cry, of course, but back of it all would be that sense of the world's travail and tragedy, made personal by her own part in it.

Julia, the second maid, was instructed to show Mr. Drake into the little drawing room. Jean came down early with her knitting, and sat on the deep-rose Davenport. The curtains were not drawn. There was always the chance of a sunset view. Julia was to turn on the light when she brought in the tea.

There was the whir of a bell, the murmur of voices. Jean sat tense. Then as her caller entered, she got somewhat shakily on her feet.

But the man in the door was not Derry Drake!

Temple Bailey

In his intrusive and impertinent green, pinched-in as to waist, and puffed-out as to trousers, his cheeks red with the cold, his brown eyes bright with eagerness, Ralph Witherspoon stood on the threshold.

"Of all the good luck," he said, "to find you in."

She shook hands with him and sat down.

"I thought you had gone back to Bay Shore. You said yesterday you were going."

"I got my orders in the nick of time. We are to go to Key West. I am to join the others on the way down."

"How soon?"

He sat at the other end of the davenport. "In three days, and anything can happen in three days."

He moved closer. She had a sense of panic. Was he going to propose to her again, in this room which she had set aside so sacredly for Derry Drake?

"Won't you have some tea?" she asked, desperately. "I'll have Julia bring it in."

"I'd rather talk."

But she had it brought, and Julia, wheeling in the tea-cart, offered a moment's reprieve. And Ralph ate the Lady-bread-and-butter, and the little pound cakes with the nuts and white frosting which had been meant for Derry, and then he walked around the tea-cart and took her hand, and for the seventh time since he had met her he asked her to marry him.

"But I don't love you." She was almost in tears.

"You don't know what love is—I'll teach you."

"I don't want to be taught."

"You don't know what it means to be taught—"

Jean had a stifling sense as of some great green tree bending down to crush her. She put out her hand to push it away.

In the silence a bell whirred—.

Derry Drake, ushered in by Julia, saw the room in the rosy glow of the lamp. He saw Ralph Witherspoon towering insolently in his aviator's green. He saw Jean, blushing and perturbed. The scene struck cold against the heat of his anticipation.

He sat down in one of the rose-colored chairs, and Julia brought more tea for him, more Lady-bread-and-butter, more pound cakes with nuts and frosting.

Ralph was frankly curious. He was also frankly jealous. He was aware that Derry had met Jean for the first time at his mother's dinner dance. And Derry's millions were formidable. It did not occur to Ralph that Derry, without his millions, was formidable. Ralph's idea of a man's attractiveness for women was founded on his belief in their admiration of good looks, and their liking for the possession of, as he would himself have expressed it, "plenty of pep" and "go." From Ralph's point of view Derry Drake was not handsome, and he was utterly unaware that back of Derry's silver-blond slenderness and apparent languidness were banked fires which could more than match his own.

And there was this, too, of which he was unconscious, that Derry's millions meant nothing to Jean. Had he remained the shabby son of the shabby old man in the Toy Shop, her heart would still have followed him.

So, fatuously hopeful, Ralph stayed. He stayed until five, until half-past five. Until a quarter of six.

And he talked of the glories of war!

Derry grew restless. As he sat in the rose-colored chair, he fingered a tassel which caught back one of the curtains of the wide window. It was a silk tassel, and he pulled at one strand of it until it was flossy and frayed. He was unconscious of his work of destruction, unconscious that Jean's eyes, lifted now and then from her knitting, noted his fingers weaving in and out of the rosy strands.

Ralph talked on. With seeming modesty he spoke of the feats of other men, yet none the less it was Ralph they saw, poised like a bird at incredible heights, looping the loop, fearless, splendid—beating the air with strong wings.

Six o'clock, and at last Ralph rose. Even then he hesitated and hung back, as if he expected that Derry might go with him. But Derry, stiff and straight beside the rose-colored chair, bade him farewell!

And now Derry was alone with Jean!

They found themselves standing close together in front of the fire. The garment of coldness and of languor which had seemed to enshroud Derry had dropped from him. The smile which he gave Jean was like warm wine in her veins.

"Well—?"

"I asked you to come—to say—that I am,—sorry—," her voice breaking. "Daddy told me that he knew why—you couldn't fight—"

"I didn't intend that he should tell."

"He didn't," eagerly, "not your reasons. He said it was a—confidence, and he couldn't break his word. But he knew that you were brave. That the things the world is saying are all wrong. Oh, I ought to go down on my knees."

Her face was white, her eyes deep wells of tears.

"It is I," he said, very low, "who should be on my knees—do you know what it means to me to have you tell me this?"

"I wasn't sure that I ought to write. To some men I couldn't have written—"

His face lighted. "When your note came—I can't tell you what it meant to me. I shouldn't like to think of what this day would have been for me if you had not written. Everybody is calling me—a coward. You know that. You heard Witherspoon just now pitying me, not in words, but his manner."

"Oh, Ralph," how easily she disposed of him. "Ralph crows, like a—rooster."

They looked at each other and tried to laugh. But they were not laughing in their hearts.

He lifted her hand and kissed it—then he stood well away from her, anchoring himself again to the silken tassel. "Now that you know a part," he said, from that safe distance, "I'd like to tell you all of it, if I may."

As he talked her fingers were busy with her knitting, but there came moments when she laid it down and looked up at him with eyes that mirrored his own earnestness.

"It—it hasn't been easy," he said in conclusion, "but—but if you will be my friend, nothing will be hard."

She tried to speak—was shaken as if by a strong wind, and her knitting went up as a shield.

"My dear, you are crying," he said, and was on his knees beside her.

And now they were caught in the tide of that mighty wave which was sweeping the world!

When at last she steadied herself, he was again anchored to the rose-colored tassel.

"You—you must forgive me—but—it has been so good to talk it out—to some one—who cared. I had never dreamed until that night in the Toy Shop of anybody—like you. Of anybody so—adorable. When your note came this morning, I couldn't believe it. But now I know it is true. And that night of Cinderella you were so—heavenly."

It was a good thing that Miss Emily came in at that moment—for his eloquence was a burning flood, and Jean was swept up and on with it.

The entrance of Emily, strictly tailored and practical, gave them pause.

"You remember Mr. Drake, don't you, Emily?"

Emily did, of course. But she had not expected to see him here. She held out her hand. "I remember that he was coming back for more of your Lovely Dreams."

"I want all of her dreams," said Derry, and something in the way that he said it took Miss Emily's breath away. "Please don't sell them to anyone else. You have a wholesale order from me."

Miss Emily looked from one to the other. She was conscious of something which touched the stars—something which all her life she had missed, something which belongs to youth and ecstasy.

"Wholesale orders are not in my line," she said. "You can settle that with Jean."

She surveyed the tea-wagon. "I'm starved. And if I eat I shall spoil my dinner."

"I can ring for hot water, Emily, and there are more of the pound cakes."

"My dear, no. I must go upstairs and dress. Your father sent for my bag, and Julia says it is in my room."

She bade Derry a cheerful good-bye, and left them alone.

"I must go, too," said Derry, and took Jean's hand. He stood looking down at her. "May I come tomorrow?"

"Oh,—yes—"

"There's one thing that I should like more than anything, if we could go to church together—to be thankful that—that we've found each other—"

Tears in the shining eyes!

"Why are you crying?"

"Because it is so—sweet."

"Then you'll go?"

"I'd love it."

He dropped her hand and got away. She was little and young, so divinely innocent. He felt that he must not take unfair advantage of that mood of exaltation.

He drove straight downtown and ordered flowers for her. Remembering the nun's dress, he sent violets in a gray basket, with a knot on the handle of heavenly blue.

The flowers came while Jean was at dinner. Emily was in

Hilda's place, a quiet contrast in her slenderness and modest black to Hilda's opulence. Dr. McKenzie had not had time to dress.

"I am so busy, Emily."

"But you love the busy-ness, don't you? I can't imagine you without the hours crammed full."

"Just now I wish that I could push it away as Richards pushed it—"

Jean looked up. "But Dr. Richards went to France, Daddy."

"I envy him."

"Oh, do you—?" Then her flowers came, and she forgot everything else.

The Doctor whistled as Julia set the basket in front of Jean. "Ralph is generous."

Jean had opened the attached envelope and was reading a card. A wave of self-conscious color swept over her cheeks. "Ralph didn't send them. It—it was Derry Drake."

"Drake? How did that happen?"

"He was here this afternoon for tea, and Ralph, and Emily— only Emily was late, and the tea was cold—"

"So you've made up?"

"We didn't have to make up much, Daddy, did we?" mendaciously.

Miss Emily came to the rescue. "He seems very nice."

"Splendid fellow. But I am not sure that I want him sending

flowers to my daughter. I don't want anyone sending flowers to her."

Miss Emily took him up sharply. "That's your selfishness. Life has always been a garden where you have wandered at will. And now you want to shut the gate of that garden against your daughter."

"Well, there are flowers that I shouldn't care to have her pluck."

"Don't you know her well enough to understand that she'll pluck only the little lovely blooms?"

His eyes rested on Jean's absorbed face. "Yes, thank God. And thank you, too, for saying it, Emily."

After dinner they sat in the library. Doctor McKenzie on one side of the fire with his cigar, Emily on the other side with her knitting. Jean between them in a low chair, a knot of Derry's violets fragrant against the gray of her gown, her fingers idle.

"Why aren't you knitting?" the Doctor asked.

"I don't have to set a good example to Emily."

"And you do to Hilda?" He threw back his head and laughed.

"You needn't laugh. Isn't it comfy with Emily?"

"It is." He glanced at the slender black figure. He was still feeling the fineness of the thing she had said about Jean. "But when she is here I am jealous."

"Oh, Daddy."

"And I am never jealous of Hilda. If you had Emily all the time you'd love her better than you do me."

He chuckled at their hot eyes. "If you are teasing," Jean told him, "I'll forgive you. But Emily won't, will you, Emily?"

"No." Emily's voice was gay, and he liked the color in her cheeks. "He doesn't deserve to be forgiven. Some day he is going to be devoured by a green-eyed monster, like a bad little boy in a Sunday School story."

Her needles clicked, and her eyes sparkled. There was no doubt that there was a sprightliness about Emily that was stimulating.

"But one's only daughter, Emily. Isn't jealousy pardonable?"

"Not in you."

"Why not?"

"Well," with obvious reluctance, "you're too big for it."

"Oh," he was more pleased than he was willing to admit, "did you hear that, Jean?"

But Jean, having drifted away from them, came back with, "I am going to church with him tomorrow."

"Him? Whom?"

"Derry Drake, Daddy, and may I bring him home to dinner?"

"Do you think a man like that goes begging for invitations? He has probably been asked to a dozen places to eat his turkey."

"He can't eat it at a dozen places, Daddy. And anyhow I should like to ask him. I—I think he is lonely—"

"A man with millions is never lonely."

She did not attempt to argue. She felt that her father could not possibly grasp the truth about Derry Drake. Her own under-standing of his need had been a blinding, whirling revelation. He had said, "I wanted some one—who cared—." Not for a moment since then had the world been real to her. She had seemed in the center of a golden-lighted sphere, where Derry's voice spoke to her, where Derry's smile warmed her, where Derry, a silver-crested knight, knelt at her feet.

Julia came in to say that Miss Jean was wanted at the telephone.

Miraculously Derry's voice came over the wire. Was she going to the dance at the Willard? The one for the benefit of the Eye and Ear Hospital? The President and his wife would be there—the only ball they had attended this season—everybody would be there. Could he come for Jean and her father? And he'd bring Drusilla and Marion Gray. She knew Drusilla?

Jean on tiptoe. Oh, yes. But she was not sure about her father.

"But you—you—?"

"I'll ask."

She flew on winged feet and explained excitedly.

"Tonight? *Tonight*, Jean?"

"Yes, Daddy."

"But what time is it?"

"Only ten. He'll come at eleven—"

"But you can't leave Emily alone, dear."

"Emily won't mind—darling—will you, Emily?"

"Of course not. I am often alone."

It was said quietly, without bitterness, but Dr. McKenzie was quite suddenly and unreasonably moved by the thought of all that Emily had missed. He felt it utterly unfair that she should sit alone by an empty hearth while he and Jean frivolled. He had never thought of Hilda by an empty hearth—and she had been often alone—but there was this which made the difference, he would not have asked Hilda to meet his daughter's friends. She had her place in his household, but it was not the place which Emily filled.

Yet he missed her. He missed her blond picturesqueness at the dinner table, her trim whiteness as she served him in his office.

He came back to the question of Emily. "You can tell Drake we will go, if Emily can accompany us."

"But, Doctor, I'd rather not."

"Why not?"

"I'm not included in the invitation."

"Don't be self-conscious."

"And I haven't anything to wear."

"You never looked better than you do at this moment. And Jean can get you that scarf of her mother's with the jet and spangles."

"The peacocky one—oh, yes, Daddy." Jean danced back to the telephone.

Derry was delighted to include Miss Bridges. "Bring a dozen if you wish."

"I don't want a dozen. I want just Daddy and Emily."

"And me?"

"Of course—silly—"

Laughter singing along the wire. "May I come now?"

"I have to change my dress."

"In an hour, then?"

"Yes."

"I can't really believe that we are going together!"

"Together—"

CHAPTER X

A MAN WITH MONEY

White and silver for Jean, the peacocky scarf making Emily shine with the best of them, Dr. McKenzie called away at the last moment, and promising to join them later; Derry catching his breath when he saw his violets among Jean's laces; Drusilla wondering a little at this transfigured Derry; Marion Gray settling down to the comfort of a chat with Emily—what had these to do with a Tin Soldier on a shelf?

"How is your father, Derry?"

"Better, Drusilla. He has a fine nurse. Dr. McKenzie sent her."

"And I have Emily," Jean sang from the corner of the big car where Derry had her penned in, with the fragrance of her violets sweeping over him as he sat next to her. "I want Emily always, but Daddy has to have a nurse in the office, and Emily won't give up her toys. And in the meantime Hilda and I are ready to scratch each other's eyes out. Please keep her as long as you can on your father's case, Mr. Drake."

"Say 'Derry,'" he commanded under cover of the light laughter of the women.

"Not before—everybody—"

"Whisper it, then."

"Derry, Derry."

His pulses pounded. During the rest of the drive, he spoke to his other guests and seemed to listen, but he heard nothing—nothing but the whisper of that beloved voice.

As Derry had said, all the world of Washington was at the ball. The President and his wife in a flag-draped box, she in black with a turquoise fan, he towering a little above her, more than President in these autocratic days of war. They looked down on men in the uniforms of the battling world—Scot and Briton and Gaul—in plaid and khaki and horizon blue—.

They looked down on women knitting.

Mrs. Witherspoon and a party of young people sat in a box adjoining Derry's. Ralph was there and Alma Drew, and Alma was more than ever lovely in gold-embroidered tulle.

Ralph knew what had happened when he saw Jean dancing with Derry. There was no mistaking the soft raptures of the youthful pair. In the days to come Ralph was to suffer wounds, but none to tear his heart like this. And so when he danced with Jean a little later he did not spare her.

"A man with money always gets what he wants."

"I don't know what you mean."

"I think you do. You are going to marry Derry Drake."

She shrank at this. She had in her meetings with Derry never looked beyond the bliss of the moment. To have Ralph's rough fingers tearing at the veil of her future was revolting.

She breathed quickly. "I shan't dance with you, if you speak of it again."

"You shall dance with me," grimly, "this moment is my own—"

She was like wax in his strong arms. "Oh, how dare you." She was cold with auger. "I want to stop."

"And I could dance forever. That's the irony of it—that I cannot make you. But if I had Drake's money, I'd make you."

"Do you think it is his money?"

"Perhaps not. But the world will think it."

"If—if he wanted me, I'd marry him if he were a beggar in the streets."

"Has it gone as far as that? But you wouldn't marry a beggar. A troubadour beneath your balcony, yes. But not a beggar. You'd want him silken and blond and singing, and staying at home while other men fought—"

She stopped at once. "If you knew what you were talking about; I'd never speak to you again. But because I was fool enough once to believe that Derry Drake was a coward, I am going to forgive you. But I shall not dance with you again; ever—"

Making her way back alone to the box, she saw with a throb of relief that her father had joined Emily and Marion Gray.

He uttered a quick exclamation as she came up. "What's the matter, daughter?"

Her throat was dry. "I can't tell you now—there are too many people. It was Ralph. I hate him, Daddy."

"My dear—"

"I do."

"But why?"

"Please, I don't want to talk about it—wait until we get home."

Looking out over the heads of the swaying crowd, she saw that Derry was dancing with Alma Drew. And it was Alma who had said at the Witherspoon dinner, "Everybody will forgive a man with money."

And that was what Ralph had thought of her, that she was like Alma—that money could buy her—that she would sell the honor of her country for gold—.

But worse than any hurt of her own was the hurt of the thing for Derry. Ralph Witherspoon had dared to point a finger of scorn at him—other people had dared—

She suffered intensely, not as a child, but as a woman.

Alma, out on the floor, was saying to Derry, "I saw you dancing with Jean McKenzie. She's a quaint little duck."

"Not a duck, Alma," he was smiling, "a white dove—or a silver swan." The look that he sent across the room to Jean was a revelation.

Like Ralph, she grew hateful. "So that's it? Well, a man with money can get anything."

He had no anger for her. Jean might blaze in his defense, but his own fires were not to be fanned by any words of Alma Drew. If he lost his fortune, Jean would still care for him. It was fore-ordained, as fixed as the stars.

So he went back to her, and when she saw him coming, the burden of her distress fell from her. The world became once more hers and Derry's, with everybody else shut out. When they had supper with the Witherspoon party joining them, and

Ralph palely repentant beside her, she even, to the utter bewilderment of her father, smiled at him, and talked as if their quarrel had never been.

Drusilla watched her with more than a tinge of envy. She was aware that her own vivid charm was shadowed and eclipsed by the white flame of Jean's youth and innocence. "And he loves her," she thought with a tug of her heartstrings; "he loves her, and there'll never be anything like it for him again."

She sat rather silently between Captain Hewes and Dr. McKenzie. Dr. McKenzie had always admired Drusilla, but tonight his attention was rather more than usual fixed upon her by a remark which Captain Hewes had made when the two men had stood alone together watching the dancers. "I have seen very little of American women—but to me Drusilla Gray seems the supreme type."

"She is very attractive."

"She is more than that. She is inspiring, the embodiment of your best ideals. When she sings one wonders that all men have not fought for democracy."

That was something to say of a woman. Doctor McKenzie wondered if it could be said of his own daughter. Set side by side with Drusilla, Jean seemed a childish creature, unstable, swayed by the emotion of the moment. Yet her fire matched Drusilla's, her dreams outran Drusilla's dreams.

Two officers passed the table.

"How any man can keep out of it," Drusilla said. "Some day I shall put on a uniform and pass for a boy—"

"Why not go over as you are?"

"They won't let me now. But some day they will. I can drive a car—there ought to be a place for me."

"There is one for me," he said, "and my decision must be made tonight. They are asking me to head a hospital staff in France. A letter came this morning, and I've got to answer it."

Her eyes went to the flame-white maiden on the other side of the table. "What does Jean say?"

"I haven't asked her. She wouldn't keep me back. But I am all she has, and it would hurt."

"It would hurt. But you are not all that she has—you might as well try to sweep back the sea as to stop what is going over there. I have been sitting here green with envy. Oh, if love might only come to me like that."

"Like what?"

"Heaven-sent—never a doubt, never a speculation; just knowing and believing—souls stripped bare of all pretence."

How splendid she was—how beautiful! He bent down to her. "Why shouldn't it come to you?"

"Men don't love me that way. They admire and respect and then love. But Jean? She's a moon maiden, luring them to—madness." She smiled up at him.

"Captain Hewes says you are the supreme type—the perfect American."

"Yes, but he thinks of me as a type. Some day perhaps he will think of me as a woman."

She brought the conversation back to Jean. "You need not let the thought of her loneliness trouble you."

"You think then that I am going to lose her?"

"You have lost her already."

Sparks burned in the Doctor's eyes. "I don't believe it. She has known him a few days—and I've given her my whole life."

"Forsaking all others," murmured Drusilla.

"Yet she loves me."

"It isn't that she loves you less—she loves him more."

"Don't," he lifted his hand. "I am not sure that I can stand it."

"It makes your way clear. That's why I have said it. There will be nothing now to keep you back from France."

Once upon a time she had said to Derry, "I can feel things, and I can make others feel." She had, perhaps, tonight, been a little cruel, but she had been cruel with a purpose.

All the way home Doctor McKenzie was very silent. When he kissed his daughter before she went upstairs, he held her close and smoothed her hair, but not a word did he say of the thing which had come to him.

He asked Emily, however, to wait a moment. "I have a letter to answer. I should like your advice."

Wondering a little, she sat down by the fire. The peacocky scarf gave out glittering lights of blue and green. She was tired and there were shadows under her eyes.

He came at once to his proposition. "I am thinking of going to France, Emily. If I do, can you stay with Jean?"

She turned her startled gaze upon him. "To France? Why?"

He told her. "They have been writing to me for weeks, and now the moment for my decision has come. I haven't said anything to Jean. But she won't keep me back. You know how she feels. But unless you can come, I can't leave her."

"I should have to be all day in my shop."

"I know, but you could be here in the evening and at night, and she could, of course, be with you in the shop, she likes that—and it would keep her from brooding. Or, if you will give up the shop, I should like to make it financially possible for you, Emily."

She shook her head. "No. You will be coming back, and then my occupation would be gone." She hesitated. "But if I come—what of Hilda?"

"She may decide to go over, too, as a nurse. We work well together."

She was silent, searching for the words which she felt that she ought to say. So that was it? They would go together, and the tongues of the world would wag. And Hilda would know that they were wagging, and would not care. But he, with his mind on bigger things, would never know, and would blunder unseeing into the net which was set for him. She felt that she ought to warn him, that the good friendship which existed between them demanded it. Yet it was a hard thing to say, and she hated it. So the moment passed.

It was he who spoke first—of Jean and Derry. "What do you think of it, Emily?"

"He is very much in love with her."

"And Jean?"

"Oh, I think you know. You saw her tonight."

He felt a sudden sense of age and loneliness. "She won't miss me, then?"

"Do you think that anyone could make up to your little Jean for the loss of her father?"

He covered his face with his hand. "You are feeling it like that?" she asked, gently.

"Yes. She is all I have, Emily. And I am jealous—desperately—desperately."

She searched for words to comfort him, and at last they came. "She will be very proud of her Daddy in France."

"Do you think she will?"

"I know it."

"And yet—I am not really worthy of all that she gives—"

She leaned forward, her white hands in her lap. Jean's comment echoed once more in his ears. "I like Emily's hands much better than Hilda's." They seemed, indeed, to represent all that was lovely in Emily, her refinement, her firmness, her gentle spirit.

"Bruce," she said—she rarely called him that—"your dear wife would never have loved you if you hadn't been worthy of love."

"I need her—to hold me to my best."

"Hold yourself to it, Bruce—" She stood up. "I must go to bed, and so must you. We have busy days before us."

He spoke impulsively. "You are a good woman, Emily—there's no one in the world that I would trust to stay with Jean but you."

She smiled a little wistfully as she went upstairs. She had perhaps comforted him, but she had left unsaid the words she should have spoken. "You must not take Hilda with you. If you take her with you, will your Jean be proud of her Daddy in France?"

CHAPTER XI

HILDA WEARS A CROWN

At two o'clock on Thanksgiving morning the light burned low in the General's room. Hilda, wide awake, was reading. Derry stopped at the door.

She rose at once and went to him.

"Is he all right, Miss Merritt?"

"Yes. He's sound asleep."

"Then you think he's better?"

"Much better."

"Good. I hope you can stay on the case. Dr. McKenzie says it is all because of your splendid care of him. I just left McKenzie, by the way. I took him and his daughter to the ball at the Willard. We had a corking time."

Her eyes saw a change in him. This was not the listless Derry with whom she had talked the day before—here were flushed cheeks and shining eyes—gay youth and gladness—.

"A corking time," Derry reiterated. "The President was there, and his wife—and we danced a lot—and—" he caught himself up. "Well, good-night, Miss Merritt."

"Good-night." She went back to the shadowed room.

Bronson, following Derry, came back in a half hour with a dry, "Is there anything I can do for you, Miss Merritt?" and then the house was still.

And now Hilda was alone with the old man in the lacquered bed. There would be no interruptions until morning. It was the moment for which she had waited ever since the hour when the General had sent her into his wife's room for a miniature of Derry, which was locked in the safe.

The suite which had belonged to Mrs. Drake consisted of three rooms—a sitting room, a bedroom and a sun-parlor which had been Derry's nursery. Nothing had been changed since her death. Every day a maid cleaned and dusted, and at certain seasons the clothes in the presses were brushed and aired and put back again. In a little safe in the wall were jewels, and the key was on the General's ring. He had given the key to Hilda when he had sent her for the miniature. His fever had been high, and he had not been quite himself. Even a nurse with a finer sense of honor might have argued, however, that her patient must be obeyed. So she knew now where his treasure was kept—behind a Chinese scroll, which when rolled up revealed the panel which hid the safe.

Hilda had never worn a jewel of value in her life. She possessed, it is true, a few trinkets, a gold ring with her monogram engraved in it, a string of Roman pearls, and a plain wrist watch. But such brilliance as that which met her startled eyes when she had first looked into the safe was beyond anything conceived by her rather limited imagination.

She opened the door between the rooms quietly, and went in, leaving a crack that she might hear any movement on the part of her patient. She crossed the sitting room in the dark. Reaching the bedroom she pulled the chain of the lamp, then set a screen to hide any ray of light which might escape.

The room was furnished with a feeling for delicate color—gold and ivory—Japanese prints—pale silks and crepes—a bit of jade—a cabinet inlaid with mother-of-pearl. But Hilda's eyes were not for these. Indeed, she knew nothing of their value, nothing, indeed, of the value of the Chinese scroll which so effectually hid the panel in the wall.

Within the safe was a large velvet box, and several smaller ones. It was from the big box that Hilda had taken the miniature, and it contained also the crown which she yearned to wear.

She called it a crown! It was a tiara of diamonds, peaked up to a point in front. There was, also, the wide collar of pearls with the diamond slides which had been worn by the painted lady on the stairs. In the smaller boxes were more pearls, long strings of them; sapphires like a midnight sky, opals, fire in a mist; rubies, emeralds—. They should have been locked in a vault at the General's bank, but he had wanted nothing taken away, nothing disturbed. Yet with that touch of fever upon him he had given the key to Hilda.

She took off her cap and turned in the neck of her white linen gown. The pearl collar was a bit small for her, but she managed to snap the three slides. She set the sparkling circlet on her head.

Then she stood back and surveyed herself in the oval mirror!

Gone was the Hilda Merritt whom she had known, and in her place was a queen with a crown! She smiled at her reflection and nodded. For once she was swayed from her stillness and stolidity. She loaded her long hands with rings, and held them to her cheeks; then, struck by the contrast of her white linen sleeve, she rummaged in one of the big closets, and threw on the bed a drift of exquisite apparel.

The gowns were all too small for her, but there was a cloak of velvet and ermine. The General's wife had worn it to the White House dinner over the gown in which she had been painted. Hilda drew the cloak about her shoulders, and laughed noiselessly. She could look like this, and she had never known it! But now that she knew——!

There was the soft click of the telephone in the General's room. Fearful lest the sound should waken her patient, she tore off the tiara, turned up the neck of her dress to hide the shining collar, dropped the cloak, pulled the chain of the lamp, then sped breathless to the shadowed room.

Dr. McKenzie was at the other end of the wire.

"I am coming over, Hilda."

"You need not,"——her voice was a whisper——"he is sound asleep."

"I want to see you for a moment. It is very important."

She hesitated. "It is very late."

"Has young Drake arrived?"

"Yes. He has gone to bed."

"I'll be there in ten minutes. You can meet me downstairs."

The General stirred. "Miss Merritt."

She hung up the receiver and went to him at once.

"Has the Doctor come?"

"No. But he has just telephoned. He will be here shortly."

His sick old eyes surveyed her. "I never saw you before without your cap——"

"No."

"You are very pretty."

She smiled down at him. "It is nice of you to say it."

"Don't wear your cap again, I don't like uniforms for women."

"But when I am on duty I must wear it. You know enough of discipline to understand that I must."

"Yes. But women don't need discipline, God bless 'em." His old eyes twinkled. "Has Derry come in?"

"Yes, and gone to bed. He asked after you."

"And it's Thanksgiving morning?"

"Yes."

"And no turkey for me. But you'll get me a glass of wine?"

"I'm not sure. I'll ask the Doctor."

She sat beside him until he again dozed. Then made her way once more to the room where the lovely gowns were piled high on the bed, and the jewels sparkled on the dressing-table. Quickly and noiselessly she put them in place. Then she tried to take off the collar, but the snaps held. She tugged and pressed, but with no result. She was afraid to pull too hard lest she break the snaps.

At last she was forced to button the collar of her linen gown above it. She smoothed her hair and put on her cap. The room as she surveyed it showed no sign of her occupation. She put out the light and returned to her patient.

She was at the front door to let the Doctor in when he arrived.

"The General is awake, and wants to see you. I'll come down when you go, and we can talk."

As they entered the shadowed room together, the old man opened his eyes. "Hello, McKenzie. Nurse, what made you put on your cap? I don't like it."

"I shouldn't dare leave it off when the Doctor's here."

"Does she have to take your orders or mine, McKenzie?"

"Mine," smiling; "that's one of the perquisites of my profession, to have all the nurses under my thumb."

"Don't you try to please your patients?"

"Yes."

"Then tell her to leave off her cap."

He began to cough. The Doctor bent over him. Hilda helped to make the old man comfortable.

When at last the General drifted into slumber, the two went down together. The hall clock pointed to four.

They stood at the foot of the great stairway. From the landing the painted lady smiled at them.

"Hilda, I am going to France."

She expressed no surprise. "When did you make up your mind?"

"In a sense it is not made up. I think I am waiting for you to confirm my decision. They want me at the head of a hospital staff, to deal with cases of shock. I should like to have you in charge of my nurses."

She meditated. "I am not sure that I care to go."

He showed his surprise. "I understood that if I went, you

would go—"

"I don't think I said that."

"Perhaps not. But it didn't occur to me that you would back out." His voice showed the irritation of a man balked in the thing he wants.

"I haven't backed out. I don't know what I want to do. I have to think it over."

He ran his fingers through his hair. "What made you change your mind?"

"I like to be comfortable. And it isn't comfortable over there."

"For Heaven's sake, Hilda—don't make yourself out as selfish as that."

"I am not any more selfish than other people, but I am honest. I don't go around deceiving myself with the idea that if I go I shall be doing something wonderful. But you—that's why you are going—to be wonderful in your own eyes, and Jean's eyes and in the eyes of the world."

"I don't think it is that," he said soberly. "I hope not. I have tried to see straight. I sometimes think it is you who are seeing crooked, Hilda."

They faced each other squarely. Her chin was slightly lifted. He caught the gleam of jewels at her throat.

"Hilda," he said, sharply, "where did you get those diamonds?"

Her hand flew up to them. She was not in the least disconcerted. "I might as well tell you. They belonged to the General's wife. I didn't have anything to do tonight, so I've been trying them on. There isn't any harm in that, is there?"

"It's rather dangerous," slowly; "why didn't you take the collar off?"

"The snap caught just as you came, and I couldn't unfasten it."

"Did the General know that you tried them on?"

"Of course not. He was asleep."

"Bend your head down, and let me look at the snap."

She leaned towards him, bringing her neck against his hand. The little curls of bright hair sprang up towards his fingers as he worked at the obstinate catch. But he did his work steadily, and as she straightened up again, he dropped the collar into her hand.

"If you will take my advice," he said, "you won't do a thing like that again. People might not understand."

"You mean that they might think I had stolen it? I am not a thief, Doctor—"

"Of course not. Do you think you have to tell me that? And are we quarrelling, Hilda?"

She swung back to her normal calm. "I am tired and cross—"

"I know you are tired. I hope the day nurse will relieve you. I can get two nurses, and let you off entirely."

She shook her head. "I'll stay here. I am interested in the case. And I want to see it through. By the way, he has asked again for wine."

"He can't have it, I told you. You must say that my orders are strict."

He held out his hand. "Then you won't go to France

with me?"

"Let me sleep on it,"—her fingers were firm on his own—"and don't scold me any more."

"Did I scold?"

"Yes."

"I am sorry."

She smiled at him. The slow smile which transformed her. "I'll forgive you. Call me up in the morning, please."

She let him out, and went silently up the stairs. The General was again awake. "I want to talk," he told her; "take off your cap, and sit where I can look at you."

He was still feverish, still not quite responsible for what he might say.

She sat with the light falling full upon her. She never made an unnecessary movement, and her stillness soothed him. She was a good listener, and he grew garrulous.

At last he spoke of his wife. "Sometimes I think she is here and I find myself speaking. A little while ago, I thought I heard her moving in her room, but when I opened my eyes you were bending over me. Sometimes I seem to hear her singing—there is never a moment that I do not miss her. If I were good enough I might hope to meet her—perhaps the Lord will let the strength of my love compensate for the weakness of my will."

So on and on in the broken old voice.

Bronson came at six, and Hilda went away to have some sleep. While the General drowsed she had put the collar safely away behind the Chinese scroll.

As she passed through the hall, she stopped for a moment at the head of the stairs. The painted lady smiled at her, the painted lady who was loved by the old man in the shadowed room.

No, Hilda was not a thief. Yet as she stood there, in the cold dawn of that Thanksgiving morning, she had it in her mind to steal from the painted lady things more precious than a pearl collar or an ermine cloak or the diamonds in a crown!

CHAPTER XII

WHEN THE MORNING STARS SANG

Jean was having her breakfast in bed. Emily had slipped downstairs to drink an early cup of coffee with the Doctor and to warn him, "Don't tell her to-day."

"Why not?"

"It will spoil her feast. Derry Drake is coming to dinner."

"The robber—"

"Do you really feel that way about it?"

"I don't know how I feel."

He rose and went to the window. "It's a rotten morning."

"It is Thanksgiving."

"I haven't much to be thankful for," moodily. "I am, you tell me, about to lose my daughter. I am, also, it would seem, to part company with my best nurse."

"Hilda?"

"Yes. I wanted her to take charge of things for me in France. She elects to stay here."

"But why?"

"She's a—woman."

"You don't mean that. And I must say that I am rather glad that she is not going."

It was out at last! She had a feeling as if she had taken a cold plunge and had survived it!

"Glad? What do you mean, Emily?"

"Every time I waked in the night, I thought of Jean and of how she would feel if Hilda went with you. Do you realize that if she goes, there are things that the world will say?"

His face was stern. "You are very brave to tell me that, Emily."

"It had to be said, and last night I shirked it."

"But Hilda is a very good nurse."

"Do you think of her only as a—good nurse?"

He turned that over in his mind. "No. In a sense she's rather attractive. She satisfies a certain side of me—."

"The best side?"

He avoided an answer to that. "When she is away I miss her."

And now Miss Emily, shaking a little, but not showing it, made him face the situation squarely.

"Have you ever thought that, missing her, you might want to marry her?"

"I have thought of it. Why not, Emily?"

"Have you thought that it would make her your Jean's—mother—?"

His startled look met her steadfast one. His mind flew back to Hilda as she had bent down to him the night before, that he might unfasten the necklace. He thought of the evil that her eyes saw in him, and in the rest of the world. He thought of Jean, and of her white young dreams.

"No," he said, as if to himself, "not that—"

She laid her hand on his arm, "Go by yourself—there's a big work over there, and you can do it best—alone."

He looked down at her, smiling a little, but smiling sadly. "If Jean's mother had lived I should not have been such a weathercock. Will you write to me—promise me that you will write."

"Of course," cheerfully. "Oh, by the way, Julia tells me that dinner will be at three, and that two soldier boys are coming. I rather think I shall like that."

He ran his fingers through his crinkled hair. "What a lot you get out of life, Emily."

"What makes you say that?"

"Little things count so much with you. You are like Jean. She is in seventh Heaven over a snowstorm—or a chocolate soda. It's the youth in her—and it's the youth, too, in you—"

She liked that, and flushed a little. "Perhaps it is because there have been so few big things, Bruce, that the little ones look big."

He had a fleeting sense of what Emily would be like with some big thing in her life—how far would it swing her from her sedate course?

"You have done me a lot of good," he said heartily when she left him to go upstairs to Jean.

Jean was still in bed. "I must run down to the shop," Emily informed her. "But I'll be back in plenty of time to dress for dinner."

"Darling—" Jean reminded her, "you must go to church."

"Of course. I shall stop on my way down."

"Pray for me, Emily." She reached out her arms. Emily came to them and they clung together. "I am so happy, darling—" Jean whispered, "but there isn't anything to tell, not really—yet—Emily—"

When Emily had gone, Jean got out her memory books. She had made of breakfast a slight affair. How could one eat in the face of such astounding events. Already this morning flowers had arrived for her, heather and American Beauties. And Derry had written on his card, "The heather because of you—the roses because of the day—"

There were two hours on her hands before church. She could dress in one—the intervening time must be filled.

Her memory books were great fat volumes kept on a shelf by themselves, and forming a record of everything that had happened to her since her first day at boarding school. They were in no sense diaries, nor could they be called scrap-books. They had, rather, been compiled with an eye to certain red-letter events—and their bulkiness had been enhanced by the insertion between the leaves of various objects not intended for such limited space. There was a mask which she had worn at Hallowe'en; the tulle which had tied her roses at graduation; a little silver ring marking a childish romance; a flattened and much-dried chocolate drop with tender associations; dance-favors, clippings, photographs, theater programs, each illumined and emphasized by a line or two of sentiment or of nonsense in Jean's girlish scrawl.

Even now, as she turned the leaves, she found herself laughing over a rhyme which her father had cut from his daily paper, and had sent in response to her wild plea for a box of something good to eat:

"Mary had a little lamb,
A little pork, a little jam,
A little egg on toast,
A little potted roast,
A little stew with dumplings white,
A little shad,
For Mary had,
A little appetite."

The big box had followed—how *dear* Daddy had always been—but had she ever wanted to eat like that?

There were letters which her father had written, pasted in, envelopes and all, to be read in certain longing moments when she had missed him and her mother. There were love letters from certain callow college boys—*love*—! She laughed now as she thought of the pale passion they had offered her.

Derry had had no word for her the night before when he had left her at her door. Her father had been with her, so Derry could only press her hand and watch her as she went in. But there had been no need for words. All the evening what they had felt had flamed between them—.

So with the desire to preserve a record of these marvellous moments which were crowding into her life, she chose a perfectly new book to be devoted to Derry. And on the first page she pasted, not the faded violet from the basket which had come to her yesterday—oh, day of days!—not the dance program on which Derry's name was most magically scrawled, nor the spring of heather, nor a handful of rose leaves from the offering of the morning—no, the very first thing that went into Jean's memory book was a frayed silken tassel that had been cut from a rose-colored curtain! She had carried down her little scissors the night before, and had snipped it, and here it was—an omen for her own rose-colored future!

Starry-eyed she lay back among her pillows.

"Oh, Polly-Ann, Polly-Ann," she said tensely, to the small cat on the cushions, "if I should ever wake up and find that it wasn't true—"

Polly-Ann stared at her with mystical green orbs. She could offer no help, but she served as a peg upon which Jean could hang her eloquence. She stretched herself luxuriously and purred.

"But it is true, Polly-Ann," Jean said, "and I am going to church with him—wasn't it beautiful that he should think of going to church with me on Thanksgiving morning, Polly-Ann?"

She dressed herself presently, making a sort of sacred rite of it—because of Derry. She was glad that she was pretty—because of Derry. Glad that her gray fur coat was becoming—glad of the red rose against it.

He came in his car, but they decided to walk.

"I always walk to church," said Jean.

"There's sleet falling," said Derry.

"I don't care," said Jean.

"Nor I," said Derry.

And so they started out together!

It was a dismal day, but they did not know it. They knelt

together in the old church. They prayed together. And when at last the benediction had been said and they stood together for a moment alone in the pew, Derry looked down at her and said, "Beloved," and the morning stars sang—!

When they went out, the sleet was coming thick and fast, and Derry's car was waiting. And when they were safe inside, he turned to her and his voice exulted, "I haven't even told you that I love you—I haven't asked you to marry me—I haven't done any of the conventional things—it hasn't needed words, and that's the wonder of it."

"Yes."

"But you knew."

"Yes."

"From the first?"

"I think it was from the first—"

"In the Toy Shop?"

"Yes."

"And you thought I was poor—and I thought you were just the girl in the shop?"

"Isn't it wonderful?"

It was more wonderful than they knew.

"Do you know that my money has always been more important to some people than I have been? I have thought they cared for me because of it."

"Ralph said last night that I cared—for the money."

She would not tell him of the other things that Ralph had said. And even as she thought of him, across the path of her rapture fell the shadow of Ralph's scorn of Derry.

He bent down to her. "Jean, if I had been that shabby boy that you first saw in the shop would you have been happy with me, in a plain little house? Would you?"

Up the streets came the people from the churches—the crowds of people who had thanked the Lord soberly, feeling meantime a bit bewildered as to the workings of His Providence. Most of them were going home to somewhat modified feasts. Many of them were having a soldier or two to dine with them. And presently these soldiers whom they feasted would be crossing the sea to that dread land of death and desolation.

Should they thank the Lord for that?

Some of the clergymen, craving light, had sought it in the Old Testament. But one, more inspired than the rest, had found it in the New.

"And there was war in Heaven; Michael and his angels fought against the dragon; and the dragon fought and his angels. And prevailed not—neither was their place found any more in Heaven."

Those who came from that church spoke of a Holy War, and were thankful that there were men in America going forth to fight the Dragon.

The two soldiers who were to dine at Dr. McKenzie's were plain young fellows from an upper county in Maryland. They were waiting somewhat awkwardly in the drawing-room when Jean arrived. She took them at once to the less formal library, left Derry with them and went upstairs to dress.

As she came into the fresh and frilly room so identified with her child life and her girl life, she stopped on the threshold.

Oh, little room, little room, the child that once lived here will never come again!

She knelt beside the bed, her face buried in her hands. No words came, but in her heart she was saying, "My beloved is mine—and I am his—"

When she went down, Dr. McKenzie was there, and Emily, and the two young soldiers had lost their awkwardness. When they found out afterwards that the young Drake who talked to them so simply and unaffectedly was DeRhymer Drake, the multi-millionaire, they refused to believe it. "He was a mighty nice chap. He didn't put on a bit of side, and the dinner was some feast."

And how could they know that Derry was envying them their cavalry yellow and their olive drab?

As for Jean, throughout the afternoon they gazed upon her as upon an enchanting vision. When they told her "Good-bye" it was the boldest who asked, with a flush on his hard cheek, if he might have a bit of the heather which she wore. "I am Scotch myself, and my mother was, and it would seem a sort of mascot."

If she hesitated for a moment it was only Derry who noticed it. And he helped her out. "It will be a proud day for the heather."

So she gave away a part of his gift, and thanked him with her eyes.

It was after the boys had gone that Derry had a talk alone with Dr. McKenzie.

"But you haven't known her a month—"

"I have wanted her all my life."

"I see—how old are you?"

"Thirty-one."

"You don't look it."

"No. And I don't feel it. Not to-day."

"And you think that she cares?"

"What do you think, sir?"

The Doctor threw up his hands. "Oh, lad, lad, there's all the wonder of it in her eyes when she looks at you."

When Derry went at last to find Jean, she was not in the library. He crossed the hall to the little drawing-room. His love sat by the fire alone.

"My darling—"

Thus she came to his arms. But even then he held her gently, worshipping her innocence and respecting it.

The next morning he brought her a ring. It was such a wonderful ring that she held her breath. She sat on the rose-colored davenport while he put it on her finger.

"If I had been the girl in the Toy Shop," she told him, "and you had been the shabby boy, you would have given me a gold band with three little stones—and I should have liked that, too."

"You shall have the gold ring some day, and it won't have stones in it—and it will be a wedding ring."

"Oh—"

"And when yon wear it I shall call you—Friend Wife—"

CHAPTER XIII

ARE MEN MADE ONLY FOR THIS?

In the afternoon the lovers made a triumphant pilgrimage to the place where they had first met. All the toys in the little shop stared at them—the clowns and the dancers in pink and yellow and the bisque babies and the glassy-eyed dogs and cats.

The white elephant was again in the window. "He seemed so lonely," Emily explained, "and with Christmas coming I couldn't feel comfortable to think of him away from it all."

Jean showed Derry her midnight camels. "I am going to do peacocks next," she told him. "I am so proud."

He bought all of the camels and a lot of other things. "We'll take them to Margaret Morgan's kiddies tomorrow; I want you to meet her."

Miss Emily found her lavish customer interesting, but demoralizing. "Run away with him, Jean," she said. "I am not used to Croesuses. He won't leave anything to sell, and then what shall I say to the people who want to buy?"

"Shut up your shop and go to tea with us at Chevy Chase," Derry suggested.

Emily smiled at him. "It is good of you to ask me, but I can't. I am not in love, and I have my day's work to do. But I think if you would like to take Jean—"

"Alone?" eagerly. "Do you think I might?"

"Why not?"

"I was almost afraid to suggest it."

"I am not a dragon. And there will never be a day like this for you again."

Jean broke in at that. "Oh, Emily, they will be wonderfuller!"

"But not this day—"

Derry knew what she meant. "How sweet you are."

Miss Emily, flushing, was a transformed Miss Emily. "Well, old people are apt to forget, and I have not forgotten."

"Darling, darling," Jean chanted. "I am going to paint dragons, and they shall all have lovely faces, and I shall call them the Not-Forgetting Dragons."

It was all very superlative. Miss Emily tried to send them away, but they still lingered. Jean set the music boxes going to celebrate the occasion, then stopped them because the only tunes they played were German tunes.

Derry laughed at her, then came to silence before a box of tin soldiers. They were little French soldiers, flat on their backs, bright with paint—

"I wonder how they feel about it?" he asked Jean.

"About what?"

"Shut up in a box, doing nothing—"

As the lovers drove away, Emily stood at the window looking after them. There was one customer in the shop, but Miss Emily had a feeling that he would keep himself amused until she was ready to wait on him. She had intuitions about the people who came to buy, and this tall spare man with the slight droop of his shoulders, his upstanding bush of gray hair, his shell glasses on a black ribbon was, she was aware, having the time of his life. No little boy could have spent more time over the toys. He fingered them lovingly as he peered through his big horn glasses.

He saw Miss Emily looking at him and smiling. "It was the white elephant that brought me in. He was made in Germany?"

"Yes."

"It is not easy to get them any more?"

"No. You see I have a little card on him 'Not for sale.'"

He nodded. "I should like to buy him—"

She shook her head. "I have refused many offers."

"I can understand that. Yet, perhaps if I should tell you?"

There was a slight trace of foreign accent in his speech. She stiffened. She felt that he was capable of calling her "Fraeulein." There was not the least doubt in her mind as to the Teutonic extraction of this gentleman who was shamelessly trying to induce her to sell her elephant.

"I can't imagine any reason that would make me change my mind."

"My father is German; he makes toys."

She showed her surprise. "Makes toys?"

"Yes. He is an old man—eighty-five. He was born in Nuremberg. Until he was twenty-five he made elephants like the one in your window. Now do you see?"

She was not sure that she did see. "Well?"

"I want him for my father's Christmas present."

"Impossible," coldly; "he is not for sale."

He was still patient. "He will make you another—many others."

He had her attention now. "Make—elephants?"

"Yes. He needs only a pattern. There are certain things he has forgotten. I should like to make him happy."

Miss Emily, hostilely convinced that it was not her business to contribute to the happiness of any octogenarian Hun, shook her head, "I'm sorry."

"Then you won't sell him?"

"Certainly not."

He still lingered. "You love your toys—I have been here before, and I have watched you. They are not just sawdust and wood and cloth and paint to you—they are real—"

"Yes."

"My father is like that. They are real to him. There's an old wax doll that was my mother's. He loves her and talks to her— Because she was made in that Germany which is dead—"

The fierceness in his voice, the flash of his eye; the thrust of his hand as if it held a rapier!

"Dead?"

"The Germany he knew died when Prussia throttled her. Her poetry died, her music—there is no echo now from the Rhine but that of—guns."

"You feel—that way—?"

"Yes."

"Then sit down and tell me—tell me—" She was eager.

"Tell you what?"

"About your father, about the toys, about the Germany that is—dead."

He was glad to tell her. It poured forth, with now and then an offending phrase, "Gott in Himmel, do they think we have forgotten? My father came to America because he loved freedom—he fought in the Civil War for freedom—he loves freedom still; and over there they are fighting for slavery. The slavery of the little nations, the slavery of those who love democracy. They want Prussia, and more Prussia, and more Prussia—" He struck his hand on the counter so that all the dolls danced.

"They are fighting to get the whole world under an iron heel— to crush—to grind—to destroy. My father reads it and weeps. He is an old man, Fraeulein, and his mind goes back to the Germany which sang and told fairy tales, and made toys; do you see?

"Yet there are people here who do not understand, who point their fingers at him, at me. Who think because I am Ulrich Stoelle that I am not—American. Yet what am I but that?"

He got up and walked around the room restlessly. "I am an American. If I was not born here, can I help that? But my heart has been moulded here. For me there is no other country. Germany I love—yes, but as one loves a woman who has been led away—because one thinks of the things she might have been, not of the thing she is."

He came back to her. "Will you sell me your elephant, Fraeulein?"

She held out her hand to him. Her eyes were wet. "I will lend him to your father. Indeed, I cannot sell him."

He took her hand in a strong grasp. "I knew you were kind. If you could only see my father."

"Bring him here some day."

"He is too old to be brought. He sticks close to his chair. But if you would come and see him? You and perhaps the young lady who waited on me when I came before, and who was here to-day with the young man whose heart is singing."

"Oh, you saw that?"

"It was there for the whole world to see, was it not? A man in love hides nothing. You will bring them then? We have flowers even in December in our hothouses; you will like that, and you shall see my father. I think you will love my father, Fraeulein."

After he had gone she wondered at herself. She had trusted her precious elephant to a perfect stranger. He might be anything, a spy, a thief, with his "Gotts in Himmel' and his "Fraeuleins" —how Jean would laugh at her for her softheartedness!

Oh, but he wasn't a thief, he wasn't a spy. He was a poet and a gentleman. She made very few mistakes in her estimates of the people who came to her shop. She had made, she was sure, no mistake in trusting Ulrich Stoelle.

Jean and Derry motoring to Chevy Chase were far away from

the world of the Toy Shop. As they whirled along the country roads the bare trees seemed to bud and bloom for them, the sky was gold.

The lovely clubhouse as they came into it was gay with big-flowered curtains and warm with its roaring fires.

As they crossed the room together, they attracted much attention. There was about them a fine air of exaltation—.

"Young blood, young blood," said an old gentleman in a corner. "Gad, I envy him. Look at her eyes—!"

But there was more than her eyes to look at. There were her cheeks, and her crinkled copper hair under the little hat, and the flower that she wore, and her white hands as she poured the tea.

They drank unlimited quantities of Orange Pekoe, and ate small mountains of toast. They were healthily happy and quite unexpectedly hungry, and the fact that they were sitting alone at the table gave the whole thing an enchanting atmosphere of domesticity.

"Ralph spoiled it the other day," Jean confided, "I had everything ready for you."

"How I hated him when I came in."

"Oh, did you?"

"Of course," and then they both laughed, and the old gentleman in the corner said to the woman who sat with him, "Let's get away. I can't stand it."

"I don't see why."

"You wouldn't see. But there was a time once when I loved a girl like that."

Drusilla and Captain Hewes coming in, after a canter through the Park, broke in upon the Paradise of the young pair.

Drusilla in riding togs still managed to preserve the picturesque quality of her beauty—a cockade in her hat, a red flower in her lapel, a blue tie against her white shirt.

"And she does it so well," Derry said, as the two came towards them. "In most women it would have an air of bad taste, but Drusilla never goes too far—"

Captain Hewes in tow showed himself a captured man. "I didn't know that American women could ride until Miss Gray showed me—today. It was rippin'."

Drusilla laughed. "It is worth more than the ride to have you say 'rippin'' like that."

"She makes fun of me," the Captain complained; "some day I shall take her over to England and show her how our gentle maidens look up to me."

"Your gentle maidens," Drusilla stated, "are driving ambulances or making munitions. When the Tommies come marching home again they will find comrades, not clinging vines."

"And they'll jolly well like it," said the big Englishman; "a man wants a woman who understands—"

This was law and gospel to Derry. "Of course. Jean, dear, may I tell Drusilla?"

"As if you had to tell me," Drusilla scoffed; "it is written all over you."

"Is it?" Derry marvelled.

"It is. The whole room is lighted up with it. You are a lucky man, Derry,"—for a moment her bright eyes were shadowed—"and Jean is a lucky girl." She leaned down and kissed the woman that Derry loved. "Oh, you Babes in the Wood—"

"By Jove," the Captain ejaculated, much taken by the little scene, "do you mean that they are going to be married?"

"Rather," Drusilla mocked him. "But don't shout it from the housetops. Derry is a public personage, and it might get in the papers."

"It is not to get in the papers yet," Derry said. "Dr. McKenzie won't let me tell Dad—he's too ill—but we told you because you are my good friend, Drusilla."

She might have been more than that, but he did not know it. When he went away with Jean, she looked after him wistfully.

"Good-bye, little Galahad," she said.

The Captain stared. "Oh, I say, do you call him that?"

She nodded.

"He's a knight in shining armor—"

"I can't understand why he's not fightin'."

"Nobody understands. There's something back of it, and meantime people are calling him a coward—"

"Doesn't look like a slacker."

"He isn't. I have sometimes thought," said wise Drusilla, "that it might be his father. He's a gay old bird, and Derry has to jack him up."

"Drink?"

"Yes. They say that Derry has followed him night after night—getting him home if he could; if not, staying with him."

"Hard lines—"

"And yet he is asking little Jean to marry him. I wonder if she will keep step with him."

"Why shouldn't she?"

"Because Derry is going to travel far and fast in the next few months," Drusilla prophesied.

Her face settled into tired lines. For the first time the Captain saw her divorced from her radiance. He set himself to cheer her.

"What is troubling you, dear woman?"

She was very frank, and she told him the truth. "I should have been glad to keep step with him myself."

He laid his hand over hers. "If you had, where would I be? From the moment I saw you, you filled my heart."

So, after all, she had been to him from the first, not a type but a woman. It had come to him like that, but not to her. "You're the bravest and best man I have ever met," she told him, "but I don't love you."

"I should be glad to wait," said the poor Captain, "until you could find something in me to like."

"I find a great deal to like," she said, "but it wouldn't be fair to give you anything less than love."

"At least you'll let me have your friendship—to take back with me."

She looked at him, startled. "Oh, you are going back?"

"I may get my orders any day. There are things I can be doing over there."

Some day she was to see him "over there," to see him against a background of fire and flame and smoke, to see him transfigured by heroism, and she was to remember then with an aching heart this moment when he had told her that he loved her.

It was dark when Derry brought Jean home. There had been a sunset and an afterglow, and a twilight, and an evening star to ravish them as they rode, to say nothing of the moon—they came to the Doctor's door quite dizzy with the joy of it.

Derry was loath to leave. "Can't we all go to a play tonight?" he asked Jean's father. "You and Miss Bridges and the two of us?"

"Certainly not. Jean has done enough to-day. She isn't made of iron."

"She is made of fire and dew," Derry flung at him, lightly.

"Heavens, has it come to that? Well, she is still my daughter. I won't have her ill on my hands."

"But, Daddy!"

"You are to have a quiet dinner with me, my dear, and go to bed—and young Lochinvar may call for you in the morning—"

Young Lochinvar was repentant. "I didn't think it would tire her."

"Henceforth you will have to think."

"I know, sir."

He was so meek that the Doctor melted. "Run along and say 'Good-bye' to her. I'll give you ten minutes."

They wanted ten eternities. But there was, of course, tomorrow. They comforted themselves with that.

At dinner, the Doctor spoke of Derry's father. "All real danger is past, but he will have to be careful."

"When is Hilda coming back?"

"She told me last night that she'd rather stay until there was no further need for a nurse. The General hates a change, and he has asked her to stay."

"Does she like it?"

"She is very comfortable."

"Derry says that his father is an old dear."

"He would think so, naturally."

There were things about the General's case which were troubling Dr. McKenzie, and of which he could not speak. The old man had, undoubtedly been given something to drink on Thanksgiving Day.

Hilda had had strict orders, and the day nurse, and the only other person who had had access to the General's room was Bronson. He had made up his mind to speak to Derry about Bronson.

The meal progressed rather silently. The Doctor was preoccupied, taciturn. Miss Emily made futile efforts at conversation. Jean dallied with her dinner.

"My dear," the Doctor commented as she pushed away her salad, "you can't live on love."

"I'm not hungry. We had tea at the Club. Drusilla was there—and—we told her."

"Told her what?"

Blushing furiously, "That Derry and I are going to be—married."

"But you are not. Not for months. If that cub thinks he can carry you off from under my eyes he is mistaken. You've got to get acquainted with each other—I have seen too many unhappy marriages."

"But we are not going to be unhappy, Daddy."

"How do you know?"

Her cheeks were blazing. Miss Emily interposed. "Don't tease her, she's too tired."

"If he is teasing, I don't care," Jean said, "but it always sounds as if he meant it."

After dinner, the Doctor laid his hand on his daughter's shoulder. "I want to talk to you, daughter."

"Is it about Derry, Daddy?"

"About myself."

Emily, understanding, left them alone. Jean sat in her low chair in front of the fire, her earnest eyes on her father. "Well, Daddy."

He patted her hand. It was hard for him to speak.

She saw his emotion. "Is—is it because I am going to marry Derry?"

"That, and more than that. Jean, dear, I must go to France—"

"To France?"

"Yes. They want me to head a hospital. I don't see how I can refuse, and keep my self-respect. But it means—leaving you."

"Leaving me—"

"My little girl—don't look like that." He reached out his arms to her.

She came, and clung to him. "How soon?"

"As soon as I can wind things up here."

"It—it seems as if I couldn't let you."

"Then you'll miss me, dearest?"

"You know I will, Daddy."

"But you will have your Derry." His jealousy forced that.

"As if it makes any difference about—you."

She hid her face against his coat. She felt suddenly that the war was assuming a new and very personal aspect. Of course men had to go. But she and her father had never been separated—not for more than a day or week, or a month when she was at the shore.

"How long, Daddy?"

"God knows, dearest. Until I am not needed."

"But—" her lip trembled.

"You are going to be my brave little girl."

"I'll try—" the tears were running down her cheeks.

"You wouldn't have me not go, would you?"

She shook her head and sobbed on his shoulder. He soothed her and presently she sat up. Quite gallantly she agreed that she would stay with Emily. If he thought she was too young to marry Derry now, she would wait. If Derry went into it, it might be easier to let him go as a lover than as a husband—she thought it might be easier. Yes, she would try to sleep when she went upstairs—and she would remember that her old Daddy loved her, loved her, and she was to ask God to bless him—and keep him—when they were absent one from the other—.

She kissed him and clung to him and then went upstairs. She undressed and said her prayers, put Polly-Ann on her cushion, turned off the light, and got into bed.

Then she lay in the dark, facing it squarely.

The things she had said to her father were not true. She didn't want him to go to France. She didn't want Derry to go. She was glad that Derry's mother had made him promise. She didn't care who called him a coward. She cared only to keep her own.

There wasn't any sense in it, anyhow. Why should Daddy and Derry be blown to pieces—or made blind—or not come back at all? Just because a barbarian had brought his hordes into Belgium? Well, let Belgium take care of herself—and France.

She shuddered deeper down into the bed. She wasn't heroic. Hilda had been right about that. She was willing to knit miles and miles of wool, to go without meat, to go without wheat, to wear old clothes, to let the furnace go out and sit shivering in one room by a wood fire, she was willing to freeze and to starve, but she was not willing to send her men to France.

She found herself shaking, sobbing—.

Hitherto war had seemed a glorious thing, an inspiring thing. She had thrilled to think that she was living in a time which matched the days of Caesar and Alexander and of Napoleon, of that first Richard of England, of Charlemagne, of Nelson and of Francis Drake, of Grant and Lee and Lincoln.

Even in fiction there had been Ivanhoe and—and Alan Breck—and even poor Rawdon Crawley at Waterloo—fighters all, even the poorest of them, exalted in her eyes by their courage and the clash of arms.

But there wasn't any glory, any romance in this war. It was machine guns and bombs and dirt, and cold and mud; and base hospitals, and men screaming with awful wounds—and gas, and horrors, and nerve-shock and—frightfulness. She had read it all in the papers and in the magazines. And it had not meant anything to her, it had been just words and phrases, and now it was more than words and phrases—.

When the hordes of people had swept into Washington, changing it from its gracious calm into a seething and unsettling center of activities, she had been borne along on the wings of enthusiasm and of high endeavor. She had scolded women who would not work, she had scorned mothers and wives who had sighed and sobbed because their men must go. She had talked of patriotism!

Well, she wasn't patriotic. Derry would probably hate her when she told him. But she was going to tell him. She wouldn't have him blown to pieces or made blind or not come back at all. And in the morning, she would beg Daddy—she would beg and beg!

As she sat up in bed and looked wildly about her, it seemed as if all the corners of the little room were haunted by specters. A long time ago she had seen Maude Adams in "L'Aiglon." She remembered now those wailing voices of the dead at Wagram. And in this war millions of men had died. It seemed to her that their souls must be pressing against the wall which divided them from the living—that their voices must penetrate the stillness which had always shut them out. "How dare you go on with it? Are men made only for this?"

She remembered now the thing that her father had said on the night after "Cinderella."

"If I had my way, it should be an eye for an eye, a tooth for a tooth. For every man that they have tortured, we must torture one of theirs. For every child mutilated, we must mutilate a child—for every woman—"

Her Daddy had said that. Her kind and tender Daddy. Was that what the war made of men? Would Daddy and Derry, when they went over, do that? Torture and mutilate? Would they, would they? And would they come back after that and expect her to love them and live with them?

Well, she wouldn't. She would *not*. She would be afraid of them—of both of them.

If they loved her, they would stay with her. They wouldn't go away and leave her to be afraid—alone and crying in the dark, with all of those dead voices.

* * * * * *

Emily tapped at the door. Came in. "My dear, my dear—. Oh, my poor little Jean."

* * * * * *

After a long time her father was there, and he was giving her a white tablet and a drink of water.

"It will quiet her nerves, Emily. I didn't dream that she would take it like this."

CHAPTER XIV

SHINING SOULS

The next morning Jean was ill. Derry, having the news conveyed to him over the telephone, rushed in to demand tragically of Dr. McKenzie, "Was it my fault?"

"It was the fault of too much excitement. Seventh heaven with you for hours, and then my news on top of it."

"What news?"

The Doctor explained. "It is going to tear me to pieces if she takes it like this. She was half-delirious all night, and begged and begged—"

"She doesn't want you to go?"

The Doctor ran his fingers through his hair. "Well, we've been a lot to each other. But she's such a little sport—and patriotic—nobody more so. She won't feel this way when she's herself again."

Derry stood drearily at the window looking out. "You think then she won't be able to see me for several days? I had planned such a lot of things."

The Doctor dropped a hand on the boy's shoulder. "Life has a way of spoiling our plans, hasn't it? I had hoped for old age with Jean's mother."

That was something for youth to think of—of life spoiling things—of lonely old age!

"I wish," Derry said, after a pause, "that you'd let me marry her before you go."

"No, no," sharply, "she's too young, Drake. And you haven't known each other long enough."

"Things move rapidly in these days, sir."

The Doctor agreed. "It is one of the significant developments. We had become material. And now fire and flame. But all the more reason why I should keep my head. Jean will be safe here with Emily. And you may go any day."

"I wish I might think so. I'd be there now if I weren't bound."

"It won't hurt either of you to wait until I come back," was the Doctor's ultimatum, and Derry, longing for sympathy, left him presently and made his way to the Toy Shop.

"If we were to wait ten years do you think I'd love her any more than I do now?" he demanded of Emily. "I should think he'd understand."

"Men never do understand," said Emily—"fathers. They think their own romance was unique, or they forget that there was ever any romance."

"If you could put in a word for us," ventured Derry.

"I am not sure that it would do any good; Bruce is a Turk."

A customer came, and Derry lingered disconsolately while Emily served her. More customers, among them a tall spare man with an upstanding bush of gray hair. He had a potted plant in his arms, wrapped in tissue paper. He set it on the counter and went away.

When Miss Emily discovered the plant, she asked Derry, "Who put it there?"

Derry described the man. "You were busy. He didn't stop."

The plant was a cyclamen, blood-red and beautiful.

Miss Emily managed to remark casually that she had loaned his father an elephant, perhaps he had felt that he ought to make some return—but he needn't—.

"*An elephant?*"

"Not a real one. But the last of my plush beauties."

She set the cyclamen on a shelf, and wrapped up the parcel of toys which Derry had bought the day before, "I may as well take them to Margaret Morgan's kiddies," he told her. "I want to tell her about Jean."

After Derry had gone, Miss Emily stood looking at the cyclamen on the shelf. It was a lovely thing, with a dozen blooms. She wished that her benefactor had stayed to let her thank him. She was not sure that she even knew where to send a note.

She hunted him up in the telephone book, and found him—Ulrich Stoelle. His hot-houses were on the old Military Road. She remembered now to have seen them, and to have remarked the house, which was peaked up in several gables, and had quaint brightly-colored iron figures set about the garden—with pointed caps like the graybeards in Rip van Winkle, or the dwarf in Rumpelstiltzkin.

When Derry's car slid up to Margaret's door, he saw the two children at an upper window. They waved to him as he rang the bell. He waited several moments and no one came to open the door. He turned the knob and, finding it unlatched, let himself in.

As he went through the hall he was aware of a strange stillness. Not a maid was in sight. Passing Margaret's room on the second floor he heard voices.

The children were alone in the nursery. He was flooded with sunlight. Margaret-Mary's pink wash frock, Teddy's white linen—yellow jonquils in a blue bow—snowy lambs gambolling on a green frieze—Bo-peeps, flying ribbons—it was a cheering and charming picture.

"How gay you are," said Derry.

"We are not gay in our hearts," Teddy told him.

"Why not?"

"Mother's crying—we heard her, and then Nurse went down and left us, and we looked out of the window and you came."

Derry's heart seemed to stop beating. "Crying?"

Even as he spoke, Margaret stood on the threshold. There were no tears, but it was worse than tears.

He started towards her, but with a gesture she stopped him.

"I am so glad you are—here," she said.

"My dear—what is it?"

She put her hand up to her head. "Teddy, dearest," she asked, "can you take care of Margaret-Mary until Cousin Derry comes back? I want to talk to him."

Teddy's grave eyes surveyed her. "You've been cryin'," he said,

"I told Cousin Derry—"

"Yes. I have had—bad news. But—I am not going to cry—any more. And you'll take care of sister?"

"I tell you, old chap," said Derry resourcefully, "you and Margaret-Mary can open my parcel, and when I come back we'll all play together."

Outside with Margaret, with the door shut on the children, he put his arm about her. "Is it Win—is he—hurt?"

"He is—oh, Derry, Derry, he is dead!"

Even then she did not cry. "The children mustn't know. Not till I get a grip on myself. They mustn't think of it as—sad. They must think of it as—glorious—that he went—that way—."

Held close in his arms, she shook with sobs, silent, hard. He carried her down to her room. The maids were gathered there—Nurse utterly useless in her grief. It came to Derry, as he bent over Margaret, that he had always thought of Nurse as a heartless automaton, playing Chorus to Teddy, yet here she was, a weeping woman with the rest of them.

He sent all of the servants away, except Nurse, and then Margaret told him, "He was in one of the French towns which the Germans had vacated, and he happened to pick up a toy—that some little child might have dropped—and there was an explosive hidden in it—and that child's toy killed him, Derry, killed him—"

"My God, Margaret—"

"They had put it there that it might kill a—child!"

"Derry, the children mustn't know how it happened. They mustn't think of him as—hurt. They know that something is the matter. Can you tell them, Derry? So that they will think of him as fine and splendid, and going up to Heaven because God loves brave men—?"

It was a hard task that she had set him, and when at last he left her, he went slowly up the stairs.

The children had strung the Midnight Camels across the room, the purple, patient creatures that Jean had made.

"The round rug is an oasis," Teddy explained, "and the jonquil is a palm—and we are going to save the dates and figs from our lunch."

"I want my lunch," Margaret-Mary complained.

Derry looked at his watch. It was after twelve. The servants were all demoralized. "See here," he said, "you sit still for a moment, and I'll go down for your tray."

He brought it up himself, presently, bread and milk and fruit.

They sat on the oasis and ate, with the patient purple camels grouped in the shade of the jonquil palm.

Then Derry asked, "Shall I tell you the story of How the Purple Camels Came to Paradise?"

"Yes," they said, and he gathered little Margaret-Mary into his arms, and Teddy lay flat on the floor and looked up at him, while Derry made his difficult way towards the thing he had to tell.

"You see, the purple camels belonged to the Three Wise Men, the ones who journeyed, after the Star—do you remember? And found the little baby who was the Christ? And because the purple camels had followed the Star, the good Lord said to them, 'Some day you shall journey towards Paradise, and there you shall see the shining souls that dwell in happiness.'"

"Do their souls really shine?" Teddy asked.

"Yes."

"Why?"

"Because of the light in Paradise—the warm, sweet light, clearer than the sunshine, Teddy, brighter than the moon and the stars—."

The children sighed rapturously. "Go on," Teddy urged.

"So the patient camels began their wonderful pilgrimage—they crossed the desert and rounded a curve of the sea, and at last they came to Paradise, and the gate was shut and they knelt in front of it, and they heard singing, and the sound of silver trumpets, and at last the gate swung back, and they saw—what do you think they saw?"

"The shining souls," said Teddy, solemnly.

"Yes, the shining souls in all that lovely light—there were the souls of happy little children, and of good women, but best of all," his voice wavered a little, "best of all, there were the souls of—brave men."

"My father is a brave man."

Was, oh, little Teddy!

"And the purple camels said to the angels who guarded the gate, 'We have come because we saw the little Christ in the manger.'

"And the angel said, 'It is those who see Him who enter Paradise,' So the patient purple camels went in and the gates were shut behind them, and there they will live in the warm, sweet light throughout the deathless ages."

"What are de-yethless ages, Cousin Derry?"

"Forever and ever."

"Is that all?"

"It is all about the camels—but not all about the shining souls."

"Tell us the rest."

He knew that he was bungling it, but at last he brought them to the thought of their father in Paradise, because the dear Lord loved to have him there.

"But if he's there, he can't be here," said the practical Teddy.

"No."

"I want him here. Doesn't Mother want him here?"

"Well—yes."

"Is she glad to have him go to Paradise?"

"Not exactly—glad."

"Was that why she was crying?"

"Yes. Of course she will miss him, but it is a wonderful thing just the same, Teddy, when you think of it—when you think of how your own father went over to France because he was sorry for all the poor little children who had been hurt, and for all the people who had suffered and suffered until it seemed as if they must not suffer any more—and he wanted to help them, and—and—"

But here he stumbled and stopped. "I tell you, Teddy," he said, as man to man, "it is going to hurt awfully, not to see him. But you've got to be careful not to be too sorry—because there's your Mother to think of."

"Is she crying now?"

"Yes. Down there on her bed. Could you be very brave if you went down, and told her not to be sorry?"

"Brave, like my Daddy?"

"Yes."

Margaret-Mary was too young to understand—she was easily comforted. Derry sang a little song and her eyes drooped.

But downstairs the little son who was brave like his father, sat on the edge of the bed, and held his mother's hand. "He's in Paradise with the purple camels, Mother, and he's a shining soul—."

It was a week before Jean went with Derry to see Margaret. It had been a week of strange happenings, of being made love to by Derry and of getting Daddy ready to go away. She had reached heights and depths, alternately. She had been feverishly radiant when with her lover. She had resolved that she would not spoil the wonder of these days by letting him know her state of mind.

The nights were the worst. None of them were as bad as the first night, but her dreams were of battles and bloodshed, and she waked in the mornings with great heaviness of spirit.

What Derry had told her of Margaret's loss seemed but a confirmation of her fears. It was thus that men went away and never returned—. Oh, how Hilda would have triumphed if she could have looked into Jean's heart with its tremors and terrors!

She came, thus, into the room, where Margaret sat with

her children.

"I want you two women to meet," Derry said, as he presented Jean, "because you are my dearest—"

"He has told me so much about you,"—Margaret put her arm about Jean and kissed her—"and he has used all the adjectives —yet none of them was adequate."

Jean spoke tensely. "It doesn't seem right for us to bring our happiness here."

"Why not? This has always been the place of happiness?" She caught her breath, then went on quickly, "You mustn't think that I am heartless. But if the women who have lost should let themselves despair, it would react on the living. The wailing of women means the weakness of men. I believe that so firmly that I am afraid to—cry."

"You are braver than I—" slowly.

"No. You'd feel the same way, dear child, about Derry."

"No. I should not. I shouldn't feel that way at all. I should die—if I lost Derry—"

Light leaped in her lover's eyes. But he shook his head. "She'd bear it like other brave women. She doesn't know herself, Margaret."

"None of us do. Do you suppose that the wives and mothers of France ever dreamed that it would be their fortitude which would hold the enemy back?"

"Do you think it did, really?" Jean asked her.

"I know it. It has been a barrier as tangible as a wall of rock."

"You put an awful responsibility upon the women."

"Why not? They are the mothers of men."

They sat down after that; and Jean listened frozenly while Margaret and Derry talked. The children in front of the fire were looking at the pictures in a book which Derry had brought.

Teddy, stretched at length on the rug in his favorite attitude, was reading to Margaret-Mary. His mop of bright hair, his flushed cheeks, his active gestures spoke of life quick in his young body—.

And his father was—dead—!

Oh, oh, Mothers of men—!

CHAPTER XV

HILDA BREAKS THE RULES

It was Dr. McKenzie who told Hilda of Jean's engagement to Derry Drake.

"I thought it best for them not to say anything to the General until he is better. So you may consider it confidential, Hilda."

"Of course."

She had come to his office to help him with his books. The nurse who somewhat inadequately supplied her place was having an afternoon off. The Doctor had been glad to see her, and had told her so. "I am afraid things are in an awful muddle."

"Not so bad that they can't be straightened out in an hour or two."

"I don't see why you insist upon staying on the General's case. I shouldn't have sent you if I had thought you'd keep at it like this."

"I always keep at things when I begin them, don't I?"

He knew that she did. It was one of the qualities which made her valuable. "I believe that you are staying away to let me see how hard it is to get along without you."

"It wouldn't be a bad idea, but that's not the reason. I am staying because I like the case." She shifted the topic away from herself.

"People will say that Jean has played her cards well."

He blazed, "What do you mean, Hilda?"

"He has a great deal of money."

"What has that to do with it?"

Her smile was irritating. "Oh, I know you are not mercenary. But a million or two won't come amiss in any girl's future— and two country houses, and a house in town."

"You seem to know all about it."

"The General talks a lot—and anyhow, all the world knows it. It's no secret."

"I rather think that Jean doesn't know it. I haven't told her. She realizes that he is rich, but it doesn't seem to have made much impression on her."

"Most people will think she is lucky to have caught him."

"He is not a fish," with rising anger, "and as for Jean, she'd marry him if he hadn't a penny, and you know it, Hilda."

Hilda considered that for a moment. Then she said, "Is it his money or his father's?"

"Belongs to the old man. Derry's mother had nothing but an irreproachable family tree."

Hilda's long hands were clasped on the desk, her eyes were upon them. "If he shouldn't like his son's marriage, he might make things uncomfortable."

"Why shouldn't he like my Jean?"

"He probably will. But there's always the chance that he may not. He may be more ambitious."

Dr. McKenzie ran his fingers through his crinkled hair. "She's good enough for—a king."

"You think that, naturally, but he isn't the doting father of an only daughter."

"If he thinks that my daughter isn't good enough for his son—"

"You needn't shout at me like that," calmly; "but he knows as well as you do that Derry Drake's millions could get him any girl."

He had a flashing sense of the coarse fiber of Hilda's mental make-up. "My Jean is a well-born and well-bred woman," he said, slowly. "It is a thing that money can't buy."

"Money buys a very good counterfeit. Lots of the women who come here aren't ladies, not in the sense that you mean it, but on the surface you can't tell them apart."

He knew that it was true. No one knows better than a doctor what is beneath the veneer of social convention and personal hypocrisy.

"And as for Jean," her quiet voice analyzed, "what do you know of her, really? You've kept her shut away from the things that could hurt her, but how do you know what will happen when you open the gate?"

Yet Emily had said—? His hand came down on top of the desk. "I think we won't discuss Jean."

"Very well, but you brought it on yourself. And now please go away, I've got to finish this and get back—"

He went reluctantly, and returned to say, "You'll come over again before I sail, and straighten things out for me?"

"Of course."

"You don't act as if you cared whether I went or not."

"I care, of course. But don't expect me to cry. I am not the crying kind." The little room was full of sunlight. She was very pink and white and self-possessed. She smiled straight up into his face. "What good would it do me to cry?"

After she had left him he was restless. She had been for so long a part of his life, a very necessary and pleasant part of it. She never touched his depths or rose to his heights. She seemed to beckon, yet not to care when he came.

He spoke of her that night to Emily. "Hilda was here to-day and she reminded me that people might think that my daughter is marrying Derry Drake for his money."

"She would look at it like that."

"When Hilda talks to me"—he was rumpling his hair—"I have a feeling that all the people in the world are unlovely—"

"There are plenty of unlovely people," said Emily, "but why should we worry with what they think?"

She was knitting, and he found himself watching her hands. "You have pretty hands," he told her, unexpectedly.

She held them out in front of her. "When I was a little girl my mother told me that I had three points of beauty—my hands, my feet, and the family nose," she smiled whimsically, "and she assured me that I would therefore never be common-place. 'Any woman may be beautiful,' was her theory, 'but only a woman with good blood in her veins can have hands and feet and a nose like yours—.' I was dreadfully handicapped in the beginning of my life by my mother's point of view. I am afraid that even now if the dear lady looks down from Heaven and sees me working in my Toy Shop she will feel the family disgraced by this one member who is in trade. It was only in the later years that I found myself, that I realized how I might reach out towards things which were broader and bigger than the old ideals of aristocratic birth and inherited possessions."

He thought of Hilda. "Yet it gave you something, Emily," he said, slowly, "that not every woman has: good-breeding, and the ability to look above the sordid. You are like Jean—all your world is rose-colored."

She was thoughtful. "Not quite like Jean. I heard a dear old bishop ask the other day why we should see only the ash cans and garbage cans in our back yards when there was blue sky above? I know there are ash cans and garbage cans, but I make myself look at the sky. Jean doesn't know that the cans are there."

"The realists will tell you that you should keep your eyes on the cans."

"I don't believe it," said Miss Emily, stoutly; "more people are made good by the contemplation of the fine and beautiful than by the knowledge of evil. Eve knew that punishment would follow the eating of the apple. But she ate it. If I had a son I should tell him of the strength of men, not of their weaknesses."

He nodded. "I see. And yet there is this about Hilda. She does not deceive herself;—perhaps you do—and Jean."

"Perhaps it is Hilda who is deceived. All the people in the world are not unlovely—all of them are not mercenary and deceitful and selfish." Her cheeks were flushed.

"Nobody knows that better than a doctor, Emily. I am conscious that Hilda draws out the worst in me—yet there is something about her that makes me want to find things out, to explore life with her—"

He was smiling into the fire. Miss Emily girded herself and gave him a shock. "The trouble with you is that you want the admiration of every woman who comes your way. Most of your patients worship you—Jean puts you on a pedestal—even I tell you that you have a soul. But Hilda withholds the admiration you demand, and you want to conquer her—to see her succumb with the rest of us."

"The rest of you! Emily, you have never succumbed."

"Oh, yes, I have. I seem to be saying, 'He may have a few weaknesses, but back of it all he is big and fine.' But Hilda's attitude indicates, 'He is not fine at all.' And you hate that and want to show her."

He chuckled. "By Jove, I do, Emily. Perhaps it is just as well that I am getting away from her."

"I wouldn't admit it if I were you. I'd rather see you face a thing than run away."

"If Eve had run away from the snake in the apple tree, she would not have lost her Eden—poor Eve."

"Poor Adam—to follow her lead. He should have said, 'No, my dear, apples are not permitted by the Food Administrator; we must practice self-denial.'"

"I think I'd rather have him sinning than such a prig."

"It depends on the point of view."

He enjoyed immensely crossing swords with Emily. There was never any aftermath of unpleasantness. She soothed him even while she criticised.

They spoke presently of Jean and Derry.

"They want to get married."

"Well, why not?"

"She's too young, Emily. Too ignorant of what life means—and he may go to France any day. He is getting restless—and he may see things differently—that his duty to his country transcends any personal claim—and then what of Jean?—a little wife—alone."

"She could stay with me."

"But marriage, *marriage*, Emily—why in Heaven's name should they be in such a hurry?"

"Why should they wait, and miss the wonder of it all, as I have missed it—all the color and glow, the wine of life? Even if he should go to France, and die, she will bear his beloved name—she will have the right to weep."

He had never seen her like this—the red was deep in her cheeks, her voice was shaken, her bosom rose and fell with her agitation.

"Emily, my dear girl—"

"Let them marry, Bruce, can't you see? Can't you see. It is their day—there may be no tomorrow."

"But there are practical things, Emily. If she should have a child?"

"Why not? It will be his—to love. Only a woman with empty arms knows what that means, Bruce."

And this was Emily, this rose-red, wet-eyed creature was Emily, whom he had deemed unemotional, cold, self-contained!

"Men forget, Bruce. You wouldn't listen to reason when you wooed Jean's mother. You were a demanding, imperative lover—you wanted your own way, and you had it."

"But I had known Jean's mother all my life."

"Time has nothing to do with it."

"My dear girl—"

"It hasn't."

She was illogical, and he liked it. "If I let them marry, what then?"

"They will love you for it."

"They ought to love you instead."

"I shall be out of it. They will be married, and you will be in France, and I shall sell—toys—"

She tried to laugh, but it was a poor excuse. He glanced at her quickly. "Shall you miss me, Emily?"

Her hands went out in a little gesture of despair. "There you go, taking my tears to yourself."

He was a bit disconcerted. "Oh, I say—"

"But they are not for you. They are for my lost youth and romance, Bruce. My lost youth and romance."

Leaning back in his chair he studied her. Her eyes were dreamy—the rose-red was still in her cheeks. For the first time he realized the prettiness of Emily; it was as if in her plea for others she had brought to life something in herself which glowed and sparkled.

"Look here," he said. "I want you to write to me."

"I am a busy woman."

"But a letter now and then—"

"Well, now and then—"

He was forced to be content with that. She was really very charming, he decided as he got into his car. She was such a gentlewoman—she created an atmosphere which belonged to his home and hearth.

When he came in late she was not waiting up for him as Hilda had so often waited. There was a plate of sandwiches on his desk, coffee ready in the percolator to be made by the turning on of the electricity. But he ate his lunch alone.

Yet in spite of the loneliness, he was glad that Emily had not waited up for him. It was a thing which Hilda might do— Hilda, who made a world of her own. But Emily's world was the world of womanly graciousness and dignity—the world in which his daughter moved, the world which had been his wife's. For her to have eaten alone with him in his office in the middle of the night would have made her seem less than he wanted her to be.

Before he went to bed, he called up Hilda. "I forgot to tell you when you were here this afternoon that I asked young Drake about Bronson. He says that it isn't possible that the old man is giving the General anything against orders. You'd better watch the other servants and be sure of the day nurse—"

"I am sure of her and of the other servants—but I still have my doubts about Bronson."

"But Drake says—"

"I don't care what he says. Bronson served the General before he served young Drake—and he's not to be trusted."

"I should be sorry to think so; he impresses me as a faithful old soul."

"Well, my eyes are rather clear, you know."

"Yes, I know. Good-night, Hilda."

She hung up the receiver. She had talked to him at the telephone in the lower hall, which was enclosed, and where one might be confidential without feeing overheard.

She sat very still for a few moments in the little booth, thinking; then she rose and went upstairs.

The General was awake and eager.

"Shall I read to you?" Hilda asked.

"No, I'd rather talk."

She shaded the light and sat beside the little table. "Did you like your dinner?"

"Yes. Bronson said you made the broth. It was delicious."

"I like to cook—when I like the people I cook for."

He basked in that.

"There are some patients—oh, I have wanted to salt their coffee and pepper their cereal. You have no idea of the temptations which come to a nurse."

"Are you fond of it—nursing?"

"Yes. It is nice in a place like this—and at Dr. McKenzie's. But there are some houses that are awful, with everybody quarrelling, the children squalling—. I hate that. I want to be comfortable. I like your thick carpets here, and the quiet, and the good service. And the good things to eat, and the little taste of wine that we take together." Her low laugh delighted him.

"The wine? You are going to drink another glass with me before I go to sleep."

"Yes. But it is our secret. Dr. McKenzie would kill me if he knew, and a nurse must obey orders."

"He need never know. And it won't hurt me."

"Of course not. But he has ideas on the subject."

"May I have it now?"

"Wait until Bronson goes to bed."

"Bronson has nothing to do with it. A servant has neither ears nor eyes."

"It might embarrass him if the Doctor asked him. And why should you make him lie?"

Bronson, pottering in, presently, was told that he would not be needed. "Mr. Derry telephoned that he would be having supper after the play at Miss Gray's. You can call him there if he is wanted."

"Thank you, Bronson. Good-night."

When the old man had left them, she said to the General, "Do you know that your son is falling in love?"

"In love?"

"Yes, desperately—at first sight?"

He laughed. "With whom?"

"Dr. McKenzie's daughter."

"What?" He raised himself on his elbow.

"Yes. Jean McKenzie. I am not sure that I ought to tell you, but somehow it doesn't seem right that you are not being told—"

He considered it gravely. "I don't want him to get married," he said at last. "I want him to go to war. I can't tell you, Miss Merritt, how bitter my disappointment has been that Derry won't fight."

"He may have to fight."

"Do you think I want him dragged to defend the honor of his country? I'd rather see him dead." He was struggling for composure.

"Oh, I shouldn't have told you," she said, solicitously.

"Why not? It is my right to know."

"Jean is a pretty little thing, and you may like her."

"I like McKenzie," thoughtfully.

She glanced at him. His old face had fallen into gentler lines. She gave a hard laugh. "Of course, a rich man like your son rather dazzles the eyes of a young girl like Jean."

"You think then it is his—money?"

"I shouldn't like to say that. But, of course, money adds to his charms."

"He won't have any money," grimly, "unless I choose that he shall. I can stop his allowance tomorrow. And what would the little lady do then?"

She shrugged. "I am sure I don't know. She'd probably take Ralph Witherspoon. He's in the race. She dropped him after she met your son."

The General's idea of women was somewhat exalted. He had an old-fashioned chivalry which made him blind to their faults, the champion of their virtues. He had always been, therefore, to a certain extent, at the mercy of the unscrupulous. He had loaned money and used his influence in behalf of certain wily and weeping females who had deserved at his hands much less than they got.

In his thoughts of a wife for Derry, he had pictured her as sweet and unsophisticated—a bit reserved, like Derry's mother—

The portrait which Hilda had subtly presented was of a mercenary little creature, lured by the glitter of gold—off with the old and on with the new, lacking fineness.

"I can stop his allowance," he wavered. "It would be a good test. But I love the boy. The war has brought the first misunderstandings between Derry and me. It would have hurt his mother."

Hilda was always restless when the name was introduced of the painted lady on the stairs. When the General spoke of his wife, his eyes grew kind—and inevitably his thoughts drifted away from Hilda to the days that he had spent with Derry's mother.

"She loved us both," he said.

Hilda rose and crossed the room. A low bookcase held the General's favorite volumes. There was a Globe edition of Dickens on the top shelf, little fat brown books, shabby with much handling. Hilda extracted one, and inserted her hand in the hollow space back of the row. She brought out a small flat bottle and put the book back.

"I always keep it behind 'Great Expectations,'" she said, as she approached the bed. "It seems rather appropriate, doesn't it?"

The old eyes, which had been soft with memories, glistened.

She filled two little glasses. "Let us drink to our—secret."

Then while the wine was firing his veins, she spoke again of Jean and Derry. "It really seems as if he should have told you."

"I won't have him getting married. He can't marry unless he has money."

"Please don't speak of it to him. I don't want to get into trouble. You wouldn't want to get me into trouble, would you?"

"No."

She filled his glass again. He drank. Bit by bit she fed the fire of his doubts of his son. When at last he fell asleep in his lacquered bed he had made up his mind to rather drastic action.

She sat beside him, her thoughts flying ahead into the years. She saw things as she wanted them to be—Derry at odds with his father; married to Jean; herself mistress of this great house, wearing the diamond crown and the pearl collar; her portrait in the place of the one of the painted lady on the stairs; looking down on little Jean who had judged her by youth's narrow standards—whose husband would have no fortune unless he chose to accept it at her hands.

Thus she weighed her influence over the sleeping sick man, thus she dreamed, calm as fate in her white uniform.

CHAPTER XVI

JEAN-JOAN

Drusilla Gray's little late suppers were rather famous. It was not that she spent so much money, but that she spent much thought.

Tonight she was giving Captain Hewes a sweet potato pie. "He has never eaten real American things," she said to Jean. "Nice homey-cooked things—"

"No one but Drusilla would ever think of pie at night," said Marion Gray, "but she has set her heart on it."

There were some very special hot oyster sandwiches which preceded the pie—peppery and savory with curls of bacon.

"I hope you are hungry," said Drusilla as her big black cook brought them in. "Aunt Chloe hates to have things go back to the kitchen."

Nothing went back. There was snow without, a white whirl in the air, piling up at street corners, a night for young appetites to be on edge.

"Jove," said the Captain, as he leaned back in his chair, "how I shall miss all this!"

Jean turned her face towards him, startled. "Miss it?"

"Yes. I am going back—got my orders today."

Drusilla was cutting the pie. "Isn't it glorious?"

Jean gazed at her with something like horror. Glorious! How could Drusilla go on, like Werther's Charlotte, *calmly cutting bread and butter*? Captain Hewes loved her, anybody with half an eye could see that—and whether she loved him or not, he was her friend—and she called his going "glorious!"

"I was afraid my wound might put me on the shelf," the Captain said.

"He is ordered straight to the front," Drusilla elucidated. "This is his farewell feast."

After that everything was to Jean funeral baked meats. The pie deep in its crust, rich with eggs and milk, defiant of conservation, was as sawdust to her palate.

Glorious!

Well, she couldn't understand Margaret. She couldn't understand Drusilla. She didn't want to understand them.

"Some day I shall go over," Drusilla was saying. "I shall drive something—it may be a truck and it may be an ambulance. But I can't sit here any longer doing nothing."

"I think you are doing a great deal," said Jean. "Look at the committees you are managing."

"Oh, things like that," said Drusilla contemptuously. "Women's work. I'm not made to knit and keep card indexes. I want a man's job."

There was something almost boyish about her as she said it. She had parted her hair on the side, which heightened the effect. "In the old days," she told Captain Hewes, "I should have worn doublet and hose and have gone as your page."

"Happy old days——."

"And I should have written a ballad about you," said Marion, "and have sung it to the accompaniment of my harp—and my pot-boilers would never have been. And we should all have worn trains and picturesque headdresses instead of shirtwaists and sports hats, and I should have called some man 'my Lord,' and have listened for his footsteps instead of ending my days in single blessedness with a type-writer as my closest companion."

Everybody laughed except Jean. She broke her cheese into small bits with her fork, and stared down at it as if cheese were the most interesting thing in the whole wide world.

It was only two weeks since they had had the news of Margaret's husband—only a month since he had died. And Winston had been Captain Hewes' dear friend; he had been Derry's. Would anybody laugh if Derry had been dead only fourteen days?

She tried, however, to swing herself in line with the others. "Shall you go before Christmas?" she asked the Captain.

"Yes. And Miss Gray had asked me to dine with her. You can see what I am missing—my first American Christmas."

"We are going to have a little tree," said Drusilla, "and ask all of you to come and hang presents on it."

Jean had always had a tree at Christmas time. From the earliest days of her remembrance, there had been set in the window of the little drawing room, a young pine brought from the Doctor's country-place far up in Maryland. On Christmas Eve it had been lighted and the doors thrown open. Jean could see her mother now, shining on one side of it, and herself coming in, in her nurse's arms.

There had been a star at the top, and snow powdered on the branches—and gold and silver balls—and her presents piled beneath—always a doll holding out its arms to her. There had been the first Rosie-Dolly, more beloved than any other; made of painted cloth, with painted yellow curls, and dressed in pink with a white apron. Rosie was a wreck of a doll now, her features blurred and her head bald with the years—but Jean still loved her, with something left over of the adoration of her little girl days. Then there was Maude, named in honor of the lovely lady who had played "Peter Pan," and the last doll that Jean's mother had given her. Maude had an outfit for every character in which Jean had seen her prototype—there were the rowan berries and shawl of "Babbie," the cap and jerkin of "Peter Pan," the feathers and spurs of "Chantecler"—such a trunkful, and her dearest mother had made them all—.

And Daddy! How Daddy had played Santa Claus, in red cloth and fur with a wide belt and big boots, every year, even last year when she was nineteen and ready to make her bow to society. And now he might never play Santa Claus again—for before Christmas had come he would be on the high seas, perhaps on the other side of the seas—at the edge of No Man's Land. And there would be no Star, no dolls, no gold and silver balls—for the nation which had given Santa Claus to the world, had robbed the world of peace and of goodwill. It had robbed the world of Christmas!

She came back to hear the Captain saying, "I want you to sing for me—Drusilla."

They rose and went into the other room.

"Tired, dearest?" Derry asked, as he found a chair for her and drew his own close to it.

"No, I am not tired," she told him, "but I hate to think that Captain Hewes must go."

"I'd give the world to be going with him."

Her hands were clasped tightly. "Would you give me up?"

"You? I should never have to give you up, thank God. You would never hold me back."

"Shouldn't I, Derry?"

"My precious, don't I know? Better than you know yourself."

Drusilla and the Captain were standing by the wide window which looked out over the city. The snow came down like a curtain, shutting out the sky.

"Do you think she loves him?" Jean asked.

"I hope so," heartily.

"But to send him away so—easily. Oh, Derry, she can't care."

"She is sending him not easily, but bravely. Margaret let her husband go like that."

"Would you want me to let you go like that, Derry?"

"Yes, dear."

"Wouldn't you want me to—cry?"

"Perhaps. Just a little tear. But I should want you to think beyond the tears. I should want you to know that for us there can be no real separation. You are mine to the end of all eternity, Jean."

He believed it. And she believed it. And perhaps, after all, it was true. There must be a very separate and special Heaven for those who love once, and never love again.

Drusilla came away from the window to sing for them—a popular song. But there was much in it to intrigue the imagination—a vision of the heroic Maid—a hint of the Marseillaise—and so the nations were singing it—.

"Jeanne d'Arc, Jeanne d'Arc,
Oh, soldats! entendez vous?
'Allons, enfants de la patrie,'
Jeanne d'Arc, la victoire est pour vous—"

There was a new note in Drusilla's voice. A note of tears as well as of triumph—and at the last word she broke down and covered her face with her hands.

In the sudden stillness, the Captain strode across the room and took her hands away from her face.

"Drusilla," he said before them all, "do you care as much as that?"

She told him the truth in her fine, frank fashion.

"Yes," she said, "I do care, Captain, but I want you to go."

"And oh, Derry, I am so glad she cried," Jean said, when they were driving home through the snow-storm. "It made her seem so—human."

Derry drew her close. "Such a thing couldn't have happened," he said, "at any other time. Do you suppose that a few years ago any of us would have been keyed up to a point where a self-contained Englishman could have asked a girl, in the face of three other people, if she loved him, and have had her answer like that? It was beautiful, beautiful, Jean-Joan—"

She held her breath. "Why do you call me that?"

"She lived for France. You shall live for France—and me."

The snow shut them in. There was the warmth of the car, of

the fur rugs and Derry's fur coat, Jean's own velvet wrap of heavenly blue, the fragrance of her violets. Somewhere far away men were fighting—there was the mud and cold of the trenches—somewhere men were suffering.

She tried not to think of them. Her cheek was against Derry's. She was safe—safe.

* * * * * *

Captain Hewes went away that night Drusilla's accepted lover. He put a ring on her finger and kissed her "good-bye," and with his head high faced the months that he must be separated from her.

"I will come back, dear woman."

"I shall see you before that," she told him. "I am coming over."

"I shall hate to have you in it all. But it will be Heaven to see you."

When he had gone, Drusilla went into Marion Gray's study.

Marion looked up from her work. She was correcting manuscript, pages and pages of it. "Well, do you want me to congratulate you, Drusilla?"

Drusilla sat down. "I don't know, Marion. He is the biggest and finest man I have ever met, but—"

"But what?"

"I wanted love to come to me differently, as it has come to Jean and Derry—without any doubts. I wanted to be sure. And I am not sure. I only know that I couldn't let him go without making him happy."

"Then is it—pity?"

"No. He means more to me than that. But I gave way to an impulse—the music, and his sad eyes. And then I cried, and he came up to me—fancy a man coming up before you all like that—"

"It was quite the most dramatic moment," said the lady who wrote. "Quite unbelievable in real life. One finds those things occasionally in fiction."

"It was as if there were just two of us alone in the world," Drusilla confessed, "and I said what I did because I simply couldn't help it. And it was true at the moment; I think it is always going to be true. If I marry him I shall care a great deal. But it has not come to me just as I had—dreamed."

"Nothing is like our dreams," said Marion, and dropped her pen. "That's why I write. I can give my heroine all the bliss for which she yearns."

Drusilla stood up. "You mustn't misunderstand me, Marion. I am very happy in the thought of my good friend, of my great lover. It is only that it hasn't quite measured up to what I expected."

"Nothing measures up to what we expect."

"And now Jean belongs to Derry, and I belong to my gallant and good Captain. I shall thank God before I sleep tonight, Marion."

"And he'll thank God—."

They kissed each other, and Drusilla went to bed, and the next morning she wrote a letter to her Captain, which he carried next to his heart and kissed when he got a chance.

CHAPTER XVII

THE WHITE CAT

Derry, going quietly to his room that night, did not stop at the General's door. He did not want to speak to Hilda, he did not want to speak to anyone, he wanted to be alone with his thoughts of Jean and that perfect ride with her through the snow.

He was, therefore, a little impatient to find Bronson waiting up for him.

"I thought I told you to go to bed, Bronson."

"You did, sir, but—but I have something to tell you."

"Can't it wait until morning?"

"I should like to say it now, Mr. Derry." The old man's eyes were anxious. "It's about your father—"

"Father?"

"Yes. I told you I didn't like the nurse."

"Miss Merritt? Well?"

"Perhaps I'd better get you to bed, sir. It's a rather long story, and you'd be more comfortable."

"You'd be more comfortable, you mean, Bronson." The impatient note had gone out of Derry's voice. Temporarily he pigeon-holed his thoughts of Jean, and gave his attention to this servant who was more than a servant, more even than a friend. To Derry, Bronson wore a sort of halo, like a good old saint in an ancient woodcut.

Propped up at last among his pillows, pink from his bath and in pale blue pajamas, Derry listened to what the old man had to say to him.

Bronson sat on the edge of a straight-backed chair with Muffin at his knees. "From the first day I had a feeling that she wasn't just—straight. I don't know why, but I felt it. She had one way with the General and another with us servants. But I didn't mind that, not much, until she went into your mother's room."

"My mother's room?" sharply. "What was she doing there, Bronson?"

"That's what I am going to tell you, sir. You know that place on the third floor landing, where I sits and looks through at your father when he ain't quite himself, and won't let me come in his room? Well, there was one night that I was there and watched her—"

Derry's quick frown rebuked him. "You shouldn't have done that, Bronson."

"I had a feeling, sir, that things were going wrong, and that the General wasn't always himself. I shouldn't ever have said a thing to you, Mr. Derry," earnestly, "if I hadn't seen what I did."

He cleared his throat. "That first night I saw her open the door between your father's room and the sitting room, and she did it careful and quiet like a person does when they don't want anybody to know. The sitting room was dark, but I went down and stood behind the curtain in the General's door, and I could see through, and there was a light in your mother's room and a screen set before it."

"I took a big chance, but I slid into the sitting room, and I could see her on the other side of the screen, and she had opened the safe behind the Chinese scroll, and she was trying on your mother's diamonds."

"What!"

Bronson nodded solemnly. "Yes, sir, she had 'em on her head and her neck and her fingers—."

"You don't mean—that she took anything."

"Oh, no, sir, she's no common thief. But she looked at herself in the glass and strutted up and down, up and down, up and down, bowing and smiling like a—fool."

"Then the telephone rang, and I had to get out pretty quick, before she came to answer it. I went to bed, but I didn't sleep much, and the next night I watched her again. I watch every night."

Derry considered the situation. "I don't like it at all, Bronson. But perhaps it was just a woman's vanity. She wanted to see how she looked."

"Well, she's seen—and she ain't going to be satisfied with that. She'll want to wear them all the time—"

"Of course, she can't, Bronson. She isn't as silly as to think she can."

"Perhaps not, sir." Bronson opened his lips and shut them again.

"There's something else, sir," he said, after a pause. "I've found out that she's giving the General things to drink."

"Hilda?" Derry said, incredulously. "Oh, surely not, Bronson, The Doctor has given her strict orders—."

"She's got a bottle behind the books, and she pours him a glass right after dinner, and another before he goes to sleep, and—and—you know he'd sell his soul for the stuff, Mr. Derry."

Derry did know. It had been the shame of all his youthful years that his father should stoop to subterfuge, to falsehood, to everything that was foreign to his native sense of honor and honesty, for a taste of that which his abnormal appetite demanded.

"If anyone had told me but you, Bronson, I wouldn't have believed it."

"I didn't want to tell you, but I had to. You can see that, can't you, sir?"

"Yes. But how in the world did she know where the diamonds were?"

"He gave her his key one day when I was there—made me get it off his ring. He sent her for your picture—the one that your mother used to wear. I thought then that he wasn't quite right in his head, with the fever and all, or he would have sent me. But a woman like that—"

"Dr. McKenzie has the greatest confidence in her."

"I know, sir, and she's probably played square with him—but she ain't playing square here."

"It can't go on, of course. I shall have to tell McKenzie."

Bronson protested nervously. "If she puts her word against mine, who but you will believe me? I'd rather you saw it yourself, Mr. Derry, and left my name out of it."

"But I can't sit on the steps and watch."

"No, sir, but you can come in unexpected from the outside—
when I flash on the third floor light for you."

Derry slept little that night. Ahead of him stretched twenty-
four hours of suspense—twenty-four hours in which he would
have to think of this thing which was hidden in the big house
in which his mother had reigned.

In the weeks since he had met Jean, he had managed to thrust
it into the back of his mind—he had, indeed, in the midst of
his happiness, forgotten his bitterness, his sense of injustice—
he wondered if he had not in a sense forgotten his patriotism.
Life had seemed so good, his moments with Jean so
transcendent—there had been no room for anything else.

But now he was to take up again the burden which he had
dropped. He was to consider his problem from a new angle.
How could he bring Jean here? How could he let her clear
young eyes rest on that which he and his mother had seen?
How could he set, as it were, all of this sordidness against her
sweetness? Money could, of course, do much. But his promise
held him to watchfulness, to brooding care, to residence
beneath this roof. His bride would be the General's daughter,
she would live in the General's house, she would live, too,
beneath the shadow of the General's tragic fault.

Yet—she was a brave little thing. He comforted himself with
that. And she loved him. He slept at last with a desperate
prayer on his lips that some new vision might be granted him
on the morrow.

But the first news that came over the telephone was of Jean's
flitting. "Daddy wants me to go with him to our old place in
Maryland. He has some business which takes him there, and
we shall be gone two days."

"Two days?"

"Yes. We are to motor up."

"Can't I go with you?"

"I think—Daddy wants me to himself. You won't mind, Derry—some day you'll have me all the time."

"But I need you now, dearest."

"Do you really," delightedly. "It doesn't seem as if you could—"

"If you knew how much."

She could not know. He hung up the receiver. The day stretched out before him, blank.

But it passed, of course. And Hilda, having slept her allotted number of hours, was up in time to superintend the serving of the General's dinner. Later, Derry stopped at the door to say that he was going to the theater and might be called there. The General, propped against his pillows and clothed in a gorgeous mandarin coat, looked wrinkled and old. The ruddiness had faded from his cheeks, and he was much thinner.

Hilda, sitting by the little table, showed all the contrast of youth and bloom. Her long hands lay flat on the table. Derry had a fantastic feeling, as if a white cat watched him under the lamp.

"Are you going alone, son?" the General asked.

"Yes."

"Why don't you take a girl?" craftily.

Derry smiled.

"The only girl I should care to take is out of town."

The white cat purred. "Lucky girl to be the only one."

Derry's manner stiffened. "You are good to think so."

After Derry had gone, Hilda said, "You see, it is Jean McKenzie. The Doctor said that he and Jean would be up in Maryland for a day or two. She has a good time. She doesn't know what it means to be poor, not as I know it. She doesn't know what it means to go without the pretty things that women long for. You wouldn't believe it, General, but when I was a little girl, I used to stand in front of shop windows and wonder if other girls really wore the slippers and fans and parasols. And when I went to Dr. McKenzie's, and saw Jean in her silk dressing gowns, and her pink slippers and her lace caps, she seemed to me like a lady in a play. I've worn my uniforms since I took my nurse's training, and before that I wore the uniform of an Orphans' Home. I—I don't know why I am telling you all this—only it doesn't seem quite fair, does it?"

He had all of an old man's sympathy for a lovely woman in distress. He had all of any man's desire to play Cophetua.

"Look here," he said. "You get yourself a pink parasol and a fan and a silk dress. I'd like to see you wear them."

She shook her head. "What should I do with things like that?" Her voice had a note of wistfulness. "A woman in my position must be careful."

"But I want you to have the things," he persisted.

"I shouldn't have a place to wear them," sadly. "No, you are very good to offer them. But I mustn't."

The General slept after that. Hilda read under the lamp—a white cat watched by a little old terrier on the stairs!

And now the big house was very still. There were lights in the halls of the first and second floors. Bronson crouching in the darkness of the third landing was glad of the company of the painted lady on the stairs. He knew she would approve of what he was doing. For years he had served her in such matters as this, saving her husband from himself. When Derry was too small, too ignorant of evil, too innocent, to be told things, it was to the old servant that she had come.

He remembered a certain night. She was young then and new to her task. She and the General had been dining at one of the Legations. She was in pale blue and very appealing. When Bronson had opened the door, she had come in alone.

"Oh, the General, the General, Bronson," she had said. "We've got to go after him."

She was shaking with the dread of it, and Bronson had said, "Hadn't you better wait, ma'am?"

"I mustn't. We stopped at the hotel as we came by, and he said he would run in and get a New York paper. And we waited, and we waited, and he didn't come out again, and at last I sent McChesney in, and he couldn't find him. And then I went and sat in the corridor, thinking he might pass through. It isn't pleasant to sit alone in the corridor with the men—staring at you—at night. And then I asked the man at the door if he had seen him, and he said, 'yes,' that he had called a cab, and then I came home."

They had gone out again together, with Bronson, who was young and strong, taking the place of the coachman, McChesney, because Mrs. Drake did not care to have the other servants see her husband at times like these. "You know how good he is," had been her timid claim on him from the first, "and you know how hard he tries." And because Bronson knew, and because he had helped her like the faithful squire that he was, she had trusted him more and more with this important but secret business.

She had changed her dress for something dark, and she had worn a plain dark hat and coat. She had not cried a tear and she would not cry. She had been very brave as they travelled a beaten path, visiting the places which the General frequented, going on and on until they came to the country, and to a farmhouse where they found him turning night into day, having roused the amazed inmates to ask for breakfast.

He had paid them well for it, and was ready to set forth again with the dawn when his wife drove in.

"My dear," he had said, courteously, as his little wife's face peered out at him from the carriage, "you shouldn't have come."

Sobered for the moment, he had made a handsome figure, as he stood with uncovered head, his dark hair in a thick curl between his eyes. The morning was warm and he carried his overcoat on his arm. His patent leather shoes and the broadcloth of his evening clothes showed the dust and soil of his walk through the fields. He had evidently dismissed his cab at the edge of the city and had come crosscountry.

His wife had reached out her little hand to him. "I came because I was lonely. The house seems so big when you are— away—"

It had wrung Bronson's heart to see her smiling. Yet she had always met the General with a smile and with the reminder of her need of him. There had been never a complaint, never a rebuke—at these moments. When he was himself, she strove with him against his devils. But to strive when he was not himself, would be to send him away from her.

Her hands were clasped tightly, and her voice shook as she talked on the way back to the husband who seemed so unworthy of the love she gave.

Yet she had not thought him unworthy. "If I can only save

him," she had said so many times. "Oh, Bronson, I mustn't let him go down and down, with no one who loves him to hold him back."

In the years that had followed, Bronson had seen her grow worn and weary, but never hopeless. He had seen her hair grow gray, he had seen the light go out of her face so that she no longer smiled as she had smiled in the picture.

But she had never given up the fight. Not even at the last moment. "You will stay with him, Bronson, and help Derry."

And now this other woman had come to undo all the work that his beloved mistress had done. And there in the shadowed room she was weaving her spells.

Outside, snug against the deadly cold in his warm closed car, Derry waited alone for Bronson's signal.

There was movement at last in the shadowed room. The General spoke from the bed. Hilda answered him, and rose. She arranged a little tray with two glasses and a plate of biscuits. Then she crossed the room towards the bookcase.

Bronson reached up his hand and touched the button which controlled the lights on the third floor. He saw Hilda raise a startled head as the faint click reached her. She listened for a moment, and he withdrew himself stealthily up and out of sight. If she came into the hall she might see him on the stairs. He had done what he could. He would leave the rest to Derry.

"What's the matter?" the General asked.

"I thought I heard a sound—but there's no one up. This is our hour, isn't it?"

She brought the bottle out from behind the books. Then she came and stood by the side of the bed.

"Will you drink to my happiness, General?"

She was very handsome. "To our happiness," he said, eagerly, and unexpectedly, as he took the glass.

Hilda, pouring out more wine for herself, stood suddenly transfixed. Derry spoke from the threshold. "Dr. McKenzie has asked you repeatedly not to give my father wine, Miss Merritt."

He was breathing quickly. His hat was in his hand and he wore his fur coat. "Why are you giving it to him against the Doctor's orders?"

The General interposed. "Don't take that tone with Miss Merritt, Derry. I asked her to get it for me, and she obeyed my orders. What's the matter with that?"

"Dr. McKenzie said, explicitly, that you were not to have it."

"Dr. McKenzie has nothing to do with it. You may tell him that for me, I am not his patient any longer."

"Father—"

"Certainly not. Do you think I am going to take orders from McKenzie—or from you?"

"But, Miss Merritt is his nurse, under his orders."

"She is not going to be his nurse hereafter. I have other plans for her."

Derry stood staring, uncomprehending. "Other plans—"

"I have asked her to be my wife."

Oh, lovely painted lady on the stairs, has it come to this? Have your prayers availed no more than this? Have the years in which you sacrificed yourself, in which you sacrificed your son, counted no more than this?

Derry felt faint and sick. "You can't mean it, Dad."

"I do mean it. I—am a lonely man, Derry. A disappointed man. My wife is dead. My son is a slacker—"

It was only the maudlin drivel of a man not responsible for what he was saying. But Derry had had enough. He took a step forward and stood at the foot of the bed. "I wouldn't go any farther if I were you, Dad. I've not been a slacker. I have never been a slacker. I am not a coward. I have never been a coward. I am going to tell you right now why I am not in France. Do you think I should have stayed out of it for a moment if it hadn't been for you? Has it ever crossed your mind that if you had been half a man I might have acted like a whole one? Have you ever looked back at the years and seen me going out into the night to follow you and bring you back? I am not whining. I loved you, and I wanted to do it; but it wasn't easy. And I should still be doing it; but of late you've said things that I can't forgive. I've stood by you because I gave a promise to my mother—that I wouldn't leave you. And I've stayed. But now I shan't try any more. I am going to France. I am going to fight. I am not your son, sir. I am the son of my mother."

Then the General said what he would never have said if he had been himself.

"If you are not my son, then, by God, you shan't have any of my money."

"I don't want it. Do you think that I do? I shall get out of here tonight, and I shan't come back. There is only one thing that I want besides my own personal traps—and that is my mother's picture on the stairs."

The General was drawing labored breaths. "Your mother's picture—?"

"Yes, it has no place here. Do you think for as instant that you can meet her eyes?"

There was a look of fright on the drawn old face. "I am not well, give me the wine."

Derry reached for the bottle. "He shall not have it."

Hilda came up to him swiftly. "Can't you see? He must. Look at him."

Derry looked and surrendered. Then covered his face with his hands.

*　*　*　*　*　*

All that night, Derry, trying to pack, with Bronson in agitated attendance, was conscious of the sinister presence of Hilda in the house. There was the opening and shutting of doors, her low orders in the halls, her careful voice at the telephone, and once the sound of her padded steps as she passed Derry's room on her way to her own. The new doctor came and went. Hilda sent, at Derry's request, a bulletin of the patient's condition. The General must be kept from excitement; otherwise there was not reason for alarm.

But Derry was conscious, as the night wore on, and Bronson left him, and he sat alone, of more than the physical evidences of Hilda's presence; he was aware of the spiritual effect of her sojourn among them. She had stolen from them all something that was fine and beautiful. From Derry his faith in his father. From the General his constancy to his lovely wife. The structure of ideals which Derry's mother had so carefully reared for the old house had been wrecked by one who had first climbed the stairs in the garb of a sister of mercy.

He saw his father's future. Hilda, cold as ice, setting his authority aside. He saw the big house, the painted lady smiling no more on the stairs. Hilda's strange friends filling the rooms, the General's men friends looking at them askance, his mother's friends staying away.

Poor old Dad, poor old Dad. All personal feeling was swept away in the thought of what might come to his father. Yet none the less his own path lay straight and clear before him. The time had come for him to go.

BOOK TWO

THROUGH THE CRACK

"I will go to the wars! I will go to the wars!" the Tin Soldier cried as loud as he could, and he threw himself from the shelf. . . .

What could have become of him? The old man looked, and the little boy looked. "I shall find him," the old man said, but he did not find him. For the Tin Soldier had fallen through a crack in the floor, and there he lay as in an open grave.

CHAPTER XVIII

THE BROAD HIGHWAY

The Doctor's house in Maryland was near Woodstock, and from the rise of the hill where it stood one could see the buildings of the old Jesuit College, and the river which came so soon to the Bay.

In his boyhood the priests had been great friends of Bruce McKenzie. While of a different faith, he had listened eagerly to the things they had to tell him, these wise men, the pioneers of missionary work in many lands, teachers and scholars. His imagination had been fired by their tales of devotion, and he had many arguments with his Covenanter grandfather, to whom the gold cross on the top of the college had been the sign and symbol of papacy.

"But, grandfather, the things we believe aren't so very different, and I like to pray in their chapel."

"Why not pray in your own kirk?"

"It's so bare."

"There's nothing to distract your thoughts."

"And I like the singing, and the lights and the candles—"

"We need no candles; we have light enough in our souls."

But Bruce had loved the smell of the incense, and the purple and red of the robes, and, seeing it all through the golden haze of the lights, his sense of beauty had been satisfied, as it was not satisfied in his own plain house of worship.

Yet it had been characteristic of the boy as it was of the man that neither kirk nor chapel held him, and he had gone through life liking each a little, but neither overmuch.

Something of this he tried to express to Jean as, arriving at Woodstock in the early afternoon, they passed the College. "I might have been a priest," he said, "if I hadn't been too much of a Puritan or a Pagan. I am not sure which held me back—"

Jean shuddered. "How can people shut themselves away from the world?"

"They have a world of their own, my dear," said the Doctor, thoughtfully, "and I'm not sure that it isn't as interesting as our own."

"But there isn't love in it," said Jean.

"There's love that carries them above self—and that's something."

"It is something, but it isn't much," said his small daughter, obstinately. "I don't want to love the world, Daddy. I want to love Derry—"

The Doctor groaned. "I thought I had escaped him, for a day."

"You will never escape him," was the merciless rejoinder, but she kissed him to make up for it.

In spite of the fact of her separation for the moment from her lover, she had enjoyed the ride. There had been much wind, and a little snow on the way. But now the air was clear, with a sort of silver clearness—the frozen river was gray-green between its banks, there were blue shadows flung by the bare trees. As they passed the College, a few black-frocked fathers and scholastics paced the gardens.

Jean wished that Derry were there to see it all. It was to her a place of many memories. Most of the summers of her little girlhood had been spent there, with now and then a Christmas holiday.

The house did not boast a heating plant, but there were roaring open fires in all the rooms, except in the Connollys' sitting room, which was warmed by a great black stove.

The Connollys were the caretakers. They occupied the left wing of the house, and worked the farm. They were both good Catholics, and Mrs. Connolly looked after the little church at the crossroads corner, where the good priests came from the College every week to say Mass. She was a faithful, hard-working, pious soul, with her mind just now very much on her two sons who had enlisted at the first call for men, and were now in France.

She talked much about them to Jean, who came into the kitchen to watch her get supper. The deep, dark, low-ceiled room was lighted by an oil lamp. The rocking chair in which Jean sat had a turkey-red cushion, and there was another turkey-red cushion in the rocking chair on the other side of the cookstove. They ate their meals on the table under the lamp. It was only when guests were in the house that the dining room was opened.

The Doctor and Jim Connolly were at the barn, where were kept two fat mules, a fat little horse, a fat little cow, and a pair of fat pigs. There were also a fat house dog, and a brace of plump pussies, for the Connollys were a plump and comfortable couple who wanted everything about them comfortable, and who had had little to worry them until the coming of the war.

Yet even the war could not shake Mrs. Connolly's faith in the rightness of things.

"I was glad to have our country get into it, and to have my sons go. If they had stayed at home, I shouldn't have felt satisfied."

"Didn't it nearly break your heart?"

Mrs. Connolly, beating eggs for an omelette, shook her head. "Women's hearts don't break over brave men, Miss Jean. It is the sons who are weak and wayward who break their mothers' hearts—not the ones that go to war."

She poured the omelette into a pan. "When I have a bad time missing them, I remember how the Mother of God gave her blessed Son to the world. And He set the example, to give ourselves to save others. No, I don't want my boys back until the war is over."

Jean said nothing. She rocked back and forth and thought about what Mary Connolly had said. One of the fat pussies jumped on her lap and purred. It was all very peaceful, all as it had been since some other cook made omelettes for the little aristocrat of an Irish grandmother who would not under any circumstances have sat in the kitchen on terms of familiarity with a dependent. The world had progressed much in democracy since those days. Those who had fought in this part of the country for liberty and equality had not really known it. They had seen the Vision, but it was to be given to their descendants to realize it.

Jean rocked and rocked. "I hate war," she said, suddenly. "I didn't until Daddy said he was going, and then it seemed to come—so near—all the time I am trying to push the thought of it away. I wouldn't tell him, of course. But I don't want him to go."

"No, I wouldn't tell him. We women may be scared to death,

but it ain't the time to tell our men that we are scared."

"Are you scared to death, Mrs. Connolly?"

The steady eyes met hers. "Sometimes, in the night, when I think of the wet and cold, and the wounded groaning under the stars. But when the morning comes, I cook the breakfast and get Jim off, and he don't know but that I am as cheerful as one of our old hens, and then I go over to the church, and tell it all to the blessed Virgin, and I am ready to write to my boys of how proud I am, and how fine they are—and of every little tiny thing that has happened on the farm."

Thus the heroic Mary Connolly—type of a million of her kind in America—of more than a million of her kind throughout the world—hiding her fears deep in her heart that her men might go cheered to battle.

The omelette was finished, and the Doctor and Jim Connolly had come in. "The stars are out," the Doctor said. "After supper we'll walk a bit."

Jean was never to forget that walk with her father. It was her last long walk with him before he went to France, her last intimate talk. It was very cold, and he took her arm, the snow crunched under their feet.

Faintly the chimes of the old College came up to them. "Nine o'clock," said the Doctor. "Think of all the years I've heard the chimes, I have lived over half a century—and my father before me heard them—and they rang in my grandfather's time. Perhaps they will ring in the ears of my grandchildren, Jean."

They had stopped to listen, but now they went on. "Do you know what they used to say to me when I was a little boy?

"The Lord watch
Between thee and—me—"

"My mother and I used to repeat it together at nine o'clock, and when I brought your mother here for our honeymoon— that first night we, too, stood and listened to the chimes—and I told her what they said.

"Men drift away from these things," he continued, with something of an effort. "I have drifted too far. But, Jean, will you always remember this, that when I am at my best, I come back to the things my mother taught her boy? If anything should happen, you will remember?"

She clung to his arm. She had no words. Never again was she to hear the chimes without that poignant memory of her father begging her to remember the best—.

"I have been thinking," he said, out of a long silence, "of you and Derry. I—I want you to marry him, dear, before I go."
"Before you go—Daddy—"

"Yes. Emily says I have no right to stand in the way of your happiness. And I have no right. And some day, perhaps, oh, my little Jean, my grandchildren may hear the chimes—"

White and still, she stood with her face upturned to the stars. "Life is so wonderful, Daddy."

And this time she said it out of a woman's knowledge of what life was to mean.

They went in, to find that the Connollys had retired. Jean slept in a great feather-bed. And all the night the chimes in the College tower struck the hours—

In the morning, Jean went over to the church with Mrs. Connolly. It was Saturday, and things must be made ready for the services the next day. Jean had been taught as a child to kneel reverently while Mrs. Connolly prayed. To sit quietly in a pew while her good friend did the little offices of the altar.

Jean had always loved to sit there, to wonder about the rows of candles and the crucifix, to wonder about the Sacred Heart, and St. Agnes with the lamb, and St. Anthony who found things when you lost them, and St. Francis in the brown frock with the rope about his waist, and why Mrs. Connolly never touched any of the sacred vessels with bare hands.

But most of all she had wondered about that benignant figure in the pale blue garments who stood in a niche, with a light burning at her feet, and with a baby in her arms.

Mary—

Faintly as she gazed upon it on this winter morning, Jean began to perceive the meaning of that figure. Of late many women had said to her, "Was my son born for this, to be torn from my arms—to be butchered?"

Well, Mary's son had been torn from her arms—butchered—her little son who had lain in a manger and whom she had loved as much as any less-worshipped mother,—and he had told the world what he thought of sin and injustice and cruelty, and the world had hated him because he had set himself against these things—and they had killed him, and from his death had come the regeneration of mankind.

And now, other men, following him, were setting themselves against injustice and cruelty, and they were being killed for it. But perhaps their sacrifices, too, would be for the salvation of the world. Oh, if only it might be for the world's salvation!

She walked quite soberly beside Mrs. Connolly back to the house. She took her knitting to the kitchen. Mrs. Connolly was knitting socks. "I don't mind the fighting as much as I do the chance of their taking cold. And I'm afraid they won't have the sense to change their socks when they are wet. I have sent them pairs and pairs—but they'll never know enough to change—

"It is funny how a mother worries about a thing like that," she continued. "I suppose it is because you've always worried about their taking cold, and you've never had to worry much about their being killed. I always used to put them to bed with hot drinks and hot baths, and a lot of blankets, and I keep thinking that there won't be anybody to put them to bed."

Jean knitted a long row, and then she spoke. "Mrs. Connolly, I'm going to be married, before Daddy leaves for France."

"I am happy to hear that, my dear."

"I didn't know it until last night—Daddy wasn't willing. I—I feel as if it couldn't be really true—that I am going to be married, Mrs. Connolly."

There was a tremble of her lip and clasping of her little hands.

Mary Connolly laid down her work. "I guess you miss your mother, blessed lamb. I remember when she was married. I was young, too, but I felt a lot older with my two babies, and Jim and I were so glad the Doctor had found a wife. He needed one, if ever a man did—for he liked his gay good time."

"Daddy?" said Jean, incredulously. It is hard for youth to visualize the adolescence of its elders. Dr. McKenzie's daughter beheld in him none of the elements of a Lothario. He was beyond the pale of romance! He was fifty, which settled at once all matters of sentiment!

"Indeed, he was gay, my dear, and he had broken half the hearts in the county, and then your mother came for a visit. She didn't look in the least like you, except that she was small and slender. Her hair was dark and her eyes. You have your father's eyes and hair.

"But she was so pretty and so loving—and you never saw such a honeymoon. They were married in the spring, and the orchards were in bloom, and your father filled her room with apple blossoms, and the first day when Jim drove them up from the station, your father carried her _n his arms over the threshold and up into that room, and when she came down, she said, 'Mary Connolly, isn't life—wonderful?'"

"Did she say that, Mrs. Connolly, really? Daddy always teases me when I go into raptures. He says that I think everything is wonderful from a sunset to a chocolate soda."

"Well, she did, too. Her husband was the most wonderful man, and her baby was the most wonderful baby—and her house was the most wonderful house. You make me think of her in every way. But you won't have apple blossoms for your honeymoon, my dear."

"No. But, oh, Mrs. Connolly—it won't make any real difference."

"Not a bit. And if you'll come up here, Jim and I will promise not to be in the way. Your mother said we were never in the way. And I'll serve your meals in front of the sitting-room fire. They used to have theirs out of doors. But you'll be just as much alone, with me and Jim eating in the kitchen."

It was very easy after that to tell Mrs. Connolly all about it. About Derry, and how he had fallen in love with her when he had thought she was just the girl in the Toy Shop. But there were things which she did not tell, of the shabby old gentleman and of the shadow which had darkened Derry's life.

Then when she had finished, Mary Connolly asked the thing which everybody asked—"Why isn't he fighting?"

Jean flushed. "He—he made a promise to his mother."

"I'd never make my boys promise a thing like that. And if I did, I'd hope they'd break it."

"Break it?" tensely.

"Of course. Their honor's bigger than anything I could ever ask them. And they know it."

"Then you think that Derry ought to break his promise?"

"I do, indeed, my dear."

"But——. Oh, Mrs. Connolly, I don't know whether I want him to break it."

"Why not?"

With her face hidden. "I don't know whether I could let him—go."

"You'd let him go. Never fear. When the moment came, the good Lord would give you strength—"

There were steps outside. Jean leaned over and kissed Mary Connolly on the cheek. "You are such a darling—I don't wonder that my mother loved you."

"Well, you'll always be more than just yourself to me," said Mary. "You'll always be your mother's baby. And after I get lunch for you and the men I am going back to the church and ask the blessed Virgin to intercede for your happiness."

So it was while Mary was at church, and the two men had gone to town upon some legal matter, that Jean, left alone, wandered through the house, and always before her flitted the happy ghost of the girl who had come there to spend her honeymoon. In the great south chamber was a picture of her mother, and one of her father as they looked at the time of their marriage. Her mother was in organdie with great balloon sleeves, and her hair in a Psyche knot. She was a slender little thing, and the young doctor's picture was a great contrast in its blondness and bigness. Daddy had worn a beard then, pointed, as was the way with doctors of his day, and he looked very different, except for the eyes which had the same teasing twinkle.

The window of this room looked out over the orchard, the orchard which had been bursting with bloom when the bride came. The trees now were slim little skeletons, with the faint gold of the western sky back of them, and there was much snow. Yet so vivid was Jean's impression of what had been, that she would have sworn her nostrils were assailed by a delicate fragrance, that her eyes beheld wind-blown petals of white and pink.

The long mirror reflecting her showed her in her straight frock of dark blue serge, with the white collars and cuffs. The same mirror had reflected her mother's organdie. It, too, had been blue, Mary had told her, but blue with such a difference! A faint forget-me-not shade, with a satin girdle, and a stiff satin collar!

Two girls, with a quarter of a century between them. Yet the mother had laughed and loved, and had looked forward to a long life with her gay big husband. They had had ten years of it, and then there had been just her ghost to haunt the old rooms.

Jean shivered a little as she went downstairs. She found herself a little afraid of the lonely darkening house. She wished that Mary would come.

Curled up in one of the big chairs, she waited. Half-asleep and half-awake; she was aware of shadow-shapes which came and went. Her Scotch great-grandfather, the little Irish great-grandmother; her copper-headed grandfather, his English wife, her own mother, pale and dark-haired and of Huguenot strain, her own dear father.

From each of these something had been given her, some fault, some virtue. If any of them had been brave, there must have been handed down to her some bit of bravery—if any of them had been cowards—

But none of them had been cowards.

"We came to a new country," said the great-grandparents. *"There were hardships, but we loved and lived through them—"*

"The Civil war tore our hearts," said the grand-parents. *"Brother hated brother, and friend hated friend, but we loved and lived through it—"*

"We were not tested," said her own parents. *"You are our child and test has come to you. If you are brave, it will be because we have given to you that which came first to us—"*

Jean sat up, wide-awake—*"I am not brave,"* she said.

She stood, after that, at a lower window, watching. Far down the road a big black motor flew straight as a crow towards the hill on which the Doctor's house stood. It stopped at the gate. A man stepped out. Jean gave a gasp, then flew to meet him.

"Oh, Derry, Derry—"

He came in and shut the door behind him, took her in his arms, kissed her, and kissed her again. "I love you," he said, "I love you. I couldn't stay away—"

It seemed to Jean quite the most wonderful thing of all the wonderful things that had happened, that he should be here in this old house where her parents had come for their honeymoon—where her own honeymoon was so soon to be—

She saved that news for him, however. He had to tell her first of how he had taken the wrong road after he had left Baltimore. He had gone without his lunch to get to her quickly. No, he wasn't hungry, and he was glad Mary Connolly was out, "I've so much to say to you."

Then, too, she delayed the telling so that he might see the farm before darkness fell. She wrapped herself in a hooded red cloak in which he thought her more than ever adorable.

The sun rested on the rim of the world, a golden disk under a wind-blown sky. It was very cold, but she was warm in her red cloak, he in his fur-lined coat and cap.

She told him about her father's honeymoon, hugging her own secret close. "They came here, Derry, and it was in May. I wish you could see the place in May, with all the appleblooms.

"It seems queer, doesn't it, Derry, to think of father honeymooning. He always seems to be making fun of things, and one should be serious on a honeymoon."

She flashed a smile at him and he smiled back. "I shall be very serious on mine."

"Of course. Derry, wouldn't you like a honeymoon here?"

"I should like it anywhere—with you—"

"Well," she drew a deep breath, "Daddy says we may—"

"We may what, Jean-Joan?"

"Get married—"

"Before he goes?"

"Yes."

She leaned forward to get the full effect of his surprise, to watch the dawn of his delight.

But something else dawned. Embarrassment? Out of a bewildering silence she heard him say, "I am not sure, dear, that it will be best for us to marry before he goes."

She had a stunned feeling that, quite unaccountably, Derry was failing her. A shamed feeling that she had offered herself and had been rejected.

Something of this showed in her face. "My dear, my dear," he said, "let us go in. I can tell you better there."

Once more in the warm sitting room with the door shut behind them, he lifted her bodily in his arms. "Don't you know I want it," he whispered, tensely. "Tell me that you know—"

When he set her down, his own face showed the stress of his emotion. "You are always to remember this," he said, "that no matter what happens, I am yours, yours—always, till the end of time."

Instinctively she felt that this Derry was in some way different from the Derry she had left the day before. There was a hint of masterfulness, a touch of decision.

"Will you remember?" he repeated, hands tight on her shoulders.

"Yes," she said, simply.

He bent and kissed her. "Then nothing else will matter." He placed a big chair for her in front of the fire, and drew another up in front of it. Bending forward, he took her hands. "I am glad I found you alone. What luck it was to find you alone!"

He tried then to tell her what he had come to tell. Yet, after all there was much that he left unsaid. How could he speak to her of the things he had seen in his father's shadowed house? How fill that delicate mind with a knowledge of that which seemed even to his greater sophistication unspeakable?

So she wondered over several matters. "How can he want to marry Hilda? I can't imagine any man wanting Hilda."

"She is handsome in a big fine way."

"But she is not big and fine. She is little and mean, but I could never make Daddy see it."

He wondered if McKenzie would see it now.

Mary Connolly, coming in through the back door to her warm kitchen, heard voices. Standing in the dark hall which connected the left wing with the house, she could see through into the living room where Jean sat with her lover.

There was much dark wood and the worn red velvet—low bookshelves lining the walls, a grand piano on a cover by the window. In the dimness Jean's copper head shone like the halo of a saint. Mary decided that Derry was "queer-looking," until gathering courage, she went in and was warmed by his smile.

"He hasn't had any lunch, Mary," Jean told her, "and he wouldn't let me get any for him."

"I'll have something in three whisks of a lamb's tail," said Mary with Elizabethan picturesqueness, and away she went on her hospitable mission.

"Marrying just now," said Derry, picking up the subject, where he had dropped it, when Mary came in, "is out of the question."

"Did you think that I was marrying you for your money?"

"No. But two months' pay wouldn't buy a gown like this,"— he lifted a fold with his forefinger—"to say nothing of your little shoes." He dropped his light tone. "Oh, my dear, can't you see?"

"No. I can't see. Daddy would let us have this house, and I have a little money of my own from my mother, and—and the Connollys would take care of everything. and we should see the spring come, and the summer."

He rose and went and stood with his back to the fire. "But I shan't be here in the spring and summer."

She clasped her hands nervously. "Derry, I don't want you to go."

"You don't mean that."

"I do. I do. At least not yet. We can be married—and have just a little, little month or two—and then I'll let you go—truly."

He shook his head. "I've stayed out of it long enough. You wouldn't want me to stay out of it any longer, Jean-Joan."

"Yes, I should. Other men can go, but I want to keep you—it's bad enough to give—Daddy—. I haven't anybody. Mary Connolly has her husband, but I haven't anybody—" her voice broke—and broke again—.

He came over and knelt beside her. "Let me tell you something," he said. "Do you remember the night of the Witherspoon dinner? Well, that night you cut me dead because you thought I was a coward—and I thanked God for the women who hated cowards."

"But you weren't a coward."

"I know, and so I could stand it—could stand your scorn and the scorn of the world. But what if I stayed out of it now, Jean?

"What if I stayed out of it now? You and I could have our little moment of happiness, while other men fought that we might have it. We should be living in Paradise, while other men were in Hell. I can't see it, dearest. All these months I have been bound. But now, my dear, my dear, do you love me enough not to keep me, but to let me go?"

There was a beating pause. She lifted wet eyes. "Oh, Derry, darling, I love you enough—I love you—"

Thus, in a moment, little Jean McKenzie unlatched the gate which had shut her into the safe and sunshiny garden of pampered girlhood and came out upon the broad highway of life, where men and women suffer for the sake of those who travel with them, sharing burdens and gaining strength as they go.

Dimly, perhaps, she perceived what she had done, but it was not given to her to know the things she would encounter or the people she would meet. All the world was to adventure with her, throughout the years, the poor distracted world, dealing death and destruction, yet dreaming ever of still waters and green pastures.

CHAPTER XIX

HILDA SHAKES A TREE

When Dr. McKenzie and Jim Connolly arrived, Derry said apologetically as he shook hands with the Doctor, "You see, you can't get rid of me—but I have such a lot of things to talk over with you."

It was after Jean had gone to bed, however, that they had their talk, and before that Derry and Jean had walked in the moonlight and had listened to the chimes.

There had, perhaps, never been such a moon. It hung in a sky that shimmered from horizon to horizon. Against this shimmering background the college buildings were etched in black—there was a glint of gold as the light caught the icicles and made candles of them.

In the months to come that same moon was to sail over the cantonment where Derry slept heavily after hard days. It was to sail over the trenches of France, where, perhaps, he slept not at all, or slept uneasily in the midst of mud and vermin. But always when he looked up at it, he was to see the Cross on the top of the College, and to hear the chimes.

They talked that night of the things that were deep in their hearts. She wanted him to go—yes, she wanted him to go, but she was afraid.

Temple Bailey

"If something should happen to you, Derry."

"Sometimes I wonder," he said, in his grave, young voice, "why we are so—afraid. I think we have the wrong focus. We want life, even if it brings unhappiness, even if it brings suffering, even if it brings disgrace. Anything seems better than to—die—"

"But to have things stop, Derry." She shuddered. "When there's so much ahead."

"Perhaps they don't stop, dear."

"If I could only believe that—"

"Why not? Do you remember 'Sherwood,' where Blondin rides through the forest singing:

"Death, what is death?" he cried,
"I must ride on—"

His face was lifted to the golden sky. She was never to forget the look upon it. And with a great ache and throb of passionate renunciation, she told herself that it was for this that the men of her generation had been born, that they might fight against the powers of darkness for the things of the spirit.

She lay awake a long time that night, thinking it out. Of how she had laughed at other women, scolded, said awful things to them of how their cowardice was holding the world back. She had thought she understood, but she had not understood. It was giving your own—your own, which was the test. *Oh, let those who had none of their own to give keep silent.*

With her breath almost stopping she thought of those glorious young souls riding on and on through infinite space, the banner of victory floating above them. No matter what might come to the world of defeat or of disaster, these souls would never know it, they had given themselves in the cause of humanity—for them there would always be the sound of silver trumpets, the clash of cymbals, the song of triumph!

Downstairs, Dr. McKenzie was listening with a frowning face to what Derry had to tell him.

"Do you mean to say that Hilda was giving him—wine?"

"Yes. Bronson told me. But he didn't want you to depend upon his unsupported testimony. So we fixed up a scheme, and I stayed outside until he flashed a light for me; and then I went in and caught her."

"It is incredible. Why should she do such a thing? She has always been a perfect nurse—a perfect nurse, Drake." He rose and walked the floor. "But deliberately to disobey my orders—what could have been her object?"

Derry hesitated.

"I haven't told you the worst."

Doctor McKenzie stopped in front of him. "The worst?"

"Dad is going to marry her."

"What?"

Derry repeated what he had said.

The Doctor dropped into a chair. "Who told you?"

"Dad."

"And she admitted that it was—true?"

"Yes."

Derry gave the facts. "He wasn't himself, of course, but that doesn't change things for me."

The Doctor in the practice of his profession had learned to conceal his emotions. He concealed now what he was feeling, but a close observer might have seen in the fading of the color in his cheeks, the beating of his clenched fist on the arm of his chair, something of that which was stirring within him.

"And this has been going on ever since she went there. She has had it in mind to wear your mother's jewels—" Derry had graphically described Bronson's watch on the stairs—"to get your father's money. I knew she was cold-blooded, but I had always thought it a rather admirable quality in a woman of her attractive type."

Before his eye came the vision of Hilda's attractiveness by his fireside, at his table. And now she would sit by the General's fire, at his table.

"She didn't say a word," Derry's young voice went on, "when he told me that I was no longer—his son. I can't tell you how I felt about her. I've never felt that way about anyone before. I've always liked people—but it was as if some evil thing had swooped down on the old house."

The lad saw straight! That was the thought which suddenly illumined Dr. McKenzie's troubled mind. Hilda was not beautiful. So beauty of body could offset the ugliness of her distorted soul.

"And so I am poor," Derry was saying, heavily, "and I must wait to marry Jean."

The red surged up in the Doctor's face. He jerked himself forward in his chair. "You shall not wait. After this you are my son, if you are not your father's."

He laid his hand on Derry's shoulder. "I've money enough, God knows. And I shan't need it. It isn't a fortune, but it is enough to make all of us comfortable for the rest of our days—and I want Jean to be happy. Do you think I am going to let Hilda Merritt stand between my child and happiness?"

"It's awfully good of you, sir," Derry's voice was husky with feeling, "but—"

"There are no 'buts.' You must let me have my own way; I shall consider it a patriotic privilege to support one soldier and his little wife."

He was riding above the situation splendidly. He even had visions of straightening things out. "When I go back I shall tell Hilda what I think of her, I shall tell her that it is preposterous—that her professional reputation is at stake."

"What will she care for her professional reputation when she is my father's wife?"

The thought of Hilda with the world, in a sense, at her feet was maddening. The Doctor paced the floor roaring like an angry lion. "It may not do any good, but I've got to tell her what I think of her."

Derry had a whimsical sense of the meeting of the white cat and this leonine gentleman—would she purr or scratch?

"The sooner you and Jean are married the better. If Hilda thinks she is going to keep you and Jean apart she is mistaken."

"Oh—did she know of the engagement?"

"Yes," the Doctor confessed. "I told her the other day when she came to fix the books."

"Then that accounts for it."

"For what?"

"Dad's attitude. I thought it was queer he should fly up all in a moment. She wanted to make trouble, Doctor, and she has made it."

Long after Derry had gone to bed, the Doctor sat there pondering on Hilda's treachery. He was in some ways a simple man—swayed by the impulse of the moment. The thought of deliberate plotting was abhorrent. In his light way he had taken her lightly. He had laughed at her. He had teased Jean, he had teased Emily, calling their intuition jealousy. Yet they had known better than he. And why should not women know women better than men know them? Just as men know men in a way that women could never know. Sex erected barriers— there was always the instinct to charm, to don one's gayest plumage; even Hilda's frankness had been used as a lure; she knew he liked it. Would she have been so frank if she had not felt its stimulus to a man of his type? And, after all, had she really been frank?

Such a woman was like a poisonous weed; and he had thought she might bloom in the same garden with Jean—until Emily had told him.

He turned to the thought of Emily with relief. Thank God he could leave Jean in her care. If Derry went, there would still be Emily with her sweet sanity, and her wise counsels.

He felt very old as he went upstairs. He stood for a long time in front of his wife's picture. How sweet she had been in her forget-me-not gown—how little and tender! Their love had burned in a white flame—there would never be anything like that for him again.

He waked in the morning, however, ready for all that was before him. He was a man who dwelt little on the past. There was always the day's work, and the work of the day after.

His appetite for the work of the coming day was, it must be confessed, whetted somewhat by the thought of what he would say to Hilda.

They had an early breakfast, with Jean between her father and Derry and eating nothing for very happiness.

There was the start in the opal light of the early morning, with a faint rose sky making a background for the cross on the College, and the chimes saying "Seven o'clock."

Jim and Mary Connolly came out in the biting air to see them off. Then Mary went over to the church to pray for Jean and Derry. But first of all she prayed for her sons.

The Doctor, arriving at his office, at once called up Hilda.

"I must see you as soon as possible."

"What has Derry Drake been telling you?"

"How do you know that he has told me anything?"

"By your voice. And you needn't think that you are going to scold me."

"I shall scold you for disobeying orders. I thought you were to be trusted, Hilda."

"I am not a saint. You know that. And I am not sure that I want you to come. I shall send you away if you scold."

She hung up the receiver and left him fuming. Her high-handed indifference to his authority sent him storming to Derry, "I've half a mind to stay away."

"I think I would. It won't do any good to go—"

But the Doctor went. He still hoped, optimistically, that Hilda might be induced to see the error of her ways.

She received him in the blue room, where the General's precious porcelain was set forth in cabinets. It was a choice little room which had been used by Mrs. Drake for the reception of special guests. Hilda was in her uniform, but without her cap. It was as if in doffing her cap, she struck her first note of independence against the Doctor's rule.

He began professionally. "Doctor Bryer telephoned this morning that his attendance of the case had been only during my absence. That he did not care to keep it unless I definitely intended to withdraw. I told him to go ahead. I told him also that you were a good nurse. I had to whitewash my conscience a bit to say it, Hilda—"

Her head went up. "I am a good nurse. But I am more than a nurse, I am a woman. Oh, I know you are blaming me for what you think I have done. But if you stood under a tree and a great ripe peach hung just out of your reach, could you be blamed for shaking the tree? Well, I shook the tree."

She was very handsome as she gave her defense with flashing eyes.

"The General asked me to marry him, and that's more than you would ever have done. You liked to think that I was half in love with you. You liked to pretend that you were half in love with me. But would you ever have offered me ease and rest from hard work? Would you ever have thought that I might some day be your daughter's equal in your home? Oh, I have wanted good times. I used to sit night after night alone in the office while you and Jean went out and did the things I was dying to do. I wanted to go to dances and to the theater and to supper with a gay crowd. But you never seemed to think of it. I am young and I want pretty clothes—yet you thought I was satisfied to have you come home and say a few careless pleasant words, and to tease me a little. That was all you ever did for me—all you ever wanted.

"But the General wants more than that. He wants me here in

the big house, to be his wife, and to meet his friends. He had a man come up the other day with a lot of rings, and he bought me this." She showed the great diamonds flashing on her third finger. "I have always wanted a ring like this, and now I can have as many as I want. Do you blame me for shaking the tree?"

He sat, listening, spellbound to her sophistry. But was it sophistry? Wasn't some of it true? He saw her for the first time as a woman wanting things like other women.

She swept out her hand to include the contents of the little room. "I have always longed for a place like this. I don't know a thing about china. But I know that all that stuff in the cabinet cost a fortune. And it's a pretty room, and some day when I am the General's wife, I'll ask you here to take tea with me, and I'll wear a silver gown like your daughter wears, and I think you'll be surprised to see that I can do it well."

He flung up his hand. "I can't argue it, Hilda. I can't analyze it. But it is all wrong. In all the years that you worked for me, while I laughed at you, I respected you. But I don't respect you now."

She shrugged. "Do you think I care? And a man's respect after all is rather a cold thing, isn't it? But I am sorry you feel as you do about it. I should have been glad to have you wish me happiness."

"Happiness—" His anger seemed to die suddenly. "You won't find happiness, Hilda, if you separate a son from his father."

"Did he tell you that? I had nothing to do with it. His father was angry at his—interference."

He stood up. "We won't discuss it. But you may tell him this. That I am glad his son is poor, for my daughter will marry now the man and not his money."

"Then he will marry her?"

"Yes. On Christmas Day."

She wished that she might tell him the date of her own wedding, but she did not know it. The General seemed in no hurry. He had carefully observed the conventions; had hired a housekeeper and a maid, and there was, of course, the day nurse. Having thus surrounded his betrothed with a sort of feminine bodyguard, he spoke of the wedding as happening in the spring. And he was hard to move. As has been said, the General had once commanded a brigade. He was immensely entertained and fascinated by the lady who was to be his wife. But he was not to be managed by her. She found herself, as he grew stronger, quite strangely deferring to his wishes. She found herself, indeed, rather unexpectedly dominated.

She came back to the Doctor. "Aren't you going to wish me happiness?"

"No. How can I, Hilda?"

After he had left her, she stood very still in the middle of the room. She could still see him as he had towered above her—his crinkled hair waving back from his handsome head. She had always liked the youth of him and his laughter and his boyish fun.

The rich man upstairs was—old—.

CHAPTER XX

THE VISION OF BRAVE WOMEN

And now the Tin Soldier was to go to the wars!

Derry, swinging downtown, found himself gazing squarely into the eyes of the khaki-clad men whom he met. He was one of them at last!

He was on his way to meet Jean. The day before they had gone to church together. They had heard burning words from a fearless pulpit. The old man who had preached had set no limits on his patriotism. The cause of the Allies was the cause of humanity, the cause of humanity was the cause of Christ. He would have had the marching hymn of the Americans "Onward, Christian Soldiers." His Master was not a shrinking idealist, but a prophet unafraid. "Woe unto thee, Chorazin! Woe unto thee, Bethsaida! . . . It shall be more tolerable for Tyre and Sidon in the day of Judgment than for you. And thou, Capernaum, which art exalted unto Heaven, shall be brought down to hell . . ."

"I am too old to go myself," the old man had said, "but I have sent my sons. In the face of the world's need, no man has a right to hold another back. Personal considerations which might once have seemed sufficient must now be set aside. Things are at stake which involve not only the honor of a nation but the honor of the individual. To call a man a coward in the old days was to challenge his physical courage. To know him as a slacker in these modern times is to doubt the quality of his mind and spirit. 'I pray thee have me excused' is the word of one lost to the high meanings of justice—of love and loyalty and liberty—"

Stirring words. The lovers had thrilled to them. Derry's hand had gone out to Jean and her own hand clasped it. Together they saw the vision of his going forth, a shining knight, girded for the battle by a beloved woman—saw it through the glamour of high hopes and youthful ardor!

A troop of cavalry on the Avenue! Jackies in saucer caps, infantry, artillery, aviation! Blue and red and green cords about wide-brimmed hats. Husky young Westerners, slim young Southerners, square-chinned young Northerners—a great brotherhood, their faces set one way—and he was to share their hardships, to be cold and hungry with the best of them, wet and dirty with the worst. It would be a sort of glorified penance for his delay in doing the thing which too long he had left undone.

He was to have lunch with Jean in the House restaurant—he was a little early, and as he loitered through the Capitol grounds, in his ears there was the echo of fairy trumpets— "*trutter-a-trutt, trutter-a-trutt—*"

The old Capitol had always been for Derry a place of dreams. He loved every inch of it. The sunset view of the city from the west front; the bronze doors on the east, the labyrinthine maze of the corridors; the tesselated floors, the mottled marble of the balustrades; the hushed approach to the Supreme Court; the precipitous descent into the galleries of House and Senate, the rap of the Speaker's gavel—the rattle of argument as political foes contended in the legislative arena; the more subdued squabbles on the Senate floor; the savory smell of food rising from the restaurants in the lower regions; the climb to the dome, the look of the sky when one came out at the top; Statuary Hall and its awesome echoes; the Rotunda with its fringe of tired tourists, its frescoed frieze—Columbus, Cortez,

Penn, Pizarro—; the mammoth paintings—Pocahontas, and the Pilgrims, De Soto, and the Surrender of Cornwallis, the Signing of the Declaration, and Washington's Resignation as Commander-in-Chief—Indian and Quaker, Puritan and Cavalier—these were some of the things which had ravished the eyes of the boy Derry in the days when his father had come to the Capitol to hobnob with old cronies, and his son had been allowed to roam at will.

But above and beyond everything else, there were the great mural paintings on the west wall of the House side, above the grand marble staircase.

"Westward the Course of Empire takes its way—!"

Oh, those pioneers with their faces turned towards the Golden West! The tired women and the bronzed men! Not one of them without that eager look of hope, of a dream realized as the land of Promise looms ahead!

Derry had often talked that picture over with his mother. "It was such men, Derry, who made our country—men unafraid —North, South, East and West, it was these who helped to shape the Nation's destiny, as we must help to shape it for those who come after us."

It was in front of this picture that he was to meet Jean. He had wanted to share with her the inspiration of it.

She was late, and he waited, leaning on the marble rail which overlooked the stairway. People were going up and down passing the picture, but not seeing it, their pulses calm, their blood cold. The doors of the elevators opened and shut, women came and went in velvet and fur, laughing. Men followed them, laughing, and the picture was not for them.

Derry wondered if it were symbolic, this indifference of the crowd. Was the world's pageant of horrors and of heroism thus unseen by the eyes of the unthinking?

And now Jean ascended, the top of her hat first—a blur of gray, then the red of the rose that he had sent her, a wave of her gray muff as she saw him. He went down to meet her, and stood with her on the landing. Beneath the painting, on one side, ran the inscription, "No pent up Utica confines our powers, but the boundless Continent is ours," on the other side, "The Spirit moves in its allotted space; the mind is narrow in a narrow sphere."

Thousands of men and women came and went and never read those words. But boys read them, sitting on the stairs or leaning over the rail—and their minds were carried on and on. Old men, coming back after years to read them again, could testify what the words had meant to them in the field of high endeavor.

Jean had seen the painting many times, but now, standing on the upper gallery floor with Derry, it took on new meanings. She saw a girl with hope in her eyes, a young mother with a babe at her breast; homely middle-aged women redeemed from the commonplace by that long gaze ahead of them; old women straining towards that sunset glow. She saw, indeed, the Vision of Brave Women. "If it could only be like that for me, Derry. Do you see—they go with their husbands, those women, and I must stay behind."

"You will go with me, beloved, in spirit—"

They fell into silence before the limitless vista.

And now more people were coming up the stairs, a drawling, familiar voice—Alma Drew on the landing below. With her a tall young man. She was turning on him all her batteries of charm.

Alma passed the picture and did not look at it, she passed the lovers and did not see them. And she was saying as she passed, "I don't know why any man should be expected to fight. I shouldn't if I were a man."

Jean drew a long breath. "There, but for the grace of God, goes Jean McKenzie."

Derry laughed. "You were never like that. Not for the least minute. You were afraid for the man you loved. It isn't fear with Alma."

But the thought of Alma did not trouble them long. There was too much else in their world today. As they walked through the historic halls, they had with them all the romance of the past—and so Robert Fulton with his boats, Pere Marquette with his cross and beads, Frances Willard in her strange old-fashioned dress spoke to them of the dreams which certain inspired men and women have translated into action.

They talked of these things while they ate their lunch. The black waiter, who knew Derry, hovered about them. His freedom, too, had been the culmination of a dream.

"Men laugh at the dreamers," Derry said, "then honor them after they are dead."

"That's the cruelty, the sadness of it, isn't it?"

"Not to the dreamer. Do you think that Pere Marquette cared for what smaller minds might think, or Frances Willard? They had their vision backed by a great faith in the rightness of things, and so Marquette followed the river and planted the cross, and Frances Willard blazed the way for the thing which has come to pass."

After lunch they motored to Drusilla's. They used one of Dr. McKenzie's cars. Derry had ceased to draw upon his father's establishment for anything. He lived at the club, and met his expenses with the small balance which remained to his credit in the bank.

"You can give Jean whatever you think best," he told the Doctor, "but I shall try to live on what I have until I go, and then on my pay."

"Your pay, my dear boy, will just about equal what you now spend in tips."

"I think I shall like it. It's an adventure for rich men when they have to be poor. That's why a lot of fellows have gone into it. They are tired of being the last word in civilization. They want to get down to primitive things."

"Mrs. Witherspoon can't imagine Derry Drake without two baths a day."

"Can't she? Well, Mrs. Witherspoon may find that Derry Drake is about like the rest of the fellows. No better and no worse. There is no disgrace in liking to be clean. The disgrace comes when one kicks against a thing that can't be helped."

In the Doctor's car, therefore, they arrived at Drusilla's.

"We have come to tell you that we are going to be married."

"You Babes in the Wood!"

"Will you come to the wedding?

"Of course I'll come. Marion, do you hear? They are going to be married."

"And after that, Drusilla,"—he smiled as he phrased it—"your Tin Soldier will go to the wars."

Jean glanced from one to the other. "Is that what she called you—a Tin Soldier?"

"It is what I called myself."

Marion having come forward to say the proper thing, added, "Drusilla's going, too."

"Drusilla?"

"Yes, with my college unit—to run errands in a flivver."

The next day, encountering Derry on the street, Drusilla opened her knitting bag and brought out a tiny parcel. "It's my wedding gift to you. I found it in Emily's toy shop."

It was a gay little French tin soldier. "For a mascot;" she told him, seriously. "Derry, dear, I shall not try to tell you how I feel about your marriage to Jean. About your going. If I could sing it, you'd know. But I haven't any words. It—it seems so—perfect that the Tin Soldier should go—to the wars—and that the girl he leaves behind him should be a little white maid like—Jean."

Thus Drusilla, with a shake in her voice, renouncing a—dream.

Derry, who was on his way to Margaret's showed the tin soldier to Teddy and his little sister. "He is going to the wars."

"With you?"

"Yes."

"When are you going?"

"As soon as I can—"

"I should think you wouldn't like to leave us."

"Well, I don't. But I am coming back."

"Daddy didn't come back."

"But some men do."

"Perhaps God doesn't love you as much as He did Daddy, and

He won't want to keep you."

"Perhaps not—"

The things which the child had spoken stayed with Derry all that day. His feeling about death had always been that of a man who has long years before him. He had rather jauntily conceded that some men die young, but that the chances in his case were for a green old age. He might indeed have fifty years before him, and in fifty years one could—get ready—age had to do with serious things, people were peaceful and prepared.

But to get ready now. To face the thing squarely, saying, "I may not come back—there are, indeed, a thousand chances that I shall not come." Lacking those fifty years in which to grow towards the thought of dissolution, what ought one to do? Should a man make himself fit in some special fashion?

There was, too, the thought of those whom he might leave behind. Of Jean—his wife—whom he would leave. She would break her heart—at first. And then—? Would she remember? Would she forget? Would he and those millions of others who had gone down in battle become dim memories—pale shadows against the vivid background of the hurrying world?

He felt that he could not, must not speak of these things to Jean. So he talked of them to Emily.

"If anything should happen to me," he said, "I couldn't, of course, expect that Jean would go on—caring—. And if there should ever be anyone else—I—I should want her to be happy."

"Don't try to be magnanimous," Miss Emily advised. "You are human, and it isn't in the heart of man to want the woman he loves ever to turn to another. Let the years take care of that. But you can be very sure of one thing—that no one will ever take your place with Jean."

"But she may marry."

"Why should you torture yourself with that? You have given her something that no one else can ever give—the wonder and rapture of first love. And the heroes of a war like this will be in a very special manner set apart! 'A glorious company, the flower of men, to serve as models for the mighty world!'"

She laid her hand on his shoulder. "You must think now only of love and life and of coming back to Jean."

He reached up his hand and caught hers in a warm clasp. "Do you know you are the nearest, thing to a mother that I've known since I lost mine?"

He spoke, too, rather awkwardly, of the feeling about—getting ready.

"I have always thought that if I tried to live straight—I've thought, too, that it wouldn't come until I was old—that I should have plenty of time—and that by then, I should be more—spiritual."

"You will never be more spiritual than you are at this moment. Youth is nearer Heaven than age. I have always thought that. As we grow old—we are stricken by—fear—of poverty, of disease—of death. It is youth which has faith and hope."

Before he left her, he gave her a sacred charge. "If anything happens, I know what you'll be to—Jean—and I can't tell you what a help you've been this morning."

She was thrilled by that. And after he left her she thought much about him. Of what it would have meant to her to have a son like that.

Women had said to her, "You should be glad that you have no boy to send—." But she was not glad. Were they mad, these mothers, to want to hold their boys back? Had the days of peace held no dangers that they should be so afraid for them now?

For peace had dangers—men and women had been worshipping false gods. They had set up a Golden Calf and had bowed before it—and their children, lured by luxury, emasculated by ease of living, had wanted more ease, more luxury, more time in which to—play!

And now life had become suddenly a vivid Crusade, with everybody marching in one direction, and the young men were manly in the old ways of strength and heroism, and the young women were womanly in the old way of sending their lovers forth, and in a new way, when, like Drusilla, they went forth themselves to the front line of battle.

To have children in these days, meant to have something to give. One need not stand before suffering humanity empty-handed!

War was a monstrous thing, a murderous thing—but surely this war was a righteous one—a fire which would cleanse the world. Men and women, because of it, were finding in themselves something which could suffer for others, something in themselves which could sacrifice, something which went beyond body and mind, something which reached up and touched their souls.

So, in the midst of darkness, Miss Emily had a vision of Light. After the war was over, things could never be as they had been before. The spirit which had sent men forth in this Crusade, which had sent women, would survive, please God, and show itself in a greater sense of fellowship—of brotherhood. Might not men, even in peace, go on praying as they were praying it now in war, the prayer of Cromwell's men, "Oh, Lord, it's a hard battle, but it's for the rights of the common people—" Might not the rich young men who were learning to be the brothers of the poor, and the poor young men who were learning in a large sense of the brotherhood of the rich—might these not still clasp hands in a sacred cause?

Yes, she was sorry that she had no son. Slim and gray-haired, a little worn by life's struggle, her blood quickened at the thought of a son like Derry. The warmth of his handclasp, the glimpse of that inner self which he had given her, these were things to hold close to her heart. She had known on that first night that he was—different. She had not dreamed that she should hold him—close.

Rather pensively she arranged her window. It was snowing hard, and in spite of the fact that Christmas was only three days away, customers were scarce.

The window display was made effective by the use of Jean's purple camels—a sandy desert, a star overhead, blazing with all the realism of a tiny electric bulb behind it, the Wise Men, the Inn where the Babe lay, and in a far corner a group of shepherds watching a woolly flock—.

Her cyclamen was dead. A window had been left open, and when she arrived one morning she had found it frozen.

She had thanked Ulrich Stoelle for it, in a pleasantly worded note. She had not dared express her full appreciation, lest she seem fulsome. Few men in her experience had sent her flowers. Never in all the years of her good friendship with Bruce McKenzie had he bestowed upon her a single bloom.

Several days had passed, and there had been no answer to the note. She had not really expected an answer, but she had thought he might come in.

He came in now, with a great parcel in his arms. He was a picturesque figure in an enveloping cape and a soft hat pulled down over his gray hair, and with white flakes powdered over his shoulders.

"Good morning, Miss Bridges," he said; "did you think I was

never coming?"

His manner of assuming that she had expected him quite took Emily's breath away. "I am glad you came," she said, simply. "It is rather dreary, with the snow, and this morning I found my cyclamen frozen on the shelf."

He glanced up at it. "We have other flowers," he said, and, with a sure sense of the dramatic effect, untied the string of his parcel.

Then there was revealed to Miss Emily's astonished eyes not the flowers that she had expected, but four small plush elephants, duplicates in everything but size of the one she had loaned to Ulrich, and each elephant carried on his back a fragrant load of violets cunningly kept fresh by a glass tube hidden in his trappings.

"There," said Ulrich Stoelle, "my father sent them. It is his taste, not mine—but I knew that you would understand."

"But," Miss Emily gasped, "did he make them?"

"Most certainly. With his clever old fingers—and he will make as many more as you wish."

Thus came white elephants back to Miss Emily's shelves. "It seems almost too good to be true," she said, sniffing the violets and smiling at him.

"Nothing is too good to be true," he told her, "and now I have something to ask. That you will come and see my father."

"With pleasure."

He glanced around the empty shop. "Why not now? There are no customers—and the gray light makes things dreary—. And it is spring in my hothouses—there are a thousand cyclamens for the one you have lost, a thousand violets for every one on the backs of these little elephants—narcissus and daffodils—. Why not?"

Why not, indeed? Why not, when Adventure beckoned, go to meet it? She had tied herself for so many years to the commonplace and the practical.

And so Miss Emily closed her shop, and went in Ulrich's car, leaving a card tucked in the shop door, "Will reopen at three."

It was at one o'clock that Dr. McKenzie came and found that door shut against him. He shook the knob with some impatience, and stamped his foot impotently when no one answered. His orders had come and he must leave for France tomorrow. He had not told Jean, he had come to Emily to ask her to break the news—.

He stood there in the snow feeling quite unexpectedly forlorn. Heretofore he had always been able to put his finger on Emily when he had wanted her. He had needed only to beckon and she had followed.

And how could he know that she was at that very moment following other beckonings? That she had responded to a call that was not the call of selfish need, but of a subtle under-standing of her rare charm. Bruce McKenzie had, perhaps, subconsciously felt that Emily would be fortunate to have a place by his fireside, to bask in his presence—Ulrich Stoelle leading Emily through the moist fragrance of his hot-houses counted himself blessed by the gods to have her there. "You see," he said, "that here it is spring."

It was indeed spring, with birds singing, not in cages, but free to fly as they pleased; with the sound of water, as a little artificial stream wound its way over moss-covered rocks set where it might splash and fall over them—with ferns bending down to it and tiny flashing fish following it.

"My father did that," Ulrich explained, "when he was younger and stronger. But now he sits in his chair and works at his toys."

The workshop of Franz Stoelle was entered through the door of the last hothouse; he had thus always a vista of splashing color—red and purples and yellows—great stretches, and always with the green to rest his eyes; with the door opened between there came to him the fragrance, and the singing of birds, and the sound of the little stream.

He sat in a big chair, bent a little, plump and ruddy-faced, with a fringe of white hair. He wore horn spectacles—and a velvet coat. He rose when Emily entered, elegant of manner, in spite of his rotundity.

"So it is the lady of the elephants, Ulrich? When you telephoned I thought it was too good to be true."

"Your son says that nothing is too good to be true," Emily told him, sitting down in the chair that Ulrich placed for her, "but I have a feeling that this will all vanish in a moment like Aladdin's palace—" She waved her hands towards the shelves that went around the room. "I never expected to see such toys again."

For there they were—the toys of Germany. The quaint Noah's arks, the woolly dogs and the mewing cats—the moon-faced dolls.

"I don't see how you have made them all."

"Many of them were made years ago, Fraeulein, and I have kept them for remembrance, but many of them are new. When my son told me that it was hard for you to get toys, I gathered around me a few old friends who learned their trade in Nuremberg. We have done much in a few days. We will do more. We are all patriotic. We will show the Prussians that the children of America do not lack for toys. What does the Prussian know of play? He knows only killing and killing and killing."

The old man beat his fist upon the table, "Killing!"

"You see," Ulrich said to Emily, "there are many of us who feel that way. Yet unthinking people cannot see that we are loyal, that our hearts beat with the hearts of those who have English blood and French blood and Italian blood and Dutch blood in their veins, and who have but one country—America."

The old man had recovered himself. "We are not here to talk of killing, but of what I and my friends shall make for you. And you are to have lunch with us? I have planned it, and I won't take 'no,' Fraeulein. You and I have so much to say to each other."

Emily wondered if it were really her middle-aged and prosaic self who sat later at the table, being waited on by a very competent butler, and deferred to by the two men as if she were a queen.

It was she and the old man who did most of the talking, but always she was conscious of Ulrich's attentive eyes, of the weight of the quiet words which he interjected now and then in the midst of his father's volubility.

"Germany, my mother, is dead," wailed the old man. "I have wept over her grave; those who wage this war against humanity are bastards, the real sons and daughters of that sweet old Germany are here in America—they have come to their foster-mother, and they love her.

"If I had been younger," he went on, "I should have fought. My son would have fought. But as it is we can make toys—and we shall say to the Prussians across the sea, 'You have killed our mother—your people are no longer our people, nor your God our God.'"

Ulrich took Emily home. She carried with her a Noah's Ark,

and a precious pot of cyclamen. She had chosen the cyclamen out of all the rest. "It is such a cheerful thing blooming in my shop."

"There are other cheerful things in your shop," he told her.

As she met his smiling eyes, she smiled back, "Do you mean that I am a cheerful thing?"

"A rose, mein Fraeulein, when your cheeks are red, like this."

Emily, alone at last in the Toy Shop, took off her hat in front of the mirror and saw her red cheeks. She set the cyclamen safely in a warm corner. The four elephants with their fragrant freight of violets made an exotic and incongruous addition to the Christmas scene in the window.

Bruce McKenzie, coming in, asked, 'Where did you get them?"

"The elephants? Ulrich Stoelle brought them. Do you know him?"

"Yes. But I didn't know that you did."

"His father makes toys. I lent him my white elephant, and he made these—"

She spoke without self-consciousness, and McKenzie's mind was on his own matters, so they swept away from the subject of Ulrich Stoelle. "Emily," Bruce said, "I have my orders. Tomorrow at twelve I must leave for France."

She gazed at him stupidly. "Tomorrow—?"

"Yes."

"But—Jean—?"

"I haven't told her. I don't know how to tell her."

"You won't be here for the wedding—?"

"No."

"It will break her heart."

"You needn't tell me that. Don't I know it?" His voice was sharp with the tension of suppressed emotion.

He dropped into a chair, then jumped up and placed one for her. "Sit down, sit down," he said, "and don't make me forget my manners. Somehow this thing gets me as nothing has ever gotten me before. It isn't that I mind going—I mind hurting —Jean—"

"You have always hated to hurt people," Emily said. "In some ways it's a sign of weakness."

"Don't scold," he begged. "I know I'm not much of a fellow, but you'll be sorry for me a little, won't you, Emily?"

She did not melt as he had expected to the appeal in his voice. "The thing we have to think of now," she said, "is not being sorry for you, but how we can get Jean married before twelve o'clock tomorrow—"

"Oh, of course we can't."

"Of course we can—if we make up our minds to it, and it's the only thing to do."

"But nothing is ready."

"Things can be made ready. They can stand up in the rose drawing-room at ten, and you can give her away."

He looked at her admiringly. "I didn't know that you had so

much initiative."

She might have told him that it was a quality on which she rather prided herself, but that hitherto it had not seemed to attract him. "There are several things as yet undiscovered by you," she remarked casually, as she locked up her toys.

Watching her, he wondered idly if there were really worlds to discover in Emily. It might be interesting to—find out—.

"Shall you miss me?" he asked.

"Of course. And now if you'll see that the back shutters are barred, we'll be ready to go."

Thus she checked his small attempt at sentiment, and on the way home they talked about Jean. "If Derry goes, you and she must live together in my house. Let that be understood. I'd rather have her with you than with anyone else in the whole wide world."

Thus again the sacred charge, but this time not as a favor, but in lordly fashion, as one who claims a right.

Jean and Derry were having tea at the club, but could not be reached by phone. "They had probably motored out into the country," Emily decided. "We'll have to do things before they come."

The things that she did were stupendous.

She had a florist up in two hours—and the rose-colored drawing room was rosier than ever, and as fragrant as a garden.

She telephoned the clergyman—"At ten o'clock tomorrow."

She telephoned the caterer—"A wedding breakfast—"

She telephoned the dressmaker—"Miss McKenzie's gown—"

She telephoned Margaret and Marion Gray—.

"Is there anyone else?" she asked the Doctor. "I suppose we really ought to tell the General."

"Certainly not."

"But Bronson—? Derry will want him."

"If he can keep a secret—yes."

Jean and Derry, arriving after dark, were swept into a scene of excitement.

Florists on the stairs!

A frenzied dressmaker waiting with Jean's wedding gown!

Maids with mops and men with vacuums!

Julia and the cook helping at loose ends and dinner late!

What did it all mean?

"It means," said the Doctor, "that you are going to be married, my dear, at ten o'clock in the morning."

"But why, Daddy—" fear showed in her eyes—

"Ask Emily."

"Is he—going away,—Emily?"

"Yes, dear."

"But he mustn't. Derry, do you hear? He is going to France—and he mustn't—"

Derry took her trembling hands in his firm clasp. "He must

go, you know that, dearest." His touch steadied her.

He leaned down to her and sang:—

"Jeanne D'Arc, Jeanne D'Arc—
Jeanne D'Arc, la victoire est pour vous."

Her head went up. The color came back to her cheeks.

"Of course," she said, and put away childish things that she might measure up to the stature of her lover's faith in her.

And it was Jean, the Woman, who talked long that night with her father before he went to France.

CHAPTER XXI

DERRY'S WIFE

It snowed hard the next morning. The General, waking, found the day nurse in charge. Bronson came in to get him ready for his breakfast. There was about the old man an air of suppressed excitement. He hurried a little in his preparations for the General's bath. But everything was done with exactness, and it was not until the General was shaved and sitting up in his gorgeous mandarin robe that Bronson said, "I'd like to go out for an hour or two this morning, if you can spare me, sir—"

"In this snow? I thought you hated snow. You've always been a perfect pussy cat about the cold, Bronson."

"Yes, sir, but this is very important, sir."

The General ran his eye over the spruce figure.

"And you are all dressed up. I hope you are not going to be married, Bronson."

It was an old joke between them. Bronson was a pre-destined bachelor, and the General knew it.

But he liked to tease him.

"No, sir. I'll be back in time to look after your lunch, sir."

The General had been growing stronger, so that he spent several hours each day in his chair. When Bronson had gone, he rose and moved restlessly about the room. The day nurse cautioned him. "The Doctor doesn't want you to exert yourself, General Drake."

He was always courteous, but none the less he meant to have his own way. "Don't worry, Miss Martin. I'll take the responsibility."

He shuffled out into the hall. When she would have followed, he waved her back. "I am perfectly able to go alone," he told her.

She stood on the threshold watching him. She was very young and she was a little afraid of him. Her eyes, as she looked upon him, saw an obstinate old man in a gay dressing gown. And the man in the gay dressing gown felt old until he faced suddenly his wife's picture on the stairs.

It had been weeks since he had seen it, and in those weeks much had happened. Her smiling presence came to him freshly, as the spring might come to one housed through a long winter, or the dawn after a dark night.

"Edith!"

He leaned upon the balustrade. The nurse, coming out, warned him. "Indeed, you'd better stay in your room."

"I'm all right. Please don't worry. You 'tend to your knitting, and I'll take care of myself."

She insisted, however, on bringing out a chair and a rug. "Perhaps it will be a change for you to sit in the hall," she conceded, and tucked him in, and he found himself trembling a little from weakness, and glad of the support which the chair gave him.

It seemed very pleasant to sit there with Edith smiling at him. For the first time in many weeks his mind was at rest. Ever since Hilda had come he had felt the pressure of an exciting presence. He felt this morning free from it, and glad to be free.

What a wife Edith had been! Holding him always to his highest and best, yet loving him even when he stumbled and fell. Bending above him in her beautiful charity and understanding, raising him up, fostering his self-respect in those moments of depression when he had despised himself.

What other woman would have done it? What other woman would have kept her love for him through it all? For she had loved him. It had never been his money with her. She would have clung to him in sickness and in poverty.

But Hilda loved his money. He knew it now as absolutely as if she had said it. For the first time in weeks he saw clearly. Last night his eyes had been opened.

He had been roused towards morning by those soft sounds in the second room, which he had heard more than once in the passing weeks. In his feverish moments, it had not seemed unlikely that his wife might be there, coming back to haunt, with her gentle presence, the familiar rooms. There was, indeed, her light step, the rustle of her silken garments—.

Half-asleep he had listened, then had opened his eyes to find the night-lamp burning, Hilda's book under it and Hilda gone!

The minutes passed as still his ears were strained. There was not a sound in the house but that silken rustle. He wondered if he sought Edith if she would speak to him. He rose and reached for his dressing gown.

Hilda had grown careless; there was no screen in front of the second door, and the crack was wide. The General standing in the dark saw her before his wife's mirror, wearing his wife's jewels, wrapped in the cloak which his wife had worn—triumphant—beautiful!

It was that air of triumph which repelled him. It was a discordant note in the Cophetua theme. He had liked her in her nurse's white. In the trappings which did not belong to her she showed herself a trifle vulgar—less than a lady.

He had crept back to bed, and wide-awake, he had worked it all out in his mind. It was his money which Hilda wanted, the things that he could give her; he meant to her pink parasols and satin slippers, and diamonds and pearls and ermines and sables, and a check-book, with unlimited credit everywhere.

And to get the things that she wanted, she had given him that which had stolen away his brains, which might indeed have done more than that—which might have killed his soul.

He had heard her come in, but he had simulated sleep. She had seated herself by the little table, and had gone on with her book. Between his half-closed eyes he had studied her—seeing her with new eyes—the hard line of her lips, the long white hands, the heaviness of her chin.

Then he had slept, and had waked to find the day nurse on duty. He felt that he should be glad never to see Hilda again. He dreaded the night when he must once more speak to her.

He was very tired sitting there in his chair. The rug had slipped from his knees. He tried to reach for it and failed. But he did not want to call the day nurse. He wanted some one with him who—cared. He raised his poor old eyes to the lady in the picture. He was cold and tired.

He wished that Bronson would come back—good old Bronson, to pull up the rug. He wished that Derry might come.

A door below opened and shut. Some one was ascending the

stairs. Some one who walked with a light step—some one slim and youthful, in a white gown—!

"Edith—?"

But Edith's hair had not been crinkled and copper-colored, and Edith would have come straight up to him; she would not have hesitated on the top step as if afraid to advance.

"Who are you?"

"Jean—"

"Jean?"

"Derry's wife."

"Come here." He tried to reach out his hand to her, but could not. His tongue felt thick—.

She knelt beside his chair. Her head was bare. She wore no wrap. "We were married this morning. And my own father has gone—to France—and I wanted a father—"

"Did Derry tell you to come?"

"Bronson begged me. He was at the wedding—"

"Old Bronson?" He tried to smile, but the smile was twisted.

She was looking up at him fearfully, but her voice did not falter. "I came to tell you that Derry loves you. He doesn't want your money, oh, you know that he doesn't want it. But he is going away to the—war, and he may be killed, so many men are—killed. And he—loves you—"

"Where is he?"

"I wouldn't let him come. You see, you said things which were hard for him to forgive. I was afraid you might say such things again."

He knew that he would never say them. 'Tell him that—I love him." He tried to sit up. "Tell him that he is—my son."

He fell back. He heard her quick cry, "Bronson—"

Bronson came running up the stairs, and the nurse who had watched the scene dazedly from the threshold of the General's room ran, too.

Weighted down by a sense of increasing numbness he lifted his agonized eyes to Jean. "Stay with me—stay—"

Hilda, waked by the day nurse, raged. "You should have called me at once when he left his room. Why didn't you call me?"

"Because I felt myself competent to manage the case."

"You see how you have managed it—I will be down in a minute. Get everybody out—"

Her composed manner when she came down showed nothing of that which was seething within her.

She found Jean in bridal-white sitting by the bed and holding the General's hand. The doctor had been sent for, Derry had been sent for—things were being swept out of her hands. She blamed it, still hiding her anger under a quiet manner, on Jean.

"He has had a stroke. It was probably the excitement of your coming."

The day nurse intervened. "It was before she came, Miss Merritt, that I saw him reach for the rug. I was puzzled and started to investigate, and then I saw her on the stairs—" She smiled at Jean. Never in her limited young life had the day nurse seen such a lovely bride, and she did not in the least like Miss Merritt.

Derry coming a little later held Jean's hand in his while he faced Hilda. "What does the doctor say?"

The truth came reluctantly. "He may be unconscious for days. He may never wake up—"

"I do not think we shall need your services—. I will send you a check for any amount you may name."

"But—"

"Whatever claim you may have upon him will be settled when he is in a condition to settle anything; until then, my wife and I shall stay—"

Hilda went upstairs and packed her bag. So her house of dreams tumbled about her. So she left behind her the tiara and the pearl collar with the diamond slides, and the velvet cloak with the ermine collar. Poor Hilda, with her head held high, going out of the shadowed house.

And taking Hilda's place, oh, more than taking her place, was Jean—and this was her wedding day. The little rose-colored drawing room had needed all of its rose to counteract the gray of the world outside, with the snow and Daddy's car standing ready to take him to the station.

But always there had been the thought of Derry to uphold her, and the wonder of their love. Nothing could rob her of that.

He had held her in his arms the night before, and had said, "Tomorrow we shall be in Woodstock, and shall listen to the chimes—"

And now it was tomorrow, and they were here in this great grim house with Death at the door.

Quite miraculously Emily arrived, and she and Bronson made a boudoir of Derry's sitting-room. They filled it with flowers, as was fitting for a bridal-bower. Jean's little trunk had been sent on to Woodstock, but there was her bag, and a supply of things which Emily brought from home.

A new night nurse came, and Miss Martin was retained for the day. The snow still fell, and the old man in the lacquered bed was still unconscious, his stertorous breathing sounding through the house.

And it was her wedding day!

They dined in the great room where Derry's ancestors gazed down on them. Emily was there, and it was a bridal feast, with things ordered hurriedly. Bronson, too, had seen to that. But they ate little. Emily talked and Derry ably supplemented her efforts.

But Jean was silent. It was all so different from what one might expect—! She still wore her white dress. It was a rather superlative frock with much cobwebby lace that had been her mother's, and in the place of her own small string of pearls was the longer string which had been her father's last gift to her. She had worn no veil, her crinkled copper hair in all its beauty had been uncovered.

"I can't believe that the lovely, lovely lady at the other end of the table is my wife," Derry told Miss Emily.

Jean smiled at him. She felt as if she were smiling from a great distance—and she had to look at him over a perfect thicket of orchids. "Shall I always have to sit so far away from you, Derry?" she asked in a very small voice.

"My dearest, no—" and he came and stood behind her, and reached for her little coffee cup and drank where her lips had touched, shamelessly, before the eyes of the sympathetic and romantic Miss Emily.

And now Emily had gone! And at last Jean and Derry were alone in the bridal bower, and Jean was telling Derry again what his father had said. "He begged me to stay—"

Their eyes met. "Dearest, dearest," Derry said, "what is life doing to me?"

"It has given you me, Derry"—such a little, little whisper.

"My beloved—yes."

The next morning they talked it over.

"What am I to do? He needs me more than ever—"

"There must be some way out, Derry."

But what way? The Tin Soldier had jumped from the shelf, but he had fallen through a crack! And the war was going on without him—!

CHAPTER XXII

JEAN PLAYS PROXY

Christmas morning found the General conscious. He was restless until Jean was brought to him. He had a feeling that she had saved him from Hilda. He wanted her where he could see her. "Don't leave me," he begged.

She slipped away to eat her Christmas dinner with Derry and Emily and Margaret. It was an early dinner on account of the children. They ate in the big dining room, and after dinner there was a tree, with Ulrich Stoelle playing Father Christmas. It had come about quite naturally that he should be asked. It had been unthinkable that Derry could enter into the spirit of it, so Emily had ventured to suggest Ulrich. "He will make an ideal Santa Claus."

But it developed that he was not to be Santa Claus at all. He was to be Father Christmas, with a wreath of mistletoe instead of a red cap.

Teddy was intensely curious about the change. "But why isn't he Santa Claus?" he asked.

"Well, Santa Claus was—made in Germany."

"Oh!"

"But now he has joined the Allies and changed his name."

"Oh!"

"And he wears mistletoe, because mistletoe is the Christmas bush, and red caps don't really mean anything, do they?"

"No, but Mother—"

"Yes?"

"If Santa Claus has joined the Allies what will the little German children do?"

What indeed?

Jean had trimmed a little tree for the General, and the children carried it up to him carefully and sang a carol—having first arranged on his table, under the lamp, the purple camels, to create an atmosphere.

> "We three kings of Orient are,
> Bearing gifts we traverse far
> Field and fountain, moor and mountain,
> Following yonder star—"

"Yonner 'tar," piped Margaret-Mary.

"Yon-der-er ste-yar," trailed Teddy's falsetto.

> "Oh, star of wonder, star of might,
> Star with royal beauty bright,
> Westward leading, still proceeding,
> Guide us to the perfect light—"

Twenty-four hours ago Hilda's book had lain where the purple camels now played their little part in the great Christmas drama. In the soul of the stricken old man on the bed entered something of the peace of the holy season.

"Oh, 'tar of wonner—"

"Ste-yar of wonder-er—" chimed the little voices.

When the song was finished, Margaret-Mary made a little curtsey and Teddy made a manly bow, and then they took their purple camels and left the tree on the table with its one small candle burning.

The General laid his left hand over Jean's—his right was useless—and said to Derry: "Your mother's jewels are my Christmas gift to her. No matter what happens, I want her to have them."

The evening waned, and the General still held Jean's hand. Every bone in her body ached. Never before had she grown weary in the service of others. She told herself as she sat there that she had always been a sort of sugar-and-spice-and-everything-nice sort of person. It was only fair that she should have her share of hardness.

The nurse begged her in a whisper to leave the General. "He won't know." But when Jean moved, that poor left hand tightened on hers and she shook her head.

Then Derry came and sat with his arm about her.

"My darling, you must rest."

She laid her head against her husband's shoulder, as he sat beside her. After a while she slept, and the nurse unlocked the clinging old fingers, and Derry carried his little wife to bed.

And so Christmas passed, and the other days, wonderful days in spite of the shadow which hung over the big house. For youth and love laugh at forebodings and they pushed as far back into their minds as possible, the thought of the thing which had to be faced.

But at last Derry faced it. "It is my self-respect, Jean."

They were sitting in her room with Muffin, wistful and devoted, on the rug at Jean's feet. The old dog, having been banished at first by Bronson, had viewed his master's wife with distrust. Gradually she had won him over, so that now, when she was not in the room, he hunted up a shoe or a glove, and sat with it until she came back.

"It is my self-respect, Jean-Joan."

She admitted that. "But—?"

"I can't stay out of the fighting and call myself a man. It has come to that with me."

She knew that it had come to that. She had thought a great deal about it. She lay awake at night thinking about it. She thought of it as she sat by the General's bed, day after day, holding his hand.

The doctor's report had been cautious, but it had amounted to this—the General might live to a green old age, some men rallied remarkably after such a shock. He rather thought the General might rally, but then again he might not, and anyhow he would be tied for months, perhaps for years, to his chair.

The old man was giving to his daughter-in-law an affection compounded of that which he had given to his wife and to his son. It was as if in coming up the stairs in her white gown on her wedding day, Jean had brought a bit of Edith back to him. For deep in his heart he knew that without her, Derry would not have come.

So he clung pathetically to that little hand, which seemed the only anchor in his sea of loneliness. Pathetically his old eyes begged her to stay. "You won't leave me, Jean?" And she would promise, and sit day after day and late into the night, holding his hand.

And as she sat with him, there grew up gradually within her a conviction which strengthened as the days went by. She could tell the very moment when she had first thought of it. She had left the General with Bronson while she went to dress for dinner. Derry was waiting for her, and usually she would have flown to him, glad of the moment when they might be together. But something halted her at the head of the stairs. It was as if a hand had been put tin front of her, barring the way.

The painted lady was looking at her with smiling eyes, but back of the eyes she seemed to discern a wistful appeal—"I want you to stay. No matter what happens I beg that you will stay."

But Jean didn't want to stay. All the youth in her rebelled against the thing that she saw ahead of her. She yearned to be free—to live and love as she pleased, not a prisoner in that shadowed room.

So she pushed it away from her, and so there came one morning a letter from her father.

"Drusilla went over on the same boat. It was a surprising thing to find her there. Since I landed, I haven't seen her. But I met Captain Hewes in Paris, and he was looking for her."

"I had never known how fine she was until those days on the boat. It was wonderful on the nights when everything was darkened and we were feeling our way through the danger zone, to have her sing for us. I believe we should all have gone to the bottom singing with her if a submarine had sunk us."

"I am finding myself busier than I have ever been before, finding myself, indeed, facing the most stupendous thing in the world. It isn't the wounded men or the dead men or the heart-breaking aspect of the refugees that gets me, it is the sight of the devastated country—made barren and blackened into hell not by devils, but by those who have called themselves men. When I think of our own country, ready soon to bud and bloom with the spring, and of this country where spring will come and go, oh, many springs, before there will be bud and bloom, I am overwhelmed by the tragic contrast. How can we laugh over there when they are crying here? Perhaps more than anything else, the difference in conditions was brought home to me as I motored the other day through a country where there was absolutely no sign of life, not a tree or a bird—except those war birds, the aeroplanes, hovering above the horizon."

"Well, as we stopped our car for some slight repairs, there rose up from a deserted trench, a lean cat with a kitten in her mouth. Oh, such a starved old cat, Jean, gray and war-worn. And her kitten was little and blind, and when she had laid it at our feet, she went back and got another. Then she stood over them, mewing, her eyes big and hungry. But she was not afraid of us, or if she was afraid, she stood her ground, asking help for those helpless babies."

"Jean, I thought of Polly Ann. Of all the petted Polly Anns in America, and then of this starved old thing, and they seemed so typical. You are playing the glad game over there, and it is easy to play it with enough to eat and plenty to wear, and away from the horror of it all. But how could that old pussy-cat be glad, how could she be anything but frightened and hungry and begging my help?"

"Well, we took her in. We had some food with us, and we gave her all she could eat, and then she curled up on a pile of bags in the bottom of the car, and lay there with her kittens, as happy as if we were not going lickety-split over the shell-torn spaces."

"And that your tender heart may be at rest, I may as well tell you that she and the kittens are living in great content in a country house where one of the officers who was in the car with us is installed. We have named her Dolores, but it is ceasing to be appropriate. She is no longer sad, and while she is on somewhat slim fare like the rest of us, she is a great hunter and catches mice in the barn, so that she is growing strong and smooth, and she is not, perhaps, to be pitied as much as Polly Ann on her pink cushion."

"And here I am writing about cats, while the only thing that is really in my heart is—You."

"Ever since the moment I left you, I have carried with me the vision of you in your wedding gown—my dear, my dear. Perhaps it is just as well that I left when I did, for I am most inordinately jealous of Derry, not only because he has you, but because he has love and life before him, while I, already, am looking back."

"My work here is, as you would say, 'wonderful.' How I should like to hear you say it! There are things which in all my years of practice, I have never met before. How could I meet them? It has taken this generation of doctors to wrestle with the problem of treating men tortured by gas, and with nerves shaken by sights and sounds without parallel in the history of the world."

"But I am not going to tell you of it. I would rather tell you how much I love you and miss you, and how glad I am that you are not here to see it all. Yet I would have all Americans think of those who are here, and I would have you help until it—hurts. You must know, my Jean, how moved I am by it, when I ask you, whom I have always shielded, to give help until it hurts—"

"I have had a letter from Hilda. She wants to come over. I haven't answered the letter. But when I do, I shall tell her that there may be something that she can do, but it will not be with me. I need women who can see the pathos of such things as that starved cat and kittens out there among the shell-holes, and Hilda would never have seen it. She would have left the cat to starve."

Jean found herself crying over the letter. "I am not helping at all, Derry."

"My dear, you are."

"I am not. I am just sitting on a pink cushion, like Polly Ann—"

It was the first flash he had seen for days of her girlish petulance. He smiled. "That sounds like the Jean of yesterday."

"Did you like the Jean of yesterday better than the Jean of to-day?"

"There is only one Jean for me—yesterday, today and forever."

* * * * * *

She stood a little away from him. "Derry, I've been thinking and thinking—"

He put a finger under her chin and turned her face up to him. "What have you been thinking, Jean-Joan?"

"That you must go—and I will take care of your father."

"You?"

"Yes. Why not, Derry?"

"I won't have you sacrificed."

"But you want me to be brave."

"Yes. But not burdened. I won't have it, my dear."

"But—you promised your mother. I am sure she would be glad to let me keep your promise."

She was brave now. Braver than he knew.

"I can't see it," he said, fiercely. "I can see myself leaving you with Emily, in your own house—to live your own life. But not to sit in Dad's room, day after day, sacrificing your youth as I sacrificed my childhood and boyhood—my manhood—. I am over thirty, Jean, and I have always been treated like a boy. It isn't right, Jean; our lives are our own, not his."

"It is right. Nobody's life seems to be his own in these days. And you must go—and I can't leave him. He is so old, and helpless, Derry, like the poor pussy-cat over there in France. His eyes are like that—hungry, and they beg—. And oh, Derry, I mustn't be like Polly Ann, on a pink cushion—."

She tried to laugh and broke down. He caught her up in his arms. Light as thistledown, young and lovely!

She sobbed on his heart, but she held to her high resolve. He must go—and she would stay. And at last he gave in.

He had loved her dearly, but he had not looked for this, that she would give herself to hardness for the sake of another. For the first time he saw in his little wife something of the heroic quality which had seemed to set his mother apart and above, as it were, all other women.

BOOK THREE

THE BUGLE CALLS

The wooden trumpeters that were carved on the door blew
with all their might, so that their cheeks were much larger than
before. Yes, they blew "Trutter-a-trutt—trutter-a-trutt—" . . .

CHAPTER XXIII

THE EMPTY HOUSE

Jean's world was no longer wonderful—not in the sense that it had once been, with all the glamour of girlish dreams and of youthful visions.

She had never thought of life as a thing like this in the days when she had danced down to the confectioner's, intent on good times.

But now, with her father away, with Derry away, with the city frozen and white, and with not enough coal to go around, with many of the rooms in the house shut that fuel might be conserved, with Margaret and the children and Nurse installed as guests at the General's until the weather grew warmer, with Emily transforming her Toy Shop into a surgical dressings station, and with her father-in-law turning over to her incredible amounts of money for the Red Cross and Liberty Bonds and War Stamps, life began to take on new aspects of responsibility and seriousness.

She could never have kept her balance in the midst of it all, if Derry had not written every day. Her father wrote every day, also, but there were long intervals between his letters, and then they were apt to arrive all at once, a great packet of them, to be read and re-read and passed around.

But Derry's letters, brought to her room every morning by

Bronson, contained the elixir which sent her to her day's work with shining eyes and flushed cheeks. Sometimes she read bits of them to Bronson. Sometimes, indeed, there were only a few lines for herself, for Derry was being intensively trained in a Southern camp, working like an ant, with innumerable other ants, all in olive-drab, with different colored cords around their hats.

Sometimes she read bits of the letters to Margaret at breakfast, and after breakfast she would go up to the General and read everything to him except the precious words which Derry had meant for her very own self.

And then she and the General would tell each other how really extraordinary Derry was!

It was a never-failing subject, of intense interest to both of them. For there was always this to remember, that if the world was no longer a radiant and shining world, if the day's task was hard, and if now and then in the middle of the night she wept tears of loneliness, if there were heavy things to bear, and hard things and sad things, one fact shone brilliantly above all others, Derry was as wonderful as ever!

"There was never such a boy," the General would chant in his deep bass.

"Never," Jean would pipe in her clear treble.

And when they had chorused thus for a while, the General would dictate a letter to Derry, for his hand was shaky, and Jean would write it out for him, and then she would write a letter of her own, and after that the day was blank, and the night until the next morning when another letter came. So she lived from letter to letter.

"You have never seen Washington like this," she wrote one day in February, "we keep only a little fire in the furnace, and I am wearing flannels for the first time in my life. We dine in sweaters, and the children are round and rosy in the cold. And the food steams in the icy air of the dining room, and you can't imagine how different it all is—with the servants bundled up like the rest of us. We keep your father warm by burning wood in the fireplace of his room, and we have given half the coal in the cellar to people who haven't any."

"I am helping Cook with the conservation menus, and it is funny to see how topsy-turvy everything is. It is perfectly patriotic to eat mushrooms and lobsters and squabs and ducklings, and it is unpatriotic to serve sausages and wheat cakes. And Cook can't get adjusted to it."

She will insist upon bacon for breakfast, because well-regulated families since the Flood have eaten bacon—and she feels that in some way we are sacrificing self-respect or our social status when we refrain.

"Your father is such an old dear, Derry. He has war bread and milk for lunch, and I carry it to him myself in the pretty old porcelain bowl that he likes so much."

"It was one day when I brought the milk that he spoke of Hilda. 'Where is she?'"

"I told him that she was still in town, and that you had given her a check which would carry her over a year or two, and he said that he was glad—that he should not like to see her suffer. The porcelain bowl had reminded him of her. She had asked him once what it cost, and after she had found out, she had never used it. She evidently stood quite in awe of anything so expensive."

"Your mother and I are getting to be very good friends, dearest. When I am dreadfully homesick for you, I go and sit on the stairs, and she smiles at me. It is terribly cold in the hall, and I wrap myself up in your fur coat, and it is almost like having your arms around me."

She was surely making the best of things, this little Jean, when she found comfort in being mothered by a painted lady on the stairs, and in being embraced by a fur coat which had once been worn by her husband!

She kept Derry's tin soldier, which Drusilla had given him, on her desk. "You shall have him when you go to France, but until then he is a good little comrade, and I say; 'Good-morning' to him and 'Good-night.' Yet I sometimes wonder whether he likes it there on the shelf, and whether he is crying, 'I want to go to the wars—'"

She was very busy every morning in Emily's room, working on the surgical dressings. She hated it all. She hated the oakum and the gauze, the cotton and the compresses, the pneumonia jackets and the split-irrigation pads, the wipes, the triangulars, the many-tailed and the scultetus. Other women might speak lightly of five-yard rolls as dressing for stumps, of paper-backs "used in the treatment of large suppurating wounds." Jean shivered and turned white at these things. Her vivid imagination went beyond the little work-room with its white-veiled women to those hospitals back of the battle line where mutilated men lay waiting for the compresses and the wipes and the bandages, men in awful agony—.

But the lesson she was learning was that of harnessing her emotions to the day's work; and if her world was no longer wonderful in a care-free sense, it was a rather splendid world of unselfishness and self-sacrifice, although she was not conscious of this, but felt it vaguely.

She wore now, most of the time, her nun's frock of gray, which had seemed to foreshadow something of her future on that glorified day when Derry had first come to her. She had laid away many of her lovely things, and one morning Teddy remarked on the change.

"You don't dwess up any more."

Nurse stood back of his chair. "Dress—"

"Dur-wess."

"Don't you like this dress, Teddy?"

"I liked the boo one."

"Blue—"

"Ble-yew, an' the pink one, and all the shiny ones you used to wear at night."

"Blue dresses and pink dresses and shiny dresses cost a lot of money, Teddy, and I shouldn't have any money left for Thrift Stamps."

Thrift stamps were a language understood by Teddy, as he would not have understood the larger transactions of Liberty Bonds. He and the General held long conversations as to the best means of obtaining a large supply of stamps, and the General having listened to Margaret who wanted the boy to work for his offering, suggested an entrancing plan. Teddy was to feed the fishes in the dining-room aquarium, he was to feed Muffin, and he was to feed Polly Ann.

It sounded simple, but there were difficulties. In the first place he had to face Cook, and Cook hated to have children in the kitchen.

"But you'd have to face more than that if you were grown up and in the trenches. And Hodgson is really very kind."

"Well, she doesn't look kind, Mother."

"Why not?"

"Well, she doesn't smile, and her face is wed."

"Red, dear."

"Ur-ed—. And when I ask her for milk for Polly, she says 'Milk for cats,' and when she gets it out, she slams the 'frigerator door."

"Refrigerator, dear."

"Rif-iggerator."

But in the main Teddy went to his task valiantly. He conserved bones for Muffin and left-over corn-meal cakes. Polly Ann dined rather monotonously on fish boiled with war-bread crusts, on the back of Cook's big range. Hodgson was conscientious and salted it and cooled it, and kept it in a little covered granite pail, and it was from this pail that Teddy ladled stew into Polly Ann's blue saucer. "Mother says it is very good of you, Hodgson, to take so much trouble."

Hodgson, whose face was redder than ever, as she broiled mushrooms for lunch, grunted, "I'd rather do it than have other people messin' around."

Teddy surveyed her anxiously. "You don't mind having me here, do you, Hodgson?"

His cheeks were rosy, his bronze hair bright, his sturdy legs planted a trifle apart, Polly's dish in one hand, the big spoon in the other. "No, I don't mind," she admitted, but it was some time before she acknowledged even to herself how glad she was when that bright figure appeared.

Feeding the fishes presented few problems, and gradually thrift stamps filled the little book, and there was a war stamp, and more thrift stamps and more war stamps, and Muffin and Polly Ann waxed fat and friendly, and were a very lion and lamb for lying down together.

Then there came a day when Teddy, feeding the fishes in the

aquarium, heard somebody say that Hodgson's son was in the war.

He went at once to the kitchen. "Why didn't you tell me?" he asked the cook, standing in front of her where she sat cutting chives and peppers and celery on a little board for salad.

"Tell you what?"

"That your boy was in Fwance."

Hodgson's red face grew redder, and to Teddy's consternation, a tear ran down her cheek.

He stood staring at her, then flew upstairs to his mother. "Cook's cryin'."

"Teddy—"

"She is. Because her son is in Fwance."

After that when he went down to get things for Muffin and Polly Ann, he said how s'prised he was and how nice it was now that he knew, and wasn't she pr-roud? And he fancied that Hodgson was kinder and softer. She told him the name of her son. It was Charley, and she and Teddy talked a great deal about Charley, and Teddy sent him some chocolate, and Hodgson told Margaret. "He's a lovely boy, Mrs. Morgan. May you never raise him to fight."

"I should want him to be as brave as his father, Hodgson."

"Yes. My boy's brave, but it was hard to let him go." Then, struck by the look on Margaret's face, she said, "Forgive me, ma'am; if mine is taken from me, I'd like to feel as you do. You ain't makin' other people unhappy over it."

"I think it is because my husband still lives for me, Hodgson."

Hodgson cried into her apron. "It ain't all of us that has your faith. But if I loses him, I'll do my best."

And so the painted lady on the stairs saw all the sinister things that Hilda had brought into the big house swept out of it. She saw Hodgson the cook trying to be brave, and bringing up Margaret's tea in the afternoons for the sake of the moment when she might speak of her boy to one who would understand; she saw Emily, coming home dead tired after a hard day's work, but with her face illumined. She saw Margaret smiling, with tears in her heart, she saw Jean putting aside childish things to become one of the women that the world needed.

Brave women all of them, women with a vision, women raised to heroic heights by the need of the hour!

The men, too, were heroic. Indeed, the General, trying to control his appetite, was almost pathetically heroic. He had given up sugar, although he hated his coffee without it, and he had a little boy's appetite for pies and cakes.

"When the war is over," he told Teddy, "we will order a cake that's as high as a house, and we will eat it together."

Teddy giggled. "With frostin'?"

"Yes. I remember when Derry was a lad that we used to tell him the story of the people who baked a cake so big that they had to climb ladders to reach the top. Well, that's the kind of cake we'll have."

Yet while he made a joke of it, he confessed to Jean. "It is harder than fighting battles. I'd rather face a gun than deny myself the things that I like to eat and drink."

Bronson was contributing to the Red Cross and buying Liberty Bonds, and that was brave of Bronson. For Bronson was close, and the hardest thing that he had to do was to part with his money, or to take less interest than his rather canny investments had made possible.

And Teddy, the man of his family, came one morning to his mother. "I've just got to do it," he said in a rather shaky voice.

"Do what, dear?"

"Send my books to the soldiers."

She let him do it, although she knew how it tore his heart. You see, there were the Jungle Books, which he knew the soldiers would like, and "Treasure Island," and "The Swiss Family Robinson," and "Huckleberry Finn." He brought his fairy books, too, and laid them on the altar of patriotism, and "Toby Tyler," which had been his father's, and "Under the Lilacs," which he adored because of little brown-faced Ben and his dog, Sancho.

He was rapturously content when his mother decided that the fairy books and Toby and brown-faced Ben might still be his companions. "You see the soldiers are men, dear, and they probably read these when they were little boys."

"But won't I wead them when I grow up, Mother?"

"You may want to read older books."

But Teddy was secretly resolved that age should not wither nor custom stale the charms of the beloved volumes. And that he should love them to the end. His mother thought that he might grow tired of them some day and told him so.

"I can wead them to my little boys," he said, hopefully, "and to their little boys after that," and having thus established a long line of prospective worshippers of his own special gods, he turned to other things.

General Drake, growing gradually better, went now and then

in his warm closed car for a ride through the Park. Usually Jean was with him, or Bronson, and now and then Nurse with the children.

It was one morning when the children were with him that he said to Nurse: "Take them into the Lion House for a half hour, I'll drive around and come back for you."

Nurse demurred. "You are sure that you won't mind being left, sir?"

"Why not?" sharply. "I am perfectly able to take care of myself."

He watched them go in, then he gave orders to drive at once to the Connecticut Avenue entrance.

A woman stood by the gate, a tall woman in a long blue cloak and a close blue bonnet. In the clear cold, her coloring showed vivid pink and white. The General spoke through the tube; the chauffeur descended and opened the door.

"If you will get in," the General said to the woman, "you can tell me what you have to say—"

"Perhaps I should not have asked it," Hilda said, hesitating, "but I had seen you riding in the Park, and I thought of this way—I couldn't of course, come to the house."

"No." He had sunk down among his robes. "No."

"I felt that perhaps you had been led to—misunderstand." She came directly to the point. "I wanted to know—what I had done—what had made the difference. I couldn't believe that you had not meant what you said."

He stirred uneasily. "I have been very ill—"

Her long white hands were ungloved, the diamonds that he

had given her sparkled as she drew the ring off slowly. "I felt that I ought to give you this—if it was all really over."

"It is all over. But keep it—please."

"I should like to keep it," she admitted frankly, "because, you see, I've never had a ring like this."

It was the Cophetua and Beggar Maid motif but it left him cold. "Hilda," he said, "I saw you that night trying on my wife's jewels. That was my reason."

She was plainly disconcerted. "But that was child's play. I had never had anything—it was like a child—dressing up."

"It was not like that to me. I think I had been a rather fatuous fool—thinking that there might be in me something that you might care for. But I knew then that without my money—you wouldn't care—"

"People's motives are always mixed," she told him. "You know that."

"Yes, I know."

"You liked me because I was young and made you feel young. I liked you because you could give me things."

"Yes. But now the glamour is gone. You make me feel a thousand years old, Hilda."

"Why?" in great surprise.

"Because I know that if I had no wealth to offer you, you would see me for what I am, an aged broken creature for whom you have no tenderness—"

It was time for him to be getting back to the Lion House. They stopped again at the gate. "If you will keep the ring," he said, "I shall be glad to think that you have it. Jean gays Derry gave you a check. If it is not enough to buy pink parasols, will you let me give you another?" He was speaking with the ease of his accustomed manner.

"No; I am not an—adventuress, though you seem to think that I am, and to condemn me for it."

"I condemn you only for one thing—for that flat bottle behind the books."

"But you wanted it."

"For that reason you should have kept it away. You should have obeyed orders."

"You asked me to doff my cap, so I—doffed my discipline." She was standing on the ground, holding the door open as she talked; again he was aware of the charm of her pink and white.

"Good-bye, Hilda." He reached out his hand to her.

She took it. "I am going to France."

"When?"

"As soon as I can." She stepped back and the door was shut between them. As the car turned, Hilda waved her hand, and the General had a sense of sudden keen regret as the tall cloaked figure with its look of youth and resoluteness faded into the distance.

When he reached the Lion House the children were waiting. "Did you hear him roar?" Teddy asked as he climbed in.

"No."

"Well, he did, and we came out 'cause it fwightened Peggy."

"Frightened—" from Nurse.

"Fr-ightened. But I liked the leopards best."

"Why?"

"Because they're pre-itty."

"You can't always trust—pretty things."

"Can't you tre-ust—leopards—General Drake?"

The General was not sure, and presently he fell into silence. His mind was on a pretty woman whom he could not trust.

That night he said to Jean, "Hilda is going to France."

"Oh—how do you know?"

"I met her in the Park."

He was sitting, very tired, in his big chair. Jean's little hand was in his.

"Poor Hilda," he said at last, looking into the fire, as if he saw there the vision of his lost dreams.

"Oh, no—" Jean protested.

"Yes, my dear, there is so much that is good in the worst of us, and so much that is bad in the best—and perhaps she struggles with temptations which never assail you."

Jean's lips were set in an obstinate line. "Daddy was always saying things like that about Hilda."

"Well, we men are apt to be charitable—to beauty in distress." The General was keenly and humorously aware that if Hilda had been ugly, he might not have been so anxious about the pink parasol. He might not, indeed, have pitied her at all!

And now in Jean's heart grew up a sharply defined fear of Hilda. In the old days there had been cordial dislike, jealousy, perhaps, but never anything like this. The question persisted in the back of her mind. If Hilda went to France, would she see Daddy and weave her wicked spells. To find the General melting into pity, in spite of the chaos which Hilda's treachery had created, was to wonder if Daddy, too, might melt.

She wrote to Derry about it.

"I would try and see her if I knew what to say, but when I even think of it I am scared. I never liked her, and I feel now as if I should be glad to pin together the pages of my memory of her, as I pinned together the pages of one of my story books when I was a little girl. There was a shark under water in the picture and two men were trying to get away from him. I hated that picture and shivered every time I looked at it, so I stuck in a pin and shut out the sight of it.

"Your father has had two letters from her since the day when he saw her in the Park. Bronson always brings the mail to me, and you know what a distinctive hand Hilda writes, there is no mistaking it. Your father dropped the letters into the fire, but she ought not to write to him, Derry, and I should like to tell her so.

"But if I told her, she would laugh at me, and that would be the end of it. For you can't rage and tear and rant at a thing that is as cold as stone. Oh, my dearest, I need you so much to tell me what to do, and yet I would not have you here—"

"I met Alma Drew the other day, and she said, as lightly as you please, 'Do you know, I can't quite fancy Derry Drake in the trenches.'"

"I looked at her for a minute before I could answer, and then I said, 'I can fancy him with his back to the wall, fighting a thousand Huns—!'"

"She shrugged her shoulders, 'You're terribly in love.'"

"'I am,' I said, and I hope I said it calmly, 'but there's more than love in a woman's belief in her husband's bravery—there's respect. And it's something rather—sacred, Alma.' And then I choked up and couldn't say another word, and she looked at me in a rather stunned fashion for a moment, and then she said, 'Gracious Peter, do you love him like that?' and I said, 'I do,' and she laughed in a funny little way, and said, 'I thought it was his millions.'"

"I was perfectly furious. But you can't argue with such people. I know I was as white as a sheet. 'If anything should happen to Derry,' I said, 'do you think that all the money in the world would comfort me?'"

"She stopped smiling. 'It would comfort me,' then suddenly she held out her hand. 'But I fancy you're different, and Derry is a lucky fellow.' which was rather nice and human of her, wasn't it?"

Life is growing more complicated than ever here in Washington. The crowds pour in as if the Administration were a sort of Pied Piper and had played a time, and the people who have lived here all their lives are waking to something like activity. Great buildings are going up as if some Aladdin had rubbed a lamp—. None of us are doing the things we used to do. We don't even talk about the things we used to talk about, and we go around in blue gingham and caps, and white linen and veils, and we hand out sandwiches to the soldiers and sailors, and drive perfectly strange men in our cars on Government errands, and make Liberty Bond Speeches from many platforms, and all the old theories of what women should do are forgotten in the rush of the things which must be done by women. It is as if we had all been bewitched and turned into somebody else.

Well, I wish that Hilda could be turned into somebody else. Into somebody as nice as—Emily—. But she won't be. She hasn't been changed the least bit by the war, and everybody else has, even Alma, or she wouldn't have said that about your being lucky to have me. Are you lucky, Derry?

"And when Hilda sets her mind on a thing—. Oh, I can't seem to talk of anything but Hilda—when she sets her mind on anything, she gets it in one way or another—and that's why I am afraid of her."

Derry wrote back.

"Don't be afraid of anything, Jean-Joan. And it won't do any good to talk to Hilda. I don't want you to talk to her. You are too much of a white angel to contend against the powers of darkness."

"As for my luck in having you, it is something which transcends luck—it just hits the stars, dearest."

"I wonder what the fellows do who haven't any wives to anchor themselves to in a time like this? Through, all the day I have this hour in mind when I can write to you—and I think there are lots of other fellows like that—for I can see them all about me here in the Hut, bending over their letters with a look on their faces which isn't there at any other time."

"By Jove, Jean-Joan, I never knew before what women meant in the lives of men. Here we are marooned, as it were, on an island of masculinity, yet it isn't what the other fellows think of us that counts, it is what you think who are miles away. Always in the back of our minds is the thought of what you expect of us and demand of us, and added to what we demand and expect of ourselves, it sways us level. We don't talk a great deal about you, but now and then some fellow says, 'My wife,' and we all prick up our ears and want to hear the rest of it."

"It is a great life, dearest, in spite of the hard work, in spite of the stress and strain. And to me who have known so little of the great human game it is a great revelation."

"In the first place, there has been brought to me the knowledge of the joy of real labor. I shall never again be sorry for the man who toils. You see, I had never toiled, not in the sense that a man does whose labor counts. I was always a rather anxious and lonely little boy, looking after my father and trying to help my mother, and feeling a bit of a mollycoddle because I had a tutor and did not go to school with the other chaps. In the eyes of the world I was looked upon as a lucky fellow, but I know now what I have missed. In these days I am rubbing elbows with fellows who have had to hustle, and I am discovering that life is a great game, and that I have missed the game. If Dad had been different, he might have pushed me into things, as some men with money push their sons, making them stand on their own feet. But Dad liked an easy life, and he was perhaps entitled to ease, for he had struggled in his younger years. But I have never struggled. I have always had somebody to brush my clothes and to bring my breakfast, and I think I have had a sort of hazy idea that life was like that for everybody—or if it wasn't, then the people who couldn't be brushed and breakfasted by others were much to be pitied."

"Oh, I've been a Tin Soldier, Jean-Joan, left out not only of the war but of life. I've been on the shelf all these years in our big house, with the wooden trumpets blowing, 'Trutter-a-trutt' while other men have striven."

"When I first came here I had a sort of detached feeling." I had no experiences to match with the experiences of other men. I had never had to rush in the morning to catch a subway, I had never eaten, to put it poetically, by candlelight, so that I might get to the store by eight. I had never sold papers, or plowed fields, or stood behind a counter. I had never sat at a desk, I had never in fact done anything really useful, I had just been rich, and that isn't much of a background as I am beginning to see it here—.

"I find myself having a rather strange feeling of exaltation as the days go by, because for the first time I am a cog in a great machine, for the first time I am toiling and sweating as I rather think it was intended that men should toil and sweat. And the friends that I am making are the sign and seal of the levelling effects of this great war. Not one of the men of what you might call my own class interests me half as much as Tommy Tracy, who before he entered the service drove the car of one of Dad's business associates. I have often ridden behind Tommy, but he doesn't know it. And I don't intend that he shall. He rather fancies that I am a scholarly chap torn from my books, and he patronizes me on the strength of his knowledge of practical things."

"Tommy likes to eat, and he talks a great deal about his mother's cooking. He says there was always tripe for Sunday mornings, and corned beef and cabbage on Mondays, and Monday was wash-day!"

"I wish you could hear him tell what wash-day meant to him. It is a sort of poem, the way he puts it. He doesn't know that it is poetry, though Vachell Lindsay would, or Masters, or some of those fellows."

"It seems that he used to help his mother, because he was a strong little fellow, and could turn the wringer, and they would get up very early because he had to go to school, and in the spring and summer they washed out of doors, under a tree in the yard, and his mother's eyes were bright and her cheeks were red and her arms were white, and she was always laughing. There's a memory for a man on the battlefield, dearest, a healthy, hearty memory of the day's work of a boy, and of a bright-eyed mother, and of a good dinner at the end of hours of toil."

"Perhaps with such a mother it isn't surprising that Tommy has made so much of himself. He has aspirations far beyond driving some other man's car, and if he keeps on he'll have a little flivver of his own before he knows it—when the war ends, and he can strike out, with his energy at the boiling point."

"There are a lot of men who have belonged not to the idle rich, but to the idle poor, and the discipline of this life is just the thing for them as it is for me. It rather contradicts the kindergarten idea of play as a preparation for life. These busy men, forced to be busy, are a thousand times more self-respecting than if left to lead the listless lives that were theirs before their country called them. I wonder if, after all, Kipling isn't right, and that the hump and hoof and haunch of it all isn't obedience? Not slavish obedience, but obedience founded on a knowledge of one's place and value in the pack?"

Jean, striving to follow Derry's point of view, found herself floundering.

"I am glad you like it, but I don't see how you can. And you mustn't say that you've always been a Tin Soldier on a shelf. I won't have it. And you have played the game of life just as bravely as Tommy Tracy, only your problems were different— And if you can't remember wash days you can remember other days—. But I like to have you tell me about it, because I can see you, listening to Tommy and laughing at him. I adore your laugh, Derry, though I shouldn't be telling you, should I—? I have pasted the picture you sent me of you and Tommy in my memory book and have written under it, 'When you and I were young, Tommy' and I've drawn a cloud of steam above Tommy, with washboilers—and tubs—and cabbages and soap suds, and his mother's face smiling in the midst of it all—. And in your cloud is your mother smiling, too, with her little crown on her head, and gold spoons for a border—and a frosted cake with candles—and a mountain of ice-cream. Perhaps you have other memories, but I had to do the best I could with my poor little rich boy—"

It was about this time that Jean's memory book! became chaotic. Most of the things in it had to do with Derry, a bit of pine from a young plume which Derry had sent her from the south—triangles cut from the letter paper on which he sometimes wrote—post-cards to say "Good-morning," telegrams to say "Good-night"—a service pin with its one sacred star.

There were reminders, too, of the things which were happening across the sea, a cartoon or two, a small reproduction of a terrible Raemaeker print; verse, much of it—

* * * * * *

They have taken your bells, O God,
The bells that hung in your towers,
That cried your grace in a lovely song,
And counted the praying hours!

The little birds flew away!
They will tell the clouds and the wind,
Till the uttermost places know
The sin that the Hun has sinned!

* * * * * *

Jean thought a great deal about the Huns. She always called them that. She hated to think about them, but she had to. She couldn't pin the pages together, as it were, of her thoughts. And the Huns were worse than the sharks that had frightened her in her little girl days. Oh, they were much worse than sharks, for the shark was only following an instinct when it killed, and the Huns had worked out diabolically their murderous, monstrous plan.

In the days when she had argued with Hilda, she had been told of the power and perfection of Prussian rule. "Everything is at loose ends in America," had been Hilda's accusation.

"Well, what if it is?" Jean had flung back at her hotly. "Having things in place isn't the end and aim of happiness. Just because a house is swept and garnished isn't any sign that it is a blissful habitation. When I was a child I used to visit my two great-aunts in Maryland. I loved to go to Aunt Mary's, but I dreaded Aunt Anne's. And the reason was this. Everything in Aunt Anne's house went by clock-work, and everything was polished and scrubbed and dusted within an inch of its life. When we arrived, we scraped our shoes before we kissed Aunt Anne, and when we departed, we felt that she literally swept us out——. We had hours for everything, and nobody thought of doing as she pleased. It was always as Aunt Anne pleased, and the meals were always on time, and nobody was ever expected to be late, and if she was late she was scolded or punished; and nobody ever dared throw a newspaper on the floor, or go out to the kitchen and make fudge, or pop corn by the sitting-room fire. Yet Aunt Anne was so efficient that her house-keeping was the admiration of the whole State.

"But we loved Aunt Mary's. She would come smiling down the stone walk to meet us, and she would leave the morning's work undone to wander with us in the fields or woods. And we had some of our meals under the trees, and some of them in the house, and when we made taffy, and it stuck to things, Aunt Mary smiled some more and said it didn't matter. And we loved the freedom of our life, and we went to Aunt Mary's as often as we could, and stayed away when we could from Aunt Anne's."

"And that's the way with America. It isn't perfect, it isn't efficient, but it is a lovely place to live in, because in a sense we can live as we please."

"Did you ever know a man who wanted to go back to slavery? As a slave he was fed and clothed and kept by his master, with no thought of responsibility——. Yet it was freedom he wanted, even though he had to go hungry now and then for the sake of it——"

"I like law and order," Hilda said. "We don't always have it here."

"I'd rather be a gipsy on the road," had been Jean's passionate declaration, "and free, than a princess with a 'verboten' sign at all the palace gates."

* * * * * *

There were wisps of gauze, too, in her memory book, a red cross, drawings in which were caricatured some of the women who worked in the surgical dressing rooms.

"Emily," Jean asked, as she showed one of the pictures to her friend, "do such women come because it's fashion or because they really feel—?"

"I fancy their motives are mixed," said Emily, "and you mustn't think because they wear high heels and fluff their hair out over their ears that they haven't any hearts."

"No, I suppose not," Jean admitted, "but I wonder what they think the veils are for when they fluff out their hair.

"And their rings," she went on. "You see, when they all have on white aprons and veils you can't tell whether they are Judy O'Grady or the Colonel's lady—so they load their hands with diamonds. As if the hands wouldn't tell the tale themselves. Why, Emily, if you and Hilda were hidden, all but your hands, the people would know the Colonel's lady from Judy O'Grady."

Emily smiled abstractedly, she was counting compresses. She stopped long enough to ask, "Is Hilda still in town?"

"Yes. I saw her yesterday on the other side of the street. I didn't speak, but some day when I get a good opportunity I am going to tell her what I think of her."

But when the opportunity came she did not say all that she had meant to say!

She went over one morning to her father's house to get some

papers which he had left in his desk. The house had been closed for weeks and the hall, as she entered it, was cold with a chill that reached the marrow of her bones—it was dim with the half-gloom of drawn curtains and closed doors. Even the rose-colored drawing-room as she stood on the threshold held no radiance—it had the stiff and frozen look of a soulless body. Yet she remembered how it had throbbed and thrilled on the night that Derry had come to her. The golden air had washed in waves over her.

She shivered and went over to the window. She pulled up a curtain and looked out upon the grayness of the street. The clouds were low, and a strong wind was blowing. Those who passed, bent to the wind. She was slightly above the level of the street, and nobody looked up at her. She might have been a ghost in the ghostly house.

Well, she had to get the papers. She turned to face the gloom, and as she turned she heard a sound in the room above her.

It was the rather startling sound of muffled steps. She dared not go into the hall. She felt comparatively safe by the window—. If—anything came, she could open the window and call.

But she did not call, for it was Hilda who came presently on rubber-heels and stood in the door.

"I thought I heard some one," she said, calmly.

"How did you get in?" was Jean's abrupt demand.

"I had my key. I have never given it up."

"But this is no longer your home."

"It was never home," said Hilda, darkly. "It was never home. I lived here with you and your father, but it was never home."

Jean, more than ever afraid of this woman, had a sudden sense of something tragic in the fact of Hilda's homelessness.

"I don't quite see what you mean," she said, slowly.

"You couldn't see," Hilda told her, "and you will never see. Women like you don't."

"We didn't get on very well together," Jean said, almost timidly, "but that was because we were different."

"It wasn't because we were different that we didn't get on," Hilda said. "It was because you were afraid of me. You knew your father liked me."

With her usual frankness she spoke the truth as she saw it.

"I was not afraid," Jean faltered.

"You were. But we needn't talk about that. I am going to France."

"When?"

"As soon as I can get there. That's why I came here. To take away some things I wanted."

"Oh—"

"And one of the things I wanted was the picture of your father which hung in your room. I have taken that. You can get more of them. I can't. So I have taken it."

They faced each other, this shining child and this dark woman.

"But—but it is mine—Hilda."

"It is mine now, and if I were you, I shouldn't make a fuss about it."

"Hilda, how dare you!" Jean began in the old indignant way, and stopped. There was something so sinister about it all. She hated the thought that she and Hilda were alone in the empty house—

"Hilda, if you go to France, shall you see Daddy?"

"I shall try. I had a letter from him the other day. He told me not to come. But I am going. There is work to do, and I am going."

Jean had a stunned feeling, as if there was nothing left to say, as if Hilda were indeed a rock, and words would rebound from her hard surface.

"But after all, you didn't really care for Daddy—"

"What makes you say that?"

"You were going to marry the General."

"Well, I wanted a home. I wanted some of the things you had always had. I'm not old, and I am tired of being a machine."

For just one moment her anger blazed, then she laughed with something of toleration.

"Oh, you'd never understand if I talked a year. So what's the use of wasting breath?"

She said "Good-bye" after that, and Jean watched her go, hearing the padded steps—until the front door shut and there was silence.

After that, with almost a sense of panic, she sped through the empty rooms, finding the papers after a frantic search, and gaining the street with a sense of escape.

Yet even then, it was sometime before her heart beat normally, and always after that when she thought of Hilda, it was against the chill and gloom of the empty house, with that look upon her face of dark resentment.

CHAPTER XXIV

THE SINGING WOMAN

Somewhere in France, Drusilla had found the Captain. Or, rather, he had found her. He had come upon her one rainy afternoon, and had not recognized her in her muddy uniform, with a strap under her chin. Then all at once he had heard her voice, crooning a song to a badly wounded boy whose head lay in her lap.

The Captain had stopped in his tracks. "Drusilla—"

The light in her eyes gave him his welcome, but she waved him away.

The boy died in her arms. When she joined her lover, she was much moved. "It is not my work to look after the wounded; I carry blankets and things to refugees. But now and then—it happens. A shell burst in the street, and that poor lad—! He asked me to sing for him—you see, I have been singing for them as they go through, and he remembered—"

He was holding both of her hands in his. "Dear woman, dear woman—" There were people all about them, but there were no conventions in war times, and nobody cared if he held her hands.

Her face was dirty, her hair wind-blown. She was muddy and without a trace of the smartness for which she had been famous. She was simply a hard-worked woman in clothes of masculine cut, yet never had she seemed so beautiful to her lover. He bent and kissed her in the market-place. He was an undemonstrative Englishman, but there was that in her eyes which carried him away from self-consciousness.

"I saw McKenzie in Paris," he said. "He told me that you were here."

"We came over together. Did you get my letter?"

"I have had no letters. But now that I have you, nothing matters."

"Really? Somehow I don't feel that I deserve it."

"Deserve what?"

"All that you are giving me. But I have liked to think of it. It has been a prop to lean on—"

"Only that—?"

"A shield and a buckler, dearest, a cross held high—" Her breath came quickly.

* * * * * *

They sat side by side on the worn doorstep of a shattered building and talked.

"I am in a shack—a *baraque*,—they call it," Drusilla told him, "with three other women. We have fixed up one room a little better than the others, and whenever the men come through the town some of them drift in and are warmed by our fire, and I sing to them; they call me 'The Singing Woman.'"

She did not tell him how she had mothered the lads. She was not much older than some of them, but they had instinctively recognized the maternal quality of her interest in them. With all her beauty they had turned to her for that which was in a sense spiritual.

Hating the war, Drusilla yet loved the work she had to do. There was, of course, the horror of it, but there was, too, the stimulus of living in a world of realities. She wondered if she were the same girl who had burned her red candles and had served her little suppers, safe and sound and far away from the stress of fighting.

She wondered, too, if women over there were still thinking of their gowns, and men of their gold. Were they planning to go North in the summer and South in the winter? Were they still care-free and comfortable?

People over here were not comfortable, but how little they cared, and how splendid they were. She had seen since she came such incredibly heroic things—men as tender as women, women as brave as men—she had seen human nature at its biggest and best.

"I have never been religious," she told the Captain, earnestly; "our family is the kind which finds sufficient outlet in a cool intellectual conclusion that all's right with the world, and it doesn't make much difference what comes hereafter. You know the attitude? 'If there is future life, we shall be glad to explore, and if there isn't, we shall be content to sleep!'

"But since I have been over here, I have carried a little prayer-book, and I've read things to the men, and when I have come to that part 'Gladly to die—that we may rise again,' I have known that it is true, Captain—"

He laid his hand over hers. "May I have your prayer-book in exchange for mine?" He was very serious. With all his heart he loved her, and never more than at this moment when she had thrown aside all reserves and had let him see her soul.

She drew the little book from her pocket. It was bound in red leather, with a thin black cross on the cover. His own was in khaki.

"I want something else," he said, as he held the book in his hand.

"What?"

"This." He touched a lock of hair which lay against her cheek. "A bit of it—of you—"

A band of *poilus*—marching through the street, saw him cut it off. But they did not laugh. They had great respect for a thing like that—and it happened every day—when men went away from their women.

They separated with a promise of perhaps a reunion in Paris, if he could get leave and if she could be spared. Then she drove away through the mud in her little car, and he went back to his men.

Thus they were swept apart by that tide of war which threatened to submerge the world.

Drusilla, arriving late at her *baraque*, made tea, and sat by an infinitesimal stove.

She found herself alone, for the other women were away on various errands. She uncovered all the glory of her lovely hair, and in her little mirror surveyed pensively the ragged lock over her left ear.

A man like that, oh, a man like that. What more could a woman ask—than love like that?

Yet even in the midst of her thought of him, came the feeling that she was not predestined for happiness. She must go on riding over rough roads on her errands of mercy. Nothing must interfere with that, not love or matters of personal preference—nothing.

She was very tired. But there was no time for rest. A half dozen kilted Highlanders hailed her through the open door and asked for a song. She gave them "Wee Hoose Amang the Heather—" standing on the step. It was still raining. and they took with them a picture of a girl with glorious uncovered hair, and that cut tell-tale lock against her cheek.

Drusilla watching them go, wondered if she would ever see them again, with their pert caps, the bare knees of them—the strong swing of their bodies.

She stretched her arms above her head. "Oh, oh, I'm tired—"

She went in and poured another cup of tea. She left the door open. Indeed it always stood open that the room might shine its welcome.

Snatching forty winks, she waked to find a woman standing over her—a tall woman in a blue cloak and bonnet, who held in her hand a dripping umbrella.

She felt that she still dreamed. "It can't be Hilda Merritt?"

"Yes, it is." Hilda set the umbrella in the wood box. "I knew you were here."

"Who told you?"

"Dr. McKenzie."

"Oh, you are with him, then?"

"He won't have me. That's why I came to you."

"To me?"

"Yes. I want you to tell him not to—turn me away."

Drusilla showed her bewilderment. "But, surely nothing that I could say would have more weight with him than your own arguments."

"You are his kind. He'd listen. Things that you say count with him."

"I don't know what you mean."

"Well, I've offended him. And he won't forgive me. Not even for the sake of the work. And I'm a good nurse, Miss Gray. But he's as hard as nails. And—and he sent me away."

"Oh, I'm sorry," Drusilla said gently. Hilda was a dark figure of tragedy, as she sat there statuesquely in her blue cloak.

"You could make him see how foolish it is to refuse to have a good worker; men may die whom I could save. He thinks that—those things don't mean anything to me, that I am arguing from a personal standpoint. He wouldn't think that of you."

"I'll do what I can, of course," Drusilla said slowly. She was not sure that she wanted to get into it, but she was sorry for Hilda.

"Won't you have a cup of tea," she said impulsively, "and take off your cloak? I am afraid I haven't seemed a bit hospitable. I was so surprised."

Hilda gave a little laugh. "I'm not used to such courtesies—so I didn't miss it. But I should like the tea, and something to eat with it. I left Dr. McKenzie's hospital early this morning, and I haven't eaten since—I didn't want anything to eat—"

She watched Drusilla curiously as she set forth the food. "It must seem strange to you to live in a room like this."

"I like it."

"But you have always had such an easy life, Miss Gray."

Drusilla smiled. "It may have looked easy to you. But I give you my word that keeping up with the social game is harder than this."

"You say that," Hilda told her crisply, "not because it's true, but because it sounds true. Do you mean to tell me that you like to be muddy and dirty and live in a place like this?"

"Yes, I like it." Something flamed in the back Of Drusilla's eyes. "I like it because it means something, and the other didn't."

"Well, I don't like it," Hilda stated. "But nursing is all I am fit for. I came over with a lot of other nurses, and they tell me at the hospital I am the best of the lot—and in war times you can't afford to miss the experience. But then I am used to a hard life, and you are not."

"Neither are the men in the trenches used to it. That's the standard I apply to myself—for every hard thing I am doing, it is ten times harder for them. I wish all the people at home could see how wonderful they are."

"That's Jean McKenzie's word—wonderful. Everything was wonderful, and now she has married Derry Drake."

"Yes, she has married Derry," Drusilla stood staring into the little round stove.

She roused herself presently. "I call them Babes in the Wood. They seem so young, and yet Derry isn't really young—it is only that there's such a radiant air about him."

Hilda's bitterness broke forth. "Why shouldn't he be radiant? Life has given him everything. It has given her everything; in a way it has given you everything. I am the one who goes without—it looks as if I should always go without the things I want."

"Don't think that," Drusilla said in her pleasant fashion. "Nobody is set apart—and some day you will see it. Did you know that Derry may be over now at any time, and that Jean is to stay with the General?"

"Yes," Hilda moved restlessly. There came to her a vision of the big house, of the shadowed room, of the room beyond, and of herself in a tiara, with ermine on her cloak.

What a dream it had been, and she had waked to this!

She rose. "If Dr. McKenzie doesn't take me back he may be sorry. Will you write to him?"

"I shall see him Saturday—in Paris. I have promised to dine with him. Captain Hewes is coming, too, if he can."

Hilda, going away in the rain, dwelt moodily on Drusilla's opportunities. If only she, too, might dine in Paris with men like Dr. McKenzie and Captain Hewes. There were indeed, men who might ask her to dine with them, but not as Drusilla had been asked, as an equal and as a friend.

The way was long, the road was muddy. There was not much to look towards at the end. It was not that she minded the dreadfulness of sights and sounds—she had been too much in hospitals for that. But she hated the ugliness, the roughness, the grinding toil.

Yet had she been with Dr. McKenzie, she would have toiled gladly for him. There would have been the sight of his crinkled copper head, the sound of his voice, his teasing laugh to sustain her. And now it was Drusilla who would see him, who would sit with him at the table, who would tempt his teasing laugh.

Well—if he didn't take her back, he would be sorry. There had been a patient in the hospital who in his delirium had whispered things. When he had come to himself, she had told him calmly, "You are a spy." He had not whitened, but had measured her with a glance. "Help me and you shall see the Emperor. There will be nothing too good for you."

Drusilla, after Hilda's departure, sat by her little stove and thought it over. She divined something which did not appear on the surface. She was glad that she had promised to plead Hilda's cause. The woman's face haunted her.

And now the other workers who shared Drusilla's shack returned, bringing news of many wounded and on the way. Then came the darkness of the night, the long line of ambulances, the ghastly procession that trailed behind.

And all through the night Drusilla sang to men who rested for a moment on their weary way, out of the shadows came eager voices asking for this song and that—then they would pass on, and she would throw herself down for a little sleep, to rouse again and lift her voice, while the other women poured the coffee.

She was hoarse in the morning, and white with fatigue, but when one of the women said, "You can't keep this up, Drusilla, you can't stand it," she smiled. "They stand it is the trenches, and some of them are so tired."

She was as fresh as paint, however, on Saturday, when she met Dr. McKenzie in Paris. "I have had two hot baths, and all my clothes are starched and ironed and fluted by an adorable Frenchwoman who opened her house for me," she announced as she sat down with him at a corner table. "I never wore fluted things before, but you can't imagine how civilizing it is after you've been letting yourself down."

The Doctor was tired, and he looked it. "No one has starched and fluted me."

"Poor man. I'm glad you ran away from it all for a minute with me. Captain Hewes thought he might be able to come. But I haven't heard from him, have you?"

"No. But he may blow in at any moment. It seems queer, doesn't it, Drusilla, that you and I should be over here with all the rest of them left behind."

She hesitated, then brought it out without prelude. "Hilda came to see me."

"To see you? Why?"

"She is broken-hearted because you won't let her work with you."

"I told her I could not. And she hasn't any heart to break."

"I wonder if you'd mind," Drusilla ventured, "telling me what's the matter."

"A rather squalid story," but he told it. "She wanted to marry the General."

"Poor thing."

He glanced at her in surprise. "Then you defend her?"

"Oh, no—no. But think of having to marry to get the—the fleshpots, and to miss all of the real meanings. I talked to Hilda for a long time, and somehow before she left she made me feel sorry. She wants so much that she will never have. And she will grow hard and bitter because life isn't giving her all that she demands."

"Did she ask you to plead her cause?"

"Yes," frankly. "She feels that you ought to give her another chance."

He ran his fingers through his crinkled hair. "I don't want her. I'm afraid of her."

"Afraid?"

"She sees the worst that is in me, and brings it to the surface. And when I protest, she laughs and insists that I don't know myself. That I am a sort of Dr. Jekyll, with the Mr. Hyde part of me asleep—"

"And you let her scare you like that?"

He nodded. "Every man has a weak spot, and mine is wanting the world to think well of me."

"Think well of yourself. What would Jean say if she heard you talking like this?"

"Jean?" she was startled by the breaking up of his face into deep lines of trouble. "Do you know what she is doing, Drusilla? She is staying in that great old house playing daughter to the General."

"Marion says the General's affection for her is touching—he doesn't want her out of his sight."

"And because he doesn't want her out of his sight, she must stay a prisoner. I say that he hasn't done anything to deserve such devotion, Drusilla. He hasn't done anything to deserve it."

"You are jealous."

"No. It isn't that. Though I'll confess that something pulls at my heart when I think of it—. But I want her to be happy."

"I think she is happy. Life is giving her the hard things—but you and I would not be without the—hard things; we have reached out our hands for them, because the world needs us.

Are you going to deny your daughter that?"

"Oh, I suppose not. But I hate it. Women ought to be happy—care-free, not shut up in sick rooms or running around in the rain."

"Oh, you men, how little you know what makes a woman happy." She stopped, and half rose from her chair. "Captain Hewes is coming."

"I don't know that I am glad, Drusilla," the Doctor turned to survey the beaming officer, "for now you won't have eyes or ears for me."

But she was glad.

While the Captain held her hand in his as if he would never let her go, she told him about being fluted and starched. "I don't look as dishevelled as I did the other day."

"You looked beautiful the other day," he assured her with fervor, "but this is better, because you are rested and some of the sadness has gone out of your eyes."

Dr. McKenzie watched them enviously, "I realize," he reminded them, "that I am the fifth wheel, or any other superfluous thing, but you can't get rid of me. I am homesick—somebody's got to cheer me up."

"We don't want to get rid of you," Drusilla told him, smiling.

But he knew that her loveliness was all for the Captain. She was lighted up by the presence of her betrothed, made exquisite, softer, more womanly. Love had come slowly to Drusilla, but it had come at last.

When the Doctor left them, he was in a daze of loneliness. He wanted Jean, he wanted sympathy, understanding, good-comradeship.

For just one little moment temptation assailed him. There was of course, Hilda. She would bring with her the atmosphere of familiar things which he craved. There would be the easy give and take of speech which was such a relief after his professional manner, there would be his own teasing sense of how much she wanted, and of how little he had to give. There would be, too, the stimulus to his vanity.

A broken-hearted Hilda, Drusilla had said. There was something provocative in the situation—elements of drama. Why not?

He thought about it that night when once more back at his work he and his head nurse discussed a case of shell shock—a pitiful case of fear, loss of memory, complete prostration.

The nurse was a plain little thing, very competent, very quiet. She was, perhaps, no more competent than Hilda in the mechanics of her profession, but she had qualities which Hilda lacked. She was not very young, and there were younger nurses under her. Yet in spite of her plainness and quietness, she wielded an influence which was remarkable. The whole hospital force was feeling the effect of that influence. It was as if every nurse had in some rather high and special way dedicated herself—as nuns might to the conventual life, or sisters of charity to the service of the poor. There was indeed a heroic aspect to it, a spiritual aspect, and this plain little woman was setting the pace.

And Hilda, coming in, would spoil it all. Oh, he knew how she would spoil it. With her mocking laugh, her warped judgments, her skeptical point of view.

No, he did not want Hilda. The best in him did not want her, and please God, he was giving his best to this cause. However he might fail in other things, he would not fail in his high duty towards the men who came out of battle shattered and broken, holding up their hands to him for help.

"I am going to let Miss Shelby have the case," the plain little nurse was saying, "when he begins to come back. She will give him what he needs. She is so strong and young, so sure of the eternal rightness of things—and she's got to make him sure."

The Doctor nodded. "Some of us are not sure—"

She agreed gravely. "But we are learning to be sure, aren't we, over here? Don't you feel that all the things you have ever done are little compared to this? That men and women are better and bigger than you have believed?"

"If anyone could make me feel it," he said, "it would be you."

When she had gone, he wrote letters.

He wrote to Jean—he wrote every day to Jean.

He wrote to Hilda.

"You are splendidly fitted for just the thing that you are doing. Men come and go and you care for their wounds. But we have to care here for more than men's bodies, we care for their minds and souls—we piece them together, as it were. And we need women who believe that God's in his Heaven. And you don't believe it, Hilda. I fancy that you see in every man his particular devil, and like to lure it out for him to look at—"

He stopped there. He could see her reading what he had written. She would laugh a little, and write back:

"Are you any better than I? If I am too black to herd with the white sheep, what of you; aren't you tarred with the same brush—?"

He tore up the letter and sent a brief note. Why explain what he was feeling to Hilda? She was of those who would never know nor understand.

And he felt the need tonight of understanding—of sympathy.

And so he wrote to Emily.

CHAPTER XXV

WHITE VIOLETS

Bruce McKenzie's letter arriving in due time at the Toy Shop, found Emily very busy. There were many women to be instructed how to do things with gauze and muslin and cotton, so she tucked the letter in her apron pocket. But all day her mind went to it, as a feast to be deferred until the time came to enjoy it.

In the afternoon Ulrich Stoelle arrived, bearing the inevitable tissue paper parcel.

"Do you know what day it is?" he asked.

"Thursday."

"There are always Thursdays. But this is a special Thursday."

"Is it?"

"And you ask me like that? It is a Thursday for valentines."

"Of course. But how could you expect me to remember? Nobody ever sends me valentines."

"My father has sent you one." It was a heart-shaped basket of pink roses; "but mine I couldn't bring. You must come and see it. Will you dine with us tonight?"

"Oh, I am so busy."

"You are not too busy for that. Let your little Jean take charge."

Jean, all in white with her white veil and red crosses was more than ever like a little nun. She was remote, too, like a nun, wrapped not in the contemplation of her religion, but of her love.

She still made toys, and the proceeds of the sale of Lovely Dreams had been contributed by herself and Emily for Red Cross purposes. There were rows and rows of the fantastic creatures behind glass doors on the shelves, and for Valentine's Day Jean had carved and painted pale doves which carried in their beaks rosy hearts and golden arrows and whose wings were outspread—.

There were also on the shelves the white plush elephants which Franz Stoelle and his friends had made, and which were, too, being sold to swell the Red Cross fund.

Thus had the Toy Shop come into its own. "I have enough to live on," Emily had said, "at least for a while, and I am taking no more chances for future living, than the men who give up everything to fight."

So enlisted in this cause of mercy as men had enlisted in the cause of war, Miss Emily led where others followed, and the old patriarch of all the white elephants, who had been born in a country of blood and iron, looked down on women working to heal the wounds which his country had made.

"Let your little Jean look after things," Ulrich repeated.

"Do you mind, my dear?"

"Mind what, Emily—?"

"If I go with Mr. Stoelle—to see his father about the—toys."

"Darling—no;" Jean kissed her. "I don't mind in the least, and the ride will do you good."

"But you are not going to see my father about toys," Ulrich told her, twinkling, as he followed her to the back of the shop.

"Do you think I was going to tell her that?"

She put on her coat and hat and off she went with Ulrich, leaving still unread in the pocket of the big apron the letter which Bruce McKenzie had written her.

All the way out Ulrich was rather silent. It was not, however, the silence of moodiness or dullness, it was rather as if he wanted to hear her speak. It was, indeed, a responsive, stimulating silence, and she glowed under his glance.

It seemed to her, as she talked, that these adventures with Ulrich Stoelle were in every way the most splendid thing that had happened to her. They were always unexpected, and they were packed to the brim with pleasure of a rare quality.

When they reached their destination, Ulrich took her at once to the hothouses. As they passed down the fragrant aisles, she found that all the men and gone, their day's work over; only she and Ulrich were under the great glass roof.

"Anton comes back later," Ulrich explained, "but at this hour the houses are empty, and dinner will not be ready for as hour. We have it all to ourselves, Emily."

Her name, spoken with so much ease, without a sign of self-consciousness, startled her. Her inquiring glance showed her that he was utterly unaware that he had spoken it. Her breath came quickly.

The birds sang and the stream sang, and suddenly her heart

began to sing.

You see it had been so many years since Emily had known romance;—indeed, she had never known it—there had always been, in her mother's time, her sense of the proper thing, and her sense of duty, and her sense of making the best of things— and now for the first time in her life there was no make- believe. This was a world of realities, with Ulrich leading the way, his hands gathering flowers for her.

He stopped at last at the entrance of a sort of grotto where great ferns towered—at their feet was a bed of white violets.

"You see," he said, "I could not bring it. I came here this morning to pick the violets—for you—to let them say, 'I love you'—"

Even the birds seemed silent, and the little stream!

"And suddenly they spoke to me, 'Let her see us here, where you have so often thought of her. Tell her here that you love her—'

"How much I love you," and now she found her hands in his, "I cannot tell you. It seems to me that the thought of you as my wife is so exquisite that I cannot believe it will ever come to pass. And I have so little to offer you. Even my name is hated because it is a German name, and my old house is German, and my father—

"But my heart's blood is for America. You know that, and so I have dared to ask it, not that you will love me now, but that you may come to think of loving me, so that some day you will care a little."

The birds were singing madly, the streams were shouting— Emily was trembling. Nobody had ever wanted her like this— nobody had ever made her feel so young and lovely and— wanted—. She had had a proposal or two, but there had been always the sense that she had been chosen for certain staid and sensible qualities; there had been nothing in it of red blood and rapture.

"If you should come to us, to me and my father, you would be a queen on a throne. If you could love me just a little in return—"

She could not answer, she just stood looking up at him, and suddenly his arms went around her. "Tell me, beloved."

* * * * * *

An hour later they went in to his father, and after that Emily was lifted up on the wings of an enthusiasm which left her breathless, but beatified. "I knew when I first saw you what we desired," said the old man, "and my son knew. All that I have is yours both now and afterwards—"

Dinner was a candle-lighted feast, with heart-shaped ices at the end.

"How sure you were," Emily told her lover, smiling.

"I was not sure. But I set the stage for success. It was only thus that I kept up my courage. There were so many chances that the curtain might drop on darkness—," his hand went over hers. "If it had been that way, I should have let the ices melt and the violets die—."

After dinner they went over the house. "Why should we wait," Ulrich had said, "you and I? There is nothing to wait for. Tell me what you want changed in this old house, and then come to it, and to my heart."

It was, she found, such a funny old place. It had been furnished by men, and by German men at that. There was heaviness and stuffiness, and all the bric-a-brac was fat and puffy, and all the pictures were highly-colored, with the women in them blonde and buxom, and the men blond and bold—.

But Ulrich's room was not stuffy or heavy. The windows were wide open, and the walls were white, and the cover on the canopy bed was white, and there were two pictures, one of Lincoln and one of Washington, and that was all.

"And when I have your picture, it will be perfect," he told her. "Where I can see you when I wake, and pray to you before I go to sleep."

"But why," she probed daringly, "do you want my picture?"

"Because you are so—beautiful—"

It was not to be wondered that such worship went to Miss Emily's head. She slipped out of the dried sheath of the years which had saddened and aged her, and emerged lovely as a flower over which the winter has passed and which blooms again.

"I don't want to change anything," Emily told her lover as they went downstairs, "at least not very much. I shall keep all of the lovely old carved things—with the fat cupids."

As she lay awake that night, reviewing it all, she thought suddenly of Bruce McKenzie's letter in her apron pocket. The apron was in the Toy Shop, and it was not therefore until the next morning that she read the letter.

In it Dr. McKenzie asked her to marry him.

"I should like to think that when I come back, you will be waiting for me, Emily. I am a very lonely man. I want someone who will sympathize and understand. I want someone who will love Jean, and who will hold me to the best that is in me, and you can do that, Emily; you have always done it."

It was a rather touching letter, and she felt its appeal strongly. Indeed, so stern was her sense of self-sacrifice, that she had an almost guilty feeling when she thought of Ulrich. If he had not come into her life at the psychological moment, she might have given herself to Bruce McKenzie.

But the letter had come too late. Oh, how glad she was that she had left it in her apron pocket!

She answered it that night.

"I am going to be very frank with you, Bruce, because in being frank with you I shall be frank with myself. If Ulrich Stoelle had not come into my life, I should probably have thought I cared for you. Even now when I am saying 'no,' I realize that your charm has always held me, and that the prospect of a future by your pleasant fireside holds many attractions. But since you left Washington, something has happened which I never expected, and all of my preconceived ideas of myself have been overturned. Bruce, I am no longer the Emily you have known—a little staid, gray-haired, with pretty hands, but with nothing else very pretty about her; a lady who would, perhaps, fill gracefully, a position for which her aristocratic nose fits her. I am no longer the Emily of the Toy Shop, wearing spectacles on a black ribbon, eating her lunches wherever she can get them. No, I am an Emily who is young and beautiful, a sort of fairy-tale Princess, an Emily who, if she wishes, shall sit on a cushion and sew a fine seam, but who doesn't wish it because she hates to sew, and would much rather work in her silver-bell-and-cockle shell garden—oh, such a wonderful garden as it is!

"And I am all this, Bruce, I am young and beautiful and all the rest, because I am seeing myself through the eyes of my lover.

"He is Ulrich Stoelle, as I have said, and you mustn't think because his name is German that he is to be cast into outer darkness. He is as American as you with your Scotch blood, or as I with my English blood. And he is as loyal as any of us. He is too old to be accepted for service, but he is giving time and money to the cause.

"And he loves me rapturously, radiantly, romantically. He doesn't want me as a cushion for his tired head, he doesn't want me because he thinks it would be an act of altruism to provide a haven for me in my old age, he wants me because he thinks I am the most remarkable woman in the whole wide world, and that he is the most fortunate man to have won me.

"And you don't feel that way about it, Bruce. You know that I am not beautiful, there is no glamour in your love for me. You know that I am not wonderful, or a fairy Princess—. And you are right and he is wrong. But it is his wrongness which makes me love him. Because every woman wants to be beautiful to her lover, and to feel that she is much desired.

"You will ask why I am telling you all this. Well, there was one sentence in your letter which called it forth. You say that you want me because I will hold you to the best that is in you.

"Oh, Bruce, what would you gain if I held you? Wouldn't there be moments when in spite of me you would swing back to women like Hilda? You are big and fine, but you are spoiled by feminine worship—it is a temptation which assails clergymen and doctors—who have, as it were, many women at their feet.

"Does that sound harsh? I don't mean it that way. I only want you to come into your own. And if you ever marry I want you to find some woman you can love as you loved your wife, someone who will touch your imagination, set you on fire with dreams, and I could never do it.

"Yet even as I finish this letter, I am tempted to tear it up and tell you only of my real appreciation of the honor you have conferred upon me in asking me to be your wife. I know that you are offering me more in many ways than Ulrich Stoelle. I don't like his name, because something rises up in me against

Teuton blood and Teuton nomenclature. But he loves me, and you do not, and because of his love for me and mine for him, everything else seems too small to consider.

"Oh, you'd laugh at his house, Bruce, but I love even the fat angels that are carved on everything from the mahogany chests to the soup tureens. It is all like some old fairy-tale. I shall make few changes; it seems such a perfect setting for Ulrich and his busy old gnome of a father.

"When you get this, pray for my happiness. Oh, I do want to be happy. I have made the best of things, but there has been much more of gray than rose-color, and now as I turn my face to the setting sun, I am seeing—loveliness and light—"

She read it over and sealed it and sent it away. It was several weeks before it reached Doctor McKenzie. He was very busy, for the spring drive of the Germans had begun, and shattered men were coming to him faster than he could handle them. But he found time at last to read it, and when he laid it down he sat quite still from the shock of it.

And the next time he saw Drusilla he said to her, "Emily Bridges is going to be married, and she is not going to marry me."

"I am glad of it," Drusilla told him.

"My dear girl, why?"

"Because you don't love her, and you never did."

CHAPTER XXVI

THE HOPE OF THE WORLD

The great spring drive of the Germans brought headlines to the papers which men and women in America read with dread, and scoffed at when they talked it over.

"They'll never get to Paris," were the words on their lips, but in their hearts they were asking, "Will they——?"

Easter came at the end of March, and Good Friday found Jean working very early in the morning on fawn-colored rabbits with yellow ears. She worked in her bedroom because it was warmed by a feeble wood fire, and Teddy came up to watch her.

"The yellow in their ears is the sun shining through," Jean told him. "We used to see them in the country on the path in front of the house, and the light from the west made their ears look like tiny electric bulbs."

Margaret-Mary entranced by one small bunny with a splash of white for a cotton tail, sang, "Pitty sing, pitty sing."

"They don't weally lay eggs, do they?" Teddy ventured.

"I wouldn't ask such questions if I were you, Teddy."

"Why not?"

"Because you might find out that they didn't lay eggs, and then you'd feel terribly disappointed."

"Well, isn't it better to know?"

Jean shook her head. "I'm not sure—it's nice to think that they do lay eggs—blue ones and red ones and those lovely purple ones, isn't it?"

"Yes."

"And if they don't lay them, who does?"

"Hens," said Teddy, rather unexpectedly, "and the rab-yits steal them."

"Who told you that?"

"Hodgson. And she says that she ties them up in rags and the colors come off on the eggs."

"Well, I wouldn't listen to Hodgson."

"Why not? I like to listen."

"Because she hasn't any imagination."

"What's 'magination?"

They were getting in very deep. Jean gave it up. "Ask your mother, Teddy."

So Teddy sought his unfailing source of information. "What's 'magination, Mother."

"It is seeing things, Teddy, with your mind instead of your eyes. When I tell you about the poor little children in France who haven't any food or any clothes except what the Red Cross gives them, you don't really see them with your eyes, but your mind sees them, and their cold little hands, and their sad little faces—"

"Yes." He considered that for a while, then swept on to the things over which his childish brain puzzled.

"Mother, if the Germans get to Paris what will happen?"

He saw the horror in her face.

"Do you hate the Germans, Mother?"

"My darling, don't ask me."

After he had gone downstairs, Margaret got out her prayer-book, and read the prayers for the day.

"Oh, merciful God, who hast made all men and hatest nothing that thou hast made, nor desirest the death of a sinner, but rather that he should be converted and live, have mercy on all Jews, Turks, infidels and heretics, and take from them all ignorance, hardness of heart, and contempt of Thy word, and so fetch them home, blessed Lord, to Thy flock, that they may be saved—"

She shut the book. No, she could not go on. She did not love her enemies. She was not in the least sure that she wanted the Germans to be saved!

On Easter morning, however, Teddy was instructed to pray for his enemies. "We mustn't have hate in our hearts."

"Why mustn't we, Mother?"

"Well, Father wouldn't want it. We hate the evil they do, but we must pray that they will be shown their wickedness and repent."

"If they re-pyent will they stop fighting?"

"My dearest, yes."

"How would they stop?"

Jean, who was ready for church and waiting, warned, "You'd better not try to give an answer to that, Margaret, there isn't any."

Teddy ignored her. "How would they stop, Mother?"

"Well, they'd just stop, dear—"

"Would they say they were sorry?"

Would William of Prussia ever be sorry?

"Can God stop it, Mother?"

Margaret wrenched her mind away from the picture which his words had painted for her, the Kaiser on his knees! *Miserere mei, Deus—*

With quick breath, "Yes, dear."

"Then why doesn't He stop it, Mother?"

Why? Why? Why? Older voices were asking that question in agony.

"He will do it in His own good time, dearest. Perhaps the world has a lesson to learn."

With Teddy walking ahead with nurse, Jean proclaimed to Margaret, "I shan't pray for them."

"I know how you feel."

"Shall you?"

"Yes," desperately, "I must."

"Why must you?"

"Because of—Win," Margaret said simply. In her widow's black, with her veil giving her height and dignity, she had never been more beautiful. "Because of Win, I must. There are wives in Germany who suffer as I suffer—who are not to blame. There are children, like my children, asking the same questions—. This drive has seemed to me like the slaughter of sheep, with a great Wolf behind them, a Wolf without mercy, sending them down to destruction, to—death—"

"And the Wolf—?"

Margaret raised her hand and let it drop, "God knows."

And now soldiers were being rushed overseas. Trains swept across the land loaded with men who gazed wistfully at the peaceful towns as they passed through, or chafed impotently when, imprisoned in day coaches, they were side-tracked outside of great cities.

And on the battle line those droves and droves of gray sheep were driven down and down—to death—by the Wolf.

The war was coming closer to America. A look of care settled on the faces of men and women who had, hitherto, taken things lightly. Fathers, who had been very sure that the war would end before their sons should go to France, faced the fact that the end was not in sight, and that the war would take its toll of the youth of America. Mothers, who had not been sure of anything, but had hidden their fears in their hearts, stopped reading the daily papers. Wives, who had looked upon the camp experiences of their husbands as a rather great adventure, knew now that there might be a greater adventure with a Dark Angel. The tram-sheds in great cities were crowded with anxious relatives who watched the troops go through, clutching at the hope of a last glimpse of a beloved face, a few precious moments in which to say farewell.

Yes, the war was coming near!

Derry wrote that he might go at any moment, but hoped for a short furlough. It was on this hope that Jean lived. She worked tirelessly, making the much-needed surgical dressings. When Emily tried to get her to rest, Jean would shake her head.

"Darling, I must. They are bringing the wounded over."

"But you mustn't get too tired."

"I want to be tired. So that I can sleep."

She was finding it hard to sleep. Often she rose and wrote in her memory book, which was becoming in a sense a diary because she confided to its pages the things she dared not say to Derry. Some day, perhaps, she might show him what she had written. But that would be when the war was over, and Derry had come back safe and sound. Until then she would have to smile in her letters, and she did not always feel like smiling!

But that was what Derry called them, "Smiling letters!"

"They smile up at me every morning, Jean."

So she wrote to him bravely, cheerfully, of her busy days, of how she missed him, of her love and longing, but not a word did she say of her world as it really was.

But there was no laughter in the things she said to the old memory book.

"I don't like big houses—not houses like this, with grinning porcelain Chinese gods at every turn of the hall, and gold dragons on the bed-posts. There are six of us here besides the servants, yet we are like dwarfs in a giant palace. Perhaps if we had the usual fires it wouldn't seem quite so forlorn. But the china in the cabinets is so cold—and the ceilings are so high—and the marble floors—."

"Perhaps if everyone were happy it would be different. But only Emily is happy. And I don't see how she can be. She is going to marry a Hun! Of course, he isn't really, and he'd be a darling dear if it weren't for his German name, and his German blood, and the German things he has in his house. But Emily says she loves his house, that it speaks to her of a different Germany—of the sweet old gay Germany that waltzed and sang and loved simple things. It seems so funny to think of Emily in love—she's so much older than people are usually when they are engaged and married."

"But Emily is the only happy one, except the children, and I sometimes think that even they have the shadow on them of the dreadful things that are happening. Margaret-Mary tries to knit, and tires her stubby little fingers with the big needles, and Teddy, poor chap, seems to feel that he must be the man of the family and take his father's place, and he is pathetically careful of his mother."

"I wonder if Margaret feels as I do about it all? She is so sweet and smiling—and yet I know how her heart weeps, and I know how she longs for her own house and her own hearth and her own husband—"

"Oh, when my Derry comes back safe and sound—and he will come back safe, I shall say it over and over to myself until I make it true—when Derry comes back, we'll build a cottage, with windows that look out on trees and a garden—and there'll be cozy little rooms, and we'll take Polly Ann and Muffin—and live happy ever after—"

"I wonder how father stands it to be always with people who are sick? I never knew what it meant until now. The General is an old dear—but sometimes when I sit in that queer room of his with its lacquer and gold and see him in his gorgeous dressing gown, I feel afraid. It is rather dreadful to think that he was once young and strong like Derry, and that he will never be young and strong again."

"Oh, I want the war to end—I want Derry, and sunshine and well people. It seems a hundred years since I did anything just for the fun of doing it. It seems a million years since Daddy and I drove downtown together and drank chocolate sodas—"

"But then nobody is drinking chocolate sodas—at least no one is doing it light-heartedly. You can't be light-hearted when the person you love best in the world is going to war. You can be brave, and you can make your lips laugh, but you can't make your heart laugh—you can't—you can't—"

"I talk a great deal to the women who come to Emily's Toy Shop. And I am finding out that some of those that seem fluffy-minded are really very much in earnest. There is one little blonde, who always wears white silk and chiffon, she looks as if she had just stepped from the stage. And at first I simply scorned her. I felt that she would be the kind to leave ravellings in her wipes, and things like that. But she doesn't leave a ravelling. She works slowly, but she does her work well—. But now and then her hands tremble and the tears fall; and the other day I went and sat down beside her and I found out that her husband is flying in France, and that her two brothers are at the front—. And one of them is among the missing; he may be a prisoner and he may be dead—. And she is trying to do her bit and be brave. And now I don't care if she does wear her earlocks outside of her veil and load her hands with diamonds—she's a dear—and a darling. But she's scared just as I am—and as Mary Connolly is, and as all the women are, though they don't show it—. I wonder if Joan of Arc was afraid—in her heart as the rest of us are? Perhaps she wasn't, because she was in the thick of it herself, and we aren't. Perhaps if we were where we could see it and have the excitement of it all, we should lose our fear. "

"But when women tell me that the women have the worst of it—that they must sit at home and weep and wait, I don't believe it. We suffer—of course, and there's the thought of it all like a bad dream, and when we love our loved ones—it is heartbreak. But the men suffer, daily, in all the little things. The thirst and the vermin, and the cold and wet—and the noise—and the frightfulness. And they grow tired and hungry and homesick,—and death is on every side of them, and horror—. Some of the women who come to the shop sentimentalize a lot. One woman recited, 'Break, break, break—, the other day, and the rest of them cried into the gauze, *cried for themselves*, if you please: 'For men must work and women must weep.' And then my little blonde told them what she thought of them. Her name is 'Maisie,' wouldn't you know a girl like that would be called 'Maisie'?"

"'If you think,' she said, 'that you suffer—what in God's name will you think before the war is over? It hasn't touched you. You won't know what suffering means until your men begin to come home. You talk about hardships; not one of you has gone hungry yet—and the men over there may be cut off at any moment from food supplies, and they are always at the mercy of the camp cooks, who may or may not give them things that they can eat. And they lie out under the stars with their wounds, and if any of you has a finger ache, you go to bed with hot water bottles and are coddled and cared for. But our boys,—there isn't anyone to coddle them—they have to stick it out. And we've got to stick it out—and not be sorry for ourselves. Oh, why should we be sorry for ourselves!' The tears were streaming down her cheeks when she finished, and a gray-haired woman who had wept with the others got up and came over to her. 'My dear,' she said, 'I shall never pity myself again. My two sons are over there, and I've been thinking how much I have given. But they have given their young lives, their futures—their bodies, to be broken—' And then standing right in the middle of the Toy Shop that mother prayed for her sons, and for the sons of other women, and for the husbands and lovers, and that the women might be brave."

"Oh, it was wonderful"—as she stood there like a white-veiled prophetess, praying.

"Yet a year ago she would have died rather than pray in public. She is a conservative, aristocratic woman, the kind that doesn't wear rings or try to be picturesque—and she has always kept her feelings to herself, and said her prayers to herself—or in church, but never in all her life has she been so fine as she was the other day praying in the Toy Shop."

"Yet in a way I am sorry for myself. Not for me as I am to-day, but for the Jean of Yesterday, who thought that patriotism was remembering Bunker Hill!"

"Of course in a way it is that—for Bunker Hill and Lexington and Valley Forge are a part of us because our grandfathers were there, and what they felt and did is a part of our feeling and doing."

"I have always thought of those old days as a sort of picture—the embattled farmers in their shirt-sleeves and with their hair blowing, and the Midnight Ride, and the lantern in the old North Church—and the Spirit of '76. And it was the same with the Civil War; there was always the vision of cavalry sweeping up and down slopes as they do in the movies, and of the bugles calling, and bands playing 'Marching through Georgia' or 'Dixie' as the case might be—and flags flying—isn't it glorious to think that the men in gray are singing to-day, 'The Star Spangled Banner' with the rest of us?"

"But my thoughts never had anything to do with money, though I suppose people gave it then, as they are giving now. But you can't paint pictures of men and women making out checks, and children putting thrift stamps in little books, so I suppose that in future the heroes and heroines of the emptied pocket-books will go down unsung—"

"It isn't a bit picturesque to give until it hurts, but it helps a lot. I saw Sarah Bernhardt the other day in a wonderful little play where she's a French boy, who dies in the end—and she dies, exquisitely, with the flag of France in her arms—the faded, lovely flag—I shall never forget. The tears ran down my cheeks so that I couldn't see, but her voice, so faint and clear, still rings in my ears—"

"If she had died clutching a Liberty Bond or wearing a Red Cross button, it would have seemed like burlesque. Yet there are men and women who are going without bread and butter to buy Liberty Bonds, and who are buying them not as a safe investment, as rich men buy, but because the boys need the money. And there ought to be poems written and statues erected to commemorate some of the sacrifices for the sake of the Red Cross."

"Yet I think that, in a way, we have not emphasized enough the picturesque quality of this war, not on this side. They do it in France—they worship their great flyers, their great generals, their crack regiments, everything has a personality, they are tender with their shattered cathedrals as if something human had been hurt, and the result is a quickening on the part of every individual, a flaming patriotism which as yet we have not felt. We don't worship anything, we don't all of us know the words of 'The Star Spangled Banner'; fancy a Frenchman not knowing the words of the 'Marseillaise' or an Englishman forgetting 'God Save the King.' We don't shout and sing enough, we don't cry enough, we don t feel enough—and that's all there is to it. If we were hot for the triumph of democracy, there would be no chance of victory for the Hun. Perhaps as the war comes nearer, we shall feel more, and every day it is coming nearer—"

It was very near, indeed. Thousands of those gray sheep were lying dead on the plains of Picardy—the Allies fought with their backs to the wall—Americans who had swaggered, secure in the prowess of Uncle Sam, swaggered no longer, and pondered on the parable of the Wise and Foolish Virgins.

Slowly the nation waked to what was before it. In America now lay the hope of the world. The Wolf must be trapped, the sheep saved in spite of themselves, those poor sheep, driven blindly to slaughter.

The General was not quite sure that they were sheep, or that they were being driven. He held, rather, that they knew what they were about—and were not to be pitied.

Teddy, considering this gravely, went back to previous meditations, and asked if he prayed for his enemies.

"Bless my soul," said the old gentleman, "why should I?"

"Well, Mother says we must, and then some day they'll stop and say they are sorry—"

The General chuckled, "Your mother is optimistic."

"What's 'nopt'mistic?"

"It means always believing that nice things will happen."

"Don't you believe that nice things will happen?"

"Sometimes—"

"Don't you believe that the war will stop?"

"Not until we've thrown the full force of our fighting men into it—at what a sacrifice."

"Can't God make it stop?"

"He can, but He won't, not if He's a God of justice," said this staunch old patriot, "until America has brought them to their knees—"

"Will they say they are sorry then?"

"It won't make very much difference what they say—"

But Teddy, having been brought up to understand the things which belong to an officer and a gentleman, had his own ideas on the subject. "Well, I should think they'd ought to say they were sorry—."

CHAPTER XXVII

MARCHING FEET

The end of April brought much rain; torrents swept down the smooth streets, and the beauty of the carefully kept flower beds in the parks was blurred by the wet.

The General, limping from window to window, chafed. He wanted to get out, to go over the hills and far away; with the coming of the spring the wander-hunger gripped him, and with this restless mood upon him he stormed at Bronson.

"It's a dog's life."

"Yes, sir," said Bronson, dutifully.

"It is dead lonesome, Bronson, and I can't keep Jean tied here all of the time. She is looking pale, don't you think she is looking pale?"

"Yes, sir. I think she misses Mr. Derry."

"Well, she'll miss him a lot more before she gets him back," grimly. "He'll be going over soon—"

"Yes, sir."

"I wish I were going," the old man was wistful. "Think of it, Bronson, to be over there—in the thick of it, playing the

Temple Bailey

game, instead of rotting here—"

It was, of course, the soldier's point of view. Bronson, being hopelessly civilian, did his best to rise to what was expected of him. "You like it then, sir?"

"Like it? It is the only life. We've lost something since men took up the game of business in place of the game of fighting."

"But you see, sir, there's no blood—in business." Bronson tried to put it delicately.

"Isn't there? Why, more men are killed in accidents in factories than are killed in war—murdered by money-greedy employers."

"Oh, sir, not quite that."

"Yes, quite," was the irascible response. "You don't know what you are talking about, Bronson. Read statistics and find out."

"Yes, sir. Will you have your lunch up now, sir?"

"I'll get it over and then you can order the car for me."

"But the rain—?"

"I like rain. I'm not sugar or salt."

Bronson, much perturbed, called up Jean. "The General's going out."

"Oh, but he mustn't, Bronson."

"I can't say 'mustn't' to him, Miss," Bronson reported dismally. "You'd better see what you can do—"

But when Jean arrived, the General was gone!

"We'll drive out through the country," the old man had told his chauffeur, and had settled back among his cushions, his cane by his side, his foot up on the opposite seat to relieve him of the weight.

And it was as he rode that he began to have a strange feeling about that foot which no longer walked or bore him lightly.

How he had marched in those bygone days! He remembered the first time he had tried to keep step with his fellows. The tune had been Yankee Doodle—with a fife and drum—and he was a raw young recruit in his queer blue uniform and visored cap—.

And how eager his feet had been, how strongly they had borne him, spurning the dust of the road—as they would bear him no more—.

There were men who envied him as he swept past them in the rain, men who felt that he had more than his share of wealth and ease, yet he would have made a glad exchange for the feet which took them where they willed.

He came at last to one of his old haunts, a small stone house on the edge of the Canal. From its wide porch he had often watched the slow boats go by, with men and women and children living in worlds bounded by weather-beaten decks. To-day in the rain there was a blur of lilac bushes along the tow path, but no boats were in sight; the Canal was a ruffled gray sheet in the April wind.

Lounging in the low-ceiled front room of the stone house were men of the type with whom he had once foregathered—men not of his class or kind, but interesting because of their very differences—human derelicts who had welcomed him.

But now, for the first time he was not one of them. They eyed his elegances with suspicion—his fur coat, his gloves, his hat— the man whose limousine stood in front of the door was not

Temple Bailey

one of them; they might beg of him, but they would never call him "Brother."

So, because his feet no longer carried him, and he must ride, he found himself cast out, as it were, by outcasts.

He ordered meat and drink for them, gave them money, made a joke or two as he limped among them, yet felt an alien. He watched them wistfully, seeing for the first time their sordidness, seeing what he himself had been, more sordid than any, because of his greater opportunities.

Sitting apart, he judged them, judged himself. If all the world were like these men, what kind of world would it be?

"Why aren't you fellows fighting?" he asked suddenly.

They stared at him. Grumbled. Why should they fight? One of them wept over it, called himself too old—.

But there were young men among them. "For God's sake get out of this—let me help you get out." The General stood up, leaned on his cane. "Look here, I've done a lot of things in my time—things like this—" his arm swept out towards the table, "and now I've only one good foot—the other will never be alive again. But you young chaps, you've got two good feet—to march. Do you know what that means, to march? Left, right, left, right and step out bravely—. Yankee Doodle and your heads up, flags flying? And you sit here like this?"

Two of the men had risen, young and strong. The General's cane pounded—he had their eyes! "Left, right, left, right—all over the world men are marching, and you sit here—"

The years seemed to have dropped from him. His voice rang with a fire that had once drawn men after him. He had led a charge at Gettysburg, and his men had followed!

And these two men would follow him. He saw the dawn of

their resolve in their faces. "There's fine stuff in both of you," he said, "and the country needs you. Isn't it better to fight than to sit here? Get into my car and I'll take you down."

"Aw, what's eatin' you," one of the older men growled. "What game's this? Recruitin'?"

But the young men asked no questions. They came—glad to come. Roused out of a lethargy which had bound them. Waked by a ringing old voice.

The General was rather quiet when he reached home. Jean and Bronson, who had suffered torments, watched him with concerned eyes. And, as if he divined it, he laid his hand over Jean's. "I did a good day's work, my dear. I got two men for the Army, and I'm going to get more—"

And he did get more. He went not only in the rain, but in the warmth of the sun, when the old fruit trees bloomed along the tow path, and the backs of the mules were shining black, and the women came out on deck with their washing.

And always he spoke to the men of marching feet—. Now and then he sang for them in that thin old voice whose thinness was so overlaid by the passion of his patriotism that those who listened found no flaw in it.

> "He has sounded forth the trumpet that has never called retreat, He is sifting forth the hearts of men before his Judgment seat, O be swift my soul to answer him, be jubilant my feet, Our God is marching on—"

There was no faltering now, no fumbled words. With head up, singing—"Be jubilant, my feet—"

Sometimes he took Jean with him, but not always. "There are places that I don't like to have you go, my dear, but those are where I get my men."

At other times when he came out to where she sat in the car there would flash before his eyes the vision of his wife's face, as she, too, had once sat there, waiting—

Sometimes he took the children, and rode with them on a slow-moving barge from one lock to another, with the limousine meeting them at the end.

So he travelled the old paths, innocently, as he might have travelled them throughout the years.

Yet if he thought of those difficult years, he said never a word. He felt, perhaps, that there was nothing to say. He took to himself no credit for the things he was doing. If age and infirmity had brought to him a realization of all that he had missed, he was surely not to be praised for doing that which was, obviously, his duty.

Yet it gave him a new zest for life, and left Jean freer than she had been before. It left her, too, without the fear of him, which had robbed their relationship of all sense of security.

"You see, I never knew," she wrote in her memory book, "what might happen. I had visions of myself going after him in the night as Derry had gone and his mother. I used to dream about it, and dread it."

Yet she had said nothing of her dread to Derry in her smiling letters, and as men think of women, he had thought of her in the sick room as a guardian angel, shining and serene.

* * * * * *

And now, faint and far came to the men in the cantonments the sound of battles across the sea. The bugles calling them each morning seemed to say, "Soon, soon, you will go, you will go, you will go—"

To Derry, listening, it seemed the echo of the fairy trumpets,

"Trutter-a-trutt, trutter-a-trutt, you will go, you will go, you will go—"

It was strange how the thought of it drew him, drew him as even the thoughts of Jean his bride did not draw—. He remembered that years ago he had smiled with a tinge of tolerant sophistication over the old lines:

"I could not love thee, dear, so much, Loved I not honor more—"

Yet here it was, a truth in his own life. A woman meaning more to him than she could ever have meant in times of peace, because he could go forth to fight for her, his life at stake, for her. It was for her, and for other women that his sword was unsheathed.

"If only they could understand it," he wrote to Jean. "You haven't any idea what rotten letters some of the women write. Blaming the men for going over seas. Blaming them for going into it at all. Taking it as a personal offense that their lovers have left them. 'If you had loved me, you couldn't have left me,' was the way one woman put it, and I found a poor fellow mooning over it and asked him what was the matter. 'It isn't a question of what we want to do, it is a question of what we've got to do, if we call ourselves men,' he said. But she couldn't see that, she was measuring her emotions by an inch rule.

"But, thank God, most of the women are the real thing—true as steel and brave. And it is those women that the men worship. It is a masculine trait to want to be a sort of hero in the eyes of the woman you love. When she doesn't look at it that way, your plumes droop!"

And now the bugles rang with a clearer note—not, "You will go, you will go—" but, "Do not wait, do not wait, do not wait."

The cry from abroad was Macedonian. "Come over and help

us!" It was to America that the ghosts of those fighting hordes appealed.

> "Take up our quarrel with the foe,
> To you from falling hands we throw
> The torch—be yours to hold it high.
> If ye break faith with us who die,
> We shall not sleep, though poppies grow
> In Flanders' field—"

Gradually there had grown up in the hearts of simple men a flaming response to that sacred charge. Men whose dreams had never reached beyond a day's frivolity, found springing up in their souls a desire to do some deed to match that of the other fellow who slept "in Flanders field."

"To you from falling hands we throw the torch—be yours to hold it high—," the little man who had measured cloth behind a counter, the boy who had sold papers on the streets, the bank clerk who had bent over his books, the stenographer who had been bound to the wheel of everlasting dictation, were lighted by the radiance of that vision, "to hold it high—."

"Gee, I never used to think," said Tommy Tracy, "that I might have a chance to do a stunt like that."

"Like what?" Derry asked.

Tommy found it a thing rather hard to express. "Well, when you've been just a common sort of chap, to die—for the other fellow—"

So men's bodies grew and their muscles hardened. But their souls grew, too, expanding to the breadth and height of the things which were waiting for them to do across the sea.

And one morning Derry was granted a furlough, and started home. He sent no word ahead of him. He wanted to come upon them unawares. To catch the light that would be on

Jean's face when she looked up and saw him.

There was rain and more rain when at last he arrived in Washington. The trees as his taxi traversed the wide avenues showed clear green, melting into vistas of amethyst and gray. The parks as he passed were starred with the bright yellow and pinks of flowering shrubs. Washington, in spite of the rain, was as lovely as a woman whose color blooms behind a veil.

He came into the great house unannounced, having his key with him. The General was out for a ride, the children with him, Margaret and Emily and Jean away, the servants in the back of the house.

Derry, going up the stairs, two steps at a time, stopped on the landing with head uncovered to greet his mother.

Oh, lovely painted lady, is this the little white-faced lad you loved, the big bronzed man, fresh from hardships, strong in the sense of the thing he has to do?

No promise made to you could hold him now. He has weighed your small demands is the balance with the world's great need.

He did not tarry long. Straight as an eagle to its mate, he swept through the hall and knocked at the door of Jean's room. There was no response. He knocked again, turned the handle, entered, and found the room empty. The tin soldier on the shelf shouted, "Welcome, welcome—comrade," but Derry had no ears to hear. Everywhere were signs of Jean; her fat memory book open on her desk, the ivory and gold appointments of her dressing table, her pink slippers, her prayer book—his own picture with flowers in front of it as before a shrine.

"My dear, my darling," his heart said when he saw that. What, after all, was he that she should worship him?

Impatient, he rang for Bronson, and the old man came—bewildered, hurried, joyful. "It's a great surprise, sir, but it's good to see you."

"It's good to see you, Bronson. Where's Miss Jean?"

"At Miss Emily's shop, sir."

"As late as this?"

"Sometimes later. She tries to get home in time for dinner."

"Where's Dad?"

"Driving with the children, and the ladies are out on war work."

A year ago women had played bridge at this hour in the afternoon, but there was no playing now.

"Don't tell Dad that I am here. I'll come back presently with Mrs. Drake."

And now down the hall came an old gray dog, wild with delight, outracing Polly Ann, who thought it was a play and leaped after him—Muffin had found his master!

But Derry left Muffin, left Bronson, left Polly Ana, a wistful trio at the front door. He must find Jean!

The day was darkening, and a light burned far back on the Toy Shop. Derry, standing outside, saw a room which was the very wraith of the gay little shop as he had left it—with its white tables, its long counters piled high with finished dressings; the white elephants in a spectral row behind glass doors on the top shelf the only reminder of what it once had been.

He saw, too, a small nun-like figure behind the counter, a

figure all in white, with a white veil banded about her forehead and flowing down behind.

All of her bright hair was hidden, her eyes were on the compresses that she was counting. It seemed to him that there was a sharpened look on the little face.

He had not expected this. He had felt that he would find her glowing as she had been on that first night when he had followed his father through the rain—his dream had been of crinkled copper hair, of silver and rose, of youth and laughter and lightness—.

Her letters had been like that—gay, sparkling—there had been times when they had seemed almost too exuberant, times when he had wondered if she had really waked to the seriousness of the great struggle, and the part he was to play in it.

Yet now he saw signs of suffering. He opened the door. "Jean," he cried.

With the blood all drained from her face, she stared at him as if she saw a specter—"Derry," she whispered.

With his strong arms, he lifted her over the counter. "Jean-Joan, Jean-Joan—"

When at last she released herself, it was to laugh through her tears. "Derry, pull down the shades; what will people think?"

He cared little what people would think. And, anyway, very few people were passing at that late hour in the rain. But he pulled them down, and when he came back, he held her off at arm's length. "What have you been doing to yourself, dearest? You are a feather-weight."

"Well, I've been working."

"How does it happen that you are here alone?"

"Emily had to go down to order supplies, and Margaret went to a Liberty Loan meeting. I often stay like this to count and tie."

"Don't you get dreadfully tired?"

"Yes. But I think I like to get tired. It keeps me from thinking too much."

He drew her to him. "Take off your veil," he said, almost roughly. "I want to see your hair."

Divested of her headcovering, she was more like herself, but even then he was not content. He loosed a hairpin here and there and ran his fingers through the crinkled gold. "If you knew how I've dreamed of it, Jean-Joan. '

But he had not dreamed of the dearness of the little face. "My darling, you have been pining, and I didn't know it."

"Well, didn't you like my smiling letters?"

"So that was it? You've been trying to cheer me up, and letting yourself get like this."

"I didn't want to worry you."

"Didn't you know that I'd want to be worried with anything that pertained to you? What's a husband for, dearest, if you can't tell him your troubles?"

"Yes, but a soldier-husband, Derry, is different. You've got to keep smiling—"

Her lips trembled and she clung to him. "It is so good to have you here, Derry."

She admitted, later, that she had confided her troubles to her memory book. "There weren't any big things, really—just missing you and all that—"

He was jealous of the memory book. "I shall read every word of it."

"Not until you come back from the war—and then we can laugh at it together."

They fell into silence after that. With his arms about her he thought that he might not come back, and she clinging to him had the same thought. But neither told the other.

"Do you know," she said at last, sitting up and sticking the hairpins into her crinkled knot. "Do you know that it's almost time for dinner, and that the General will wonder where I am?"

"I told Bronson not to tell him."

"Oh, really, Derry? Let's make it a great surprise."

Providentially the General was late. He and the children came home to find the house quite remarkably illumined, and Margaret flushed and excited, and in white.

"Is it a party, Mother?" Teddy asked, lending his shoulder manfully to the General's hand, as, with the chauffeur on the other side, they helped the old man up the stairs.

"No, but on such a rainy night Bronson and I thought we'd have a little feast. Don't you think that would be fun?"

The General was tired. "I had planned not to come down again—"

"Please do," she begged,

Bronson, knowing his master's moods, was on tip-toe with anxiety. "I've your things all laid out, sir."

"Well, well, I'll see."

Teddy, somewhat out of breath as they reached the top landing was inspired to remark, "We'll be 'spointed if you don't come down—"

"You want me, eh?"

"Yes, I do. There isn't any other man—'

The General chuckled. "Well, that's reason enough—. You can count on me, Ted, for masculine support."

The table was laid for six. Teddy appearing presently in the dining room pointed out the fact to Bronson, who was taking a last look.

"Is Margaret-Mary coming down?"

"She may later, for the sweets."

"Those aren't her spoons and forks."

"Well, well," said Bronson, "so they aren't"; but he did not have them changed.

The General in his dinner coat, perfectly groomed, immaculate, found Jean in rose and silver waiting for him.

"How gay we are," he said, and pinched her cheek.

Teddy in white linen and patent leathers also approved. "You've got on your spangly dwess, and it makes you pwetty—"

"Oh, Ted, is it just my clothes that make me pretty?"

"I didn't mean that. Only tonight you're so nice and— shining."

She shone, indeed, with such effulgence, that it was a wonder that the General did not suspect. But he did not, even when she said, "We have a surprise for you."

"For me, my dear?"

"Yes. A parcel—it came this afternoon. We want you to untie the string."

"Where is it?" Teddy demanded.

"On the table in the blue room."

Teddy rushed in ahead of the rest, came back and reported, "It's a big one."

It was a big one, cone-shaped and tied up in brown paper. It was set on a heavy carved table, a length of tapestry was under it and hid the legs of the table.

"It looks like a small tree," the General remarked. "But why all this air of mystery?"

He was plainly bored by the fuss they were making. He was tired, and he wanted his dinner.

But Jean, in an excited voice, was telling him to cut the string, and Bronson was handing him a knife.

And then—the paper dropped and everybody was laughing, and Teddy was screaming wildly and he was staring at the khaki-clad upper half of a tall young soldier whose silver-blond hair was clipped close, and whose hand went up in salute.

"It's Cousin Derry. It's Cousin Derry," Teddy was shouting, and Margaret-Mary piped up, "It's Tousin Dee."

Derry stepped out from behind the table, where leaning forward and wrapped up he had lent himself to the illusion, and put both hands on the General's shoulders. "Glad to see me, Dad?"

"Glad; my dear boy—" It was almost too much for him.

Yet as supported by his son's arm, they went a moment later into the dining room, he had a sense of renewed strength in the youth and vigor of this youth who was bone of his bone, flesh of his flesh. If his own feet could not march here were feet which would march for him.

There were flowers on the table, most extravagantly, for these war times, orchids; and there were tall white candles in silver holders.

Jean shining between the candles was a wonder for the world to gaze upon. Derry couldn't keep his eyes off her. This was no longer a little nun of the Toy Shop, yet he held the vision of the little nun in his heart, lest he should forget that she had suffered.

He talked to them all. But beating like a wave against his consciousness was always the thought of Jean. Of the things he had to tell her which he could tell to no one else. He knew now that he could reveal to her the depths of his nature. He had withheld so much, fearing to crush her butterfly wings, but she was not a butterfly. They had been playing at cross purposes, and writing letters that merely skimmed the surface of their emotions. It had taken those moments in the Toy Shop to teach them their mistake.

Teddy, feeling that the occasion called for a relaxing of the children-should-be-seen-and-not-heard rule, asked questions.

"How long can you stay?"

"Ten days."

"Are you going to Fwance?"

"I hope so."

"Mother says I've got to pray for the Germans."

"Teddy," Margaret admonished.

"Well, I rather think I would," Derry told him. "They need it."

This was a new angle. "Shall you hate to kill them?"

There was a stir about the table. The old man and the women seemed to hang on Derry's answer.

"Yes, I shall hate it. I hate all killing, but it's got to be done."

He spoke presently, at length, of what many men thought of war.

"We are red-blooded enough, we Americans, but I think we hate killing the other man rather more than we fear being killed. It's sickening—bayonet practice. Killing at long range is different. The children of my generation were trained to tender-heartedness. We looked after the birds and rescued kittens, and were told that wars were impossible—long wars. But war is not impossible, and it has come upon us, and we are finding that men must be brave not merely in the face of losing their own lives, but in the face of taking the lives of—others. I sometimes wonder what it must have seemed to those Germans who went first into Belgium. Some of them must have been kind—some of them must have asked to be shot rather than be set at the work of butchery.

"I sometimes think," he pursued, "that if we could give moving pictures of the war just as it is—in all its horror and hideousness—show the pictures in every little town in every country in the world, that war would stop at once. If the Germans could see themselves in those towns in Belgium —if the world could see them. If we could see men mowed down—wounded, close up, as our soldiers see them. If our people should be forced to look at those pictures, as the people of war-ridden countries have been forced to gaze upon realities, money would be provided and men provided in such amounts and numbers that those who began the war would be forced to end it on the terms the world would set for them.

"The fact that men are going into this war in spite of their aversion to killing shows the stuff of which they are made. It is like drowning kittens," he smiled a little. "It has to be done or the world would be overrun by cats."

Teddy, wide-eyed, was listening. "Do people drown kittens?" he asked. "Oh, I didn't think they would." It was a sad commentary on the conditions of war that he was more heavily oppressed by the thought of drowned little cats than by the murder of men.

"My dear fellow," Derry said, "we won't talk about such things. I must beg your pardon for mentioning it."

The talk flowed on then in lighter vein. "Ralph Witherspoon is in town," Jean vouchsafed. "He had a bad fall and was sent home to get over it. Mrs. Witherspoon has asked me there to dine. I shall take you with me."

"I didn't know that people were dining out in these times."

"Mrs. Witherspoon prides herself on her conservation menus. She says that she serves war things, that she gives us nothing to eat that the men need, and she likes her friends about her."

"We shall miss Drusilla," Derry said. "I've been worried about her since the Huns recaptured those towns in France."

"Daddy wrote that she is not far from his hospital, doing splendid work, and that the men adore her."

"They would," said Derry. "She is a great-hearted creature. I can fancy her singing to them over there. You know what a wonder she was at that sort of thing—"

After dinner the General was eager to have his son to himself. "The women will excuse us while we smoke and talk."

Derry's eyes wandered to Jean. "All right," he said with an effort.

The General's heart tightened. His son was his son. The little girl in silver and rose was in a sense an outsider. She had not known Derry throughout the years, as his father had known him. How could she care as much?

Yet she did care. He realized how Derry's coming had changed her. He heard her laugh as she had not laughed in all the weeks of loneliness. She came up and stood beside Derry, and linked her arm in his and looked up at him with shining eyes.

"Isn't he—wonderful?" she asked, with a catch of her breath.

"Oh, take her away," the old gentleman said. "Go and talk to her somewhere."

Derry's face brightened. "You don't mind?"

"Of course not," stoutly. "Bronson says that the rain has stopped. There's probably a moon somewhere, if you'll look for it."

Margaret went up to put the children to bed. Emily, promising to come back, withdrew to write a letter. The old man sat alone.

He limped into the blue room, and gazed indifferently around on its treasures. Once he had cared for these plates and cups—his quest for rare porcelains had been eager.

And now he did not care. The lovely glazed things were for the eye, not for the heart. He would have given them all for the touch of a loving hand, for a voice that grew tender—.

There was the patter of little feet on the polished floor. Margaret-Mary in a diminutive blue dressing gown and infinitesimal slippers, with her curls brushed tidily up from the back of her neck and skewered with a hairpin, came over and laid her hand on his knee. "Dus a itte 'tory?" she asked ingratiatingly. She adored stories.

He picked her up, and she curled herself into the corner of his arm.

Her mother found her there. "Mother's naughty little girl," she said, "to run away—"

"Let her stay," the General begged. "Somehow my heart needs her tonight."

CHAPTER XXVIII

SIX DAYS

Four days of Derry's furlough had passed, four palpitating days, and now the hours that the lovers spent together began to take on the poignant quality of coming separation. Every moment counted, nothing must be lost, nothing must be left unsaid, nothing must be left undone which should emphasize their oneness of thought and purpose.

They read together, they walked together, they rode together, they went to church together. If they included the General in their plans it was because they felt his need of them, not theirs of him. They lived in a world created to survive for ten days and then to collapse like a pricked bubble—

And it was because of the dread of collapse that Jean began to plan a structure of remembrance which should endure after Derry's departure.

"Darling," she said, "there are only six days—What shall we do with them?"

THE FIFTH DAY

It was Sunday, and in the morning they went dutifully to church. They ate their luncheon dutifully with the whole family, and motored dutifully afterwards with the General. Then at twilight they sought the Toy Shop.

They had it all to themselves, and they had told Bronson that they would not be home for dinner. So Jean made chocolate for Derry as she had made it on that first night for his father. They toasted war bread on the electric grill, and there were strawberries.

They were charmed with their housekeeping. "It would have been like this," Derry said—all eyes for her loveliness, "if you had been the girl in the Toy Shop and I had been the shabby boy—"

Jean pondered. "I wonder if a big house is ever really a home?"

"Not ours. Mother tried to make it—but it has always been a sort of museum with Dad's collections."

"Do you think that some day we could have a little house?"

"We can have whatever you want." His smile warmed her.

"Wouldn't you want it, Derry?"

"If you were in it."

"Let's talk about it, and plan it, and put dream furniture in it, and dream friends—"

"More Lovely Dreams?"

"Well, something like that—a House o' Dreams, Derry, without any gold dragons or marble balls or queer porcelain things; just our own bits of furniture and china, and a garden, and Muffin and Polly Ann—" Her eyes were wistful.

"You shall have it now if you wish."

"Not until you can share it with me—"

And that was the beginning of their fantastic pilgrimage. In the time that was left to them they were to find a house of dreams, and as Jean said, expansively, "all the rest."

"We will start tonight," Derry declared. "There's such a moon."

It was the kind of moon that whitened the world; one swam in a sea of light. Derry's runabout was a fairy car. Jean's hair was molten gold, her lover's pale silver—as with bare heads, having passed the city limits, they took the open road.

It was as warm as summer, and there were fragrances which seemed to wash over them in waves as they passed old gardens and old orchards. There was bridal-wreath billowing above stone fences, snow-balls, pale globes among the green, beds of iris, purple-black beneath the moon.

They forded a stream—more silver, and a silver road after that.

"Where are we going?" Jean breathed.

"I know a house—"

It was a little house set on top of a hill, where indeed no little house should be set, for little houses should nestle, protected by the slopes back of them. But this little house was set up there for the view—the Monument a spectral shaft, miles away, the Potomac broadening out beyond it, the old trees of the Park sleeping between. This was what the little house saw by night; it saw more than that by day.

It was not an empty house. One window was lighted, a square of gold in a lower room.

They did not know who lived in the house. They did not care. For the moment it was theirs. Leaving the car, they sat on the grass and surveyed their property.

"Of course it is ours," Jean said, "and when you are over there, you can think of it with the moon shining on it."

"I like the sloping roof," her lover took up the refrain, "and the big chimney and the wide windows."

"I can sit on the window seat and watch for you, Derry, and there will be smoke coming out of the chimney on cold days, and a fire roaring on the hearth when you open the door—"

They decided that there ought to be eight rooms—, and they named them. The Log-Fire Room; The Room of Little Feasts; the Place of Pots and Pans—

"That's the first floor," said Jean.

"Yes."

The upper floor was harder—The Royal Suite; The Friendly Boom, for the dream maid of all work; The Spare Chamber—

"My grandmother had a spare chamber," Jean explained, "and I always liked the sound of it, as if she kept her hospitality pressed down and running over—"

Derry, who had written it all by the light of the moon, held his pencil poised. "There is one more," he said, "the little room towards the West—"

Jean hesitated for the breadth of a second. "Well, we may need another," she said, and left it nameless.

The door opened and a man came out. If he saw them, they meant nothing to him—a pair of lovers by the wayside; there were many such.

He paced back and forth on the gravel walk. They could hear

the crunch of it under his feet. They saw the shining tip of his cigar—smelt its fragrance—.

Again the door opened, to frame a woman. She called and her voice was young.

"Dearest, it is late. Are you coming in?"

His young voice answered. His far-flung cigar-end trailed across the darkness, his eager steps gave quick response—the door was shut—.

"Oh, Derry, I'd call you like that—"

"And I should come."

The light went out on the lower floor, and presently in a room above a window was illumined.

THE SIXTH DAY

A dream house must have dream furniture. There are old shops in Alexandria, where, less often than in earlier years, one may find treasures, bow-legged chairs and gate-legged tables, yellowed letters written by famous pens, steel engravings which have hung in historic halls, pewter and plate, Luster and Sevres, Wedgwood and Willow, Chippendale and Hepplewhite, Adams and Empire, everything linked with some distinguished name, everything with a story, real or invented. One may buy an ancestor for a song, or at least the portrait of one, and silver with armorial bearings, and no one will know if you do not tell them that your heirlooms have come from a shop.

And Alexandria, as all the world knows, is reached from Washington by motor and trolley, train or ferry.

It was by ferry that the lovers preferred to go in the glory of this May morning, feeling the breeze fresh in their faces as with a motley crowd they stood on the lower deck and looked towards the old town.

Thus they came to the wharves, flanked by ancient warehouses in a straggly row along the water line. The windows of these ancient edifices had looked down on Revolutionary heroes, the old brick walls had echoed to the sound of fife and drum—the old streets had once been thronged by men in blue and buff. Since those days the quaint little city had basked in the pride of her traditions. She had tolerated nothing modern until within this very year she had waked to find that her red-coat enemy was now her friend, that the roads which George Washington had travelled were being trod once more by marching men; that in the church where he had worshipped prayers were being said once more for men in battle.

And into the shops, with their storied antiques, drifted now men in olive-drab and men in blue, and men in forester's green, who laughed at the flint locks and powder horns, saluted the Father of his Country whenever they passed his picture, gazed with reverence on ancient swords and uniforms, dickered for such small articles as might be bought out of their limited allowances, and paid in the end, cheerfully, prices which would have been scorned by any discriminating buyer.

"There must be a table for the Log-Fire Room," Jean told her husband, "and a fire-bench, not too high, and a big chair for you, and another chair for me—"

"And a stool for your little feet—."

"And a desk for you, Derry."

"And an oval mirror with a gold frame, for me to see your face in, Jean-Joan—"

Then there was a four-poster bed with pineapples, and an

Adams screen, an old brass-bound chest, the most adorable things in Sheffield and crystal, and to crown it all, a picture of George Washington—a print, faintly colored, with the country's coat of arms carved on the frame.

Yet not one thing did they buy except a quite sumptuous and splendid marriage coffer which suggested itself at once as the only wedding present for Emily.

The price took Jean's breath away. "But, dearest—"

"Nothing is too good for Emily, Jean-Joan."

* * * * * *

That night Derry drew a picture of the house in Jean's memory book.

"I'll put a garden in front—"

"How can you put in a garden, Derry, when there isn't one?"

She wore a lace robe and a lace cap, and there were pink ribbons threaded in, and her cheeks were pink. "You can't put in a garden until there is one, Derry. When we find it, it must be a lovesome garden, with the old-fashioned flowers, and a fountain with a cupid—and a fish-pond."

With this settled, he proceeded, with facile pen, to furnish the house. There was the Log-Fire Room, with the print of George Washington over the mantel, with Jean's knitting on the table; Muffin on one side of the fire, and Polly Ann on the other. He even started to put Jean in one of the big chairs, but she made him rub it out. "Not yet, Derry. You see, I am not living in it yet. I am living here, with you alive and loving—"

He caught her to him. "When you are away from me," she whispered, "I'll live in it—and you'll be there—and I shall never feel alone—"

Yet later, Derry coming in unexpectedly after a talk with his father, found her sobbing with her head on the fat old book.

"My darling—"

"It isn't that I am unhappy, Derry—. It is just for that one little minute, I wanted it to be real—"

THE SEVENTH DAY

It was on the morning of the seventh day that a letter came from Drusilla.

"*Dear Babes in the Wood*:

"I am writing this to tell you that the next time I see Captain Hewes, I am going to marry him. That sounds a little like a hold-up, doesn't it? But it is the way we are doing things over here. He has wanted it for so long, and I am beginning to know that I want it, too. It has been hard to tell just what was really best in the face of all that is happening. It has seemed sometimes as if it were a sacrilege to think of love and life in the midst of death and destruction.

"I shan't have any trousseau; I shan't have a wedding journey. He will just blow in some day, and the chaplain will marry us, and the little old cure of this village will give us his blessing.

"I never expected to be married like this. You know the kind of mind I have. I must always see the picture of myself doing things, and there had always been a sort of dream of some great church with a blur of gold light at the far end, and myself floating up the aisle in a cloud of white veil, and a hushed crowd and the organ playing.

"And it won't be a bit like that. I shall wear a uniform and a flannel shirt, and I'll be lucky if my boots are not splashed with mud. It will seem queer to be married with my boots on, as men died in old romances.

"Perhaps by the time this reaches you, Drusilla Gray will be Drusilla Hewes, and so I ask your blessing, and your prayers.

"I should never have asked for your prayers a year ago. I should have been thanking you for your wedding present of glass and silver, and asking you to dine with me on Tuesday or Thursday as the case might be. But now, the only thought that holds me is whether God will give my Captain back to me, and the hope that if not, I may have the strength to bear it—.

"I am sure that Derry will feel the sublimity of it all when he comes—death is so near, yet so little feared; the men know that tonight or tomorrow they may be beyond the shadows, and it holds them to something bigger than themselves.

"But be sure of this, my dears, that when Derry goes the seas will not part you—. Spirit touches spirit, space has nothing to do with it. Often when I am alone, the Captain comes to me, speaks to me, cheers me; I think if he should die in battle, he would still come.

"If ever I have a home of my own, I shall build an altar not to the Unknown God but to the God whom I had lost and have found again. I go into old churches here to pray, and it is no longer a matter of feeling, no longer a matter of form, it is something more than that.

"And now I can't ask you to dance at my wedding, but I can ask you to wish me happiness and a long life with my lover, or failing that, the strength to give him up—"

She signed herself, "Always loving you both, DRUSILLA."

"Such a dear letter," said Jean.

"And such a different Drusilla. Do you think that the Drusilla of the old days would have built an altar?"

And it was because of Drusilla's letter that Derry took Jean that afternoon to the great Library with the gold dome and guided her to a corridor made beautiful by the brush of an artist who had painted "The Occupations of the Day"; in one lunette a primitive man and woman knelt before a pile of stones on which burned a sacred flame. Above them was blue sky—flowers grew within reach of their hands—the fields stretched beyond.

"We must build an altar, dearest."

"In our hearts—"

"And in our House of Dreams—"

THE EIGHTH DAY

There was no getting out of the Witherspoon dinner, and it was when Ralph greeted Jean that he said to her, "You are lovelier than ever."

She smiled at him. "It is because my heart is singing—"

"Do you feel like that?"

She nodded. "In three days the song will cease—the lights will go out, and the curtain will fall—the end of the world will come."

"Drake goes in three days?"

"He goes back to camp. I don't expect to see him again before he sails."

"Lucky fellow."

"To go?"

"To have you."

"Please don't."

"Let me say this—that I acted like a cad; I'd like to feel that you've forgiven me."

"I have forgotten, which is better, isn't it?"

"How sweet you are—and all the sweetness is Derry's. Well, when I go over, will you pray for me, my dear?"

He was in dead earnest. "There are so few women—who pray—but I rather fancy that you must—"

All around them was surging talk. "How strange it seems," Jean said, "that we should be speaking of such things, here—"

"No," Ralph said, "it is not strange. I have a feeling that I shan't come back."

Alma Drew on the other side of him claimed his attention. "War is the great sensational opportunity. And there are people who like patriotism of the sound-the-trumpet-beat-the-drum variety—"

"You said that rather cleverly, Alma," Ralph told her, "but you mustn't forget that was the kind of patriotism our forefathers had, and it seemed rather effective."

"Men aren't machines," Jean said hotly. "They are flesh and blood, and so are women—a fife and drum or a bag-pipe means more to them than just crude music; the blood of their ancestors thrilled to the sound."

"As savages thrill to a tom-tom."

They stared at her.

"It is all savage," Alma said, crisply and coolly, "We are all murderers. We are teaching our men to run Germans through with bayonets, and trying to make ourselves think that they aren't breaking the sixth commandment. Yet in times of peace, when a man kills he goes to the electric chair—"

It was Derry who answered that. "If in times of peace I heard you scream and saw you set upon by thieves and murderers, and stood with my hands in my pockets while you were tortured and killed, would you call my non-interference laudable?"

"That's different."

"It is the same thing. The only difference lies in the fact that thousands of defenceless women and little children are calling. Would you have the nation stand with its hands in its pockets?"

Alma, cold as ice, challenged him: "Why should they call to us? We'll be sorry some day that we went into it."

Out of a dead silence, a man said: "Not long ago, I went into a sweet shop in England. A woman came in with two children. They were rosy children and round. They carried muffs.

"She bought candy for them—and when she gave it to them, I saw that they had—no hands—"

A gasp went round the table.

"They were Belgian children."

That night Jean said to Derry with a sternness which set strangely upon her, "We must have friends in our House of Dreams. The latchstrings will always be out for people like Emily and Marion, and Drusilla, and Ulrich and Ralph—"

"Yes—"

"But not for Hilda and Alma."

THE NINTH DAY

It was on the ninth day that Derry waked his wife at dawn. "I've ordered the car. It rained in the night, and now—oh, there was never such a morning; there may never be such a morning for us again."

"What time is it, Derry?"

"Sunrise time—come and see."

Her window faced the east, and she saw all the pearl of it, and the faint rose and the amethyst and gold.

"We shall eat our breakfast ten miles from town," Derry said, as their car carried him out into the country, "and there's a lovesome garden—"

"With old-fashioned flowers and a fountain and a Cupid?"

"With all that—and more—"

The garden belonged to an old woman. For years and years she had planted flowers—tulips and hyacinths and poppies and lilies and gladiolus and larkspur and phlox and ladyslipper— there had always been a riot of color.

She had an old gardener, and she would stand over him, leaning on her silver-topped ebony cane, with a lace scarf covering her hair, and would point out the places to plant things.

But now in her garden she had strawberries and Swiss chard

and sweet herbs, and rows and rows of peas and young onions and potatoes, with a place left for corn at the back, and tomatoes in every spare space.

And there was lettuce, and an asparagus bed, and everything on this May morning was shouting to the sun.

"I had always thought," said the old lady to Derry, when he presented Jean, "that a vegetable garden was uninteresting. But it is a little world—with class distinctions of its own, if you please. All the really useful vegetables we call common; it is the ones we can do without which are the aristocrats. The potatoes and cabbages and onions are really important, but I am proudest of my young peas and my peppers and cucumbers and tomatoes, and that's the way of the world, isn't it? If there was only an aristocracy things would stop, but the common folk could go on alone until the end of time."

She gave Jean a blue bowl to pick strawberries in; and Derry dug asparagus—the creamy shoots were tipped with pale purple and pink, deepening into green where they had stood too long in the sun.

"Aren't there any flowers?" Jean was anxious.

"Come and see." The old woman went ahead of them, her cane tap-tapping on the stone flags.

She opened a gate which was flanked by brick walls. "These," she said, whimsically, "are my jewels."

All the sweetness which had once spread over her domain was concentrated here, fragrance and flame—roses, iris, peonies—honeysuckle—ruby and emerald, amethyst and gold; a Cupid riding a swan, with water pouring from his quiver into a shallow marble basin.

"I should not have dared keep this, if it had not been for the other—" the old woman told them. "I am very sure that in these days God walks in vegetable gardens—"

For breakfast they had strawberries and radishes, thin little corn cakes—and two fresh eggs from the chickens which most triumphantly occupied the conservatory.

"This is the only way I can do my bit," the old lady explained, "by helping with the world's food supply. My eyes are bad and I cannot sew, my fingers are twisted and I cannot knit, and Dennis is old—but we plan the garden and plant—"

And that night Jean said to Derry, "I am glad there were flowers to make it lovesome—and I am glad there were vegetables to make it right."

So he drew a waving field of corn back of the dream cottage, and tomatoes and peas to the right and left—with onions in a stiff row along the border, and potatoes storming the hillside. But the gate which led to the Lovesome Garden was open wide, so that one might see the Cupid as he rode his swan.

THE LAST DAY

It was on the tenth day that Derry said, "We have our house and the furniture for it, and we have built an altar, and found our friends, and we have planted a garden—what shall we do on the last day?"

And Jean said, rather unexpectedly, "We will go to the circus."

"To the circus?"

"Yes. And take the children—they are dying to go, and Margaret can't. It is up to you and me, Derry."

Even Nurse was to stay behind. "We'll have them all to ourselves."

Derry was dubious, a little hurt. "It seems rather queer, doesn't it, on our last day?"

"I—I think I should like it better than anything else, Derry."

And so they went.

It was warm with a hint of showers in the air, and both of the children were in white. Jean was also in white. They rode in the General's limousine to where the big tent with all its flags flying covered a vast space.

"Cousin Derry, Mother said I might have some peanuts."

"All right, old man."

"And Margaret-Mary mustn't. But there are some crackers in a bag."

It was all most entrancing, the gilded wagons, the restless beasts behind their bars, the spotted ponies, the swaying elephants, the bands playing, the crowds streaming—.

Teddy held tight to Jean's hand. Margaret-Mary was carried high on Derry's shoulder. All of her curls were bobbing, and her eyes were shining. Now and then she dropped a light kiss on the silver blond hair of her cavalier.

"Tousin Dee," she murmured, affectionately.

"She's an adorable kiddie," Derry told Jean as they found their seats.

"Cousin Derry," Teddy reminded him, "don't forget the peanuts."

And now the trumpets blared and the drums boomed, and the great parade writhed like a glittering serpent around the huge circle, then broke up into various groups as the performance began in the rings.

After that one needed all of one's eyes. Teddy sat spellbound for a while, but found time at last to draw a long breath. "Cousin Derry, that is the funniest clown—"

"The little one?"

"The big one; oh, well, the little one, too."

Silence again while the elephants did amazing things in one ring, with Japanese tumblers in another, with piebald ponies beyond, and things being done on trapezes everywhere.

Teddy slipped his hand into Derry's. "It's—it's almost like having Daddy," he confided. "I know he's glad I'm here."

Derry's big hand closed over the small one. "I'm glad, too, old chap."

Margaret-Mary having gazed her fill, slept comfortably in Jean's arms.

"Let me hold her," Derry said.

Jean shook her head. "I love to have her here."

She had taken off her hat, and as she bent above the child her hair made a halo of gold. In the midst of all the tawdriness she was a still and sacred figure—a Madonna with a child.

Teddy, when he reached home, told the General all about it.

"It was be-yeutiful—but Cousin Jean cwied—"

"Cried?"

"I saw a tear rwunning down her cheek, and it splashed on Margaret-Mary's nose—"

And that night Derry said, "My darling, what shall I draw in our book?"

"The thing that you want most to remember, Derry."

So he drew her all in white, bending over a child of dreams.

* * * * * *

The next morning, she told him "Good-bye." They had come along to the Toy Shop for their farewell, so that there was only the old white elephant to see her tears, and the Lovely Dreams to be sorry for her.

Yet her head was held high at the very last, and she was not sorry for herself. "I am glad and proud to have you go, dearest. I am glad and proud—"

And after he had gone, she worked until lunch time on the bandages and wipes, and rode with the General in the afternoon, with her hand in his, knowing that it comforted him.

But very late that night, when every one else is the big house was fast asleep, she crept out into the hall in her lace robe and lace cap and pink slippers and stood beneath the picture of the painted lady. "He will come back," she said. "He must come back—and—oh, oh, Derry's mother in Heaven—you must tell me how to live—without him—."

CHAPTER XXIX

"AND, AFTER ALL, HE CAME TO THE WARS!"

A perfect day, with men lying dead by thousands on the battlefield; twilight, with a young moon; night and the stars—

Drusilla's throat was dry with singing—there had been so many hurt, and she had found that it helped them to hear her, so when a moaning, groaning, cursing ambulance load stopped a moment, she sang; when walking wounded came through sagging with pain and dreadful weariness, she sang; and when night fell, and an engine was stalled, and she took in her own car a man who must be rushed to the first collecting station, she found herself still singing—. And this time it was "The Battle Hymn of the Republic."

The man propped up beside her murmured, "My Captain liked that—he used to sing it—"

"Yes?" She was listening with only half an ear. There were so many Captains.

"He was engaged to an American."

She listened now. "Your Captain—?"

"Captain Hewes."

She guided the car steadily. "Dawson Hewes?"

"Yes. Do you know him?"

"I—I am the girl he is going to marry—"

He froze into silence. She bent towards him. "What made you say—*was*—?"

"He's—gone West—"

"Dead?"

"Yes."

"When?" She still drove steadily through the dark.

"To-day."

She looked up at the stars. So—he would never come blowing in with the sweet spring winds.

"I'd rather have been—shot—than to have told you that—" the man beside her was saying, "but, you see, I didn't know you were the girl—"

"Of course you couldn't. You mustn't blame yourself."

She delivered her precious charge at the hospital and put up her car for the night. Standing alone under the stars she wondered what she should do next. There was no one to tell— the women who had worked with her in the town which had since been recaptured by the Germans had gone to other towns. But she had stayed as near the front as possible, and she had never felt lonely because at any moment her lover might come—there had always been the thought that he might come—.

And now he would never come!

She had a room in the house of an old woman, all of whose

sons were in the war. So far two of them had escaped death. But the old woman said often, fatalistically, "They will not always escape—but it will be for France."

The old woman had soup on the fire for Drusilla's supper. The room was faintly lighted. "What is it?" she asked, as the girl dropped down on the doorstep.

"My Captain is dead—"

The old woman rose and stood over her. "It comes to all."

"I know."

"Will you eat your soup? When the heart fails, the body must have strength."

Drusilla covered her face with her bands. The room was very still. The old woman went back to her chair by the fire and waited. At last she rose and filled a small bowl with the soup— she broke into it a small allowance of bread. Then she came and sat on the step beside the girl.

"Eat, Mademoiselle," she said, with something like authority, and Drusilla obeyed. And when she gave back the bowl, the old woman set it on the floor, and drew the girl's head to her breast.

And Drusilla lay there, crying softly, a lonely American mothered by this indomitable old woman of France.

Days passed, days in which men came and men went and Drusilla sang to them. And now new faces were seen among the tired and war-worn ones. Eager young Americans, pressing forward towards the front, found a countrywoman in the little town; and they wrote home about her. "She's a beauty, by jinks, and when she sings it pulls the heart out of you. She's the kind you want to say your prayers to."

So her fame went forth and took on gradually something of the supernatural—her tall, straight slenderness, her steady eyes, her halo of red hair grew to have a sort of sacred significance, like that of some militant young saint.

Then came a day when Derry's regiment marched through the town to the trenches, spent an interval and came back, awed by what it had seen, but undaunted.

Drusilla, sitting on the doorstep of the stone house, saw a tall figure striding down the street. He stopped to speak to an old woman and doffed his hat, showing a clipped silver-blond head.

Drusilla went flying through the dusk. ' Derry, Derry!"

He stared and stared again. "Is it you?" he asked. Nothing was vivid now about Drusilla except her hair.

"Yes."

He took her hands in his. "My dear girl." It was hard for either of them to speak.

"Did Bruce McKenzie tell you that my Captain has—gone West?"

"I had a letter. I haven't seen him. His hospital isn't far from here, I understand."

"Just outside. He—he has been a great help—to me, Derry."

She took him back to her doorstep and they sat down.

"Tell me about Jean."

He tried to tell her, wavered a little and spoke the truth. "The hardest thing was leaving her. I don't mind the fighting. I don't mind anything but the fact that she's over there and I'm over here. But it had to be—of course."

"Yes, everything had to be, Derry. I am believing that more and more. When my Captain went—I found how much I cared. I hadn't always been sure. But I am sure now, and I am sure, too, that he knows—"

"Love—in these times, Derry—isn't building a nest—and singing songs in the tree tops on a May morning; it goes beyond just the man and the woman; it even goes beyond the child. It goes as far as the future of mankind. What the future of the world will be depends not so much on how much you love Jean or she loves you, or on how much I loved and was loved, but on how much that love will mean to the world. If we can't give up our own for the sake of the world's ideal then love hasn't meant what it should to you and to me, Derry—"

She rose as a group of men approached. "They want me to sing for them. You won't mind?"

"My dear girl, I have heard of you everywhere. I believe that some of the fellows say their prayers to you at night—"

She stood up and sang. Her hair caught the light from the room back of her. She gave them a popular air or two, a hymn, "The Marseillaise—"

He missed nothing in her then. In spite of her paleness, the old fire was there, the passion of patriotism—there was, too, a new note of triumphant faith.

She needed no candles now, no red and white and blue for a background—she did not even need her beauty, her voice was enough—

When she sat down and the men had gone she said to Derry, "Do you remember when I last sang the 'Marseillaise' for you?"

"Yes."

He brought out from his pocket a tiny object and set it on the step, so that the light from the open door shone on it.

"You gave it to me, Drusilla."

"Oh, my little tin soldier."

"And after all, he came to the wars—"

Very proudly the little soldier shouldered his musket.

He had indeed come to the wars, and the winds of France blew upon him, the stars of France were over his head, the soil of France was beneath his feet.

Trutter-a-trutt, trutter-a-trutt—blew all the bugles of France, and the little tin soldier was at last content!

Derry had, too, in his pocket a letter from Jean; he read to Drusilla the part that belonged to her.

"Tell Drusilla that there's a chair in our dream house for her. I often shut my eyes and see her in it, and I see Daddy and you, Derry, all home safe from the war and the world at peace—"

"Safe and at home and the world at peace—. Will the time ever come, Derry?"

"You know it will come. It must—"

It was three days later that Dr. McKenzie motored over for a late supper with Drusilla and Derry. They were served by the old woman who had mothered the lonely girl.

"To think," the Doctor said, as they sat at their frugal board, "to think that we three should be here in the midst of all this; and yet a year ago I was wondering what to do with the rest of my life, Drusilla was running around telling people what kind of pictures to put on their walls, and what kind of draperies to put at their windows, and Derry was trying to pretend that he was not an elegant idler; and now—we are seeing a world made over—"

"You are seeing the world of men made over," said Drusilla, "but the most wonderful thing is seeing the women made over."

"I don't want to see the women made over," the Doctor groaned. "They are nice enough as it is. I want my little Jean gay and smiling—and Derry tells me that she is a nun in a white veil."

"She is more than that," Derry said, and a great light came into his eyes. "I sometimes feel that she and Drusilla are holding hands across the sea—two brave women in different spheres."

Drusilla, wise Drusilla pondered. "Perhaps the war will teach men like Bruce that women aren't playthings—"

"Don't be too hard on me, Drusilla."

"I am not hard. I am telling the truth."

"I'll forgive you, because in these weeks you've taught me a lot—" Bruce McKenzie's world would not have recognized in this tired and serious gentleman its twinkling, teasing man of medicine. Weary feet on the stones—

"I must go to them," Drusilla said.

She went out on the step. They saw the men cluster about her—French and English, Scotch—a few Americans.

Her voice soared:

"In the beauty of the lilies, Christ was born across the sea, With the glory in his bosom which transfigures you and me. As he died to make men holy, let us die to make men free—While God is marching on—"

"Look," said the Doctor. "Do you see their faces, Derry?"

Gazing up at her as if they drank her in, the men listened. She was the daughter of a nation of dreamers, the daughter of a nation *which made its dreams come true.*

Tired and spent, they saw in her hope personified. They saw America coming fresh and unworn to fight a winning battle to the end. So they turned their faces towards Drusilla. She was more to them than a singing woman. Behind her stood a steadfast people—and God was marching on.

ABOUT THE AUTHOR

Irene Temple Bailey (c.1885 - July 6, 1953) was an American novelist and short story writer.

Beginning around 1902, Temple Bailey was contributing stories to national magazines such as The Saturday Evening Post, Cavalier Magazine, Cosmopolitan, American Magazine, McClure's, Woman's Home Companion, Good Housekeeping, McCall's and others.

In 1914, Bailey wrote the screenplay for the Vitagraph Studios film "Auntie" and two of her books were filmed. She also had three of her books on the list of bestselling novels in the United States in 1918, 1922, and 1926 as determined by the New York Times.

Choose from Thousands of 1stWorldLibrary Classics By

A. M. Barnard
Ada Leverson
Adolphus William Ward
Aesop
Agatha Christie
Alexander Aaronsohn
Alexander Kielland
Alexandre Dumas
Alfred Gatty
Alfred Ollivant
Alice Duer Miller
Alice Turner Curtis
Alice Dunbar
Allen Chapman
Alleyne Ireland
Ambrose Bierce
Amelia E. Barr
Amory H. Bradford
Andrew Lang
Andrew McFarland Davis
Andy Adams
Angela Brazil
Anna Alice Chapin
Anna Sewell
Annie Besant
Annie Hamilton Donnell
Annie Payson Call
Annie Roe Carr
Annonaymous
Anton Chekhov
Archibald Lee Fletcher
Arnold Bennett
Arthur C. Benson
Arthur Conan Doyle
Arthur M. Winfield
Arthur Ransome
Arthur Schnitzler
Arthur Train
Atticus
B.H. Baden-Powell
B. M. Bower
B. C. Chatterjee
Baroness Emmuska Orczy
Baroness Orczy
Basil King
Bayard Taylor
Ben Macomber
Bertha Muzzy Bower
Bjornstjerne Bjornson

Booth Tarkington
Boyd Cable
Bram Stoker
C. Collodi
C. E. Orr
C. M. Ingleby
Carolyn Wells
Catherine Parr Traill
Charles A. Eastman
Charles Amory Beach
Charles Dickens
Charles Dudley Warner
Charles Farrar Browne
Charles Ives
Charles Kingsley
Charles Klein
Charles Hanson Towne
Charles Lathrop Pack
Charles Romyn Dake
Charles Whibley
Charles Willing Beale
Charlotte M. Braeme
Charlotte M. Yonge
Charlotte Perkins Stetson
Clair W. Hayes
Clarence Day Jr.
Clarence E. Mulford
Clemence Housman
Confucius
Coningsby Dawson
Cornelis DeWitt Wilcox
Cyril Burleigh
D. H. Lawrence
Daniel Defoe
David Garnett
Dinah Craik
Don Carlos Janes
Donald Keyhoe
Dorothy Kilner
Dougan Clark
Douglas Fairbanks
E. Nesbit
E. P. Roe
E. Phillips Oppenheim
E. S. Brooks
Earl Barnes
Edgar Rice Burroughs
Edith Van Dyne
Edith Wharton

Edward Everett Hale
Edward J. O'Biren
Edward S. Ellis
Edwin L. Arnold
Eleanor Atkins
Eleanor Hallowell Abbott
Eliot Gregory
Elizabeth Gaskell
Elizabeth McCracken
Elizabeth Von Arnim
Ellem Key
Emerson Hough
Emilie F. Carlen
Emily Bronte
Emily Dickinson
Enid Bagnold
Enilor Macartney Lane
Erasmus W. Jones
Ernie Howard Pie
Ethel May Dell
Ethel Turner
Ethel Watts Mumford
Eugene Sue
Eugenie Foa
Eugene Wood
Eustace Hale Ball
Evelyn Everett-green
Everard Cotes
F. H. Cheley
F. J. Cross
F. Marion Crawford
Fannie E. Newberry
Federick Austin Ogg
Ferdinand Ossendowski
Fergus Hume
Florence A. Kilpatrick
Fremont B. Deering
Francis Bacon
Francis Darwin
Frances Hodgson Burnett
Frances Parkinson Keyes
Frank Gee Patchin
Frank Harris
Frank Jewett Mather
Frank L. Packard
Frank V. Webster
Frederic Stewart Isham
Frederick Trevor Hill
Frederick Winslow Taylor

Friedrich Kerst
Friedrich Nietzsche
Fyodor Dostoyevsky
G.A. Henty
G.K. Chesterton
Gabrielle E. Jackson
Garrett P. Serviss
Gaston Leroux
George A. Warren
George Ade
Geroge Bernard Shaw
George Cary Eggleston
George Durston
George Ebers
George Eliot
George Gissing
George MacDonald
George Meredith
George Orwell
George Sylvester Viereck
George Tucker
George W. Cable
George Wharton James
Gertrude Atherton
Gordon Casserly
Grace E. King
Grace Gallatin
Grace Greenwood
Grant Allen
Guillermo A. Sherwell
Gulielma Zollinger
Gustav Flaubert
H. A. Cody
H. B. Irving
H.C. Bailey
H. G. Wells
H. H. Munro
H. Irving Hancock
H. R. Naylor
H. Rider Haggard
H. W. C. Davis
Haldeman Julius
Hall Caine
Hamilton Wright Mabie
Hans Christian Andersen
Harold Avery
Harold McGrath
Harriet Beecher Stowe
Harry Castlemon
Harry Coghill
Harry Houidini

Hayden Carruth
Helent Hunt Jackson
Helen Nicolay
Hendrik Conscience
Hendy David Thoreau
Henri Barbusse
Henrik Ibsen
Henry Adams
Henry Ford
Henry Frost
Henry James
Henry Jones Ford
Henry Seton Merriman
Henry W Longfellow
Herbert A. Giles
Herbert Carter
Herbert N. Casson
Herman Hesse
Hildegard G. Frey
Homer
Honore De Balzac
Horace B. Day
Horace Walpole
Horatio Alger Jr.
Howard Pyle
Howard R. Garis
Hugh Lofting
Hugh Walpole
Humphry Ward
Ian Maclaren
Inez Haynes Gillmore
Irving Bacheller
Isabel Cecilia Williams
Isabel Hornibrook
Israel Abrahams
Ivan Turgenev
J.G.Austin
J. Henri Fabre
J. M. Barrie
J. M. Walsh
J. Macdonald Oxley
J. R. Miller
J. S. Fletcher
J. S. Knowles
J. Storer Clouston
J. W. Duffield
Jack London
Jacob Abbott
James Allen
James Andrews
James Baldwin

James Branch Cabell
James DeMille
James Joyce
James Lane Allen
James Lane Allen
James Oliver Curwood
James Oppenheim
James Otis
James R. Driscoll
Jane Abbott
Jane Austen
Jane L. Stewart
Janet Aldridge
Jens Peter Jacobsen
Jerome K. Jerome
Jessie Graham Flower
John Buchan
John Burroughs
John Cournos
John F. Kennedy
John Gay
John Glasworthy
John Habberton
John Joy Bell
John Kendrick Bangs
John Milton
John Philip Sousa
John Taintor Foote
Jonas Lauritz Idemil Lie
Jonathan Swift
Joseph A. Altsheler
Joseph Carey
Joseph Conrad
Joseph E. Badger Jr
Joseph Hergesheimer
Joseph Jacobs
Jules Vernes
Julian Hawthrone
Julie A Lippmann
Justin Huntly McCarthy
Kakuzo Okakura
Karle Wilson Baker
Kate Chopin
Kenneth Grahame
Kenneth McGaffey
Kate Langley Bosher
Kate Langley Bosher
Katherine Cecil Thurston
Katherine Stokes
L. A. Abbot
L. T. Meade

L. Frank Baum
Latta Griswold
Laura Dent Crane
Laura Lee Hope
Laurence Housman
Lawrence Beasley
Leo Tolstoy
Leonid Andreyev
Lewis Carroll
Lewis Sperry Chafer
Lilian Bell
Lloyd Osbourne
Louis Hughes
Louis Joseph Vance
Louis Tracy
Louisa May Alcott
Lucy Fitch Perkins
Lucy Maud Montgomery
Luther Benson
Lydia Miller Middleton
Lyndon Orr
M. Corvus
M. H. Adams
Margaret E. Sangster
Margret Howth
Margaret Vandercook
Margaret W. Hungerford
Margret Penrose
Maria Edgeworth
Maria Thompson Daviess
Mariano Azuela
Marion Polk Angellotti
Mark Overton
Mark Twain
Mary Austin
Mary Catherine Crowley
Mary Cole
Mary Hastings Bradley
Mary Roberts Rinehart
Mary Rowlandson
M. Wollstonecraft Shelley
Maud Lindsay
Max Beerbohm
Myra Kelly
Nathaniel Hawthrone
Nicolo Machiavelli
O. F. Walton
Oscar Wilde

Owen Johnson
P.G. Wodehouse
Paul and Mabel Thorne
Paul G. Tomlinson
Paul Severing
Percy Brebner
Percy Keese Fitzhugh
Peter B. Kyne
Plato
Quincy Allen
R. Derby Holmes
R. L. Stevenson
R. S. Ball
Rabindranath Tagore
Rahul Alvares
Ralph Bonehill
Ralph Henry Barbour
Ralph Victor
Ralph Waldo Emmerson
Rene Descartes
Ray Cummings
Rex Beach
Rex E. Beach
Richard Harding Davis
Richard Jefferies
Richard Le Gallienne
Robert Barr
Robert Frost
Robert Gordon Anderson
Robert L. Drake
Robert Lansing
Robert Lynd
Robert Michael Ballantyne
Robert W. Chambers
Rosa Nouchette Carey
Rudyard Kipling
Saint Augustine
Samuel B. Allison
Samuel Hopkins Adams
Sarah Bernhardt
Sarah C. Hallowell
Selma Lagerlof
Sherwood Anderson
Sigmund Freud
Standish O'Grady
Stanley Weyman
Stella Benson
Stella M. Francis

Stephen Crane
Stewart Edward White
Stijn Streuvels
Swami Abhedananda
Swami Parmananda
T. S. Ackland
T. S. Arthur
The Princess Der Ling
Thomas A. Janvier
Thomas A Kempis
Thomas Anderton
Thomas Bailey Aldrich
Thomas Bulfinch
Thomas De Quincey
Thomas Dixon
Thomas H. Huxley
Thomas Hardy
Thomas More
Thornton W. Burgess
U. S. Grant
Upton Sinclair
Valentine Williams
Various Authors
Vaughan Kester
Victor Appleton
Victor G. Durham
Victoria Cross
Virginia Woolf
Wadsworth Camp
Walter Camp
Walter Scott
Washington Irving
Wilbur Lawton
Wilkie Collins
Willa Cather
Willard F. Baker
William Dean Howells
William le Queux
W. Makepeace Thackeray
William W. Walter
William Shakespeare
Winston Churchill
Yei Theodora Ozaki
Yogi Ramacharaka
Young E. Allison
Zane Grey